The Accounting Dwarf

CAL HUTTON

To my parents

The promise of tomorrow

is bound by

the choices of today.

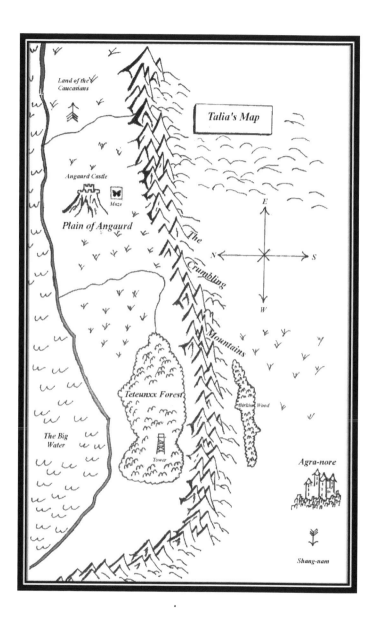

Talia's Map

Land of the
Caucasians

Angaurd Castle

Maze

Plain of Angaurd

The

Crumbling

Mountains

Teteunxx Forest

Birkin Wood

The Big
Water

Tower

Agra-nore

Shang-nam

E

N — S

W

5

CONTENTS

A PUFF OF SMOKE

As Kirin strode up to the bar of the Blue Admiral Inn, a hush followed him. The landlady, her eyes narrowing, put down the glass she was cleaning. He slapped his palm down and demanded a tankard of freshest milk, at her earliest convenience. While the landlady was fetching a fresh pitcher, he slowly looked round the dark interior of the inn taking a special interest in, but without seeming to, the Tax Goblin drinking by himself in the corner. Kirin's gaze returned to the freshly poured tankard, he ran a finger down its cool surface before grabbing it and draining it in one go, he then slammed it down hard on to the bar and let out a long satisfying sigh. Around the inn the general hubbub resumed.

Removing his backpack he gestured for the landlady to come closer and whispered. "Don't suppose an Accounting Dwarf could get a bite to eat and a little privacy could he?" Kirin indicated the Tax Goblin with a nod of his head.

The landlady, after a glance in the corner, raised an eyebrow at the dwarf, sizing him up. He was darkly dressed except for a tan coloured leather jerkin, the kind with a hood. His hair was black, short and spiky and his brown skin glowed with a fine sheen from walking under a long, hot sun. He had generous lips at home in a smile that seemed at odds with his serious looking, large, brown eyes.

"Accounting Dwarf you say?" said the landlady. "Well that's as maybe but you haven't paid for the milk yet."

Looking up Kirin saw his milk moustache in the mirror and quickly wiped it away with the back of his hand. "Seems to me, the owner of a place like this, Mrs eh..."

"Elsie Sturridge is the name. Proprietress of the Blue Admiral Inn." She pronounced the word proprietress like she was especially proud of it.

"Well it seems to me, Mrs Sturridge," whispered Kirin, "that it might be in the interest of such a *proprietress*, to trade a night's lodgings for an overhaul of her ledger by a *fully Chartered,* Accounting Dwarf."

The landlady's eyes widened. "Chartered did you—"

"Ahem!" Kirin coughed then added in a loud voice. "Perhaps you have somewhere with more eh, space where a tired traveller could rest his weary bones?" Kirin raised an eyebrow.

Without an up to date audit Tax Goblins invariably overestimated annual tax bills. The landlady after a hasty glance to the corner, nodded to Kirin. "Ah, indeed yes, eh, you must have had a long journey master dwarf. I have a private function room, eh less noisy, which I'm sure you'll find more comfortable. I'll have some food and refreshment brought to you." The landlady winked and led Kirin to an adjacent room.

"OK so here's the deal," said Kirin, "bring me the books and that means both sets of ledgers," Kirin tapped the side of his nose, "and I'll recalibrate your assets, reduce your liabilities and draw up a new profit and loss account for you. I guarantee you'll be satisfied."

"Really!" The landlady paused. "It's been so long since a Chartered—"

"OK. OK." said Kirin. "Now if you could just bring the food I'll get started." He gave the landlady a large smile. "Oh and of course your receipts, invoices, credit notes and current cash value as of close of business today."

"Eh? Oh, yes, yes of course master dwarf," said the landlady.

"Oh and another one of these." Kirin indicated the tankard to the departing landlady.

Shortly after the landlady returned, this time by another door and with two large books one under one arm. In her other hand she carried an old shoe box, bulging with bits of paper. Behind her came a barmaid bearing a large plate of small sandwiches, a bowl of fruit and a fresh tankard of milk. The landlady placed the books on the table leaving her hand lingering on one as she caught his eye. Kirin nodded and waved the woman away.

The landlady hovered by the door as the barmaid scurried out. "Eh, anything else you require, eh, master dwarf?"

Kirin looked up. "The name's Kirin. Kirin Numbercruncher."

His name wasn't really Numbercruncher but as someone trying to deflect attention away from his family, an obviously fake name allowed him to conceal his true identity whilst being up front about it. And besides he quite liked the sound of it.

Kirin opened the first book, the official ledger. Inside he found, frankly a mess. Not just any old mess, it was a multicoloured, smudged, half illegible mess. Assets mislabelled, profits added up wrong and liabilities half rubbed out as if they could be made to disappear. Kirin sighed. That they thought it was all right to use coloured pens did not bode well. He was going to have to do an inventory. This was definitely going to take longer than he had anticipated. He chuckled as he recalled his mother explaining to him Hofstadter's Law: A task always takes longer than you expect, even when you take into account Hofstadter's Law.

He began at the beginning, as his mother had taught him. He reached into a specially constructed pocket of his jerkin and took out a long, thin metal case. It was old and the once black writing on it had faded, blending in with the grey metal, but he knew what it had once said. He laid it carefully on the table and opened it, inside were four long, silver pens each with a different coloured tip. These had belonged to his mother and had been her parting gift to him. They were the tools of his trade but over and above that they also represented the tradition of Chartered Accountancy that stretched back untold generations. And now with this, his first job, he Kirin, was part of that history. The hairs on the back of his neck stood to attention.

Kirin glanced at the plate of sandwiches. Someone had taken the trouble to cut all the crusts off, and quarter them into little squares, though he did see a suspiciously dark looking smudge on one. Selecting the adjacent sandwich he took a bite. Savouring the taste for a moment, he nodded to himself, then popped the rest of the sandwich in his mouth and selected the green tipped pen, the one he used for making notes. There were going to be a lots of note taking before he could even begin to create fresh accounts.

His mother, Riverna, had not only taught him accountancy. He smiled as he remembered that old book on Euclidean Geometry. It had gotten so worn out that his father, Shalako, had had to rebind it. Ever since he'd been old enough to read he'd been fascinated by books, and not just school books. He would lose himself for hours in the stories from different worlds and past times, full of wondrous invention and heroic imaginings. It was only later that he learned his parents had spent what little money they had buying them second-hand, right here in Shang-nam. That in a way was a reflection of Kirin's problem, it was the cost of studying mathematics at university which was Kirin's dream and in a roundabout way the reason he had come to Shang-nam.

* * * *

Closing the book, he went to take the last sandwich, noticing that the smudged one was already gone. He smiled, job well done. He stretched and yawned. It turned out that Mrs Sturridge had a reasonably nice little business, and now one that was officially in profit. He got up, feeling the stiffness in his legs as he walked to the door. He spotted the landlady drying glasses behind the bar. The rest of the inn was nearly empty just a few stragglers, perhaps staying the night like himself, but definitely no Tax Goblins.

"All done then?" The landlady asked hopping excitedly from foot to foot.

Kirin nodded. "If you could show me to my room, I'd like to get some sleep."

"Of course, of course. Eh, Isabel?" The landlady waved a towel in the barmaid's direction. "The eh..." She mouthed the word 'books' at Kirin.

Kirin tilted his head back towards the function room behind him.

"And eh, everything's....?"

"Oh yes indeed everything's..." echoed Kirin.

The landlady scurried past Kirin into the function room.

"This way master dwarf." Isabel, who it turned out was the landlady's daughter, escorted Kirin to his room up a creaky, wooden staircase that didn't quite drown out the small yelps of delight coming from below. Inside the small but comfortable looking room Isabel handed Kirin the candle and with a quick curtsey and a slight giggle, was gone. Kirin put his pack down, undressed carelessly and let himself collapse on to the strange, soft bed. He was struggling to keep his eyes open but was not quite ready for sleep, not just yet. Stretching over to his pack he took out a small folded up brochure, the reason he had come to Shang-nam. He started to read it once more, devouring every word, making sure there was nothing he had missed, even though he must have read it a hundred times already.

QUEST FOR THE TRAL-FE-TIGORE

Queen Zehalani wishes to make known to all her subjects of the Fourth Kingdom the following:

Accounting Dwarfs wanted for financial quest to join existing team of six Accounting Dwarfs (Certified). The team will be searching for the legendary Tral-fe-tigore. All participating members[†] of the quest will receive twice the standard accountancy rate[††] amounting to but not exceeding a dozen gold pieces! Upon successful completion of the quest, a gold and jewels bonus, 'beyond your wildest dreams' will be paid to each member[†] of the team.

The legendary Tral-fe-tigore will solve all the Kingdoms current economic difficulties: ogre health care, illegal tax havens, the troll problem...

The Quest itself of course was a fake. His parents had explained that whenever there was a severe downturn in the economic cycle the Quest for the Tral-fe-tigore usually reared its ugly head. Now was such a time and the brochures were flying. It was just a myth. The point of it though, was that it proved a useful distraction from the Kingdoms financial problems till things just kind of got better on their own. Kirin's interest in the quest lay in the fact that as an alternative to the (up to) twelve gold pieces on offer to even unsuccessful quest members, they could claim certain goods and services as supplied by the state. Crucially this included higher education.

Kirin shook himself back to the present. He couldn't afford any mistakes, pulling out his application he began reading it carefully. Of course all this was relatively easy, keeping his secret hidden might prove just a little bit tougher. At breakfast the next morning he would find out just how tough.

* * * *

"Yes it's a nice little business you've got here Mrs Sturridge," said Kirin for the umpteenth time to the landlady of the Blue Admiral Inn, who's excitement was more than two stationary feet could contain. "No. No more pancakes thank you. I've already had an ample sufficiency."

Kirin patted his stomach, he had the distinct impression that Mrs Elsie Sturridge believed him to be in need of feeding up. While it was nice to have his accountancy skills appreciated, he was finding the landlady's attention a little overpowering. He did not wish to hurt her feelings but he was, after all, trying to keep a low profile. His parents had repeatedly stressed the importance of this simple enough task upon him, however he was now finding it easier said than done. Initially he'd tried engaging with the landlady in idle chitchat. Indeed he'd learned that the Blue Admiral Inn had, until recently, gone under the rather drab appellation of the 'Dog and Duck'. She thought the name change added more local colour for the tourists. Indeed she wanted to know if this was perhaps the reason for her inn's new-found profitability. Kirin sighed and told her that in all honesty he could not positively say that it was not. After a slight pause the landlady seemed to consider this a good thing. Unfortunately for Kirin, her continual hopping from one foot to another was drawing every eye in the inn. The woman just could not keep still.

Kirin sighed. "There is one thing you could do for me, if it's not too much trouble?"

"More pancakes?"

"Eh, no," smiled Kirin, "but I'll be leaving shortly so if you could perhaps make up a packed lunch for me? Eh, perhaps some of those excellent smoked salmon sandwiches?"

"Oh right away master dwarf," beamed the landlady and immediately scurried away with barely a hop in sight.

Kirin settled down to finish his breakfast in peace, the pancakes were actually very good, but as he did so a hooded figure approached his table. He wore the grey hooded jerkin of a Certified Accounting Dwarf. Indeed he was dressed all in grey and had a tankard of milk in one hand and in the other a long thin pipe. He paused for a moment, giving Kirin a look that spelt trouble, before producing a large a puff of smoke from his pipe. Then without so much a by-your-leave, he seated himself at Kirin's table, took a swig from the tankard of milk in his hand and, with a satisfying sigh, sat back making himself comfortable. He removed his hood revealing a handsome face dominated by inquisitive green eyes and all framed by a mop of unruly blond hair.

"I hear tell you're a Chartered Accounting Dwarf," said the stranger.

Oh dear, thought Kirin, if this wasn't trouble it would make do till it got here. And all before Kirin had even finished breakfast. It didn't do to talk to strange dwarfs without being introduced first. This was indeed maternal advice that Kirin had received, many a time. And this occasion definitely fitted the bill. As if reading his mind the stranger then spoke.

"The name's Stilgoe," he said.

Kirin realised he'd need to keep his wits about him.

"Oh? Who says so?" asked Kirin.

"What?" Stilgoe's brow furrowed. "My name—"

"No, who said I was a Chartered Accounting Dwarf."

Stilgoe let out a loud laugh. Taking another puff of his pipe he indicated with his head the landlady behind the bar. "Can't really get her to stop saying it."

Kirin couldn't help but look across at the landlady who was cleaning glasses at the bar, in between hops. Noticing Kirin's attention she beamed a smile back and waved her bar towel. Kirin instinctively waved back before stopping himself.

"So what's it to you?" asked Kirin.

"Oh just being sociable, as one Accounting Dwarf to another." Stilgoe took a long puff on his pipe. "Can't help but notice though that you aren't wearing your guild ring." He stretched his left hand out on the table. On his middle finger he wore the silver ring of a Certified Accounting Dwarf. Kirin could clearly see the accountancy insignia (an open book with a set of scales on it) and on either side, the initials S. and L.

"Oh how very pretty," said Kirin and went back to finishing off his pancakes.

"Look, practising accountancy without being licensed is not something the guild takes kindly to, if you know what I mean?" said Stilgoe.

"Excellent," said Kirin, licking his lips.

"Eh, the pancakes that is," he added.

Kirin stretched a his arms a little allowing himself a calming smile as he considered the matter. If he couldn't handle one Certified Accounting Dwarf over breakfast then he might as well give up and go home. He was a problem solver and one thing he knew about problems was, that they quite often turned out to be opportunities in disguise.

"You think this is funny? A little trip up to the University to see the Guildmaster and maybe you won't think it quite so amusing," said Stilgoe.

"Excellent suggestion," said Kirin. "I'm *really* glad I bumped into you. As it turns out I have business with the Chancellor myself. Do you know the way?"

Stilgoe slammed his pipe down on the table. All eyes turned towards them, even those of the excited landlady, who had now stopped hopping. "Oh, I know the way all right," said Stilgoe a little lamely.

Kirin leant back regarding Stilgoe for a moment then reached into his shirt searching for the bit of string that was round his neck. He withdrew the string revealing a small ring made of white gold that had been threaded through it. The ring bore the Accountancy Dwarf insignia, an open book with a set of scales like Stilgoe's but there were no initials, instead angled across the bottom were a pair of quill pens denoting his chartered status. He rolled it between his thumb and forefinger, watching the light playing upon it. But this was far more precious to him than gold, having been given to him by his dwarf mother, as it had in turn been given to her by her mother before. Stilgoe's green eyes widened.

"Now I shall be leaving within the half-hour." Kirin gave what he hoped was his most nonchalant sigh. "At which point you can guide me to the Chancellor. There's a good fellow."

Stilgoe looked round at the landlady who along with everyone else was still staring at the pair of dwarfs. He gave the landlady a little wave, at which the general hubbub in the inn resumed. "Look," said Stilgoe. "I guess we got off on the wrong foot here." He paused for a second before suddenly offering his pipe to Kirin. "Here, a peace offering, so to speak."

Kirin's momentary relief came to a crashing standstill. He smiled wanly at the proffered pipe, for of course Kirin did not smoke. Not only didn't he smoke but he couldn't smoke. The one thing all dwarfs, accounting or otherwise did, their robust constitutions not only tolerated but thrived upon the medicinal benefits of 7-leaf. For this was Kirin's great secret. He wasn't a dwarf!

One night after securing his fishing boat to the jetty by their cottage, Shalako his dwarf father, had seen movement in the estuary reed beds. It had been his half drowned birth mother, along with his six month old self. She was sick with fever and had not lasted the night. Riverna and Shalako had no children of their own and had made the decision to raise Kirin as their own. In preparation for the quest Kirin had practised with his dwarf parents all that he needed to do to pass himself off as a dwarf, including the smoking thing. Rehearsed it all till he was blue in the face. Now was the crucial test, he just hadn't expected it would come so soon.

"I don't smoke," sighed Kirin.

"What?' said Stilgoe narrowing his eyes.

"Eh, it's a little embarrassing, I don't really like to talk about it," mumbled Kirin.

"Really? Never heard of a dwarf who didn't smoke before." Stilgoe leaned in.

"I uh," Kirin swallowed, "Eh, I um, I've got this slight, really very slight problem."

"Yes?" said Stilgoe encouragingly.

"Really it's hardly worth mentioning. Doesn't really affect me but, the healer said probably best not to smoke. You understand?" whispered Kirin.

"Eh, not entirely. No," said Stilgoe.

Kirin eyed Stilgoe carefully before continuing. "You seem like a trustworthy fellow. Do I have your word, as one Accounting Dwarf to another, that it'll go no further?"

"Trustworthy is my middle name," said Stilgoe solemnly, if not entirely accurately.

Kirin looked around the inn, before whispering in Stilgoe's ear.

"I have a touch of asthma."

* * * *

Whether Stilgoe suspicions were eased or not he had agreed to escort Kirin to the University. The affable Stilgoe had even claimed to have business there himself, a coincidence that seemed a little to convenient to Kirin's way of thinking. They had just stepped out from the shadow of the inn doorway, squinting in the bright sunlight, when the landlady and Isabel came out after them, struggling with a large hamper.

"Master dwarf sir?"

They both turned round. They looked first at the hamper, then at the landlady and Isabel.

"Lunch sir?"

"Look I asked for a packed lunch, not..." words failed Kirin.

"Well, the least we can do is have a look, after Mrs Sturridge and the lovely Isabel, have taken so much time and trouble." A smiling Stilgoe gave a short nod in the lovely Isabel's direction who giggled slightly. Stilgoe opened the hamper. Inside were various bundles of sandwiches wrapped in waxed paper and all helpfully labelled. But that was just for starters. A cask of milk, bottles of ginger beer, fruit and something wrapped in muslin cloth that Kirin's nose took to be cheese. There were jars of honey and apricots and much more besides. Kirin protested, but he might as well have been talking to the wind. In the end there was to be no dissuading Mrs Sturridge, especially with an eager Stilgoe willing to help carry it.

The path to the University led away from the inn up through a wooded slope. The hamper had seemed light enough at the start, but trudging up the rough track Kirin soon began to feel the weight. After half an hour he was about to suggest they stop and eat something just to lighten the load when Stilgoe halted.

"Need a rest? A little too heavy for you perhaps?" said Kirin..

Stilgoe just laughed. "Nature's call," he said and then disappeared behind a big oak tree.

Kirin sat down on the hamper, facing back down the hill. His thoughts turned to the Quest for the Tral-fe-tigore. It wasn't too late for him to turn back, he could just change his mind, forget about the whole thing. But this was such an opportunity. He had to play it smart of course, wander around with the others for a few weeks, stay out of trouble and of course not do anything stupid. Then he would return as one of the valiant but unsuccessful heroes. Everyone would be a winner, the Kingdom would get distracted from its economic woes, and he would get his education paid for.

"Oy! What you got there then mate?"

Kirin turned around and saw two youths, about three yards away, on the slope above him. He quickly assessed them. The one who had spoken was a skinny fellow with a shock of red hair. The second youth had mousy brown hair and was shorter but seemed sturdier. Kirin looked beyond them, but couldn't see anyone else.

"Lunch," he answered.

"Well that seems like a lot of lunch for one little dwarf," said Red.

"Naw, he probably needs it," said Mousy. "Look how skinny he is. Don't think I've ever seen such a scrawny dwarf. Runt of the litter, ain't you."

With a sigh Kirin stood up. "You know, it's not too late for you to walk away. In fact there's a particularly nice inn just at the bottom of the hill." Kirin smiled and pointed, but inside he felt his heart pounding, the blood racing round his body. It was a warm day but his skin felt cold.

His father's reassuring voice echoed in his head. Stay calm, accept your fear. Let your opponent be angry. Use their strengths against them. His father had taught him many things for he had not always been a fisherman.

"Bit of a smart mouth you got there," said Red. "Well I got something that'll fix that for you."

Kirin breathed slowly, fully. He felt a tingling sensation in his fingers and toes and was intensely aware of the smallest details: leaves swaying in the wind, the rustle of some small creature in the undergrowth, the set of Red's shoulders. He slowly took two steps back from the hamper. Leaving his left leg forward, towards the hamper, his right leg trailing behind him, down the slope. Knees bent, balanced equally on the balls of both feet, arms in front of him, he waited.

Red suddenly rushed forward, launching himself over the hamper at Kirin. From facing the youth head-on, Kirin began to pivot on the balls of his feet, turning to his right. At the same time with his right hand he grabbed the youths shirt at the shoulder, as he flew at him. Kirin continued to pivot through an arc of 180 degrees using his left hand to help guide the flailing youth past him through the air, like he (Kirin) wasn't there. Kirin then let go with his right hand, and watched his opponent crash to the ground and go rolling down the slope, ending up in a crumpled heap some four or five yards down the path. Breathing slowly, Kirin pivoted on the balls of his feet to face back up the slope, and his second opponent, Mousey. His father's mantra calmly played in his head. Stay calm, accept your fear. Let your opponent be angry. Use their strengths against them.

"Oh v-very sneaky. Full of tricks you are. I can see I'm gonna have to watch you," said Mousey.

"Actually no. It's me you're going to have to watch out for."

Mousey turned to see Stilgoe behind him.

Kirin slowly moved sideways and turned slightly, widening his field of view to include both youths. Red was slowly getting to his feet.

"Really," said Kirin addressing Stilgoe. "I don't think it requires more than one Accounting Dwarf to sort out these two." He raised an eyebrow at Stilgoe.

"True," answered Stilgoe, "but why should you have all the fun?"

Mousey was now edging round the other side of hamper from Kirin. He was looking warily at both dwarfs. "Didn't realise you were Accounting... Eh. No offence meant. We were just joking. Ain't that right Sid?"

"So you're Sid," said Stilgoe who then turned to Mousey. "And what's your name?"

Sid, on his feet again, was rubbing the back of his head, which had quite a lump. "Don't tell him Karl!" he said.

Sid popped a hand over his mouth.

"You're a moron Sid, you know that?" said Karl now shoving Sid down the hill. "Look we'll just be heading off to that inn, like you said. Don't want no trouble now."

Kirin regarded them for a moment "Well, we're on friendly terms with the landlady there, so if we find out there was any trouble, we'll know who it was, won't we?'"

As the two youths disappeared out of sight Stilgoe regarded Kirin thoughtfully, then began to whistle some vaguely familiar tune, it seemed to have all the right notes but just not necessarily in the right order. The two of them picked up the hamper and continued on up the path for another ten minutes or so till they got to the top of the slope where the trees petered out and Kirin found himself looking out over a grassy plane that merged into a manicured lawn. There were a few students milling about or sitting on the grass, but Kirin's attention was focused on the dark grey stone building some 400 yards in front of him. The University. He gazed up at the giant structure, which in places was up to four stories high. Dotted along its length, apparently at random, were towers topped by golden spires. The spires may have been gleaming but they were not entirely vertical. Indeed one would have been hard pressed to find a right angle anywhere in the building. Kirin though, thought it the most perfect place in all the Fourth Kingdom.

They stopped at the main gateway, an arch five yards wide by twice that tall. Directly above the gateway was one of the main towers. Kirin gazed upwards at the grey granite, standing in its own shadow and threatening to topple down on him at any moment. He tentatively tapped the stone with a fingertip expecting sparks to fly but it remained cold and impassive. It would not yield up its secrets so easily.

"I know what you're thinking. The towers are a bit wonky, but don't worry they won't fall down," laughed Stilgoe. "We should head to the porters lodge first. He'll be able to tell us if the Chancellor is in or not."

The main gateway led into a cool dark stone passageway, at the far end of which it opened onto a courtyard basking in the sun. Stilgoe though indicated they should take a doorway off to their left where they found themselves in a gloomy chamber full of fluted granite columns each one rising up to form vaulted arches with those adjacent to it, like a forest of stone. Kirin slowed almost to a stop as he marvelled at the workmanship of the masons who had built it. The poor light obscured the detail of the ceiling which only made it all the more intriguing to Kirin.

"No time for dawdling. The porters room is just through there." Stilgoe pointed to a door at the far end of the chamber of columns. Going through it Kirin found himself in a similar passage way to the one he had first entered. "OK set her down here." Stilgoe put his end of the hamper down and Kirin followed suit. There was no courtyard at the far end of this passageway just another door. Kirin longed to explore. There was so much to see, wonders at every turn.

"Dring!"

Kirin turned to see Stilgoe at a little wooden counter, that he hadn't noticed before. There was a dark opening behind it from which strange noises were coming. On the counter were a small bell and a sign saying 'Head Porter'.

"OK. All yours, master dwarf sir." Stilgoe gave Kirin a mock bow and backed away.

A very tall man, he must have been all of five foot, stepped out of the darkness. He was wearing a tightly fitting black suit edged with red piping and adjusting a peaked cap upon his head.

"Who's been ringing my bell then?" His question was curt and his voice may have been gruff, but the eyes that sized Kirin up and down were anything but. The porter glanced over at Stilgoe, now sitting on the hamper, who seemed to find the whole situation very amusing. "You two together?"

Behind Kirin, Stilgoe was nodding.

"No," said Kirin. "Well that is we came here together but—"

"Well which is it master dwarf ? Can't very well be both now can it?"

Taking a deep breath Kirin began again. "My name is Kirin Numbercruncher and I wish to hand in my application for the Tral-fe-tigore quest to the Chancellor's office." Behind him an open mouthed Stilgoe nearly fell off the hamper. Kirin reached into his pocket and produced his crumpled brochure, pointing to the title of it. "This good fellow here," Kirin indicated with his thumb behind him, "has been helping me with my hamper."

"Hmmmm. Well then master Kirin Numbercruncher, I am Mr Arbuthnott the head porter, I think you'd better follow me." The porter then led a slightly confused Kirin to the door at the far end of the passageway. As they passed through Kirin could hear Stilgoe begin to whistle that same tune again. They went up a grand stone staircase, along a wooden panelled corridor which opened up into an enormous stately room with large golden framed pictures on the walls. Most were of imposing, stern faced scholars who seemed to be staring straight at Kirin, like he didn't belong there. Then they went down a winding staircase, and along a dark stone walled corridor till finally they stopped at a large but ordinary looking door. The porter knocked, waited a moment then opened the door and walked inside. He closed the door behind him leaving a none the wiser Kirin in the corridor. After some conversation that Kirin could not make out, despite his best efforts, the door opened and the porter indicated that Kirin should enter.

The air in the room was thick and heavy. Large ancient leaded windows filtered the sunlight which illuminated tiny swirling dust mites before falling onto the most impressive desk Kirin had ever seen.

"Please come in and sit down master dwarf," said the Chancellor.

The Chancellor did not look up. He was resplendent in black velvet robes that billowed with each flourish of his arm as he scribbled away at some, no doubt, important papers. As Kirin sat down on the small lonely chair in front of the desk the door closed almost noiselessly behind him.

"Thank you sir," said Kirin, as he fumbled with his pack, getting his application. "I've come—"

The Chancellor raised his hand, which Kirin took to mean that he should stop talking.

"Mr Arbuthnott has informed me that you wish to put your name forward for the Tral-fe-tigore quest. You are of course aware that this is the final day for applications?" He looked down his exceptionally long nose at Kirin. His face was very birdlike all the features seemed to have a sharp edge to them. His skin was dark, almost black but it was his eyes that were the most striking thing about him. They were blue, the colour of the sky on a summers day, they didn't seem to belong on that face. Perhaps they thought so too because they forever darting about, as if looking for somewhere else to be. For the moment though they were focused on some papers in front of the Chancellor.

"Application."

It was more of a command than a question, as a long bony hand stretched out from his voluptuous robes. Kirin had fortunately found his application, which he placed in the hand without delay.

"Eh, I—"

The Chancellor, now reading Kirin's application, raised his hand once more. Kirin sat in silence. He hadn't expected to see the Chancellor in person and he had the distinct impression that he had done something wrong but for the life of him he couldn't think what it was. He breathed out a large sigh which made rather more noise than he intended. As his eyes adjusted to the gloom he saw that the walls were lined with books, more books than he had ever seen before. Books of every hue, and every size. Some bound in leather with impressive gold lettering, others in some strange glossy material he had never seen before. Was it possible for one person to have read all these?

"It says here you were trained in Chartered Accountancy by your mother Riverna daughter of Sharmene."

"What? Eh, yes, she—"

"Class of 54, a competent student as I recall."

The Chancellor's blue eyes fixed themselves on Kirin as if daring him to contradict. A moment later their attention was back on his application. Kirin considered his mother way more than competent! He began to wonder how *competent* was this Chancellor if that was his assessment of his mother. His hands closed into fists, opened and clenched again. Kirin thought he heard the Chancellor mutter 'lacked commitment, pity'. His face flushed red for he knew that his mother had given up accountancy in order to bring him up. The Chancellor shuffled some papers he had been writing on, and along with Kirin's application placed them in a folder.

"Perhaps you will prove the same," said the Chancellor.

Blue eyes darted momentarily in Kirin's direction. The Chancellor then proceeded to drip some hot wax on the folder before using his ring of office to seal it. Placing the folder neatly to one side he looked up at Kirin. "You will proceed to Queen Zehalani's palace at Agra-nore where you will present yourself two days hence from now at mid-day, when the quest members will be announced." The Chancellor waved a hand dismissively and began opening a large old looking book that was lying on his desk.

Kirin sat for a moment still clenching his fists. He wanted to shout out that *the Chancellor* didn't know his mother, that *she* was the best Chartered Accounting Dwarf there was. Part of him was also dimly aware that his application had been successful, at least in this initial stage. He got up, staring blackly at the Chancellor, who appeared oblivious, engrossed in his book. All he could manage to say in a dry monotone voice was, "I don't know the way to

Agra-nore."

Without looking up the Chancellor said, "There's an official courier leaving at two o'clock. You can travel with him. Ask Mr Arbuthnott for details."

Kirin clamped his mouth shut, his lips pressed firmly together, he did not trust himself to reply. he walked out the room without looking back, pulling the door closed behind him with more force than was strictly necessary.

* * * *

"So let me get this straight. He called your mother competent." Stilgoe began laughing "And that made you angry?"

"Of course it made me angry. Who wouldn't be angry?" Kirin stared hard at Stilgoe.

Shaking his head Stilgoe said, "You don't understand." Still laughing, much to Kirin's annoyance he explained. "The Chancellor. Ha! Ha! He, he thinks pretty much *everyone* is incompetent, certainly all students." Kirin's brows were still furrowed. "Don't you get it? It was a compliment. Ha! Ha! Ha!"

A most pleasant lunch sitting on the university lawn in the warm sun was mostly wasted on Kirin. Still, a significant chunk of Mrs Sturridge's hamper was devoured between the two of them, and though it did not restore his good humour, it took the edge of his bad one. They fitted into their packs what they could and, at Stilgoe's suggestion, donated the rest to Mr Arbuthnott. Stilgoe excused himself saying he had his business to attend to but that he would see Kirin before he left. Kirin nodded, a little sorry to see this strange dwarf go.

Despite the now much lighter hamper, Kirin still struggled to carry it back to the head porter's office where the half-hearted protestations of Mr Arbuthnott melted like butter as he opened the hamper and peered inside. Kirin took the opportunity to ask about the courier but Mr Arbuthnott only waved a dismissive hand and told him not to worry, his attention now entirely consumed with the contents of the hamper. Upon catching a sniff of Mrs Sturridge's finest honeyed cheese, the head porter began praising the delights of the cuisine of the Blue Admiral Inn. Clutching a bottle of ginger beer in one hand Mr Arbuthnott insisted that Kirin had no need to worry and that he would personally ensure the return of the hamper to the Blue Admiral Inn with most excellent compliments. Kirin attempted one more time to enquire about the courier but ended up just smiling and nodding as he waited for Mr Arbuthnott to run out of words though that was beginning to look as likely as the hamper running out of food.

"Why master Kirin. Here comes the courier now, if I'm not mistaken."

Kirin turned to see a smiling Stilgoe approaching, carrying an official looking bag slung across his shoulder.

"You!"

"At your service master dwarf." A smiling Stilgoe gave Kirin a mock bow.

Lost for words Kirin's mouth was moving but it was Mr Arbuthnott who spoke. "Master Stilgoe here is the official courier of Queen Zehalani herself... amongst other duties." He nodded to Stilgoe.

Stilgoe smiled and gave a slight bow of his head towards Kirin. "I have been informed you wish to take the road to Agra-nore, master Kirin?"

Kirin nodded.

"In that case I shall be happy to guide you safely there."

SUPER IS AS SUPER DOES

In the royal palace of Agra-nore the Elf Queen Zehalani stood before the assembled beings of the Fourth Kingdom. She raised an arm and a hush spread throughout the magnificent throne room as she addressed the young dwarf before her.

"Kirin Numbercruncher, you and your six companions have been chosen to go on the quest to find the Tral-fe-tigore. This, as legend tells us, will solve all the kingdom's ills: ogre health care, tax havens, the troll problem, and of course, not only reduce the Ko-Ko bean deficit but turn it into a surplus!" At this the crowd let out a collective gasp and began cheering. The Queen raised her hand in acknowledgement and waited for silence. "Furthermore it will unlock our stored elf equity without Tax Goblins getting a look in. And as for roving bands of venture capitalists? Well, they'll be queuing up to invest in us!"

Queen Zehalani stood for a moment basking in the spontaneous applause. Kirin found himself clapping along with everyone else. Never in his life had he even imagined such breathtaking magnificence and yet here he stood surrounded by all the grand lords and ladies of the royal court resplendent in all their finery. He forced himself to breath slowly and deeply and wished silently that he was somewhere else. Anywhere else. For, as the applause waned, everyone was now staring at him. His heart felt like it was going to pound its way right out of his chest. In an effort to calm down he focused on a patch of floor in front of him and began reciting the Fibonacci sequence in his head.

The Queen raised her arm, to silence the hall once more. "To help you on this quest you are to be granted a superpower. Anything that your heart desires. But think carefully young Kirin, for this power may prove invaluable against the deadly perils that await you. Your companions have—"

Young Kirin was now waving a hand above his head in a very insistent manor. Things had suddenly gone from the merely overwhelming to significantly out of control.

"Yes?" said the Queen.

"Excuse me! Excuse me your Majesty! I'm sorry, but did you say *deadly perils?* Because there was no-one mentioned any perils to me, and certainly not deadly ones."

The Queen waved her hand dismissively. "Well obviously on a high risk/high yield quest of this nature one must expect to encounter Dividend-orcs at some point." She laughed. "That's just standard probability theory. Goes without saying really" The Queen paused, as if slightly cross with herself for actually saying it.

"Dividend-orcs your Majesty?" Kirin enquired in a slightly high pitched voice. A hard knot tied itself, then sunk into the pit of his stomach. Dividend-orcs were notorious for their single minded pursuit of profit. Kirin closed his eyes and tried to think, but all he wanted to do was hide or better still disappear entirely.

The Queen continued, still playing to the crowd. "Your companions have already chosen their superpowers, to complement the renowned fighting skills that Certified Accounting Dwarfs already possess. As the enforcers of the financial community, they have already proven themselves in the cutthroat world of merchant banking and are not afraid to indulge in a hostile takeover or two, I can tell you." At this another round of applause broke out, though mainly at the instigation of the Palace Guard spear-tips.

"So Kirin Numbercruncher, *Chartered* Accounting Dwarf, what will you choose?" asked the Queen. "To have superhuman strength? The faculty for flight? Or perhaps the power of invisibility? Make your choice Kirin Numbercruncher. And choose wisely."

Kirin had not expected to have to choose a superpower and now the possibility of coming up against Dividend-orcs? He recalled what the brochure had said. Dwarfs wanted for financial quest, it had said, no mention of special powers. A gold and jewels bonus beyond your wildest dreams, it had said, nothing about Dividend-orcs!

Kirin though not actually a dwarf, had been brought up by them, and thanks to his adopted dwarf mother Riverna, he was fully proficient with balance sheets, profit and loss accounts and tax liabilities. Also, at almost fifteen, was still small enough to easily pass for one. He had only met one Certified Accounting Dwarf, Stilgoe, the Elf Queens courier who had guided him from Shang-nam University to Agra-nore. He'd seemed a frivolous fellow, laughing and joking, always preening his mop of blond hair. Kirin believed, due to his dwarf father Shalako's *special training,* he could certainly handle anything that the likes of Stilgoe could, Dividend-orcs though were an entirely different kettle of fish.

He took a deep breath. For the time being all he needed to concern himself with, was choosing a superpower, Dividend-orcs would be a worry for another day. While Kirin racked his brain for an idea, the Queen waited with a stately, if somewhat forced smile fixed upon him. But as the delay became uncomfortably long she folded her arms and the foot tapping started, at which point her Chamberlain slowly edged away from her, side-stepping behind the nearest Palace Guard.

This was nuts! He'd never heard of anybody having superpowers before, but then he'd spent most of his life fishing on the waters of the Tervent or foraging in the nearby woods. But this was the Elf Queen, ruler of the Fourth Kingdom, that had to mean something? Did she have the ability to dispense superpowers at will? What even was a superpower anyway? She'd talked about the power of flight. People couldn't fly, but birds could so technically flight was possible?

"Argh!"

Everyone of the fine lords and ladies were looking at him, waiting for him to choose. They all must know something he didn't. And the Elf Queen had said the others had already chosen, so however impossible it sounded, it must be true. No! This was crazy superpowers didn't exist. Couldn't exist. And yet he had to choose one. The queen had mentioned invisibility which, at that moment, was very, very tempting. But still he couldn't shake the thought that this choice was important somehow, and not to be wasted. Then an idea popped into his head and, before he knew it, out of his mouth.

"Teleportation," he blurted out.

"What!" Queen Zehalani shook her head, looking at Kirin as confused as a queen can be.

Kirin, ignoring the knot in his stomach that now seemed to weigh a ton, just smiled back, and took advantage of the pause in proceedings to inspect his fingernails. The Queen looked to her Chamberlain who, peeking from behind a Palace Guard, shook his head, equally perplexed. Everyone though, was now looking at the Queen to see what she would do.

"Eh, tele what?" she said.

"Teleportation. The ability to instantly travel to a remote location," replied Kirin.

"Oh I see," said the Queen, not seeing at all. "Well of

course super-speed is a very wise choice and well compliments the—"

"Not super-speed. Teleportation." Kirin took a deep breath. "To instantaneously transport oneself from one place to another."

"Ahem! Well, if that's what you want? No-one has ever asked for that before, but we can do that for you, if you're sure?" The Queen cast a furtive look at the Chamberlain who returned a very unconvincing nod before suddenly stepping out from behind the Palace Guard. "Actually your Majesty we do have special boots that allow a person to run faster, even than an elf."

The crowd let out a collective sigh of awesomeness.

The Queen fixed her stern eye upon the Chamberlain.

Kirin sighed, shaking his head at the pair of them. "Look I don't want to be able to run faster than a man, a dwarf or even *an elf*." Kirin glanced at the Chamberlain. "I want to be able, in a flash, disappear from one place and reappear in another."

The Queen and Chamberlain looked at Kirin intensely, then conducted a mumbled conversation, out of the corners of their mouths. The gist of which was whether this Kirin was some kind of simpleton, not the right sort of person for this kind of quest at all. Kirin even thought he heard something about, 'if it wasn't for the fact that he'd been the only volunteer'.

After a few minutes the Chamberlain shuffled forward, helped by a very unqueen-like nudge in the back and began speaking very slowly. "Queen Zehalani has, most generously and to assist in the pursuit of the Tral-fe-tigore, deemed to grant the members of the Company of the Quest one superpower, but one superpower only." He paused as the crowd broke into spontaneous applause. "Now clearly Kirin Numbercruncher has requested the superpower of disappearing, the superpower of reappearing and the superpower of moving very fast to different places. And it doesn't take an Accounting Dwarf to see that that adds up to three."

Some in the crowd were nodding in agreement while counting out the superpowers on their fingers, while others applauded the Chamberlain's grasp of arithmetic and a few even laughed nervously. Kirin felt his face turning red. A million things rushed through his head but only one word managed to pass his lips.

"Sorry," he mumbled.

Queen Zehalani brushed past her chamberlain and addressed the assembly as much as Kirin.

"So young Kirin, is super-speed to be the superpower that you choose?"

"Well I suppose..." replied Kirin still franticly thinking about superpowers. "Though it would have been nice to have known about all this beforehand. For instance was there a list to choose from?" Kirin added a little sarcastically "Your Majesty."

The Queen was not used to being addressed in this manner. She attempted to give Kirin her stern eye, but Kirin just stared right back at her. The Chamberlain rushed to the defence of his monarch. "Look, do you want this superpower or not? You know you get to keep it after the quest finishes, assuming of course..."

Kirin wasn't listening. He was thinking about super-speed and the beginnings of a plan were beginning to form in his head.

The Queen having collected herself decided it was time to finalise matters. She stepped forward and addressed the assembly. "Of course if this is the power that Kirin Numbercruncher desires then so shall it be." And with that the matter was decided. The Queen gave a slight flourish of her hand and the crowd erupted in applause with barely a spear-tip required. She continued to apply her flourish and the crowd continued to cheer. When they did begin to flag, their mistake was quickly pointed out. During this the Queen talked quietly to Kirin.

"Sure you wouldn't like something more practical?

Walking through walls, triple entry book-keeping, or my favourite, shooting lightning bolts from your fingertips? Now that's a superpower! Though, you do have to be careful not to get burned." The Queen frowned slightly, rubbing her thumb against her fingertips.

Kirin just smiled and shook his head. No, this superpower was definitely the bee's knees. He had the basics of a rudimentary, cunning plan, half formed in his head and this superpower might be just what he needed to make it work.

* * * *

The lavish decoration of the palace corridor was wasted on Kirin. A small voice was mumbling somewhere superpowers aren't real but it was drowned out by the words 'teleportation' and 'super-speed' bouncing off the confines of his mind like angry wasps.

"Argh!"

If the Chamberlain and the two flanking Palace Guards heard him they paid no attention, but Kirin would not have noticed if they had. The most important moment of his life, when he was put on the spot, when he had such an opportunity, and he'd been bullied out of choosing teleportation. Still there was the cunning plan n'all but... Kirin wondered if they would they let him choose again? That didn't seem unreasonable. After all, where's the harm? He hadn't actually got it yet and if they could squeeze out all those superpowers like candy why not squeeze out one more? That little voice was still mumbling and the knot in the pit of his stomach was back. He shook his head. But teleportation was the only superpower worth having. Oh yes! Quick and easy. Just teleport there, grab the Tral-fe-tigore and zap right back. Job done. Easy-peasy. Easy... Peasy... He was missing something. The Chamberlain hadn't looked too convincing even about the super-speed thing. Everything had been too quick, too neat, too easy. Kirin tried to clear his mind by continuing his calculations on the Fibonacci sequence, but that bad feeling would not go away. It was like he'd taken a wrong turn in the dark but despite knowing this he was still marching on, when the smart thing would have been to stop and retrace his steps. Go back in time. Now there's a superpower. Time travel!

"Argh!"

He couldn't think straight. He needed to calm down.

The Chamberlain stopped beside a large ornately painted door and turned to face Kirin. The two Palace Guards either side of Kirin also stopped in unison. Kirin however, continued on, bumping into the front of the Chamberlain.

"Oh sorry," said Kirin, raising a hand in apology.

Ignoring Kirin, the Chamberlain opened the door. "The Company of the Quest awaits you inside. Tonight you dine as honoured guests of Queen Zehalani. Tomorrow the quest for the Tral-fe-tigore begins." There was perhaps the most imperceptible of bows and with that he stood aside. Kirin entered the large state room. It must have been over 100 feet across. As he looked about at the ornate ceiling and fine paintings on the walls, the door was closed behind him with a resounding thud. It must have been some kind of banqueting room for it was full of long tables, each with a dozen tall-backed golden chairs. The tables were all set out very formally with linen tablecloths and finest silverware. All expectantly waiting. Well not all. At the far end, over to his right he could now make out voices coming from behind the chairs of one table. He began walking towards it and soon saw that it had half a dozen occupants, all wearing the grey hooded jerkins of Certified Accounting Dwarfs.

The dwarf seated at the far end of the table stood up announcing herself as Talia, leader of the quest. Her long auburn hair was neatly tied in a single braid that hung down her back. She had almond shaped eyes and a wide thin mouth. When she spoke, each word was finished separately, giving her speech a clipped edge to it. Three dwarfs sat on the long side of the table facing Kirin, they did not look friendly. There were two more sitting on Talia's left with their backs to Kirin, one still had his hood up. Talia motioned for Kirin to sit between these two dwarfs which he did tentatively, as three pairs of eyes across the table burned into him.

"Welcome Kirin Numbercruncher, to the Company of the Quest." Talia's announcement was met by an overwhelming silence.

"This is a mistake," said the dwarf on Talia's right, her steady grey eyes never leaving Kirin.

"Quiet Bashka," said Talia.

Bashka turned to face Talia. "Seven's an unlucky number, an odd number. Eight would have been better." She turned to face Kirin, "or better still six."

"So suddenly you're an expert on numerology now!" said Talia.

Bashka held Talia's gaze for a moment before lowering her eyes to the table. "Just saying what everyone's thinking," she muttered before taking a swig from her tankard of milk.

The dwarf next to her stood up addressing Talia. "Look we don't need no Chartered Accountant!" He seemed to almost spit out the words. "Look at him, I don't care what anyone says, he's just gonna hold us up."

"Sit down Dargo!"

In the uneasy silence Talia fixed her gaze on Dargo till he had retaken his seat, before she spoke again. "We have not yet been formally introduced, would you have Kirin Numbercruncher here think that all Certified Accounting Dwarfs are discourteous oafs!" Dargo made to get up again but thought better of it. There were various grunts and mutterings before the group was silent. Talia then began the introductions, starting with the dwarf on her left, Freyla. She was slight of build and her fair hair was closely cropped. She was frowning, her focus seemed elsewhere. There was a nod of acknowledgement to Kirin but she said nothing. Kirin was just glad she wasn't angry with him. Talia continued introducing Bashka and Dargo, whose names Kirin had already caught and then the third dwarf sitting next to them, who was the largest dwarf Kirin had ever seen. It was not so much his height as his girth. This was Coulan, who it also happened was Dargo's brother. His eyes had never left Kirin all this time, giving the distinct impression that he was annoyed with him. And being in Coulan's bad books seemed a very bad place to be.

"And finally I believe you already know this fellow sitting next to you." The corner of Talia's mouth twitched slightly.

The fellow next to him lowered his hood, revealing a smiling Stilgoe. Kirin's mouth gaped open.

"Well I couldn't let you have all the fun, now could I?"

Things mellowed a little once the food arrived. Dwarves are definitely at their most convivial when enjoying a good meal. The courses just kept coming. Initially just platters of sandwiches and fruit, of which Kirin partook, but little did he know these were just the appetisers. Dwarfs can go days without food if need be, conversely of course they will eat to excess whenever they can. There were pies, both sweet and savoury, casseroles and pasta dishes, sword fish steaks and venison and side orders of roasted vegetables littered the table, and indeed the floor. At one point an entire roast wolf was served up to a great cheer and there was enough milk for even a dwarf of Coulan's appetite. The atmosphere was one of relaxed banter and boisterousness that came from comradeship and shared misadventure with only the occasional good natured squabble over the ownership of a certain bottle of ginger beer.

After the initial frenzy of feasting had faded, the room rang to the contented noises of well-fed dwarfs, unfortunately this was also accompanied by a great deal of out of tune singing. All in all it was not the most unpleasant way of spending a late summer's afternoon. It was at this point that Stilgoe took Kirin aside and explained a few delicate matters. Firstly, that the hunt for volunteers was just a publicity stunt and that Kirin (indeed any volunteers) weren't supposed to be going on the quest at all. It had just been a scheme dreamed up the Chamberlain to get the people enthused about the quest.

Competing questions sloshed around Kirin's head like someone was shaking him to make sense of it all. If he wasn't going on the quest would they still honour the contract? And what was going to happen to him in the meanwhile? But after all this publicity surely they would have to let him go? Perhaps it was better if he didn't go but he couldn't help but feel a little bit miffed about the whole arrangement. But it still felt like cheating somehow even if he would still be able to study mathematics at Shang-nam University, which was the point of applying in the first place. But then it occurred to Kirin, why had Dargo and Bashka still been so upset with him?

Stilgoe, who appeared to be enjoying himself, then added that, based on the strong recommendation of the Chancellor of Shang-nam University, Queen Zehalani had decided that Kirin *should* go on the quest after all. Kirin was beginning to feel like a yo-yo. Going, not going, going again! He had thought the Chancellor a queer old bird when he had first met him, very brusque, bordering on rude, when referring to his mother Riverna (whom he had taught) as merely a 'competent student'. But now why would the Chancellor of all people have insisted Kirin go on the quest?

Stilgoe seeing the look on Kirin's face just shook his head and smiled.

At this point Talia had joined them. "Have you told him the bad news yet?"

Kirin was not entirely sure if what he had just been told was bad news or not. Before Stilgoe could say anything, Kirin took control of the conversation. "Since you're in the mood for explaining, just what is the deal with this whole superpower thing the Elf Queen was talking about?"

Stilgoe and Talia looked at each other. "Told you he was smart," said Stilgoe shrugging at Talia. "You wanna break the news?"

"Yes smart enough to question the existence of superpowers but dumb enough to still believe in elves," said Talia.

"What?" said Kirin. "She's not a real elf?"

Stilgoe slapped his forehead. "No-one's a real elf. They don't exist!"

Kirin opened his mouth but then shut it again with a puzzled look on his face.

"Just because people *call* themselves, or others, all sorts of names: elves, trolls, goblins," said Stilgoe, "doesn't make it so."

Kirin smiled uncomfortably at Stilgoe's logic.

"Never mind that." Talia wasn't smiling now. "What I'm about to tell you doesn't go beyond this room. You understand?"

Kirin nodded.

"For the record, the small print of your contract agreement does not allow you to mention, discuss, or in any way disclose any information that you may encounter during the quest with any party etcetera, etcetera." Talia raised an eyebrow and waited on Kirin.

"OK! OK! I understand," said Kirin.

"The superpowers or rather the lack of them, was another of the Chamberlain's ideas," she said with a sigh. "Of course if you are ever talking to the Queen, it was her idea."

"So no superpowers. I knew it! I knew there was something fishy about that. I mean if she had all these superpowers then why would the Queen need us?" Kirin felt both elated and deflated at the same time. So much for his cunning plan.

"Well yes and no," said Stilgoe.

"I hate it when people say that," said Kirin.

"There are no superpowers but there are super gifts," said Stilgoe.

"Uh huh?" said Kirin.

"It's like this. Each of us got to choose a superpower. Well there are no actual superpowers but each of us did receive a related super gift, to help us with the quest." Stilgoe paused. "Getting the idea?"

"Continue," said Kirin.

"Take Bashka over there." Stilgoe nodded in her direction. Kirin glanced across the table where he could see Bashka eating a chicken drum stick in one hand while arm wrestling Dargo. "Her superpower was invisibility. Her super gift was a two week intensive course in camouflage techniques. She's actually pretty good. You see how it all works now?"

"I'm beginning too, tell me about the rest."

Stilgoe explained how the six of them had been in training for the last three months. Dargo's special power had been invincibility, and his super gift was a special shirt he wore next to his skin. It's fibres were of ancient design, tough, flexible and breathable like a second skin, but crucially it was almost impenetrable, resisting any attempt to puncture it. Coulan had chosen super strength. The irony of this apparently lost on Coulan. Anyway his gift had been a diet and exercise regime that had maximised his already phenomenal strength. For Freyla's power of flight, she had received a gift of an intensive aeronautics engineering course. She might not be able to fly but she knows as much about it as just about anyone in the Fourth Kingdom. Talia explained her own superpower had been to be able to swim like a dolphin. This seemed a strange choice to Kirin as dwarfs, despite being excellent sailors, generally hated going in the water. In any event her super gift was something called an aqua stick. This was a small cylindrical device about the size of your middle finger. In its centre was a mouth guard which a person gripped between their teeth and it then supplied air for up to thirty minutes breathing underwater. Stilgoe finished off his catalogue of powers and gifts with his own superpower which had been fire, or more specifically the ability to control fire. Importantly he wanted to be impervious to fire. For his trouble Stilgoe was sent on a survival course where he learned how to make fire from pretty much anything. Stilgoe did not regard this as a particularly super gift.

This was a lot to take in and as Kirin thought about it Stilgoe and Talia began discussing the plan for tomorrow. They would be getting an early start so it was time to start curtailing the festivities as there might not be too many good night's sleeps ahead of them.

"Wait a minute. What about my superpower, er, gift, I mean?" said Kirin.

Stilgoe and Talia looked up from their mini conference. "Eh, sorry Kirin. You weren't really supposed to be coming, remember? And it was all so last minute that…" Stilgoe shrugged. "You can have my fire lighter if you want?" He added, "It's just a bunch of crappy sticks."

Kirin smiled, He shook his head. "No, you should hang on to them, you never know." He wasn't disappointed, not really.

Tomorrow the quest would begin. How would he fare? Was he up to it. Would he live up to the promise his parents had said was within him? His thoughts drifted back to the evening before he left home. He was sitting with his father, Shalako, on the ramshackle jetty that poked into the Tervent river that flowed past their cottage. The sun had set behind Barrowhill and they were waiting for the first stars to appear, just like on a hundred other such nights. Kirin had asked about all the nobles at the court of Queen Zehalani. What was it that made them noble? His father had thought for a while before answering. He'd said that there were two kinds of noble. There was them that was born noble, really no different from anyone else, except that they were called Duke or Duchess or whatnot and that gave them a certain position in society. Then he said then there's the other kind of noble. That's the kind that anyone can be. They were noble, because of the things they did.

FEAR OF FLYING

They trooped out of Agra-nore in single file, Kirin bringing up the rear. It was early, just after dawn, and the dwarfs passing barely registered with the few local inhabitants who were up, scratching, yawning, and readying themselves for another day's toil. At the outskirts of town Talia, who was in the lead, snapped out the command and they all started jogging in unison. Kirin was caught momentarily off guard but quickly fell into step with the others and managed to keep up without too much trouble. A couple of hours later he was not so sure. The pace, though not fast, was unrelenting; tired and hungry, breakfast now seemed a very long time ago. Kirin had learned that the others were all Certified Accounting Dwarfs, the enforcers of the Accounting Dwarf community. As such they wore the customary grey hooded jerkins and each carried a quarterstaff as tall as their shoulder. While not necessarily great calculators, they were famed for their strength, endurance and fighting skills. As a Chartered Accounting Dwarf, Kirin's area of expertise relied more on mental prowess and his boast that he could do anything a Certified Accounting Dwarf could do, was now beginning to ring a little hollow.

Kirin recalled the inauspicious conversation with Talia before they had set out. He'd asked her, with a deal of curiosity, what was her grand plan to find the Tral-fe-tigore. She replied with a confident air that they had a map. Stilgoe smirked. Kirin looked around at the other dwarfs, most of whom found something of interest occupying them round their feet. Coulan's interest however lay in the sharpness of his knife blade, which he began testing with his thumb. With a yelp he dropped his knife and buried his thumb under an armpit. The knife, being well balanced for throwing, fell point first into Dargo's foot who doubled up in pain and in the process head-butted Coulan in the stomach. Both collapsed in a writhing heap of feet, thumbs and armpits. Ignoring the commotion Talia then announced that they also had a compass and that together with the map *and* the compass, getting the Tral-fe-tigore should be relatively straightforward. After that their only concern would be what to do with the gold and jewels bonus beyond their wildest dreams. The others all began punching the air and yelling 'Yey', with an occasional 'Yo', except of course for Coulan and Dargo who were still groaning on the ground clutching body parts.

The route Talia had planned out for them first led across the flattish fields and pastures that surrounded Agra-nore and then through the upland heaths, deserted except for a few sheep. They now found themselves winding round the side of a small hill with an increasingly steep drop on their left hand side. Kirin forced himself to look down. It was overgrown with brambles and nettles, which would at least break his fall. Suddenly the troop stopped. Kirin bumped into Dargo stepping on his foot, who then let out a surprisingly high pitched yelp.

"Sorry," mumbled Kirin.

"OK!" announced Talia. "This'll do." Talia and Bashka were saying something that Kirin couldn't quite make out. Bashka was pointing in the distance at something, she then handed Talia a small pair of binoculars. Kirin was about to ask Dargo what was happening, when he and the others started taking off their packs and, after a quick rummage, took out their elfin biscuits. To Kirin's surprise the small bundles were being launched into the air to disappear into the tangled undergrowth below. As Dargo was about to throw his Kirin put a hand on his arm. "Why are you all throwing away the elfin biscuits? They were a gift from the elves, eh, that is, the Queen."

Dargo snorted. "Their idea of a joke you mean." He eyed Kirin suspiciously. "What, you never tasted elfin biscuits?"

Kirin immediately realised he'd made a mistake. The others were all looking now. His father had once told him the best way to maintain a lie is to try and tell as much of the truth as possible.

"Eh, no," said Kirin, "my family were..."

"You're family were what?" said Dargo.

"Oh leave him be Dargo," said Freyla. "Not every dwarf family can afford elfin biscuits."

Dargo just snorted.

Kirin felt relieved and confused in equal measures.

"So," said Dargo, suddenly smiling at Kirin. "Want to try some now?"

The others began to smirk. Kirin looked at Freyla but she was just shaking her head. He decided refusing was not an option and stretched out his hand. "OK, I'll give it a go."

"Oh stop it Dargo," said Freyla. "You know that at his age he'll be elfin biscuit intolerant. Seeing him throw-up may be your idea of fun but it's not mine."

"Maybe, maybe not," said Dargo. Anyway he said he wanted to try it." He unwrapped an elfin biscuit and put it in Kirin's hand who steeled himself for something very unpleasant. Breaking off a small piece, he tentatively popped it in his mouth.

"You don't have to do this," said Freyla.

"Shhhh!" said Dargo, throwing Freyla an angry look.

Kirin began to chew tentatively. It was actually quite bland at first but then it had a distinctly bitter after taste. Really though it wasn't that bad. At least not for a him.

"Argh! Yeough!" Kirin coughed and spluttered as he turned away bending over in mock pain. He spat out some of the biscuit on to the ground and turned back with what he hoped was an angry, disgusted look on his face. Everyone burst out laughing, except Freyla. Dargo slapped Kirin on the back, causing him to swallow the remnants of the biscuit still in his mouth. Another round of laughing ensued, even Freyla joined in this time.

"The look on— Ha! Ha! Ha! When you swallowed— Ha! Ha! So funny." Dargo was bent over with laughter.

Kirin smiled a little at Dargo. It was a relief to see him laughing rather than his constant sneering, even if he was laughing at Kirin. "Well you could have warned me."

"OK," said Talia "Enough. There's still another two hours till lunch. Let's go"

While they were jogging Kirin felt a warm glow of well-being in his stomach. Gradually this spread throughout his body. His arms felt strong and powerful, his legs, like coiled springs. Half an hour ago he was wondering if he would last till lunch-time, now he felt he could run all day long. He slipped a hand inside his jerkin pocket, the remains of Dargo's elfin biscuit was still there also in all the confusion no-one, it seemed, had noticed that he hadn't thrown his own elfin biscuits away. They might prove very handy, but he would need to be more careful in future. He'd caught a lucky break this time, the quest had only just begun and there he was, nearly undone by a biscuit!

According to legend the answer to the location of the Tral-fe-tigore lay in the in the 'Tower' which stood on the western edge of the Forest of Teteunxx. From Agra-nore this was a full two day journey, passing through Birkin Wood to the foot of the Crumbling Mountains, then another day to climb them and from the summit they should be able to see the Tower. The dwarfs did not like to speak the name 'Forest of Teteunxx' referring to it as merely 'The Forest'. It was said to be a strange place, an evil place, the trees themselves unnatural. No-one lived there. It was said anyone who was foolish enough to enter would disappear never to be seen again. Though this did beg the question, who actually *they* were that had somehow managed to *say this*.

That evening when they made camp for the night, Kirin felt like an old man. His legs were throbbing agonisingly with every step and there were muscles he did not even know he had, that now ached alarmingly. The elfin biscuits had sustained his energy levels but muscles not up to the task now needed rest. He occasionally covered up to ten miles a day, roaming the woods and countryside by his home but today they must have jogged at least twice that! He dragged his aching body away from the campfire where the others were before rolling out his sleeping map, as a pretext he had asked Talia if he might study the map and compass. When no-one was looking he tentatively lay down and stretched out his legs. His face contorted with the pain as he forced himself not to make a sound, every movement now felt like a stab wound. He closed his eyes and took some deep breaths to steady himself but while he was doing this he heard a voice behind him.

"Thought you could do with some food." Freyla offered Kirin a bowl of stew.

"Thanks. Eh, just thought I'd go over Talia's map," said Kirin.

Freyla looked at the map, her face expressionless. She bent down setting the bowl beside him.

Kirin shrugged, not sure if she had seen him grimacing in pain or not. Would she tell the others? The thought of Dargo gloating over being proved right about Kirin slowing them down, brought a flush to his cheeks.

As Freyla stood up she whispered, "Rub it on your legs,

it will help." And with that she turned and walked back to her sleeping mat.

Kirin stared after her. Confused thoughts ran through his head. Rub stew on his legs? Was she crazy? Wait, she knew about his legs. Would she say anything? He watched her as she had a few words with Bashka and then take her boots off and lie down. Bashka was sitting quietly by the fire having her final smoke of the evening. If Freyla had said anything to her about him she was not reacting.

The smell of the food snapped Kirin back to how hungry he was. He began wolfing down the stew trying not to move his legs in the process. It was then he noticed on the grass beside him a small brown glass jar. He unscrewed the top. Inside was translucent ointment or salve of some kind, bringing it up to his nose, it had a faint smell of mint. This must be what she meant for him to rub on his aching legs. He looked over at Freyla, her back was to him and she appeared asleep already. The others had seemed like a rag-tag bunch but they'd outlasted him today, and they'd accomplished that without the benefit of elfin biscuits. Looking over he observed them practice sparring round the campfire, they were pretty handy with their quarterstaffs and more than that, they seemed a tight unit, each knowing their place and at ease with one another. From his detached position Kirin felt like an unwelcome intruder He was seriously doubting how well he was prepared for this quest.

He decided to check his pack before going to sleep, which contained a few items that his parents had thought might prove useful for whatever trials and tribulations might still lie in store for him. There was over a hundred feet of his father's fishing twine, a variety of fishing hooks and floats, an old wire coat hanger, and most valuable of all, a quantity of bark-ties. These were 18 inches long, thin strips of pliable bark with v-shaped notches like barbs cut along both edges, one end of the barkstrip had been softened and corded like string, which was then made into a slipknot. A few of these bark-ties were carefully placed along each of his forearms, secured by a leather wristband and all concealed by his shirt sleeves. The end with the slipknot was left protruding slightly such that with a deft pull Kirin would instantly have a bark-tie to hand. Then by slipping the barbed end of the bark-tie through the slipknot end he could quickly secure whatever he had encircled with the bark-tie. This was his father's invention, and was used in the self-defence technique he had taught Kirin.

The next day Kirin awoke at the persistent nudging of Stilgoe's boot.

"OK sleepyhead, get your stuff together. You've just time for some stew," Stilgoe nodded at the campfire, "if you're quick."

Rubbing the sleep out of his eyes Kirin just nodded. He stretched and yawned. Too late! He almost cried out in pain as he anticipated the agony from his legs, but there was nothing. His legs felt fine. Maybe a little sore but nothing compared to last night. That salve had really worked. He looked towards his pack were the small glass jar was securely stored. Smiling he got up. Deciding to have some more of that nourishing stew that helped him sleep so well, he looked around for last night's bowl, but it was nowhere to be seen.

As they set off at the same jogging pace as yesterday, Kirin fingered the remains of the elfin biscuit in his pocket. There was still two thirds of it left and he still had his own pack of six biscuits. He decided it would be best to ration them, figuring about a third of a one a day should be about right. His legs felt a little stronger today. If nothing else, this quest was going to get him in the shape of his life.

Within an hour Bashka called a halt. She indicated to Talia something on the horizon. Kirin peered into the distance, as did some of the others, but he still had no idea what Bashka had seen. Eyes like telescopes was all that

Dargo muttered. Talia held out her hand and Bashka retrieved her binoculars. Kirin had not noticed before, the little utility pouches she had on her belt. He manoeuvred himself up to be behind Bashka before they set off again.

After a little while Kirin could make out Birkin Wood on the horizon. They entered it shortly before lunch. The trees were densely packed in places, with thick undergrowth that slowed their pace to something Kirin was more used to. Initially Kirin had felt pleased about this, more comfortable in this his usual habitat, but something else was happening which alarmed him. On the open road the dwarfs were efficient and effective travellers. But not so much in the woods. Here they had a serious liability, it was the amount of noise they were making, Coulan and Bashka in particular. It was almost as if they went out of their way to step on every dry twig!

* * * *

Kirin squirmed his back against the tree, trying to get more comfortable as he relaxed after lunch. The others too were doing likewise. To his left he watched as Coulan noisily ate a large sandwich in one hand, while scratching himself with the other. Bashka was sitting directly across from him, holding a half eaten apple in one hand and, he now realised, was staring at him intently.

"Been watching you," said Bashka. "You seem pretty at home in the woods."

Kirin shrugged.

"As quiet as a little mouse you are." Bashka winked at Stilgoe.

"No sense making more noise than you need to," said Kirin.

There was a pause as Bashka continued to stare at Kirin.

"You saying I'm clumsy." There was something about Bashka's tone that seemed to draw all other sound out of the air. Everyone stopped eating, even Coulan. All eyes were bearing down on Kirin now, like he'd crossed some invisible line.

"Eh I didn't mean anything... I, eh."

Kirin felt his heart thumping noisily in his chest. Unsure what to do he struggled to his feet, wondering how you were supposed to see an invisible line anyway?

Bashka laughed, quickly followed by everyone else.

"Just messing with you Charter-mouse," said Bashka. She turned to the others laughing and sharing the joke before taking a noisy chunk out of her apple.

Kirin sat down again and decided to examine his fingernails in great detail. He got out his pocketknife and began to clean out the dirt from beneath them while the others grinned and winked at each other, pointing at him. Five minutes later Talia gave the word to move.

Kirin manoeuvred himself up next to Talia. "I was wondering sometime, when it's convenient, if you could show me some of those camouflage techniques Stilgoe said you were so good at?" asked Kirin.

"In your dreams Charter-mouse." said Bashka, who then moved off in Talia's direction. She turned her head back to Kirin. "Maybe sometime."

Kirin fell in line behind Bashka. He gave her a little more room as her pace was more sporadic slowing suddenly for a bit before speeding up again. She was still making as much noise as before, just about.

* * * *

The Crumpled Mountains marked the northern boundary of the Fourth Kingdom. Queen Zehalani laid claim to the Forest of Teteunxx and the lands beyond, but in practice the jagged peaks of the mountain range were a geographical barrier few of her subjects would even attempt, much less overcome. Looking up Kirin could see why. They were magnificent of course, a sight to behold in the setting sun, and seemed to extend as far as the eye could see, both east and west. So many peaks, so high up, they reminded him of a saw blade. Whoever had named them either had a sense of humour or was playing the long game expecting the name to be more accurate in about a million years. They didn't have to climb the peaks of course but the passes between them were not much lower. And as if that wasn't enough even the passes were all covered in a layer of snow and ice. This close, the mountains towered above him. Every time he looked up at them, the shifting shadows had rippled across their surface, changing it, like the rocks themselves had moved when he wasn't looking. Jogging along the hill path with its steep drop the previous day had been scary enough, but this was literally taking it to another level.

He wandered over to the Talia, Stilgoe and Bashka who were pouring over the map discussing the best route to take tomorrow. He rubbed his thighs, they were sore, but less so than yesterday. Now they seemed to be the least of his problems.

"So what's the plan then?" Kirin asked.

"Up and over." Stilgoe pointed to what looked like the highest peak. "Early start, so best get a good night's rest." He slapped Kirin on the back. His right hand still held the map and compass.

"Mind if I have a look?" Kirin indicated the map. Talia and Bashka who had been talking looked over. Ignoring them Kirin looked down at the map Stilgoe had handed him. Without looking up he asked, "What about the possibility of going round?" Not even focusing on the map, he swallowed and waited.

"You're kidding right?" Stilgoe pointed on the map Kirin was holding. "In the east, it continues for over a hundred miles before eventually meeting another mountain range even taller. And in the west, it eventually turns north, going all the way to the ice lands. Besides the Tower should be just over the other side."

Bashka and Talia were looking over at Kirin now, who felt her almond eyes quietly studying him.

"Don't worry Charter-mouse. It'll be a piece of cake," said Bashka.

Kirin smiled, "Just thought I'd ask."

Sitting down Kirin examined the map carefully. He placed the map directly in front of him facing the east-west mountain range with due north straight ahead of him. He lined up the compass or at least he tried to. It was saying north was slightly to the right of where the map said it was. He tapped the compass, then let it settle several times, but each time it said north was to the right of the map's north. Maybe the map wasn't quite right. He vaguely recalled reading something about magnetic north and true north? Anyway the others knew all about this stuff. What would they say? He's just making excuses because he's scared of the climb, even blaming the map and compass. Looking from the map to the mountains beyond, he could see the pass that Stilgoe had indicated. It was quite far over on the right and it really did look like one of the highest. He put aside the compass for a moment and tried to concentrate. He scanned the mountains looking for the lowest pass. There was one, but it was way over to the left. It didn't look as high. Of course there was no telling if it was any more or less dangerous.

He stood up and strolled over to Stilgoe and offered him back the map and compass but didn't say anything. Stilgoe, who was talking to Talia, took the map and said, "Oh Coulan likes to hold on to the compass." He nodded in Coulan's direction, then continued talking to Talia.

Kirin gave Coulan back the compass who greeted it like a long lost pal. He scowled at Kirin as if he had been deliberately keeping them apart. Kirin apologised though for what he was not quite sure. The hard knot in his stomach was back, it drowned out any other concerns. He went through the rest of his routines that evening in a trance. He looked to the darkening sky and the forlorn hope that perhaps bad weather tomorrow might save him but even then they'd probably still attempt the climb. He grimaced at the thought. He lay awake long after the others had turned in and it was only the sheer exhaustion of his body soothed by the salve on his legs that eventually let him fall into a fitful sleep. One where his dreams played out disastrous scenarios from simple missed footings and frayed ropes breaking, to tempestuous storms and avalanches. But all of them ending with that long, lonely fall, where he clawed helplessly at the empty air.

* * * *

Now that Kirin was actually on the ledge, it all felt very real. He was sweating despite the gusting cold wind threatening to whip him of the mountainside, like he didn't belong there. His legs were like lead weights and with every step Kirin felt his chest tighten as his breathing became shallower and his heart beat faster, like that would help. The ledge now was only wide enough for one at a time and Kirin was climbing between Stilgoe and Bashka, in the middle of the group. He kept as far to the left as he could, but the ledge was so narrow now it hardly made a difference. His left hand caressed the rock wall as if it could save him. and he kept his eyes pinned on Bashka's back, knowing if he looked down the sheer cliff he was lost.

It all seemed to happen in slow motion. On moment the ground under his feet was solid, the next he was flying. It actually felt like he was floating, cocooned in a bubble of air, that was pleasantly cool against his clammy skin. Freed from the restraints of gravity his whole being felt incredibly light. The wind had died away to the softest of breezes, and above him he could just make out the muted voices of his companions. This was not a thing to be feared. This was to be embraced, celebrated. At the back of his mind though there was a tiny black spot of gnawing doubt.

Suddenly there was an annoyingly sharp pain in his right shoulder and wrist. He looked up. Bashka had a hold of his wrist in both of her hands and bizarrely, she was also halfway off the ledge herself. His mind was oddly calm and calculating. This was not possible, her centre of gravity was below the ledge. She should be toppling down the cliff along with him. This troubled him. It was a puzzle. But he was good at solving puzzles. He could do this.

"Grab my hand!"

Kirin looked up to his left. It was Stilgoe, stretching his hand towards him. Now he too was impossibly balanced like Bashka. This was a conundrum.

"Kirin," said Stilgoe calmly "Reach up with your left hand and take my hand."

Kirin looked down at his left arm. It was wafting gently in the air like it was someone else's. Beyond it everything looked so far away that it hardly mattered.

"Don't look down Kirin," shouted Stilgoe.

"I'm losing him, I can't hold him much longer," shouted Bashka.

Kirin looked up at the two animated faces above him, slowly he forced himself to concentrate and willed his left arm to move. Slowly it began to move, stretching up, inch by inch. He knew it was important. He was not sure why? But he could do this. There was muffled shouting and screaming from up above but Kirin ignored it. The only thing that mattered was the upward movement of his arm. Another stab of pain, as a vice like force grabbed his left wrist. Suddenly the wind was buffeting his body once more and the cries of anguish, confusion, and jubilation assailed his ears. Above him he saw Stilgoe's hand gripping his arm just above the wrist, his own fingers now closed tight, clenching Stilgoe.

"I've got him," cried Stilgoe. "OK, now haul me up."

Slowly but surely Kirin was bundled back up on to the ledge. He sat there for what seemed an age, back against the ledge a heaving mass of pounding heart and heavy breathing. Looking to his left he saw Dargo lying across Bashka's legs, with Talia on top of Dargo. He started to laugh, soon they were all laughing.

THE FOREST OF TETEUNXX

They were still pretty high up, above the snow line, Kirin could feel the cold and wet creeping in as he sat with his back anchored against a rock but he didn't mind. He had gotten over the mountain! It wasn't possible but somehow he had, thanks to Bashka, Stilgoe and the others but still, *he'd* done it. And now here he was sitting on top of a mountain staring off in to the distance. He breathed in deeply. The cold mountain air felt exhilarating. The Forest of Teteunxx now lay beneath them. The only problem, it was in the wrong place. First the arguments started, then the fighting, and from there it got real messy pretty quick. But as for Kirin, he just sat watching the quarrelling dwarfs in front of him like he used to watch the behaviour of ants as a child. He felt... there was no other word for it, serene.

His gaze roamed over to his right, away from the dwarfs. to where the rock face fell sharply away forming a vertical drop of several hundred feet. Suddenly the nausea returned, that hard knot formed once more in the pit of his stomach, his head began to swim and had he not already been sitting he might have fallen. He looked away. Not cured after all. He closed his eyes taking several deep breaths, trying to get that feeling of serenity back, but it had gone.

Opening his eyes it was a mess. Bashka had actually punched Stilgoe, who was clutching his eye. Dargo was calling Talia several very uncomplimentary names which cast substantial doubt on her leadership abilities. Talia, one hand grabbing Dargo's jerkin, was asking in no uncertain terms if he could have done any better. To Kirin, being at the wrong end of the Forest of Teteunxx didn't seem like such a big deal; a molehill compared to a mountain. Coulan was sitting off in the distance. Kirin couldn't be sure but he suspected Coulan's legs were dangling over a sheer drop. Kirin's stomach churned. Bizarrely amongst all the commotion Coulan was playing with a yo-yo. While he was watching Freyla came over and crouched down by Coulan's side. He couldn't hear what they were saying but Coulan put his yo-yo down carefully and after rummaging in his pockets opened his hands showing Freyla the contents. Freyla said something before patting Coulan on the shoulder and then approached Dargo and Talia.

"A magnet." Freyla held up a small red U-shaped object.

"What!" said Talia, one hand still gripping Dargo's jerkin. Dargo also focused a puzzled expression on the diminutive metal object.

Freyla explained that among Coulan's many little toys that he was fond of, was a magnet. Which did not make for good bedfellows with his other toy, the compass. Being stuck together in Coulan's pocket had been shifting the compass off north. Even before selecting the mountain pass they had been far too east to begin with. The cumulative result was that they were maybe thirty miles east of where they should have been.

Now a whole new set of arguments and recriminations broke out. Kirin shook his head and looked down at the forest below them, examining it in greater detail. They were at its eastern edge now, but their objective the Tower, was close to the western edge and of course nowhere to be seen. Teteunxx Forest was truly unique. Not predominantly green but literally every colour under the rainbow. From up here it was beautiful, but violet trees? Reds and oranges and yellows were common in autumn, but this was midsummer. There was one other thing that caught his attention in the forest. In the distance rising straight up into the fresh blue sky, was an unmistakable thin wisp of woodsmoke.

Despite all the arguing there really was only one choice now. The slope they were on was too steep and dangerous to traverse across and going back was now was no longer an option with the ledge having given way in places. No, the only way for them now was down, and into the Forest of Teteunxx. No-one said anything about the prospect of having to travel the entire length of the forest, but it hung over the dwarfs like an ominous storm cloud. Coulan was upset of course about not getting to hold on to his toy anymore and Dargo hadn't handled explaining that very well. Stilgoe's normal good humour seemed to have deserted him as he nursed his eye, with a handkerchief of ice pressed against it, and Talia kept shouting at Bashka every time she dislodged a rock causing a mini avalanche. If Freyla had not been between them during the descent there might have been more fisticuffs. For Kirin the path down was less traumatic than the ascent but it was still no picnic. The descent took the best part of four hours and night was falling when a somewhat sullen Company of the Quest made camp by a small stream not far from the edge of the forest. After a subdued meal where no-one was much in the mood for talking Kirin went to help Freyla who was washing their supper bowls.

"That was pretty cool. I mean figuring out the whole magnet thing," said Kirin.

Freyla continued washing her bowl in the stream.

"I eh, actually thought it might be something like that," said Kirin.

Freyla stopped cleaning her bowl for a moment, before

continuing. "Is that so? When exactly was that."

"Eh, well, before we climbed the mountain," said Kirin.

Freyla turned to look at Kirin. "I see, and you thought it best not to share that information?"

"Well, um. I wasn't..."

"Guess you Chartered Accountants just like keeping all that precious knowledge to yourselves. Huh?"

With that she got up and left. Kirin scratched his head as he watched her walk back to the camp. He hadn't even thanked her for the salve she had given him.

The next day various plans were put forward and rejected, but this time all the arguing took place in muted half-voices and shouted whispers. The forest felt oppressive, malignant even. No-one said so but Kirin figured they were all thinking what he was thinking. It was listening. In daylight he got a good look at the trees which were widely spread this close to the edge of the forest. They just looked wrong. There was a beech tree, based on its leaves (even if they were orange), but there was no large rounded crown, it just shot straight up with short thin branches like a pine. And there a oak tree, the right shape but this time with a soft spongy bark and leaves, the right shape, but more blue than green. Something screwy here, unless that wasn't an beech or an oak? There was something else, something he hadn't noticed till Talia pointed it out to him. The forest was strangely quiet, there were a few birds, but no insects.

Kirin shook himself, and concentrated on the matter at hand. He hadn't proved too useful so far. Perhaps he could come up with a cunning plan. He had been listening. as they had rejected the obvious plan of simply travelling the full width of the forest to get to the Tower. No-one wanted that! What had made the initial plan viable was that they only had to venture in a few miles or so from the western edge to get to the Tower. Some had even suggested heading east and looking for a good route back over the Crumbling Mountains, but that of course meant giving up on the quest.

Kirin came up with a proposal that they split into two parties. Talia, Stilgoe and Kirin would venture into the forest on a short scouting mission to see just what perils it actually had to offer and also check out the source of the woodsmoke, which was relatively close to the edge. The three of them could travel more quickly and silently (though Kirin did not mention that) than the whole group and if there was trouble they could make a quick escape. Meanwhile the second group of Dargo, Bashka, Coulan and Freyla would remain at the edge of the forest. Indeed they could fortify their position with some traps, using Coulan's strength and Bashka's camouflage skills. In two days, at most, the scouting team would return and they would know if it was safe to proceed or abandon the quest. There were various nods of approval. Dargo grunted, he made it clear he needed to be doing something, anything, sitting about here was not an option.

Well it's a plan" said Talia not overly enthusiastically. "Anyone got any objections?" No-one raised any. "OK, but Stilgoe I want you to stay here. Dargo you're with me and Kirin here."

"Really? If you're worried about my eye..."

Talia looked at Stilgoe, whose right eye was nearly closed surrounded by an unhealthy looking purple bruise. "No. I want you in charge here. OK?"

Stilgoe nodded.

Coulan looked a little unhappy. Perhaps at the prospect of being separated from his brother especially coming so soon after losing his compass. Kirin looked at Freyla, who had said nothing all morning, her face passive with that same far-away look as when they'd first met. She walked over to Coulan. "OK, lets you and I get started on fortifications. We'll have a look, see the lay of the land." Coulan nodded and followed her.

Kirin just couldn't read her at all.

* * * *

Kirin was regretting suggesting that he be included in the scouting party. Sitting about building a fort struck him as a much cushier job at the moment. The elfin biscuits were helping and his legs were stronger now, but it was still tough going. Talia was nearly as good at moving through the forest as he was and Dargo slightly less so, resulting in their speed through the forest being faster than the group. Their pace was also helped by the sparse undergrowth and by how widely and evenly spaced apart the trees were, even though they were now deep into it. There was something else though that troubled Kirin even more, the forest floor had no game trails or even any signs of smaller creatures, it was as undisturbed as a freshly laid snowfall. The unfortunate upshot of which was, despite their best efforts, they were leaving a trail that even a blind man could follow.

They had been taking turns on point as they headed towards the smoke and Kirin was leading when he froze and held up his fist (the universal signal to those behind him to stop silently), the others all piled into the back of him. After an angry exchange of whispers concerning pre-agreed signals, Kirin explained the reason for the halt. Tracks.

They proceeded more slowly, taking extra care to make no sound, The footprints seemed to indicate three or four people, whether men, or dwarfs none of them could say. Presently they heard voices. They swung round to the left so as to approach down wind. They could hear the gurgling of water and smell the woodsmoke now but they could hear something else too. They soon found themselves stumbling through marshy ground that opened out into a river maybe fifteen yards wide. On the far side was a small jetty, though with nothing moored at it, and beyond that a clearing. They could see a camp fire with some figures huddled round it. In the distance there was what looked like a low cave from which strange sounds seemed to be coming. With the noise from the river they were too far away to hear anything useful. There was only one thing for it and Kirin said so.

"What do you mean swim!" Dargo managed to whisper and growl at the same time.

"You can swim?" said Talia.

"Eh, my father was a fisherman," said Kirin realising he'd made another blunder, as dwarfs don't swim.

"Your father can swim too?" said Talia.

"Eh, No he can't." said Kirin which was true. "Long story. This is not the time— Wait a minute Talia you've got your aqua stick thing?"

"Oh yes I do, don't I." Talia did not look very keen.

"Look it's not that far and I'll be there to help you," said Kirin.

Dargo just shrugged. "No way I go in the water," he mumbled.

"Fine." said Kirin before anyone said anything else. "You get to stay here as lookout." He looked at Talia who nodded but still didn't seem very happy. There was a further heated exchange of whispers on what signals should be used. It was settled that in the event of danger Dargo would do his blackbird impression, which was actually surprisingly good.

Their side of the river was shallow with reeds offering cover, leaving their packs behind, Kirin and Talia eased themselves into the water. Their aim was to use the jetty on the other side as cover. The water was shockingly cold but fortunately did not have much of a current. In the end Talia's lack of swimming ability was not an issue. She actually walked across the bottom of the river bed, which at its deepest, was only about ten or eleven feet. Talia's problem though, was that she kept her eyes shut the whole way across, and emerged some ten yards downriver. However once her head was above water again she quickly waded back to the cover of the jetty. Fortunately there was space enough beneath the jetty for them both to haul themselves out of the river, just about. They waited for a few minutes, making sure they had not been seen and then squirmed out on their stomachs and up the bank to get a better view. They could now clearly see the three figures, dwarfs, sitting around the campfire. They seemed grimy and unkempt, not at all like forest dwellers. Kirin and Talia settled in for the long haul. It was not comfortable but at least they were out of the river and were warming up again.

Over the next two and a half hours they picked up a fragmented picture of what was happening, as the three dwarfs were griping about their boss. In the cave beyond was a forge where they were smelting gold coins into ingots. These then got shipped back by raft on the river that flowed all the way to the western edge of the forest. A tall man who seemed to be their leader, came over for it seemed no other purpose than to vent his frustrations about his bosses the Shysters. Talia mouthed the word to herself. Kirin felt frustrated but resisted the temptation to ask. They (the Shysters) were too clever for their own good, the man said. They had the brains to come up with tax-dodging pyramid schemes, but couldn't manage the simple task of delivering a shipment of gold coins on bloody time. And if they thought he was paying dwarf wages for sitting about on their arses out of his cut, they were very much mistaken. With that he stormed off. Talia mouthed the words Money Launderers to Kirin, who had no idea what she was talking about.

At one point one of the dwarfs approached the river. Kirin and Talia quickly slithered back under the jetty, bunching up against each other just inches below the wooden planking. They held their breath. There were footsteps above them which then stopped. Kirin scrunched up on his elbows couldn't see above him but after a few seconds he heard, from his right, the unmistakable sound of a stream of liquid tinkling into the river. Kirin clamped his hand over his mouth to keep from making a sound. His body though was juddering with laughter. A punch in his ribs told that Talia did not share his amusement. The jetty above them creaked ominously and then over his left shoulder he saw a bucket, being dipped it into the river half filling it. He wasn't laughing now. The bucket withdrew and moments later the footsteps left the jetty and back to the campfire.

During the dwarfs' talk there was one name, that when it came up in conversation, caused Talia's brows to furrow. Sang-gast. It was not clear what his role was. The other dwarfs did not seem to care for him much, but what were they to read into that? It was dusk when the dwarfs fell asleep. Kirin and Talia slipped quietly back into the water and rejoined Dargo on the other side of the river.

Talia explained to Kirin what Money Launderers were. They took stolen or swindled gold and coins then melted them down into ingots. This 'new money' was untraceable and could be used to buy goods and services or invest in legitimate businesses without any awkward questions being asked about where the money came from. Money Laundering was of course illegal, but difficult to prove. If asked they could just say the dug the gold out of the ground. No need to declare its origin, no need for legitimate paperwork, no need for pesky taxes. The Shysters were drawn from all races. They were people of poor character. Essentially they swindled the honest citizens of the Fourth Kingdom out of their money. Using bogus investments they exchanged impressive but worthless certificates for cold hard coinage, preferably gold. The Shysters then skipped town and their victims, even if they realised they'd been duped, were usually too embarrassed to report the crime. The gold and coins were shipped off here to the forest somehow. Here it was all melted down into untraceable gold ingots. Talia also explained about the dwarfs. They were fallen dwarfs. Dwarfs who no longer adhered to the code. They hired themselves out as heavies doing the dirty work of others. In this case as Money Launderers.

"Why would they do such a thing?" asked Kirin.

"Economic hardship and the recession are a powerful driving forces," said Talia, shrugging.

"It's tough for everyone," growled Dargo and spat on to the ground.

"Well it's clear to see why the Fourth Kingdom is in an economic downturn," said Talia. "All its money is ending up here and in the hands of the Shysters." Talia rolled her eyes and gave Kirin a long hard look. "Hmmmm. Guess that's what comes from a capitalist, money based economy," she said.

"Yeah OK, we all want to change the system, but we're stuck with it till something better comes along," said Kirin with a sigh.

Talia was about to respond when Kirin asked, "So who's this Sang-gast?"

"Sang-gast!" said Dargo suddenly very alert.

"Shhhh!" hissed Talia.

"What's Sang-gast got to do with all this?" said Dargo ducking down slightly as if that made his voice quieter.

"Can't say for sure, but I think he's over there." Talia indicated with her head across the river.

Dargo made a low growling noise and gave the far bank of the river a very unpleasant look indeed.

Talia was of the opinion that they should rescue Sang-gast. Dargo was not. A heated, despite being whispered, discussion ensued. Talia insisted that whatever Sang-gast might or might not be *they* needed to adhere to the Dwarf code which meant not leaving him behind. Dargo held to a more flexible interpretation of the code which, when it suited him, he regarded more as guidelines.

"He's an Accounting Dwarf. We don't leave one of our own behind." Talia glared at Dargo.

"Him, I could happily leave," said Dargo. "Besides he's not one of us, not Certified."

"Oh, like Kirin here? You going leave him behind too?" said Talia.

Dargo's brows furrowed, "Besides, how do we know he's not working with them. Wouldn't put it past him." mumbled Dargo

"And we *won't know,* till we talk to him," said Talia.

"You realise that we'll likely bring the whole lot of them down on top of us. No chance of getting to the Tower after that," said Dargo.

"The Tower?" laughed Talia. "The Tower? We'll be lucky to get out of this without suffering the same fate as everyone else who's ever entered the forest!"

A wry smile did play about Dargo's lips for a moment. He shook his head, "You don't know him. I've had dealings with him before and I don't like him," he said firmly. "I say no."

Talia sighed. "OK then. It's Kirin's decision." The both turned to Kirin.

"What? You're joking, right? I mean I'm not even a—"

"You're an Accounting Dwarf. You have the casting vote," said Talia.

"A Chartered one," mumbled Dargo.

"He's an Accounting Dwarf and gets a vote," said Talia. She fixed her eyes on Dargo waiting, till eventually he nodded.

They both turned to Kirin once more. "This is a dangerous situation Kirin. If we're caught they won't want to leave any witnesses." Talia's voice trailed away in to the darkening air.

"Eh, give me a minute here guys." With that Kirin ducked down and began moving through the trees round to the left of their position. Within ten minutes he was back, facing some very angry stares.

"OK I thought if we were going to mount some kind of rescue mission, we would need some better way of getting across the river. I figured they might need a way of crossing the river themselves and as it happens they do. It looks like the river comes down from the mountains and there's a wooden bridge across it, just out of sight up to the left."

The others looked up to the left, where Kirin had pointed, for the bridge that was out of sight, then back to Kirin.

"OK a decision. Well I guess... we go rescue him." Kirin shrugged.

Dargo turned away in disgust. "We're all gonna die... for *him*."

"Probably," said Talia "But at least you won't get wet."

Dargo looked up, that wry smile was back again.

Kirin smiled along with the others, till he realised what they were actually smiling about.

It was a simple plan. Get a few hours sleep till midnight, then slip in across the bridge, grab Sang-gast, slip out again, back across the bridge then run as fast as they could back to Stilgoe and the others. What could possibly go wrong?

From their vantage point, behind some trees near the bridge, they saw the extent of the Money Launderer's operation. The clearing with the cave was actually a spur of land with the river on three sides, almost doubling back on itself. To the far right was the jetty and the campfire of the three sleeping workers and directly in front of them there was only a short path that led to the left side of the cave. The centre of the cave was dominated by a giant metal structure. It consisted of two giant A-frames made of steel girders, they stood parallel about twenty feet apart. The two A-frames were criss-crossed by smaller girders, to strengthen the whole structure and at the top they were joined together by a round, solid steel bar. A giant metal cauldron was suspended by two hooks and chains from this steel bar and there was a large fire below it. This is what they were using to smelt the gold. Money Laundering on an industrial scale.

On the front side the cauldron had a spout like a teapot and on the back side, a third metal hook and chain was attached, but this time at the bottom. This chain, operated manually via a series of pulleys, was used to tip the cauldron, spilling its molten contents into a smaller metal trough in front of it. This trough had a sluice gate that could be opened to allow the molten gold to flow down a chute into small brick moulds each about as long as your hand. There was a large, neat stash of these small golden ingots nearby.

The three night shift smelters were huddled round a small fire in front of the cauldron, quietly talking. There was no sign of the tall man or of Sang-gast. To the right of the cauldron was just a pile of scrap metal but on the left, directly across from the bridge, was a large stack of logs and a small ramshackle hut that looked as if it was likely to fall down at any minute. There was nothing else. Sang-gast and the man must be in there.

Quickly but quietly they slipped across the bridge and back into the cover of the trees. As they made their way to the cave they came across a track that led westwards into the heart of the forest. This must be where the shipments of gold coins arrived from the Fourth Kingdom. The stopped and peered into the darkness, listening. But all they heard was the unnatural quiet of Teteunxx Forest. At the side of the hut, they hunkered down behind a barrel, where they were hidden from view from the smelters. The hut which was bigger than they had realised, more of a shack really, had one grimy window at the front beside the door, which was closed. When the smelters moved out of sight Kirin crept round. He listened carefully for a minute. It seemed an eternity. He thought he could hear someone snoring. He decided to risk a look. A moment later he was back round the side of the hut with the others.

"The tall man is sleeping on a bunk to the left of the door. At the far end there's a dwarf. He's sitting at a desk with his back to the door, seems to be working on the books. Didn't see anyone else or any other exits," whispered Kirin, to a focused Talia. Dargo was nodding in the background.

"OK," whispered Talia. "We do this by the numbers. I'll go first and tackle Sang-gast. Dargo you're right behind me. You immobilise the tall guy. No excessive force OK?" Dargo moved his head in a somewhat indeterminate fashion. "Then you bring up the rear, check if we were spotted." Talia looked at Kirin, who nodded.

By the time Kirin got inside, Dargo was sitting astride a now struggling tall man in his bunk, Dargo's hand clasped firmly over the man's mouth. Quickly Kirin pulled a bark-tie from his belt and secured the man's kicking legs. Dargo tapped the man gently on the forehead with his knife. He stopped struggling. Kirin with his own knife cut off a piece of bed sheet and stuffed it into the man's mouth, with another piece of sheet he tied a gag round his mouth. Dargo got off the man, indicating he should roll over on to his front. Kirin cut another piece of bed sheet and bound the man's hands behind him. Dargo examined Kirin's bark-tie round the man's ankles.

"Handy thing that, got any more?" he asked.

"Not so many as I can waste them. Better see if Talia needs you." With that Kirin retied the man's ankles with some of the rapidly diminishing bed sheets and retrieved his bark-tie, slipping it back into his wristband with a silent thank you to his father. He quickly checked outside again before joining the others at the far end of the hut. He nodded to Talia that everything was OK. Sitting on a stool next to her was a dwarf with short grey hair and sparkling blue eyes. His face seemed both curious and anxious at the same time, his hands rested on a, now closed, small, black book.

"Dwarfs! Indeed Accounting Dwarfs no less! Thank heavens!" said Sang-gast, for it was indeed that very dwarf. He made to clap his hands till Talia grabbed his wrist. Bringing the forefinger of her other hand up to her lips." Oh of course, of course," said Sang-gast in a rather loud whisper. "You've come here to save me? Yes?"

"That remains to be seen," said Dargo his eyes fixed on

Sang-gast.

Talia flashed Dargo a look. "OK start talking Sang-gast. What's the set-up here?"

"They, they kidnapped me, forced me to do their books," said Sang-gast clutching at Talia's jerkin.

There was something about the way Sang-gast was cloying at Talia that Kirin found distasteful.

"Well from what I hear that wouldn't be the first time," said Talia, "But that's not what I asked you."

"Ah, you know of me, but I don't know you," said Sang-gast. "Your friend here, giving me the black looks, he does look familiar."

"Look we can leave the introductions till later. Right now, how many more of them are there?"

"Eh, just Thomas there," Sang-gast pointed, "and the three smelters outside."

"And the day shift?" asked Talia.

"Yes, oh yes there are another three smelters, they're sleeping just now but—"

"Is there anyone else," asked Talia. "Anyone else expected?"

"No, No that's all. You are here to rescue me aren't you?"

To Kirin this Sang-gast seemed a bit nervous but then again who wouldn't be in his situation. He popped back to the window to check outside. All was quiet. He looked round the hut, there didn't seem to be anything of much interest. Sang-gast was now telling Talia how he'd been kidnapped. Kirin looked down at Sang-gast's hands they were pressed firmly on the small black book on the desk.

"Mind if I have a look at that?" Kirin asked making to take the book. For a moment Kirin thought there was a flash of anger in Sang-gast's eyes, but his facial expression never changed.

"Oh I don't suppose it would make much sense to you. It's in code." Sang-gast held on to the book.

"Indulge me," said Kirin, "I do like all the pretty

colours you Chartered Accountants use."

Talia looked at Kirin curiously but said nothing.

"Eh, of course," said Sang-gast relinquishing the little black book. Turning to Talia he asked, "How many are you and how on earth did you find this place?"

Kirin took the book and went back to check on outside again. He flipped through its pages. Annoyingly Sang-gast was right he couldn't make any sense of it. It was all a jumble of letters and numbers. He slipped the book into his back pocket and peered out the window taking care to keep himself hidden.

Talia explained briefly about the quest and how they'd been searching for the Tower.

"The Tower?" repeated Sang-gast.

"What do you know of it?" asked Dargo.

"Nothing," said Sang-gast. "I mean there's nothing to know."

"You've seen it?" asked Talia..

"Yes, but it's at the other end of the forest you know?"

"Yes, we know," said Dargo.

"Carry on," said Talia, "What do you mean *nothing to see?*"

"When I was kidnapped they took me past it. It's just a metal framework. It has a sort of hut at the top, really nothing there at all except for the metal box at the bottom, but even that was empty. Looted years ago and left to rust no doubt. Eh, it's actually outside, across the cave with the other scrap metal waiting to be recycled."

Kirin didn't like this. He looked over from the window. There was too much talking, time enough for that later. They were pushing their luck. He looked out across the cave and could see a pile of scrap, there did appear to be a metal box of some kind there. At least Sang-gast was telling the truth about that, but he still had the feeling he was hiding more than he was telling. The more this fellow talked the more Kirin sided with Dargo's opinion of him. Kirin looked out the window again. Wait. The three smelters were out of sight but something was wrong. The murmur of the smelter's talking, punctuated by the occasional laugh, had been there in the background. Now there was nothing. No noise. What were they doing, or not doing?

"I think we may have been spotted," whispered Kirin. "I can't see them but they're not making any noise."

Talia looked up, "OK, let's go." She nodded to Dargo. Turning to Sang-gast she said, "I think you'd better come with us." Picking up her staff she indicated to Sang-gast, "And keep quiet."

They slipped out the shack, Talia and Dargo moved cautiously peering round the woodpile. Nothing. The three smelters were nowhere to be seen. Kirin had Sang-gast directly in front of him. He was sure the three smelters couldn't have slipped out the cave to warn the others, by the campfire, without him having seen.

Then it all kicked off in an avalanche of logs and dwarfs. The three smelters launched themselves at Talia and Dargo from on top of the wood pile next to the cauldron. At the same time Sang-gast stamped down heavily with his heel on Kirin's toe. Kirin lifted his foot in agony. Suddenly Sang-gast's face was right in front of him, contorted and vicious looking. Sang-gast's hands were clambering over him, round his back. Off balance on one leg Kirin fell backwards. Sang-gast, still grabbing at Kirin, toppled over on top of him and Kirin's raised knee connected with Sang-gast's stomach winding him. Kirin rolled Sang-gast off him and got to his feet, wincing with pain.

Kirin quickly saw that Dargo was in trouble. Two of the smelters had gotten him on the ground and were raining down kicks and punches upon him. Kirin kicked the nearest smelter hard at the back of his right knee, which buckled. The smelter twisted round to the left to see his attacker. As he did so Kirin grabbed the smelter's left wrist with his right hand, twisting and forcing it up behind his back. Kirin pushed. With his right leg already collapsing, the smelter went down, hard on his front. Quickly Kirin secured his wrists and then his ankles with bark-ties.

This distraction allowed Dargo to roll away and get unsteadily to his feet. The second smelter, who was nursing a nasty bruise at the side of his head, looked at his incapacitated colleague uncertainly. As Kirin and Dargo advanced, he ran, heading off in the direction of the campfire and the sleeping smelters. Dargo pursued him. Suddenly Kirin heard Sang-gast shouting. Turning Kirin saw Sang-gast at the bridge urging the other smelters to come and block their retreat. Out of nowhere the third smelter sprang past him, running towards Sang-gast at the bridge. Talia clutching a bloody hand was running after Dargo shouting at him to come back. Kirin looked at the bridge with only Sang-gast and one of the smelters defending it. He shouted for the others to head to the bridge. Talia seemed to hear him and nodded but Dargo did not and Talia was forced to run after him, eventually stopping him. But by this time the fleeing smelter had been joined by the three from the campfire, and all four were heading towards the still shouting Sang-gast at the bridge. Once there Sang-gast barked out more orders and they spread out covering their escape between the cave and the bridge. Kirin backed away from them joining Talia and Dargo in the middle of the clearing.

Sang-gast, now clearly in charge of the situation, ordered the other dwarfs to hold their positions. Kirin considered making a dash for the river, but that was not a great option for Dargo or even Talia. They moved back to the cave. For some reason the Sang-gast and his dwarfs did not attack. It was a stand-off.

BOILING THE KETTLE

Talia's hand was bleeding badly. Kirin got a bucket of clean water from the shack and washed the wound as best he could, letting it bleed clean. From what he could see, there appeared to be some nasty teeth marks between Talia's thumb and the forefinger. In answer to his questioning look Talia said, "Sang-gast. I grabbed the little weasel as he tried to run past me."

"Looks nasty," said Kirin. He took out a clean handkerchief and wrapped it round the wound tying it tightly. It really needed some Tandock leaves to stop any infection but since they had entered this strange forest Kirin had hardly seen a plant he confidently recognised.

"You should let Freyla have a look at that when we get back," said Kirin.

"Least of my worries," laughed Talia, "Though if I ever get my hands round that lying weasel's throat again..."

They joined Dargo at the front of the cave, who tossed Talia her staff, who caught it with a grimace. "Why don't they just attack us?" said Dargo looking at the Sang-gast's dwarfs spread out in front of them. They had now armed themselves with long vicious looking clubs. "They out-number us two to one."

"Maybe they're wondering why we didn't make a break for the river," said Talia slapping Dargo on the back.

"This is my fault," said Dargo. "If I hadn't lost my head, we could have made it across the bridge."

"Hey, come on," said Kirin. "What happened to, we don't leave one of our own behind."

Dargo laughed. "That's the kinda thinking that got us into this mess in the first place."

This brought a laugh from all three of them. From a distance, Sang-gast and his gang watched.

"Reinforcements!" said Talia "They're waiting on reinforcements."

"The late delivery," said Kirin.

"Exactly, why risk further injury, we've already taken out two of their number," said Talia.

"Well that settles it," said Dargo. "Waiting is not an option. I say we attack now!"

Kirin wasn't so sure, he was missing something. This was happening a lot lately. He needed time to think, to come up with a plan. Sang-gast was giving them some time, so why not use it? "Well let's call that plan B," said Kirin. "How about we see if we can come up with plan A." With that he slapped Dargo on the back and wandered off. Dargo and Talia watched curiously as Kirin strolled over to the pile of scrap metal, at the opposite end of the cave from the shack, where he sat down.

This was not a good situation. Kirin glanced out the cave at the opponents ranged against them. He shook his head. Over to his left he noticed the box Sang-gast had mentioned. He walked over to it. Crouching down he examined it. There was some faded writing on the lid, but inside it was empty. Whatever had been there, now long since gone. He sat down on the box. The whole quest was a dud, right from the start. A quest to find an empty box, but what they'd found instead was trouble, real trouble. It was only dumb luck that they hadn't entered the forest at the western edge. Sang-gast probably had dwarfs there, waiting to ambush the foolish and the unwary, to maintain Teteunxx's reputation as an evil place. A place where no-one returned from. Just to keep their dirty Money Laundering operation a secret.

Yeah lucky, thought Kirin, that's what they were. His gaze wandered round the cave till it fell upon the large neatly piled stack of gold ingots; a quest for gold and jewels beyond your wildest dreams. Well they had the gold for the moment at least, much good that it was to them. He looked across at the giant cauldron. He looked back at the gold again. The gold, or the love of gold, now that did matter... to Money Launderers. Kirin quickly got up and approached a bemused looking Talia and Dargo and began explaining his plan. Dargo growled at first but soon began nodding with Talia and by the end his wry smile was back once more.

So how do you solve a problem like Sang-gast and his dwarfs guarding the only exit? Distraction, diversion and division. But first things first, when you're making a cup of tea, you start by boiling the kettle.

Talia was on woodpile duty. The fire under the cauldron was just embers now, but they were hot embers. She began throwing logs on to the fire, churning up the embers, and soon flames began to lick up the sides of the cauldron. All the while they kept an eye on Sang-gast and his gang. He was watching all right, that was part of the plan. It all hinged on what Sang-gast would do, and Kirin, Talia and Dargo had to be ready to react.

Kirin and Dargo were at the scrap metal pile. Kirin picked up a piece of twisted pipe.

"No," said Dargo. "That's steel. Take that bit there." He indicated a piece of metal next to it.

"Why? What's the difference?" asked Kirin.

"Really? You don't know?" said Dargo. He took the piece that Kirin had in his hand. "This. This is steel. No good." He hurled it towards the back of the cave. He picked up the other piece of metal. This is iron. Melts hotter, much hotter than steel." With that he tossed it into the cauldron.

Kirin nodded, the hotter the better. Of course that bit didn't necessarily matter. In the end it didn't have to succeed at all, what was important was that Sang-gast believed it would succeed. After three or four futile attempts to tell the difference between iron and steel, Kirin got fed up asking Dargo and he swapped jobs with Talia. Things then proceeded much faster.

Kirin was now shovelling coal on to the roaring fire underneath the cauldron. It was so hot now, he had to hurl the coal from a distance. They had been at work now for half an hour. Talia and Dargo reckoned it would take an hour to melt the iron. Kirin looked across at Sang-gast, he would happily have given all this gold to know exactly what he was thinking at that moment. The dwarfs were still in position guarding the bridge and the path leading westwards into the forest. Of course Kirin and the others didn't want to escape that way. They'd be on the wrong side of the river from their friends and headed in the wrong direction. The bridge was their only way out.

The distraction part of the plan was going well. Confuse the enemy. Get them reacting, always playing catch up, stop them taking the initiative. Dargo came over to relieve Kirin from his coal shovelling duties. They had enough iron in the cauldron now. Talia also grabbed a shovel, but with this she began to dig. She dug round the front base of one the A-frame girders that supported the cauldron, digging down about two feet to the concrete base. As she did so she piled up the earth round about the hole making it about four feet deep.

While Talia was doing this Kirin began preparing the diversion. First he dragged the prostate body of the smelter dwarf over to the far edge of the cave. The side furthest away from the bridge. He then went and got the tall man, Thomas, from the shack. He was pretty heavy but by grabbing the back of his collar and lifting his front off the ground, Kirin was able to drag the man across the hard stony ground to join his former employee. There was a lot of muffled complaining about this from the gagged Thomas so Kirin thoughtfully deposited him on top of the nice soft dwarf. This good deed though just seemed to increase the complaining, now coming from both parties. Kirin shrugged, there was just no pleasing some people.

Looking up at the clear night sky he figured it must be past midnight. It had been a long day and he had not had an elfin biscuit since lunch-time, but they were in his pack which was stashed on the other side of the river opposite the jetty. He looked across at Sang-gast and his gang. What did they think he was up to with Thomas? They must be getting restless now. Time to start the diversions. With that he removed the gag from the Thomas's mouth. Kirin didn't bother to hang around, but walked casually back to the others as the air ran blue with the man's exhortations.

Dargo and Talia were now working on diversion number two. The trough in front of the cauldron had a chute that fed the molten gold into a path that led to the ingot moulds. Now they were creating a new path from the end of the chute to the base of the A-frame girder that Talia had excavated. Together Talia and Dargo had built an earth ramp between the chute and the base of the A-frame girder, and lined it with a combination of upturned moulds and gold ingots. Kirin joined in, bringing gold ingots over from the stash. He looked over at the bridge, surely Sang-gast must realise now what they were up to?

Dargo checked on the cauldron. He looked down at the other two and nodded. Talia joined Dargo round the back of it, while Kirin kept look-out. This was getting to the crucial part of the plan. They must be prepared to drop everything when the time came. Dargo and Talia pulled on the chain that went up over the bar (that joined the two A-frames) and down to the bottom of the cauldron. Thanks to a series of pulleys the cauldron slowly tipped and poured its molten iron contents into the reservoir trough in front of it. Kirin shouted when this was done, then opened the sluice gate. As Talia and Dargo rushed back round to the front of the cauldron the molten iron poured down the chute and then down their makeshift gold-lined ramp to form an increasingly deep iron puddle round the base of the A-frame girder.

"OK," said Kirin. "Now for the fun bit where we get to throw some money around." With that began diversion number three. With home-made slings, courtesy of the last of the bed sheets. The three of them began hurling what remained of the gold stash at Sang-gast and his gang. Actually only Kirin was aiming at the bridge where Sang-gast was. This part of the plan had annoyed Dargo but his and Talia's target was the river, as far from the bridge as they could throw.

This did prove the final straw and the start of the divisions. The sight of their precious gold disappearing into the river prompted one of Sang-gast's dwarfs to jump in the river to try and retrieve it. Not a wise course of action, for a non-swimmer. As he struggled to get back out to the safety of the riverbank, Sang-gast must have finally realised that his Money Laundering operation was in danger of literally melting away before his eyes. He screamed at the remaining four dwarfs, berating them to save it. In a frenzy he even started beating them with a club. The four dwarfs rushed forward except for one who was diverted by Thomas, who insisted in quite colourful language that he be set free immediately. The remaining three armed with their large clubs rushed straight at Kirin, Talia and Dargo who waited patiently.

This was the moment they had been waiting for. Three against three were good odds. But it wasn't going to stay that way for long. Each of them had two gold ingots which they aimed at their opponents' legs. Two of Sang-gast's dwarfs went down in an agonising heaps. Talia and Dargo went quickly past them stepping on top of them for good measure. Kirin had missed with his first shot and the second was just a glancing blow. Still it did force his opponent off balance. Kirin ran the other way but still had to duck a viscously swinging club. He felt the rush of air as it passed over his head, but did not look back. He kept running, following the others to the bridge.

Sang-gast stood at one side of the bridge, cursing his incompetent dwarfs. As Dargo passed him he shot a fist out sideways connecting with Sang-gast's chin, who shortly after connected with the water. They continued without breaking stride, round to where their packs were stashed. As they put them on they witnessed the pandemonium across the river. An angry Sang-gast and frustrated Thomas were shouting at each other, arguing over whose fault it was. The other dwarfs had shut down the sluice gate and destroyed the new pathway for the molten metal but closing the stable door after the horse had bolted hadn't really improved the situation. Talia, Dargo and Kirin turned and began following the trail back the way they had come. They had not gone far when they heard the screech of tortured metal followed by a horrendously heavy crash.

Dargo glanced round at Kirin, "Structural integrity of steel and heat, not a good mix." His wry smile was back.

"Save your energy," said Talia. "They may not have been chasing us before, but they will be now."

* * * *

Kirin was tired but they had to keep up the pace. There was no telling how far behind their pursuers were and by the time they found out, it might be too late. He'd managed to grab another mouthful of elfin biscuit as they started out, which was helping, but it was now the middle of the night and, apart from a little nap as the waited for nightfall, they'd been on the go since just after dawn. He thought about getting another biscuit but decided against it. It was quite possible, judging by today's escapade, that he might need all them before this quest was done.

Their jogging pace was almost hypnotic, matching his

breathing and heartbeat. There were no exchanges about the route or good natured banter; only the relentless pounding of tired feet and rhythmic wheezing of exhausted lungs. Kirin allowed his mind to wander. This had all seemed so simple when he explained it to his parents. There was never going to be any real danger, just a wander round the woods for a couple of weeks and then back to Agra-nore and thanks very much for the free education. The days before he left his father had gone over his training with him every day, his mother watching from a distance. He remembered telling his mother that final morning how he would be fine and not to worry. She had hugged him longer than normal. He had broken it off, given her a kiss on the cheek and waved goodbye. He couldn't stop thinking about that now.

Dargo stopped in front of him, Kirin ran into the back of him. Dargo said nothing he was just bent over, hands on thighs trying to catch his breath. Just ahead Talia was leaning against a tree and slid down to sit at the bottom of it. Yesterday it had taken them about six hours to get from the edge of the forest to Sang-gas's camp. They'd been going now for about three, but their pace was not what it was then. If they were lucky, they'd made it a third of the way back. Dargo seemed in worse shape than Kirin, but it was Talia who was in deep trouble. Kirin went up to her. Kneeling down he could see she was sweating profusely. This was more than just the exertions of the run. He placed the back of his hand against her forehead, the way his mother used to do. She was burning up. He examined her wound again and cleaned it as best he could with water from his canteen and cut a strip of his shirt as a fresh bandage.

Leaving an exhausted Talia, Kirin walked over to Dargo, who was still bent over breathing heavily. "It's the bite from Sang-gast. She's got an infection," he whispered

"Hey, don't worry about me," said Talia. She coughed and spluttered for a moment then laughed. "Just getting my second wind."

"Dargo", said Kirin. "We're going to have to help her."

Dargo raised one arm from his thigh and acknowledged Kirin. After a short break for some food and water they were on their way again. Talia was now supporting herself with an arm round the shoulders of the other two. Kirin was carrying her staff. In one respect they were lucky, it was a cloudless sky and they had a three quarter moon to guide them. Of course the same moon lit the way for Sang-gast and they were now making a trail that even a blind man in the dark could follow. They kept going like this for another hour, but Kirin figured they were still were at least three hours from Stilgoe and the others. They stopped for another rest and Talia sagged to the ground. She was near unconscious. Even with food, water and rest Kirin did not think she would be able to carry on. And there was no time for rest.

Dargo too was slumped his back against a tree, his eyes closed, "D'ya think," he wheezed. "D'ya think maybe they're not," he wheezed, "chasin us?"

Kirin looked back down the trail and listened as hard as he could. He could detect nothing but he remembered Sang-gast's contorted face, and there was something else but he was too tired to think what it was now. He looked across at Dargo whose eyes were open now. "They're still chasing." They could not get Talia to eat anything but did manage to get her to take a little water. Kirin stood up racking his brains for some alternative, some cunning plan. He had nothing.

Dargo got up slowly to his feet. "Guess it's come to this then." He motioned to Kirin. "Help me get her to her feet. I'll carry her."

Kirin almost laughed. "Nice gesture Dargo but you can barely stand yourself. I'd make a better job of carrying her."

Dargo winced. "It's a hard thing for a dwarf to give up, but we don't leave one of our own behind."

"Give up wh—" said Kirin as Dargo produced a gold ingot from each pocket of his jerkin and dropped them heavily by the side of the trail. Kirin thought of several different things to say but in the end just shook his head.

Kirin didn't like it but Dargo's plan made sense. He couldn't think of anything better and at least this way there was a chance. They stashed the gold, Dargo's and Talia's packs some way off the trail along with the two dwarf staffs. Kirin helped Talia on to Dargo's back. She could just about cling round his neck. That was fine. The part of the plan that Kirin was not so keen on, was the bit where he was to run off and leave them.

"You sure about this?" asked Kirin.

Dargo attempted a shrug. "She ain't heavy. Now if it was Coulan!" He rolled his eyes.

Kirin held out the compass to Dargo, telling him not to worry about trying to follow his trail but to keep checking his bearings.

Dargo scratched his head. "I thought that thing didn't work anymore?"

"It doesn't read true but it is consistent. Keep heading southeast and we will find you."

Dargo nodded and shuffled Talia's weight on his back. "You ready boss?"

Kirin nodded to them both then raced away. No longer constrained by the others he increased his speed, he even sneaked another chunk of elfin biscuit as a boost. Perhaps they should have done something different back at the camp. Taken Sang-gast prisoner with them or something? But there was nothing he could do about it now, he was running on adrenalin, and elfin biscuits! With each passing second he knew that the pursuing Sang-gast was getting closer to Talia and Dargo, but he dare not go any faster and risk injuring himself.

Dawn began to break, making it easier for him to read the trail but it also reminded him how much in need of sleep he was. He'd been on the go for almost an entire day, and most of that running. In the grey half-light all the trees now blended together in a relentless blur as he rushed by. Every so often the mad confusion of shapes would change, filling him with false hope that the trees were thinning out a little, that he must be nearing the edge of the forest.

"Argh!"

Kirin's world view had been substantially altered. He was swinging upside down about six feet above the ground suspended by one foot. He looked up or down, depending on your point of view, at his foot. Suddenly Bashka's upside down face appeared.

"Looks like my Charter-mouse trap's worked a treat," she said.

Against his will almost, Kirin smiled before saying."Get me down Bashka, the other's are in trouble."

Bashka's expression changed. She looked as if she was about to say something but then disappeared for a moment. Kirin felt himself gradually being lowered to the ground, where Bashka, loosened the loop of rope round his ankle.

"Take me to the others?" said Kirin getting up. "Quickly."

Bashka nodded, her smile now gone. "They're just over this way." She led off at a jog.

A couple of minutes later Kirin found himself at an impressive fortification constructed from sharpened wooden spikes, and cut willow rods woven into a barrier wall. Kirin was immediately assailed by questions on all sides but there was no time to waste telling the whole story. He shouted for quiet and explained just the essential facts of Talia and Dargo's plight. The way Coulan was looking at him reminded him of how Dargo had looked at Sang-gast. It was agreed that Stilgoe and Coulan should go back with Kirin, though Coulan was going no matter what was agreed. Bashka and Freyla were to remain in the fortification just in case Sang-gast and his dwarfs somehow got there before them.

The thought of running back into the forest was almost too much for Kirin. It was only the thought of not doing so that spurred him on. On the way he provided more information on all that had happened. They asked few questions and soon none at all. All three were now reserving their breathing to maximise their pace, all pretence at stealth forgotten. They were now in a race against Sang-gast and his dwarfs to see who would reach Talia and Dargo first. Kirin was struggling now to keep focused on the trail, the need for sleep was becoming overpowering. More than once he lost it, slowed to a stop and had to retrace his steps to refind the trail, much to the frustration of the others. As they got closer to where Kirin expected to find Dargo and Talia, they needed now to go slower and not just because he was losing it. Coulan and Stilgoe both protested but Kirin explained that Talia and Dargo, while heading towards them were probably not on the trail, and they risked passing each other, a few dozen yards apart. They needed three pairs of ears listening for them, which meant making less noise themselves.

Kirin, who was in the lead halted, giving the agreed hand gesture. Stilgoe and Coulan duly piled into the back of him. Then they all heard it, the sound of someone not being overly careful moving through the forest over to their right. They moved cautiously towards the sound, the only thought in their heads, who was it?

The next minute a purple faced Dargo with Talia barely clinging to his back crashed through the trees in front of them. He collapsed into Coulan's arms, a heaving mass of panting dwarf. Coulan cradled his brother, while Stilgoe and Kirin peeled an unresponsive Talia off Dargo's back and laid her gently on the ground. Stilgoe knelt down beside her and brushed the damp hair from her forehead. Kirin noticed him biting his lower lip. Then they all stopped. This time the noise was much louder though maybe a little further away.

Quickly Coulan hoisted Dargo on his back, and Stilgoe took Talia onto his. Kirin wanted to help Stilgoe but was too weak to be of any use and so instead he took point leading the way along the trail back to the others. Thanks to Coulan it was now a pretty unmistakable path. No attempt was made to disguise their presence, they crashed through the forest as fast as they could. Their pace only dictated by the slowest of them which was Stilgoe as he laboured under Talia's weight. Unsure if their pursuers were still minutes away or about to pounce upon them, they ran as if their lives depended on it.

It felt like Kirin had been running for hours. He was so tired now he couldn't think straight anymore, even the pain in his legs had faded to a dull numbness, like they were somebody else's. He just wanted to stop running, close his eyes and go to sleep. But he knew he couldn't. The only thing now was to keep on running. Each stride became an effort of will. Nothing else mattered, not the need for sleep, not the fate of Talia and Dargo, nothing. He'd stumble, catch himself just in time and try to focus once more, picking out rocks and tree roots and undulation in the path that might trip him. For if he were to fall now he wasn't sure if he'd be able to get back up again.

Whether in his dreams or in reality, Kirin was past caring which, he stumbled into the fortified position once more. He sat down leaning back against a tree, still wearing his pack. And that was the last he knew. He fell instantly asleep.

* * * *

It was about nine in the morning when Stilgoe had gently woken him. At first he was angry that they had let him sleep. He knew though that he had been spent and would have been worse than useless in the fight that followed, but even so.

Gradually from conversations he pieced together what had happened. They had just managed to keep ahead of

Sang-gast all the way back. This much he knew already. Sang-gast and his gang had attacked not ten minutes after they had gotten back. Two of the dwarfs had got caught in Bashka's traps, like Kirin had. Meanwhile Dargo had showed himself at the fortified position behind the wooden stakes. Sang-gast and the remaining four dwarfs had attacked head on. Of course Dargo was in no condition to fight, but his brother Coulan lying down out of sight, was. The two dwarfs that did made it past the stakes regretted it. Sang-gast, upon seeing Coulan had realised that it was a trap, however by then he was being attacked from the rear by Stilgoe and Bashka. It was all over in minutes, Sang-gast and two of the dwarfs escaped but not before Bashka had given him a good clout round the ear with her staff. She and Stilgoe chased them back in to the forest making sure they weren't coming back.

The story of what had happened at Sang-gast's camp, after Kirin and the others had left, was told by the captured dwarfs, via the process of having Coulan sit on them. Once he stopped sitting they were only too eager to talk. Bizarrely in the end, it was only by threatening them with another Coulan sitting, that they could get them to shut up. Apparently Sang-gast and Thomas had had a big bust-up, with a difference of opinion regarding their course of action. Thomas wanted to concentrate on salvaging the smelter whereas Sang-gast wanted to pursue them immediately. It was only the arrival of the another half dozen or so dwarfs with a shipment of gold coins that resolved things. So it was that Sang-gast, with the fresh batch of dwarfs then set out after them.

Kirin went down to the stream to have a wash. Part of him was disappointed at missing all the action, but upon reflection, considering all that had happened over the last day or so, things hadn't gone too badly. He decided to take his boots off and sitting on the bank bathed his feet in the river. He closed his eyes drifting off for a moment.

"Penny for them?"

Kirin looked up it was Freyla. She was kneeling by the river washing, what turned out to be Talia's blood stained shirt. "What? Oh, hi there," he said.

Freyla quickly worked up a lather and was soon beating the shirt against a rock. Kirin looked on not knowing what to say. After a bit he said "How's Talia?"

"She's weak, very weak, I've made her some tea from Tandock leaves but she still has a fever."

"She was bitten, on the hand by Sang-gast," he said.

She looked up and nodded.

"I feel like an idiot sleeping through the whole thing," said Kirin. "How did you get on?"

"Oh, I was with Dargo and Coulan. You didn't miss much." She scrubbed vigorously at a particularly stubborn stain. "Heard you had a run in with Sang-gast yourself."

"Yeah, strange fellow really. Very rude. Stood on my toe and didn't even apologise afterwards."

Freyla laughed.

They headed back to camp together, where they found Dargo enjoying a large bowl of stew. He gave Kirin a toothy grin. Apart from a large multicoloured bruise on his left cheek he looked none the worse for wear. Kirin suspected though he had many such bruises elsewhere. Kirin sat down beside him and got himself a bowl of stew from the pot.

"Still can't believe you were carrying two gold ingots all that way." Kirin shook his head at Dargo smiling.

Dargo shrugged. "There's an equal share in it for you." He winked at Kirin.

Kirin shook his head and nodded at the same time. They both burst out laughing. While this was happening Coulan came up behind Kirin and practically crushed the breath out of him by giving him the hardest hug of his life.

A BURDEN SHARED

They left within the hour, not daring to risk going back for Dargo and Talia's stuff, or even, to Dargo's dismay, his stash of gold. Everyone was keen to put as much distance between themselves and the forest as soon as possible. There had been a brief dispute as to what to do with their captured dwarfs. Coulan had asked them nicely not to come after them, to which they'd quite readily agreed. In addition they'd been left with their hands and feet still bound, which admittedly already restricted their capacity for pursuit. They would probably have been freed when Sang-gast returned with reinforcements but Freyla tossed a particularly blunt knife in front of them before leaving, much to Dargo's disgust.

They'd constructed a stretcher for Talia using their quarterstaffs. The fever had a firm grip of her now and she was now in a permanent state of semi-consciousness. They worked in shifts, four on, two off. As soon as they had passed the edge of the forest and were in open grassland, everyone felt better. The air itself felt fresher, cleaner, like it had just washed down from the mountains, and familiar smells like creeping thyme and lavender once more drifted through the warm summer air, even Talia seemed to breath more easily.

By mid-afternoon the relief of leaving the forest was gone, at least for Kirin. His arms felt the same way his legs had at the end of that first day of relentless jogging. He just hoped that that salve Freyla had given him worked as well on arm muscles. His legs were defiantly stronger now and they would have to be as he did not have much of the salve left and for some reason he did not want to ask Freyla for more. The terrain they were crossing was rolling grassland, they marched on throughout the day, every step eastwards, a step further away from Sang-gast and his gang. Kirin wasn't sure what the others thought but he was under no illusions, they hadn't seen the last of him. On their left, blocking their way south, was a wide flowing river that flowed westwards into the Forest of Teteunxx. As they continued east, they scanned the slopes of the Crumbling Mountains on their right, looking in vain for some easy passage across them.

The setting sun, sent their tall shadows increasingly in front of them, till twilight finally dissolved them. They continued on in the dark till they found a little stream coming down from the mountains and made their camp for the night. That was when the arguments and recriminations began.

"Look I'm just saying." Dargo sighed "And I take no pleasure in this but..." Dargo looked across to where Talia lay. "It was a mistake trying to rescue Sang-gast." He spat out the last word.

So your blaming it all on Talia," said Stilgoe, "how very convenient for you."

"What d'ya mean by that?" Dargo got to his feet.

"Hey if you want someone to blame then blame me, I voted for it," said Kirin.

"Bah!" said Stilgoe.

"Like it or not Stilgoe, Dargo was right. It was a mistake, we were lucky to get away." Kirin turned to Dargo. "But Talia was also right. She—"

"How can you say that?" said Dargo.

"As Talia said we couldn't know about Sang-gast till—"

"I knew!"said Dargo.

"What's done is done, for good or ill. We need to decide what we do now," said Freyla.

"Exactly!" said Stilgoe. "We should keep heading east, putting distance between us and—"

"Who put you in charge?" said Dargo

"No-one's put me in charge," said Stilgoe. "But if you've got a better plan then let's hear it?"

"Talia's our leader not you," said Dargo, but did not volunteer any plans, better or otherwise.

"What about the quest?" asked Coulan.

Freyla turned to Coulan, putting her hand on his arm. "The quest is over Coulan. The other end of the forest where the Tower is? That's crawling with more of Sang-gast's dwarfs. Anyone going there doesn't come back. If the Tral-fe-tigore was ever there. It's gone now. It's time to go home."

"OK," said Stilgoe. "Tomorrow we keep heading east and keep a lookout for a an easy passage south back across the mountains." He glared at Dargo, who glared right back at him.

The meeting dissolved after that. Dargo and Coulan went off to have a private huddle, while Stilgoe went off to relieve Bashka who was on look-out duty. Kirin went over to see how Talia was. Freyla was refreshing a cold compress on her forehead from a bowl of water. Talia moaned and tried to pull her blanket off. Freyla gently restrained Talia's arm till she eventually relaxed, then tucked her arm back under the blanket. She pulled the blanket back up to Talia's chin.

"How's she doing?" Kirin felt stupid. It was a stupid question.

"The fever's getting worse. I've ran out of Tandock leaves." Freyla sighed, running her hand threw her hair. She stood up. "All we can do is keep her warm. Try to break the fever."

"Tandock leaves, yes." Kirin nodded. "But what about Stalwort and a moss poultice?"

"What? You are skilled in these things?"

"Eh, not really. Do you think it might help?" Kirin looked down at Talia. She looked so pale.

"Yes it might, if we had any. I should have thought of the moss poultice myself."

"A mile or so back, there was a hollow down by the river, where a little stream ran into it. It could be shady enough for Stalwort?" said Kirin.

Freyla was nodding.

A little later Bashka joined them, she had collected some wood on her way back to build up the fire. They explained that they were going to look for some medicinal herbs for Talia. Bashka nodded, but didn't appear to be listening, She said he would sit with Talia.

Kirin and Freyla walked in silence for a while then, in answer to her earlier question, Kirin told her of how, when he was very young, he had accompanied his mother each day into the woods harvesting nuts and berries, herbs and mushrooms. His mother though a Chartered Accounting Dwarf also had a love of herbology and it was not just edible plants she knew but also ones that could heal. They lived by themselves, and though his father was a fisherman, they relied on the woods for everything else. She had tried to teach him about all the growing things and he'd picked up a little of her knowledge. He regretted now that he had not paid more attention.

They found the hollow easily enough but clouds covered the moon, and searching by starlight alone proved more difficult. They found the Sphagnum moss easily enough but not the Stalwort. They were about to give up and leave when Freyla found a couple of specimens of the shy plant. She harvested only the few leaves she required. Back at the camp Kirin watched carefully as Freyla prepared the Stalwort leaves and the moss poultice and even more carefully as Freyla cleaned Talia's wound and applied it. Bashka was very grateful to them both but then looked disappointed that there was no instant effect. Kirin knew though that such thinks take their time. Bashka said she would keep an eye on Talia and that Freyla and Kirin should get some rest.

Kirin longed for sleep, but something was still gnawing at him. He had the feeling that he was missing something. As he lay on his sleeping mat he knew he should sleep and that any attempt to try and think now was just wasted effort but he couldn't help himself. Absent-mindedly he took out Sang-gast's book from his back pocket and began reading through it. It was clearly all in code, a mixture of letters and numbers but there was a structure to it. Every double page was divided into six columns. Some of the columns were clearly amounts, with commas and decimal points. One of the columns looked like a date with eight characters separated into groups of two, two and four by slashes. Kirin was aware there was something else going on here. Why would Sang-gast take the trouble to encode it all but at the same time not hide that structural information? Leaving the column information as clues, was a mistake. Sang-gast did not strike Kirin as the type who made mistakes.

Now Kirin knew that dates and amounts are made up of numbers (0 to 9) i.e. ten possible characters. If it was a straight substitution code then these dates and amounts should still be made up of up to 10 different characters (ie the letter A is substituted for the number 1, B for 2 etc.). But the dates had at least 15 different characters! Unless he was wrong and these were not dates and amounts?

"Argh!"

Kirin was too tired to think clearly. He shut the book. One thing he did know, it was not a simple substitution code. Of that he was sure. He lay down and fell into a fitful sleep, his body battling with his mind.

* * * *

As soon as he tried to open his blanket, Kirin knew. It was like lead weights were attached to his arms. He had been so pre-occupied with that stupid book that he had forgotten to use the salve last night. Instead he'd wasted time on something that might turn out to be just Sang-gast's shopping list. Kirin knew though, that it wasn't. Sang-gast would only take the trouble to encode something that was important, very important indeed. Even so he was tempted to hurl the damn thing away, only the thought of the ensuing pain in his arms stopped him. He put some salve on his aching muscles, eight hours too late!

They got under way again still heading east. Kirin contrived to be slightly apart from the others at the start and avoided the first shift on stretcher duty. No-one said anything to him about it. Perhaps they hadn't noticed, but Kirin knew. He felt like an outsider again, more so than even that first day. Dargo was right, thought Kirin, he was holding them up, not taking his fair share of the burden, unable to pull his weight, literally. He imagined his father hanging his head unable to look him in the eye, and worse, his mother trying to give him a comforting smile. All he wanted now was for this quest to end and to go back home again. He couldn't bring himself to look at the others much less talk with them. That hour he spent walking alone, became the longest hour of his young life. It got so he couldn't wait for that first stretcher shift change. It was like he deserved the physical pain it would bring. And it was physical pain. He felt his arm being slowly pulled out its socket. He kept looking at it, expecting to see it suddenly flop away from him, his hand still attached to the stretcher pole. Half way through the hour shift he ended up using both hands. This gave him some relief but he felt the others' concerned looks burning into him. He kept his eyes down. He focused on Talia, her suffering face only a foot or so away from him. That helped. He thought of her pain, the seriousness of her condition. His pain was nothing compared to hers. His arm was not going to drop off, but she...

Somehow he got through the shift and the one after that, when he was rotated to the front of the stretcher. Then it was back to his turn for a break from stretcher duty. The sun was getting hot as it rose in the sky, and it was still an hour till noon. Kirin had his hood up and was walking alone when Stilgoe came up to him. He walked beside Kirin for a few minutes without saying anything.

"We seem to be getting closer to the river," said Stilgoe.

Kirin looked to his left. It was true, the river which had been a couple of miles away was now no more than half that distance. But it was not them getting closer to the river. It was the river getting closer to them. Peering into the distance Kirin could see the strip of flat land they were on between the Crumbling Mountains and the river begin to narrow. It looked like they were being funnelled into something. But into what? Then it struck Kirin.

Kirin pointed into the distance. "The river, I think it may have its source in the mountains."

Stilgoe's brows furrowed as his eyes squinted trying to see into the distance.

"Do you have the map?" asked Kirin

Stilgoe produced the map from inside his jerkin and unfolded it. It clearly showed the river on their left flowing westwards towards Teteunxx Forest behind them and that its source originated from the north before sharply turning to the west. This struck Kirin as strange that the river did not originate in the Crumbling Mountains in the south. But the map showed nothing coming down from the mountains. According to the map the strip of land they were on between the mountains and the river eventually opened up into the Plain of Angaurd. But now the truth was unavoidable. There was a tributary coming down from the Crumbling Mountains barring their passage forwards. They were running out of dry land and were going to have to either cross water, or go up into the mountains. Stilgoe hurried off to share the information with the others. Kirin continued walking some ten yards out to the side away from the others. He could feel their looks upon him once more but did not dare acknowledge them. He watched disinterestedly as Stilgoe, after talking with the others, then jogged off into the distance.

At noon they stopped for lunch. They were seated round eating cold rations. There was no wood anywhere near to make a fire. It was too hot anyway. There was not a cloud in the sky. Kirin ate in near silence, just nodding or shrugging or grunting some indiscriminate reply to any attempts to converse with him. The group descended into silence. Kirin felt the pressure of their stares build upon him.

"Kirin," said Stilgoe.

"What! What is it? Look I'm tired I admit it. Maybe I just don't have what it takes. I'm sorry I didn't mean to let you all down." He blurted out.

After a pause it was Bashka who spoke. "You're a swimmer, I hear tell Charter-mouse."

"What?" said Kirin

"We're all tired, exhausted but we work together as a team," said Stilgoe. "We cover for each other. And you, I don't know what's going on in your head but you've let no-one down. Freyla told me how you helped find medicine for Talia last night that might just save her." He trailed off looking at Talia lying asleep on the stretcher.

Kirin looked around at everyone his face flushed red and wiped the corner of his eye with his sleeve. He did not see any angry faces only concerned ones.

"Swimmer?" mumbled Kirin.

Their predicament was now clear for all to see. This tributary came from meltwater high up in the Crumbling Mountains, it flowed steeply down due north. But at the junction where they now were the tributary then split into two rivers. One continued flowing due north, presumably all the way to the Big Water while the other widened out and flowed westwards into Teteunxx Forest (the river they had been walking beside on their left).

Tributary. The word itself didn't sound so bad. Something less than a full blown river but maybe more than a stream. In this case though, raging torrent painted a clearer picture. They were trapped in a cul-de-sac of sorts. On their left, a wide flowing river. On their right were the Crumbling Mountains, too steep and dangerous for Talia on the stretcher. And straight ahead of them the white water of the tributary raged all the way down to the river, dashing itself carelessly against a multitude of rocks. It was impassable. The others had looked at Kirin as if he could somehow swim across it. The frustrating thing was that at its narrowest point it was only thirty feet or so across.

In their favour they did have Talia's aqua-stick. She had kept it in her jerkin pocket. It was partly used but still had air left. The problem was the current. One step in the water and even a sturdy dwarf like Coulan would be swept away to be dashed on the rocks. Kirin suggested everyone empty their packs and they sat for an hour coming up with brilliant plans that one by one ended up full of holes. Some of the plans got some of them across, but none of the plans got all of them across. And waiting where they were was not an option. In the end it was the solution to the age old problem of the fox, the chicken, and the bag of grain. How to get them all safely across the river when you can only take one at a time?

Stage one. They went down to where the tributary met the main river. Now the river was wide, forty maybe fifty yards wide, but it did not have any white water. Kirin reckoned he could swim it. Of course it still might have a treacherous current but he was willing to risk it. The others converted Talia's stretcher into a raft, or at least a floating stretcher. They had no wood other than their hawthorn quarterstaffs. These did not float well, but tying on empty canteens as flotation devices helped. Kirin always thought it strange that despite being non-swimmers dwarfs were such skilled sailors and boatmen. His father had said it concentrated the mind. They couldn't afford to make mistakes. A bit like mountain climbers, the thought of falling was just not something they contemplated. Kirin would take boats over mountains any day!

The first stage went well. Kirin crossed the river that flowed west, the current took him some 200 yards downstream, but still safely across on the north bank. Stage two was pretty much the same as stage one. Kirin crossed the second river that flowed north. Now he was on the eastern bank of both the river that flowed north and the tributary. He jogged along the bank to a place they had already spotted, a little way up from where the tributary split into the two rivers. Here there was a small tree on Kirin's side of the tributary.

Now began stage three. They had two bark ropes that they'd made in the forest. Tied together these were fifty feet in length. Coulan threw one end of this to Kirin who tied the bark rope securely round the tree. There was nothing on the west side to tie it to, so they used the next best thing to a tree, Coulan. Then Stilgoe climbed on to the rope, gripping tightly while hooking his ankles over it so that he was hanging from it upside down. He also had Talia's aqua-stick in reserve in case he fell in. Kirin too was ready to dash down to the main river if needed. Stilgoe then pulled himself across, hand over hand, safely to the other side. This plan had however, two main drawbacks; they couldn't get Talia across; and they couldn't get Coulan across.

Stage four. Actually the plan didn't have numbered stages, each stage was just referred to as the *next* stage. Anyway it involved repeating stage three for Bashka, Freyla and Dargo. This all went well so the *next* stage was to get Talia across. Talia and her stretcher/boat was still down at the river's edge. Kirin untied the rope from the tree and threw it to Coulan. At this point Coulan hurled all of their packs and gear across to the other side. They were now committed.

They all went down to where the tributary met the river. The water was still fast flowing here but there were no rocks, at least none that they could see. Coulan secured his end of the rope to Talia's stretcher-raft and then threw the rope across to Stilgoe and the others. While this was being done Kirin lowered himself in the water and let the current take him past the mouth of the tributary before swimming strongly for the bank, to join Coulan. Once Kirin was rested he and Coulan carefully lowered Talia's stretcher-raft into the water. Kirin got in the water beside her and placed the aqua-stick in her mouth, hoping there would be enough air left in it. She appeared to be breathing normally. Kirin positioned himself at the foot of the stretcher boat, leaning on it and tipping the other end up in an attempt to keep Talia's head above water. He signalled the others and they began to pull.

At first it all went horribly wrong. The current from the tributary took Talia right out into the middle of the river. Actually though this proved a blessing in disguise as the current was less strong here compared to the mouth of the tributary. Bit by bit, slowly but surely, Stilgoe and the others hauled Talia, with Kirin kicking in the water behind her, to the other bank. Eager hands grabbed the stretcher-raft, and hauled it ashore. She was fine but cold. Bashka went to get some wood for a fire. Now there was just Coulan.

This they decided to call the final stage. Having untied the rope from the stretcher/boat they threw one end back to Coulan along with Talia's aqua-stick. Coulan was too heavy for the stretcher-raft so he just secured the rope around his body and under his arms and entered the water. Taking a firm grip of the aqua stick between his teeth he signalled the others with a wave of his hand. They began to pull. For the first few steps he kept his footing but then he slipped and that was it. From then on it was a fishing contest. Coulan's hands gripped the rope tightly but his legs were thrashing uselessly about in the water searching desperately for a footing. The others were hauling him in, inch by stubborn inch, and just like the stretcher-raft before, Coulan swung out in to the middle of the river. Whether he was getting any air from the aqua-stick was unclear but at the very least it was keeping the water out of his mouth. Kirin was poised, ready to launch himself into the water if need be but in the end a bedraggled, befuddled but still breathing Coulan was hauled up on to the bank.

It was already dusk so they camped where they had landed ashore. Everyone was in good spirits and after supper and Kirin, the water having soothed his aching arms, joined in the good natured but still serious quarterstaff sparring with the others. Stilgoe taught him a few basic moves and he learned that agility was just as important as strength. They night they slept the sleep of the exhausted, even Coulan.

BREAKING AND ENTERING

Waking with clear open sunshine of a new day, Kirin felt better than he had for days. His arms still ached but it was a good kind of ache, a healing ache. Since they were right by the river he decided to take his fishing line and try his luck. Half an hour later, when Stilgoe showed up, there were five good sized catfish wrapped in large dock leaves lying on the grass under the shade of his jerkin.

Stilgoe said nothing, he picked a long stem of grass, stripping off its few stray leaves, before launching it into the air. They both watched as it arced into the river, the current then carrying it away.

They both stared to talk at the same time.

"Sorry," said Kirin "You first."

"I was just going to say. Good job getting us all across the river yesterday."

Kirin shrugged. "It was a team thing. We couldn't have done it without everyone and I mean *everyone* pulling their weight."

"The look on Coulan's face when we fished him out." Stilgoe laughed.

They both laughed, then there followed an awkward silence.

Kirin spoke first. "About yesterday, I was having a bad day—"

"Forget it," said Stilgoe. "We all have bad days and if that was yours, then trust me you've got nothing to feel bad about."

They sat for awhile.

"Now talking of bad days, am I to gather breakfast is to be cold rations again this morning."

"Well that really depends if your so called fire-lighting skills are up to scratch." Kirin indicated his jerkin lying on the grass. A curious Stilgoe lifted it aside revealing the brace of fish and began whistling that off-key tune again

As they approached the camp they saw a commotion round where Talia was. They rushed forward to be greeted by the sight of her sitting up complaining about the food. She still looked pale and weak, but her fever had broken. She was joking with the others about how she had just taken an extended nap and now everything had gone to pot. So when Stilgoe, after winking at Kirin, produced the brace of five catfish Talia declared this was why Stilgoe was second in command. Everyone laughed, even Dargo.

A good hot breakfast can work wonders of course, but there was something about being on the other side of the river. It was like an invisible barrier between them and Sang-gast. The best of it though was Talia. No-one had said anything, but they had all been worried about her. So now there was nothing to stop them heading home. If you can call the Crumbling Mountains nothing that is.

After breakfast they had another look at the map to see if it indicated which pass across the mountains might be the easiest, Talia was still weak but with another day's rest she said she would be ready to tackle them. There was much good natured banter going back and forth, for no-one minded an extra day's march in the warm sunshine. Kirin had another look at the map, examining it in more detail. He smiled as he noticed where someone had drawn the hitherto missing tributary and scribbled the words

'River Kirin' next to it. This river flowed all the way north to the top edge of the map where it simply said 'The Big Water' and marked the western edge of the Plain of Angaurd, where they now found themselves. Behind them, to the south were the Crumbling Mountains but ahead of them the terrain was flat and even, a mixture of grassland and heath, stretching all the way to the horizon. Well flat that is if you didn't count a giant rocky plateau poking up out of the middle of it whose steep sides seemed to rise up almost vertically from the plain. The map called this Angaurd Castle, it must have been a good two days walk (or one days jog) away. But this was not what had caught Kirin's eye. on the map, for round the far eastern side of the castle, hidden from their current position, was something the map referred to as the 'Maze'. A small square drawing represented this. Now there was nothing particularly special about that except at the centre of the drawing was a small blue butterfly. This meant nothing to everyone else, and looking at the map and it would have meant nothing to Kirin either, except that he had seen that same blue butterfly before. It had been on the lid of the metal box that had come from the Tower, the one he'd found in Sang-gast's camp.

This news brought much discussion. Dwarfs do like to discuss. Moot points were debated, arguments were won and lost on both sides. Even the veracity of Kirin's eyesight was called in to question. In the end it's close proximity and the need for Talia to regain her strength before tackling the mountain, swung the balance. The quest for the Tral-fe-tigore was mostly dead and buried. But mostly dead was not entirely dead. So for the time being it was a little bit alive, hanging on a hunch.

The company split into two parties. The main group, with Talia, were to head northeast at an easy walking pace. Kirin and Stilgoe were to jog due north along the east bank of the River Kirin. Their aim, to keep an eye out to the west for any unwanted company and do some more fishing before heading due east and meeting up with the rest.

It was one of those hot summer's days with barely a breath of wind. High up only a few wisps of cloud were to be seen in a vast expanse of blue. As they sat by the riverbank, Kirin explained that the most important attribute a fisherman can have is patience. Stilgoe had nodded at hearing this though Kirin got the impression he mistook patience for lazing about on a summer's afternoon. The two of them got to talking, words flowed slowly but easily, coaxed out by the summer heat. Stilgoe told Kirin of how his father had been a legaliser, those who administered the legal system of the Fourth Kingdom. A traditional dwarfish profession, he'd always been expected to follow in his father's footsteps. Kirin got the impression that his decision not to do so had disappointed his family. According to Stilgoe it was not that he lacked the intellect, it was just that his inclination was always for the open road.

When it came to the subject of Kirin's swimming prowess he stuck to as close to the truth as he could. He had been friends with a boy called Peter, and when they were very young they had learned to swim together. He assured Stilgoe that he was not a great swimmer by the standard of men, which was true enough. When they settled down to do some fishing Kirin was not quite as successful as earlier, bagging only three fish, though one of them was a medium sized trout. Much to Kirin's surprise and indeed his, Stilgoe caught a not unsubstantial catfish himself.

It was dusk when they reunited to the others. Angaurd Castle was now dominating the skyline to the north. Bashka, whose excellent eyesight was boosted by her binoculars said there looked like what could be some ancient ruins on the top of the plateaux. The remnants of the castle? The darkening light gave the plateaux a gloomy, haunting look. What had happened to the people who had lived there, had some dark catastrophe befallen them? They would get a better look at it tomorrow in the bright light of day when they would skirt its south eastern corner, where they should also see what the Maze, actually was, or if it even existed.

Kirin settled down on his sleeping mat with a full stomach and decided to have another look at Sang-gast's little black book once more. Shortly after Freyla walked over to him.

"What you doing there?" she said.

"It's Sang-gast's, it's in code" said Kirin "I'm not entirely sure but I think it might be important."

He handed the book to Freyla who sat down beside him.

She flicked through a few pages. "Perhaps you need to get inside Sang-gast's head. Figure out what makes him tick."

"Not sure I want to get inside his head."

At that moment Coulan joined them, She handed the book up to Coulan.

Turning back to Kirin she said, "Well he's a Chartered Accountant like you. I guess he thinks about profit and loss, assets and liabilities, stuff like that?"

Kirin looked anxiously up at Coulan seeing the tiny book in his large powerful hands. "Not sure I like the idea of lumping Chartered accountants like Sang-gast in with the rest of us." Kirin closed his eyes rubbing the bridge of his nose between his thumb and forefinger. The books secrets were not going to be solved tonight.

"What is it?" Freyla was addressing Coulan.

"Pretty pictures," he said.

"What! What pictures?' Kirin opened his eyes and stretched his hand up for the book.

Coulan gave Kirin an unhappy look and clutched the small book to his chest.

"It's OK Coulan. Show Kirin what you've found." Freyla placed her hand on Coulan's arm.

"I'm sorry," said Kirin, "Didn't mean to shout at you."

Coulan handed Kirin the book, somewhat reluctantly, all the time looking at Freyla who nodded encouragingly. Kirin saw that it was opened at the very last page. On it was what appeared to be a strange mix of swirling lines, geometric shapes and words and numbers all jumbled together.

"What is it?" asked Freyla.

"Oh I think it's just Sang-gast's doodles," said Kirin.

"Doodles?" she said.

"Yeah doodles. You know the random scribbles people do when they're thinking."

"Is that good?" she said.

"Possibly," he said.

As they left to bed down for the night Kirin poured over the page. Nothing obvious stood out. It was probably nothing. If there was something then his subconscious would have to work it out. He was going to sleep.

The next day they continued at walking pace, Talia said she felt up to jogging but Stilgoe said it would be best to proceed with caution and no-one contradicted him. Despite the good news of Talia's recovery a heavy stillness fell over the group that seemed to grow with every step across the Plain of Angaurd. No trees grew here and what might have been old drainage ditches and the remnants of stone boundary walls indicated that perhaps it had once been cultivated in times past. Now though it had reverted back to grassland, bracken and wild heather. The few deer and wild ponies they had seen kept to themselves on the slopes of the Crumbling Mountains. And as for people, there were none.

It was Angaurd Castle though that all eyes were drawn to, even in the bright light of day it seemed a dark and cheerless place, a relic from another age. They could all now make out the ruined walls that rose from the top of the sheer rock face in front of them. It had been a mighty fortress in its day, now laid to ruin but still impregnable thanks to its geography. Kirin could see no way up. The rock itself rose up at least 3000 feet high, with walls on top of that of maybe another few hundred feet or so, where they still stood intact. Close up it was not quite as steep as it had appeared from afar but Kirin pitied any army trying to attack from this side. Kirin had the feeling that something very bad had happened here once. The castle was more than just gloomy, it exuded a malevolent presence as though it was the source of evil that now lay upon the land. It seemed to lurk within the very stones of that ancient ruin, waiting, brooding, for anyone foolish enough to approach.

By mid afternoon they had turned the corner and could now see the Maze. This was good in more ways than one, giving them something else to focus on. It appeared to be a dense, small woodland of sorts. There also appeared to be a low building of some kind behind it. As they got closer they could see that what they took for woodland was an area of overgrown hedgerows. They decided to circle round it to the right looking for an opening, keeping the dark heights of Angaurd Castle in front of them. They felt more comfortable keeping the open heathland to their backs or as Stilgoe said it always paid to have a good exit strategy.

* * * *

They had walked all the way round the other side of the Maze and now stood between it and a long, low, two storey shell of a building made of crumbling concrete, rusting steel and shattered glass. Hardly any of its large windows were still intact. The main entrance had two large doors, or at least it used to. One of them was missing and the other hung precariously from one hinge. The wreck of the building though was not simply the ravages of time. It had been purposely destroyed by people. As they peered inside they saw a floor littered with broken glass and the remnants of the ceiling that had come down in places. Many of the walls had been partially knocked down and there were scorch marks everywhere.

"There is nothing for us here. If there ever was, then it has long since been looted." Talia's words, amid the remnants of what once had been, signalled a dejected end to their quest.

Crash!

Kirin and the others turned to see Coulan, who was bending down to pick up another rock.

"Fool of a dwarf," hissed Talia bringing her forefinger up to her mouth.

"What?" asked Coulan.

The others turned to look up at the castle towering above them, watching, listening.

"No. There still might be something," said Kirin. "We should split up, check out the building and the Maze before it gets too dark."

Talia and Stilgoe exchanged a look.

Everyone was now looking at Talia apart from Kirin who was looking at his feet.

"Stilgoe, you take Dargo, Bashka and Kirin and *check out* the Maze. I'll take—"

"My gut says it's the building," Kirin blurted out.

Talia raised an eyebrow and stared hard at Kirin. For a moment no-one said anything.

"Is that right Charter-mouse," said Bashka. "Ever consider that maybe you might have chosen the wrong branch of accountancy?" The others all laughed. Talia did not.

Kirin took this as some veiled criticism of his mother and was about to reply when Talia spoke.

"Fine! Then you're with me, along with Freyla and Coulan. And let's hope you're gut hasn't wasted two days of our time."

Kirin just nodded.

For over an hour they searched the building. The upper storey was in a bad way the flat roof had collapsed in many places, causing the second floor to end up being the first floor. The elements had been allowed free reign here. It was extremely dangerous and Talia had ordered Coulan not to even attempt going up to the second floor. Their hopes were momentarily raised when they found the vault. It had a solid steel door that was still intact. It was over three feet thick. They could tell the thickness because someone had helpfully made a large dwarf-sized hole in the concrete beside it. Inside the vault was chaos, masonry, twisted broken metal and thousands of little rectangular papers covered the floor. A steel barred door lay broken and twisted on the floor and empty shelves mocked them with riches they may once have held.

They made their way outside, Kirin trudged through the rubble lost in his thoughts. Wanting something badly enough does not make it happen. This is what happened when he abandoned logic and started taking advice from his gut. Bashka was right he should stick to his numbers. Leave this thinking on the run and going with your instinct stuff to the experts. Who was he kidding, everyone must think him such a fool. Well he'd learned his lesson. Yeah from now on it was strictly by the numbers. He sat down on the steps by the main entrance.

"Where's Coulan?" said Talia looking about. "If he's off throwing rocks again..."

"I think he wandered in to that large office." Freyla pointed to a room off the main hallway behind them. "I'll go get him."

Two minutes later she was back. "Eh, I think you guys had better come."

"What is it?" asked Talia.

"Eh, it's something you have to see," she said.

Talia strode past her, giving her a stern look, and Freyla followed with what might have been a hint of a smile. Reluctantly Kirin got up and trooped along behind them. The office had an enormous desk that had been overturned and all its drawers removed, many lying broken on the floor which was littered with more of the little bits of paper. On one wall there had been a large picture hanging at an angle on one nail. It had a white background and contained a jumble of geometric shapes, squares, circles and triangles, some filled in with bright reds, greens and yellows. This picture was now in Coulan's massive hands. But what drew the attention of Kirin and the others was not Coulan and his new toy, it was the small wall safe now revealed behind where the picture had been.

Talia, Freyla and Kirin stood in front of it and looked at each other and then back at the safe and for the first time that day all three of them smiled. The safe was about two foot square and had a handle on the front and to the left of it a small keypad comprising of the numbers 0 through 9. Talia put her hand on the handle and paused, she looked at the others, who nodded. She turned the handle, or at least tried to, it was locked. They decided to consider their options, safe cracking was after all a delicate business.

* * * *

Dargo and Stilgoe were standing in front of the safe debating the matter. They'd already been round the other side of the wall, estimating its thickness and had already determined it was made out of concrete. They were both already hot and tired from hacking their way to the centre of the Maze, only to find absolutely nothing, and were now considering how long it would take to dig out the safe and how heavy it would be to carry. Everyone else was looking to Kirin who had been pondering the problem while the others arrived at the scene. It suddenly occurred to him that this attention was not necessarily a compliment.

"I say we just smash it and see if it opens." said Coulan. There were murmurs of approval, but not from Talia.

"Look," said Kirin. "You didn't bring me along just for my business acumen and good looks."

Freyla made a snorting noise.

"Give me a moment here." Kirin turned to Bashka.

"Could you lend me your magnifying glass." Bashka looked to Talia while clutching at her utility belt. "Please." added Kirin

"Let him have it. This should be interesting," said Stilgoe.

Talia nodded.

"Thank you kindly," said Kirin giving Bashka a curt bow of his head. This time Freyla's snort was echoed by Bashka.

Kirin examined the keypad closely under the magnifying glass. He detected that three of the keys had traces of a tiny dark brown coloured stain on them. These were the numbers 2, 7 and 8. It occurred to Kirin that this stain might have been blood. He wondered briefly about what the circumstances of the last person to use this safe might have been. Undeterred he looked more closely. It seemed to him that the number 7 key was significantly more stained than the others. He thanked Bashka and handed back her magnifying glass. His gut feeling was that this was a four digit combination involving the digits 2, 7 and 8 with possibly the 7 being used twice. No, he thought, no gut feelings. This needed to be done by the numbers, literally.

He opened the inside pocket in his jerkin and removed his pen case. Opening it he removed the black pen, then returned the case to his pocket. Everyone was now watching his every move. Talia gave Stilgoe a quizzical look. Stilgoe just shrugged. Kirin held the pen delicately in his hand (with the nib cover still on), telling himself that he didn't want to disturb the keypad too much. Firstly he needed to eliminate the possibility that it was a simple three digit combination. The number of combinations for three digits was six. He felt the excitement in his fingers as he pressed the buttons with his pen, trying each combination in turn. 278, 287, 728, 782, 827, 872. Nothing!

He could feel the others disappointment, it was in the

air they breathed out behind him. Dargo and Stilgoe started arguing about how heavy tensile steel was and whether they should break the safe open here or attempt to carry it back over the Crumbling Mountains.

Kirin forced himself to focus again. He had expected that to fail. A four digit combination was always more likely. Concentrate. This was just basic mathematics. A question of combinations. A four digit combination had ten possibilities (0 to 9) for the first number, similarly ten for the second, third and fourth, giving a total number of combinations of 10 x 10 x 10 x 10 which of course was 10,000. However Kirin knew that only the digits 2, 7 and 8 were used, which shortened the odds considerably. If he was right.

First he considered the situation where there were four different numbers. Then there would be four ways of choosing the first digit, three ways of choosing the second digit, two ways of choosing the third digit and of course there would only be one digit left for the last place. i.e. 4 x 3 x 2 x 1 = 24. But if two of the digits were the same i.e. two 7's then that cut down the number of possibilities by half. So if the four digit combination consisted of the numbers 2, 7 and 8 with the 7 being used twice there were only 12 combinations!

Well that certainly cut it down from 10,000. Kirin allowed himself a small smile. He began trying them. 2778 Nope, 2787 Nah, 2877 Zip.

"This is a waste of time," said Dargo. "Is he gonna try *every* combination?"

Stilgoe sighed. "No! Let's see if Kirin Numbercruncher can live up to his name." He turned to Kirin raising a finger, "But the clock is ticking."

The others all murmured their approval apart from Dargo who just folded his arms and Coulan who looked around in vain for the clock.

Kirin continued undistracted. 7728 Nope, 7782 Nah, 7827 Zip, 7872... Kirin thought he detected a slight click.

The rest of the room suddenly tuned out, all he could hear now was the blood pumping round his body. Slowly he reached out and put his hand on the safe handle once more. He felt a tremor of excitement running through his fingers as he touched the handle. This time it turned and the safe door swung open. Kirin stood back too amazed to even look in the safe. For a moment there was complete silence broken only by a long low whistle from Stilgoe.

The only thing in the safe was a small grey looking box about four inches long by two wide and one deep. Talia was first to examine it, she held it very gingerly before passing it to Stilgoe. He looked as if he was about to do something, then felt better of it and passed it to Freyla. She stroked it surface thoughtfully before passing it to Kirin. He examined it more closely. It looked like nothing he had ever seen before, he could not even say what it was made of. It must have been some ancient artefact from the past, perfectly preserved for hundreds of years, but it looked so shiny and new, it could almost have come from the future. The surface was actually covered in grey squares marked by thin silver lines, except for one side where there was an additional large black square and next to it a small toggle switch with the words 'ON' and 'OFF' written on it.

Kirin rested his finger on the switch, he wasn't sure if was already on or off. He looked up at Talia, who nodded. Kirin pressed the switch. Nothing. He toggled the switch the other way. Again nothing. He pressed again. Still nothing. He started rapidly flipping it on and off before giving up in disgust. The mood in the room deflated. All that effort for just a bit of junk. Freyla asked to have a look at it and Kirin handed it to her.

"Could be solar powered?" she said.

"What?" said Kirin.

"I'm just saying, you know, powered by sunlight?" she said.

"You seem to know a lot about this sort of thing all of

a sudden," said Kirin.

"Who says I know! It was just a..." she said.

"Yes a...?" asked Kirin.

"Oh! Sort it yourself!" she said tossing the box at Kirin and strode away.

Kirin scratched his head as he watched her leave. He had another look at the box. If it was powered by the sun then... He went outside and sat down on the steps, where they still bathed in the setting sun, placing the box down beside him in the sunlight. While the others prepared to move out. Kirin sat watching the box for what seemed an age before he tried the switch again. Nothing, it was a dud after all.

There was still an hour's daylight left. An hour to head south, an hour to get that closer to home. As they prepared to move off Coulan picked up the picture from the office placing it under his arm.

"Leave it," said Dargo adding "It's got broken glass."

Coulan shook his head.

"You're not humphing that thing. We're on a quest here. Put it down." Dargo gave his brother one of his dark looks. Coulan did not budge.

Freyla stepped up to Coulan. She gently opened his fingers and took the picture frame from him. She then banged the frame on the ground releasing the pieces of broken glass that still clung to it. She brought out her knife and with a few deft strokes cut the picture from its frame. Coulan's howling dismay was cut off almost as soon as it started when she rolled the picture up and tucked it into the back of his pack.

They camped at dusk. No-one was keen to push things, even though the threat of Sang-gast had not gone away. As he picked his spot for the night Kirin held up the device and gave it a shake. He pressed the on/off switch again. Nothing. No wait what was that? It had beeped. It definitely beeped.

"Did you hear that?" he said.

Everyone was now looking at the device in Kirin's hand

As Kirin watched, it beeped again and this time he noticed on the black square a green dot appeared in the middle before moving off to one side and disappearing. Kirin looked up, as mystified as all the faces looking at him.

Kirin turned round to face north. The green dot though still moved off in the same direction as before. Could it be a tracker device of some sort? But then what was it tracking? Perhaps the Tral-fe-tigore? No-one knew. All they did know for sure was that it was pointing northeast, towards The Big Water. This was a journey in to the unknown, literally off the map. As scary as this was Kirin was secretly relieved that it had not pointed at Angaurd Castle. He still had a bad feeling about that place. One gut feeling had worked out today, he didn't want to put another to the test.

No-one seemed to question that the device was important. It had been locked in the safe after all. Everyone agreed that this was a long shot but then almost everyone was a Certified Accounting Dwarf and those were the kind of odds they liked. The quest for the Tral-fe-tigore was not hanging by a just a hunch anymore; it was hanging by the light of a small green dot and a faint but definite beep.

BROTHER, ROCK, HARD PLACE

"So pathfinder, are we still on track?" A grinning Stilgoe slapped Kirin playfully on the back.

Kirin lined up the tracking device with the compass. It was still indicating a direction of north by northeast or more exactly a bearing of 026 degrees. He turned raising his hand to block the late afternoon sun from his eyes, it was maybe five o'clock or so. Nodding to Stilgoe he asked, "What do you make of that?" He pointed off in the distance to a thin grey line on the horizon separating the rolling green plains from the sky. Stilgoe strained his eyes, before turning and asking for Bashka's mini binoculars.

"It's a wall, a long stone wall," said Stilgoe.

Bashka peered into the distance and held out her hand for the binoculars.

Talia was up beside them now and Stilgoe passed the binoculars to her.

"Is it to keep something in, or something out," said Talia who passed the binoculars back to Kirin, who could now see a low, dry stone wall, the kind used for marking a boundary rather than a fortification

"Maybe neither, it doesn't seem much of an obstacle," said Kirin.

"You know those are *my* binoculars," said Bashka.

Kirin handed the binoculars back to Bashka with a polite nod and a thankyou. Bashka snorted but with a smile. Another hour saw them reach the wall. It was actually on the crest of a ridge. The wall itself was only four feet high but stretched out of sight in either direction. There was a gently slope leading up to it but beyond the wall the ground fell away sharply. They could see The Big Water in the distance. Leading down to the sea the land was divided into a patchwork of fields, crops and pastures, containing a scattering of cows and sheep grazing in the remains of the day. There were also more of the low dry stone walls but these were in good repair in contrast to those on the plain above them. On their right a gentle stream cut through the fields angling southeast as it meandered its way down to the Big Water. Kirin's attention though was focused on the point where that stream flowed into the sea and the small town that nestled there.

Up above on the plain the last rays of the sun still shone, but below the ridge everywhere was now in shadow. It felt cold and there was a freshening breeze now blowing, bringing that unmistakable salty tang of the sea. They began to walk the couple of miles to the town, all kept any eye out for trouble. They were approaching civilization once more. As they marched into town they kept their wits about them while trying to appear as simple travelling strangers, the few people they did see scurried away closing doors behind them. They arrived at the central square of the town to find the very welcome sight of the Green Man Tavern. It was a large, wooden, two story building and from behind its old fashioned leaded glass windows came a warm comfortable glow. After many days on the road there was no dwarfish discussion required here, Talia led the way.

"A round of milks for some thirsty dwarfs, if you please landlord!" Talia thumped her hand down on the bar counter. The entire tavern fell silent.

"Eee. We don't have none." The landlord, a somewhat portly man, focused on the glass he was polishing, as fourteen dwarfish eyes bore into him.

"What! Whom am I addressing?" asked Talia.

"Oh, eh, Mr Albert Shivers," said the landlord.

"It says tavern on the sign doesn't it? There's cows in the fields aren't there?"

Mr Shivers nodded reluctantly at Talia's incontrovertible logic.

"Well, in that case it would not seem beyond the realm of the possible to arrange for some fresh milk to be served up for my companions and myself."

Mr Shivers put down his glass. "It's a little late in the day—"

"As Certified Accounting Dwarfs we are empowered to enforce the Trades Description Act." Talia paused. "A tavern that *doesn't* sell milk" Talia shook her head and made a tutting sound.

"Oh I don't think we want any of that sort of thing. It's just we don't get many dwarfs round these parts. Bart? Bart?" A small, neat man with a large white apron and short white hair, who had been standing just behind Mr Shivers all the while, coughed slightly. "Ah Bart, go round to Mr Franklin's and fetch a keg, eh better make that two kegs of fresh milk for our valued customers here." Bart looked like he was about to say something before changing his mind and scurrying off.

The landlord showed the dwarfs to a table, assuring them he would bring their milk over as soon as it was ready. While they waited they took the opportunity to order some food. Mr Shivers had seemed surprised when they said they'd come from the south. Past Angaurd Castle he had whispered in awe. He was scared. Of that Kirin was sure, but of what? Ghosts? He mentioned dwarfs. Perhaps he'd been getting some business from those Money Laundering dwarfs from the Forest of Teteunxx? The business of the tavern returned to normal or what passed for normal. But there were lots of mutterings and furtive looks. Was it just that they were strangers wondered Kirin? They kept their voices down as they waited for their supper. Talia had made it clear to them all that they should keep their mouths shut, especially about the quest for the Tral-fe-tigore, till they knew the lay of the land. In a lull in the general conversation they heard one man speak more loudly than perhaps he intended.

"That one doesn't look like an accounting dwarf to me." His remark clearly directed at Kirin.

In the silence that followed Dargo stood up and faced the man who was at the next table.

"You got a problem with how we look?" he asked.

"I, I'm just saying—"

"Hey, what you doin?" said Stilgoe, to Dargo. "You trying to have all the fun?"

"What," said Dargo.

"You know the rules." Stilgoe sighed. "Share and share alike, turn and turn about."

"Oh, It's your turn? Really? I thought it was mine." Dargo scratched his head for good measure.

Stilgoe just slowly shook his head. He stood up, and with a mock bow Dargo gave way to him and sat down again. "Well sir unless you wish to retract your remark about my Chartered Accountant friend here." Stilgoe gave a slight nod to Kirin, "Then I believe we have an appointment outside."

Kirin, thinking things were getting out of hand was about to say something, when Freyla gently placed her hand on his arm and shook her head. The man looked from Stilgoe to Kirin to Dargo and back to Stilgoe again. "Eh I may have been a little hasty in my remarks. No offence was meant master dwarf sir." The man sat down and bowed his head over his tankard of ale. Stilgoe continued to stare at the top of the man's head for a few moments before sitting down. The rest of the tavern broke its silence with murmured conversations. There were mentions of 'Chartered Accountant' and Kirin was suddenly getting a lot more attention now. Talia gave Stilgoe a hard look, who in return merely shrugged a little sheepishly.

After a short while tankards of fresh milk were brought to the table, and after an even shorter while they required refilling. Their food arrived and soon the sound of dwarfs enjoying their supper filled the room. People seemed to be paying them less attention now. The landlord popped over to see if everything was satisfactory. Talia nodded between mouthfuls. The landlord was attentive to Kirin in particular and let it be known that should Kirin care to peruse his accounts then eternity would not be long enough to express his gratitude. Kirin looked to Talia at this point, who nodded.

Kirin followed Mr Shivers into an adjacent room, that the latter indicated was his office. Whilst apologising for the mess, Mr Shivers brought down a large old brown leather book from a shelf, dusted it down and placed it in front of Kirin on the desk.

"Just the one?" asked Kirin.

"Oh yes. Just he one," said Mr Shivers and quickly scurried away.

There was something about the way he had said, just the one. Kirin sensed fear once more and not just of Tax Goblins. Kirin spent the next few hours redoing the accounts of the Green Man Tavern. He left them in a much healthier state, to Mr Shivers inexpressible delight. The accounts held nothing out of the ordinary apart from one item labelled as miscellaneous expenses. Normally not such a big deal, it is a term often used to cover a multitude of minor items. In this case though it accounted for exactly twenty percent of the profits!

While this was going on Talia indicated that they were looking for a boat to charter. They had previously agreed this would be a good pretext for exploring the region. Mr

Shivers enquired if they were going down the coast or across to Bank island. The map had shown no islands, so this was news to them. However they stuck to their explanation of a 'business trip' and acted non-committal as Mr Shivers directed them to the Harbour Master, as the person most able to help them in this matter. Lodging and board was on the house of course, courtesy of Kirin's services. He remarked on how rare it was to find a Chartered Accounting Dwarf these days. So rare indeed. He actually clapped his hands at one point.

The next day after a good cooked breakfast they went off to see the Harbour Master, whose office was, not unsurprisingly, down by the dock. At this point they were not sure if their quest lay here in Helsinagar (which was the name of the town) or further northeast, perhaps on this Bank island the landlord had mentioned, or even beyond. The dock was comprised of a number of jetties in the shape of a capital letter E, but on its side, with the three prongs pointing out to sea. The middle jetty was the longest, and about two thirds of the way along it, two more jetties extended sideways out from it. On one of these sideways jetties was a small shack or large hut depending upon your point of view. This was the Harbour Master's office. Walking onto the dock, Kirin found himself conveniently at the centre of a huddle of dwarfs. Concealed inside his jerkin he peered at the device while the others talked loudly, with a covering cough Kirin switched the device on then off. He peered into the distance, the water was still and calm and seemed to stretch away forever. Whatever the quest held in store for them, it was not here in Helsinagar.

A short but very stout man with a nervous expression and a peaked hat that said 'Harbour Master' on it, appeared before them. Talia looked across at Kirin, who shook his head.

"Good day sir, the Harbour Master I presume," said Talia.

"Indeed it is mistress dwarf," he said. How can I be of service?"

"We wish to charter a boat sir," said Talia.

"Oh, em, er of course, em where are you going?" he said.

"It's a business trip, up the coast to the Land of the Caucasians," interjected Stilgoe.

"Hmmm. Them's strange folk up there," he said scratching his chin.

"We shall need the boat for several days," said Stilgoe

"At least a week," said Talia.

"At least a week," echoed Stilgoe.

"Party of seven," said Talia

"Eight if you count him twice," said Stilgoe pointing at Coulan.

The Harbour Master looked at Coulan and then back to Stilgoe and Talia. He laughed nervously. "Eh, right, a week it is then. There is this vessel here," the Harbour Master began walking along the dock to where a rather dilapidated looking boat was moored. "The Papillon."

"Excellent," said Stilgoe, Talia nodded

To Kirin's mind they needed a bigger boat, "Eh, excuse me but do you have any other vessels available?'

Stilgoe coughed, nudging Kirin in the ribs with his elbow.

"This is our eh, nautical expert," said Talia dismissively.

"Well there is the Red Witch but she is a little more expensive," said the Harbour Master. "She is due in this afternoon. A sixty foot schooner. A beautiful boat, lovely lines, there's nothing faster in these waters." The Harbour Master smiled the smile of a doting father. A troubled look crossed his countenance. "But she's not for hire..."

"Well I'm sure we can come to some mutually amicable arrangement," said Stilgoe putting his arm round the Harbour Master and walking back with him to his office.

They split up into three groups. Stilgoe and Freyla conducted negotiations with the Harbour Master while

Talia and Bashka went for a casual wander around town to see what information they could pick up. Kirin, Dargo and Coulan however, were to reconnoitre the area west of the town, as this might prove a useful escape route. Kirin objected at first, thinking he could be more useful in the boat negotiations but Talia shook her head and told him she needed him to take charge of their exit strategy. Once again he realised he had crossed another one of those invisible lines.

Kirin, Dargo and Coulan strolled casually out of town travelling west on a rough dirt road, that ran parallel to the shoreline. On their left, south of the road, was open country, a patchwork of fields and pastures with a handful of small farms and homesteads scattered among them. On their right, the shoreline was about half a mile north of the road, in between was lightly wooded terrain. This was ancient woodland, not like the Forest of Teteunxx. It was Kirin's guess that all the country round here was once like this till it had been cleared, by man for planting and grazing. This stretch may have been left as a sustainable source of firewood and timber, it certainly seemed to extend for miles. They decided to leave the path and explore the woodland, while still travelling west.

It was not long before they realized the woodland had eyes upon them. And more crucially it had clumsy feet and careless voices. After a whispered conversation with Dargo and Coulan, Kirin fell back slipping away from the other two. He took cover and waited. Soon he heard the murmured discourse of what sounded like some sort of argument between two individuals. They passed by his hiding place, no more than ten feet or so away from him. Kirin followed them, being careful to stop when they stopped. After one such halt there were more raised whispers and a long pause before the two of them split up. Kirin followed the one who moved towards the road side of the woodland. He came up behind him unseen. His would-be stalker, a boy not much older than himself, was soon securely bound thanks to Kirin's bark-ties. He cried out briefly before Kirin gagged him with his last clean handkerchief. As he headed off in pursuit of the other stalker he smiled to himself remembering his mothers advise about the wisdom of always having a clean hanky. After a few minutes a snapped twig to his left stopped him in his tracks. He held his breath, gently he placed his raised foot on the ground balancing himself. He waited. There a slight rustle, he could see the other boy now and up ahead he could hear Dargo and Coulan crashing through the woodland, well walking as normal in Coulan's case. This was always part of the plan. Slowly, using the woodland as cover, Kirin snuck up on the second boy.

Then in the distance he heard some kind of ruckus with many different raised voices, among them Dargo and Coulan. Kirin reacted immediately. Under cover of the noise he tackled the second boy, who seemed unsure whether to remain hidden or take part in the action that was now unfolding. Kirin soon had him immobilised, though not gagged, and ran at a loping pace towards the commotion.

In a slight clearing Dargo was gripping one boy by his shirt, lifting him clear off the ground. The boy was kicking wildly. When one foot connected with Dargo's knee, he cried out in pain letting go of the boy who dropped to the ground like a sack of potatoes but then immediately sprang up and ran off. All the while Coulan was sitting on top of another boy, his knees either side of the boy's chest. With one arm he had pinned down one of the boy's arms. With the other he held a rock poised above the boy's head. The boy's other arm was flapping ineffectually against Coulan. Kirin watched the other boy getting away, but did not give chase.

"Coulan, stop" said Kirin.

He tried not to shout, tried to remember the tone Freyla used with him.

Coulan turned round. His right eye was gushing blood.

It looked really bad.

"What are you saying?" said Dargo, sitting rubbing his knee. "The guy nearly killed him!"

"Nearly is not the same as actually," said Kirin. "And look at him, he's just a kid. A scared kid." Turning to Coulan, Kirin said, "I know you're hurt and angry, but there's no need to hit the boy with the rock."

"Aw, let the kid have some of his own medicine," said Dargo.

Coulan was still poised rock in hand, the boy was screaming now in terror.

"Shut up Dargo. Think about how Coulan will feel... after..."

"What?" Dargo looked as if he was about to say more, but then just scowled at Kirin.

"You're his brother, you're supposed to be looking out for him!"

Dargo said nothing, his mouth shut tightly, squeezing his lips even thinner.

Coulan looked to his brother then at Kirin. "He hurt me."

"Imagine you're the other person. The one being hit. How would you feel?"

Coulan's brows furrowed. He looked to his brother once more.

"Oh leave him alone can't you? You're just confusing him." said Dargo "You know he doesn't do gushy, feely stuff."

Ignoring Dargo, Kirin tried to think. He was at a loss, then it came to him. "Coulan, imagine you are the rock." Coulan looked down at the rock in his hand as if seeing it for the first time. "That's it." encouraged Kirin. "Now imagine being hit against something or someone, *very hard*." Kirin noticed Coulan's expression change slightly. "Well done Coulan. Now imagine that nice, hand sized rock, beginning to break, crumbling apart, turning to dust within your very hand."

"What are you talking about?" said Dargo.

"Shhhh." Kirin waved his hand at Dargo, but kept his gaze fixed on Coulan. "Now imagine how that feels..."

Even the boy was quiet now, all eyes on Coulan who was looking aghast at the rock in his hand. His grip went slack and the rock slipped from it, falling to the ground. He gasped as it bounced of the hard ground. Bending over he gently picked it up, cradling it for a moment before gently placing it back down. Coulan stood up, his gaze went first to Kirin then across to his brother before settling on his feet. "I wouldn't like it."

Kirin secured the boy who had remained motionless on the ground even after Coulan had stood up. Next quest he decided he would definitely bring more bark-ties. They washed Coulan's eye with water from their canteens. The eye itself was closed up and the tissue all round it was purple. The blood came from a nasty looking gash along the line of his eyebrow, rather than from the eye itself, which hopefully was not damaged. They wouldn't know till the swelling went away. They cut a strip of fabric from Coulan's spare (and clean) shirt from his pack and formed a bandage and patch for his eye. Kirin had a feeling it might need stitches, but at least the bleeding had stopped. Dargo was limping a bit, still rubbing his knee but did not seem to be seriously injured. The very relieved boy in front of them readily answered all their questions. When they were pretty sure he had told them all he knew, which was more than enough, they let him go.

Dargo had not been happy about letting their three prisoners go, but as Kirin had explained one of them had already escaped so there was nothing to be gained by keeping them and risking the wrath of the townspeople. Releasing them showed both strength and acted as a good will gesture. Dargo reluctantly agreed but remained in a grumpy mood, rubbing his hurt knee, as they made their way back to meet the others. He was like a rough edged rock always rubbing up against something. Kirin suspected that he was even exaggerating his limp.

They decided to make their way back to town along the coast and headed for the shoreline. It was not long before they came across a small, sheltered bay. The trees here had been felled forming a clearing, many were still scattered about, lying there like abandoned giant sticks. At one side of the clearing was a small woodsman's hut. Inside there was no sign of anyone, the cobwebs and dust suggested the place had been abandoned for some time. It must have been used to clear the trees for it was full of old tools, and equipment. Dargo gave his brother a questioning look, who nodded in return.

After this they moved on reaching the edge of the woodland, and in sight of Helsinagar by about two o'clock. Dargo went into town to fetch the others while Kirin and Coulan prepared a late lunch. When the others arrived there was much to talk about. But Freyla first had a look at Coulan's eye and decided it did need stitches. To Kirin's surprise she used a common needle and thread to do this. Rather Coulan than him he thought but Coulan seemed unaffected by the whole procedure. Freyla persuaded Kirin to allow Coulan the use of his coloured accountancy pens and two blank pages in Sang-gast's notebook and his only cry of alarm was when it was all over and Kirin gently eased the book and pen out of his grasp.

Other news was not so good. Firstly Stilgoe and Freyla had negotiated a price for the boat charter subject to viewing the boat but it was a high one. The Harbour Master would only accept gold. Not going back for Dargo's stash of gold ingots, had seemed sensible at the time. Now a little gold would have come in very useful. Talia and Bashka had nothing definite to report, except that they were sure the town was gripped by fear. No-one was talking much. But one word kept getting mentioned in hushed whispers. This was confirmed by the stories told by the boys in the woods. Each of them had independently told the same story pretty much. And the bad news was it was a story about Dividend-orcs.

They'd appeared in the region some twenty years ago and had taken up residence in Angaurd Castle itself. It occurred to Kirin that perhaps they had been watching them the whole time as they made their way across the plain, first to the Maze and then to Helsinagar. But their presence was not just limited to Angaurd Castle, they had laid claim to the entire Plain of Angaurd, brandishing a property certificate, that gave them the legal right to do so. They applied prohibitive levies on anyone crossing the plain. Though if this was the case, why had they left the Company of the Quest alone? Gradually no-one could afford to live on the plain any more. The Dividend-orcs had then concentrated their financial efforts on Helsinagar town itself and the lands north of the wall. Slowly but surely their stranglehold on the town increased. It was now in so much debt that just keeping up the interest payments alone was killing the town. Dividend-orcs didn't care. They were the ultimate creditor. All that mattered to them was profit. Not people. Once the town became financially insolvent, they would asset strip it and move on to the next one.

The question was, what were they up to now. They had sent the boys to spy upon them, promising their families five percentage points relief on their interest payments for a little information. That was how they worked, always subverting, coercing others to their will, appealing to the lowest conmen denominator. That was what made them so insidious.

Kirin listened at first curiously and then with awe as the others discussed the situation like military tacticians. They assumed that the orcs had probably found the empty safe and would have surmised that something of value had been acquired and they would also know about their planned boat trip by now. In addition after the incident with the boys in the woods, the orcs would now know that, they now knew the orcs were watching them. This was a complicated game of cat and mouse and they were going to have to play this very cagily if they weren't going to end up as dead mice. Fooling Dividend-orcs was not one of your holiday games. They talked for an hour trying to come up with a something plausible. In the end it was Stilgoe and Freyla who came up with the crazy plan. Kirin had the sneaky suspicion that this wasn't for the first time. Never mind distraction, diversion and division, they was only one way to come out ahead in this situation. Not to fight them as Kirin supposed, but a scam!

Everyone was deep in thought that evening. Kirin's brain was boggling with the intricacy of the plan. He needed to switch off, think of something else. "Stilgoe?" he said. "What do you know about Dividend-orcs. Or are you going to tell me that, like elves, they don't really exist. I've just heard rumours and—" He stopped as everyone went quiet and looked towards him. He'd said something wrong again. Why hadn't he just gone to sleep.

"Oh they do exist," said Stilgoe. "They were human once, still are, only, just not quite."

"Best not to speak of such things." said Dargo his voice strangely flat and empty.

Stilgoe spoke to Talia who was sitting alongside Bashka by the fire, enjoying her pipe. "He is to play a part tomorrow, perhaps it is only right he should know."

Talia looked over at Bashka, who nodded. She then took a few deep puffs from her pipe but said nothing, it was as if she were absorbing the smoke, transforming it into words. Then after tapping out her pipe she began to speak.

"It is said the orcs's ancestors were investment bankers, financial speculators and the like; the elite of their world. In those ancient times their knowledge and power was beyond anything we can dream of now, and between them they possessed all the wealth of the world. They had even created the Ether. An unseen world which they believed more important than the real one. Some of them, it was said, locked their gold and precious things away in deep underground vaults, never even to look at. Others hoarded promissory notes beyond count, that embodied the sum of their fortunes. But the bulk of their financial capital they poured into the Ether.

In the end it was their insatiable greed that caused it all, that led the world to fall. The Fall that split the world into a million pieces a thousand years ago. Even their precious Ether came tumbling down, proving just as fragile as their world of paper promises. When that invisible world disappeared, it is said, many lost their senses, descended to some dark place and no more is known of them.

But how did it all come to fall? Well they prized intelligence above all else. But it was not enough that they possessed it, others must not. They feared that from within the ranks of the masses *others* might arise to challenge them. So they sought to make them more malleable, reduce them to forever serve their purpose. Turning a liability into an asset. For all these reasons and more they devised the Plague. They modified the common cold to deliver it, to target it. In their arrogance they believed they had conquered nature itself in all its complexity. They were wrong. Disastrously wrong.

The Plague was intended to reduce the intelligence of the populous. Even if it had succeeded perfectly the disruption to the world would have been immense, but it did not succeed perfectly. Alas for so many, it proved fatal. And for those that did survive; it was not just their intelligence that was diminished. Even the elite did not survive unscathed. For though they succeeded in preserving their own intelligence, as planned, it came at a great physical cost to their bodies, which were left stunted and enfeebled.

One good thing did come of it all, the rise of the dwarfs. For though many of our kind also perished from the Plague, those who did survive were the stronger for it. Thus we became unlooked for rivals, and worthy challengers to the orcs. But the rest of the world was reduced. Reduced in numbers, reduced in intelligence, even reduced in stature. The world became a smaller, simpler place."

THE PAYOFF CLINCHER

It was late morning when Stilgoe, Kirin and Freyla entered the Harbour Master's office, having left the others to do the hard work. Kirin was so far out of his comfort zone that climbing another mountain was beginning to look like a piece of cake. Thankfully Stilgoe and Freyla were going to be doing most of the talking. He was still troubled though about the seed money. This was what they needed for the sting operation and it was likely they would not see it again. Everyone had put in what gold coinage they had. Everyone that is except for Kirin, for he had none.

He recalled how he had removed the string from around his neck and thrust out a fist dangling his chartered accounting ring, given to him by his mother and passed on by untold generations before. The ring bore the Accountancy Dwarf insignia, an open book with a set of scales on it and angled across the bottom were a pair of quill pens denoting his chartered status. Stilgoe had said no, indeed no-one had seemed keen. But Kirin knew the dwarf motto of 'share and share alike, turn and turn about' meant he had to contribute. It was a shock when Bashka grabbed the ring. She brought out her magnifying glass and with a great deal of show examined it. Without even looking up she offered two gold coins for it. Stilgoe exploded, suggesting her valuation was below even the low-end estimate for such a valuable piece, though he expressed himself in much more colourful language. Indeed Talia had been required to restrain Stilgoe till Bashka, while putting away her magnifying glass, indicated the price was for pawning purposes only. Everyone burst out laughing, even Stilgoe. Who clapped Bashka heartily on the back as she tucked the ring into her utility belt. Kirin mouthed a silent thank you to her.

"Good day Harbour Master, I see the Red Witch is in, she looks a passable vessel right enough. Of course we shall have to inspect her." Stilgoe examined his fingernails.

"What? Oh, eh, yes indeed master dwarf. She is certainly Yarr," said the Harbour Master.

"Yarr?" whispered Kirin to Freyla.

"For an aquatic expert, your friend doesn't seem terribly knowledgeable about boats, master Stilgoe," said a voice from the shadows in the corner. The stranger stepped forward into the light and sat down casually at the table in the centre of the room. He gestured with his hand indicating that Stilgoe and the others should join him. He offered them a smile which never got even near his eyes. Stilgoe began looking all round the room as if he was trying to detect the source of an annoying insect.

"Em, er this is Ryszard, um, my sleeping partner," said the Harbour Master.

Stilgoe shrugged, still ignoring the stranger he addressed the Harbour Master, "Don't mind if my colleague examines the boat," He nodded to Freyla who ducked out the doorway.

"Eh no of course not I—"

"Listen to me dwarf, we've got more business here than a poxy boat hire," said Ryszard.

"Pray tell what business could I possibly have with a Dividend-orc," said Stilgoe.

Kirin who had been eyeing the stranger suspiciously,

stopped in his tracks. The hairs on the back of his neck stood up, he should have been feeling fear or even dread, based on their reputation, but he wasn't. There was no other word for what he was experiencing. It was excitement! He took a closer look at the stranger. Thin and scrawny looking, he was no taller than a dwarf, and though not physically intimidating, there was something about the way he looked at them, the way he was sizing them up, thought Kirin. There was intelligence there for sure, but also something else, like a cat when it's caught the mouse and is watching it squirm.

"Well let's see now, there's the levy for seven dwarfs crossing the Plain of Angaurd." Ryszard sighed. "Then there's the fine for non payment of the aforementioned levy—"

"What! What are you talking about." said Stilgoe.

"And of course interest. At twenty percent per day on these amounts. It all adds up to a pretty penny." Ryszard employed his non-smile again.

Stilgoe looked the Dividend-orc up and down and asked to see the Property Certificate. After a slight pause, which Ryszard seemed to take great pleasure in, he took a brown envelop from his pocket and presented it to Stilgoe, who opened it and examined the document in detail for some time. During this, Freyla came back, she began to ask what was going on, but Stilgoe just held up a hand to silence her.

Ryszard sighed. "Come now it is a simple enough document, even for an Accounting Dwarf."

Stilgoe ignored him and continued reading.

After what seemed like an eternity to Kirin, Stilgoe finished. He held out the document to the Harbour Master.

"You see this? All very clear in black and white. Except land registry certificates use coloured ink. This? This is just a copy. It's not legally enforceable." Stilgoe dropped the Property Certificate on the table in front of Ryszard. The

Harbour Master picked it up, looking closely at the document before turning angrily to Ryszard.

"Is this true, what he said!" said the Harbour Master.

"We have the original safe and sound!" Ryszard's voice was like a slap across the face to the Harbour Master.

"Even so, it is still a legal requirement for the party of the first part. That's you," Stilgoe pointed at Ryszard, "to show the Property Certificate to the party of the second part being levied. That's us," he pointed at himself, "when requested."

"Suddenly you seem to know a whole lot about leagalising for a Certified Accounting Dwarf." said Ryszard.

"The others are not going to be happy, we didn't bargain for this," said Freyla.

"Well let's see just how much you are going to have to bargain for. Hmmm there's seven for the levy plus another five (standard non-payment fine) then there's two days interest." Ryszard took a deep and noisy intake of breath. "Well we're talking, rounding up, eh eighteen gold pieces, coin of the realm. Oh plus the hire for the boat that's another eight. And that's if you pay now. Are you paying now?"

"Twenty six! No way will Talia go for that," said Freyla.

"Shut up, leave Talia to me," hissed Stilgoe at Freyla. "You just deliver your end. Remember we need him with us."

"And as for you," said Stilgoe, turning back to Ryszard. "You don't get a thing till we see the original of that!"

"Problems among the brethren? Perhaps I should be talking to this Talia?" said Ryszard. After a slight pause he casually added, "Of course it's possible we could come to some less financially prohibitive arrangement..."

Stilgoe looked searchingly at the Dividend-orc in front of him.

"What kind of arrangement?" said Stilgoe.

Ryszard sighed, "I believe you have the contents of a

certain safe, something that is of no use to you but may be of interest to us."

"How did—," said Freyla.

"Shut up!" said Stilgoe.

Stilgoe turned to the Dividend-orc, regarding him for a long time. "Maybe we do, maybe we don't." He leaned his hands on the table and regarded Ryszard as if reassessing him, as if he were a worthy adversary that he'd misjudged, underestimated. He maintained this look just to the edge of turning Ryszard's arrogance into uncertainty, but not beyond. "We'll meet back here in two hours and then we'll *negotiate*. Is that time enough for you?"

Ryszard nodded. What passed for a smile playing about his lips.

* * * *

As they walked back along the dock Kirin was bursting to talk, but a seemingly inadvertent brush of Freyla's arm on his had caught his attention. The slight shake of her head was enough to remind him, there might still be eyes and ears upon them. He bit his tongue, forced himself to focus on his task, simple straightforward, distraction. At the bridge over the river Stilgoe and Kirin waited, like casually chatting companions, till they saw Freyla jog safely out of town, to rendezvous with the others in the woodland. Then the two of them wandered over to the Green Man Tavern, like two tired dwarfs in need of some refreshment.

The landlord Mr Shivers was very happy to see them again, especially Kirin, nothing was too much trouble. So when they asked for the private use of his function room he was only too happy to oblige. While Stilgoe ate some bread and cheese, Kirin did a little shopping, thanks to Mr Shivers' directions he was able to obtain what they required and also arrange a financial audit for later that evening, at a certain Mrs Magellon's general store. When Kirin returned, Stilgoe got to work, writing.

As Kirin watched Stilgoe work, he consumed his lunch with a vengeance, hungrily tearing the bread apart with his teeth. All that nervous tension from the morning had sapped his energy, and besides on top of it all he was going to have a very long night. It was fascinating to see the painstaking care Stilgoe took with each letter and word. This was a different Stilgoe from the laid back dwarf he had come to know. Gradually the document took shape. To Kirin's eye it was beginning to resemble the Property Certificate that Ryszard had shown them. Stilgoe explained that, whist working for his father, he had written hundreds of such documents. They were all of the same format and structure. All he had had to remember were the details: where the land was bounded, the owners names, the witnesses and the date of the transaction. That's still a lot to remember, thought Kirin.

Freyla and Coulan arrived about an hour or so later. Lunch was served and while the others tucked into it, Kirin left to have a quiet word with Mr Shivers. As part payment for his financial audit the landlord had agreed to ship supplies along the coast road to a second party of dwarfs camped at the edge of the Forest of Teteunxx who would be waiting for them. Entirely fictitious of course. Kirin had not liked deceiving Mr Shivers that way but if the Dividend-orcs were to question the landlord, then he could answer them honestly. More distraction.

After they had all finished eating lunch the landlord returned with some good news to report, as requested he had set-up Kirin with three additional customers: Given and Sons, Dombie's Bakery and a ladies dressmaker. While the others left to rendezvous with Talia in the woods west of town, Kirin left to attend to his appointed tasks. He felt more comfortable doing something he was trained for, even if it was only his third time, but it troubled him not being with the others in case there was trouble. First on his audit list was the general store of Mrs Magellan which was then to be followed by the ladies dressmaker. He recalled his conversation with Freyla about that.

"But why a dressmaker?" he said.

"Exactly," she said.

"Exactly what? I don't understand?" he said

"Perfect," she said.

"Hurrumph!" he said.

"Look, you think you're pretty clever don't you?" she said.

"Um no, eh, that is um..." he said

"Imagine you're a Dividend-orc trying to figure what you are up to?" she said.

"Eh... Oh? Distraction!" he said.

"Having said all that, there is another matter," and with that she handed him a piece of paper.

All this mind game stuff was new territory for Kirin. Nothing his parents had taught him was even close. He thought back to how Freyla and Stilgoe had played that scene with the Dividend-orc, it had been brilliant and as for what they were planning next, well that was just mind-boggling. What they'd done back in the Forest of Teteunxx was nothing compared to this! Kirin forced himself to calm down, he needed to focus, one step at a time. He wasn't going to get anywhere worrying about what he couldn't control.

* * * *

"Oh I see you're early and you've brought some playmates with you. How nice." Stilgoe stepped inside the Harbour Master's office where Ryszard and six other Dividend-orcs were seated and standing round the table. That non-smile was still playing around the bottom half of Ryszard's face.

"Have you brought the item?" said Ryszard.

"Oh I've brought more than that," smiled Stilgoe as he sat down at the table facing Ryszard. Behind him first Freyla then Coulan entered the office. They must have known about him, but Coulan's presence, in the now quite cramped office still had an intimidating effect on the others. The pirate patch over his injured eye added a nice touch to the scowling looks he was spreading round the room. Those Dividend-orcs already standing against the wall tried to melt into it and Ryszard was no longer attempting a smile.

"Show us the item." A deep thick voice came from the Dividend-orc seated next to Ryszard.

"I don't believe you've introduced me to your side-kick here." Stilgoe grinned at the stranger.

"Th... this is Derrott, our leader," said Ryszard.

Stilgoe looked at the stranger. He had shoulder length gently flowing black hair that didn't seem to belong with a stern looking face etched with the lines of command. "Oh I see, so you're the organ grinder, so to speak," Stilgoe then regarded Ryszard, cocking his head to one side. "I guess, that makes you the performing monkey." Stilgoe laughed at his own joke. Ryszard scowled at him and started to say something but then thought better of it. Stilgoe, eyes focused on Derrott, put up a hand behind him. Freyla had to nudge Coulan who eventually twigged and placed a package on Stilgoe's palm. Stilgoe placed it on the table, enjoying the hush that had descended on the room. Slowly he began untying the string holding the sealskin covering in place.

"It came in this?" said Derrott.

"No, but we figured it might be a bit delicate," said Stilgoe as he lifted the tracking device free from its protective wrapping.

There was an audible gasp from some of those present. Stilgoe ignored it. Tossing it playfully from hand to hand he twirled it making sure they all got a good look at it. After a pause, he himself looked at it intensely, as if for the first time. "Yes. A curious thing. It does have an on/off switch as you see." At this point he made to switch it on, but didn't. "Doesn't work though."

"Give it to me!" said Derrott, his eyes glued to the device.

"Wow, hold your horses there Mr Derrott. Not so fast, where's the Property Certificate."

"What! What are you talking about. Give it to me. Let me try it," said Derrott.

Stilgoe drew back from the outstretched arms of Derrott. He passed the tracking device back to Freyla who wrapped it up tightly once again, all the while he kept his eyes fixed on Derrott.

"Didn't your little underling here tell you?" said Stilgoe. "He was supposed to bring proof of the Property Certificate, the original not just a copy. That's what this meeting was for." Derrott looked at Ryszard who at this point was as far away from smiling as a Dividend-orc can get.

"I, I didn't think he was serious!" Ryszard looked wildly from Stilgoe to Derrott.

Derrott was facing Ryszard as he spoke. "The original Property Certificate is normally kept under lock and key. Of course if you wish to view it, that can be arranged, but I must insist on seeing—"

"You can insist on nothing!" said Stilgoe, rising up and banging his fist down on the table.

The room shook with silence.

"We came here in good faith! We held up our end of the bargain! We showed you the device! We even brought the money for the boat hire!" With that Stilgoe brought a pouch of money from his jerkin pocket and slammed it down on the table.

"Look I'm sorry, that there may have been some *mix-up*," Derrott glared at Ryszard at this point, "But we're all business people here. Now I admit we seem to have gotten off on the wrong foot but—"

Stilgoe held up a hand silencing Derrott. The other Dividend-orcs exchanged looks.

"I don't want to know about your problems," said Stilgoe. "I've got enough of my own. Not everyone's happy about doing a deal with Dividend-orcs. Some of my compatriots back in the woods are pretty angry. You really shouldn't have sent those spies you know." Stilgoe shook his head. "We three here and the Chartered Accountant, we thought making a deal was the smart thing to do. We convinced the others, that it was the smart thing to do. Now what are they going to say when we come back and tell them you didn't hold up your end?"

Stilgoe leaned his hands on the table looking directly into Derrott's face. "I'll tell you what they're going to say. They'll say, you can't trust Dividend-orcs. Heck maybe they'll even say, they don't even *have* the Property Certificate!" Slowly Stilgoe stood up, picked up his pouch of coins, turned around and indicated to Freyla and Coulan that they should leave.

"Wait!" said Derrott, "We can still do this. We'll reschedule. The property Certificate is in Angaurd Castle we can have it here by tomorrow."

Stilgoe paused in the doorway, he turned round. He regarded Derrott for a moment who was half standing, half leaning on the table. Stilgoe looked slowly round the room and then walked back to the table and plopped the pouch of money back on the table. A couple of coins spilled out. He carefully popped them back in. He weighed the pouch carefully in his hand as he thought.

"Noon tomorrow. Here. We bring the device. You bring the Property Certificate. We give you the device and that takes care of the levy, the fine and all interest up to and *including* tomorrow," Stilgoe looked straight at Derrott, who nodded. "One more thing," said Stilgoe, he tipped the pouch spilling four gold pieces onto the table. "Your forgetful friend here can throw in the charter of the boat for half-price, *for our inconvenience*."

"What!" cried Ryszard. No it's eight gold pieces. You can—"

"I'm going to have some very angry dwarfs back in the woods to deal with. Saving them a few gold pieces would go a long way to smoothing over this whole *situation*." Stilgoe looked at Derrott.

"Yes, that does not seem unreasonable, after all

Ryszard should pay for his mistake." Derrott looked disdainfully at Ryszard, who glared at Stilgoe, but said nothing, his hands were squeezed tightly into fists.

* * * *

Derrott stood on the dock outside the Harbour Master's hut watching the departing backs of the three dwarfs.

"I may be out of line here sir, but you can't seriously be thinking of trusting that dwarf?" said Ryszard.

Ignoring Ryszard, Derrott summoned two of the Dividend-orcs and after a brief instruction they headed off to relieve those watching Kirin. He then spoke to another Dividend-orc called Cantana, his second in command, and was informed that since the *incident* in the woods no-one was willing to go anywhere near them, not even for ten percent. This did not seem to please Derrott who stood pensively for a moment. Cantana then suggested using the Red Witch to observe the dwarfs from the sea. Derrott considered this but then shook his head.

"Has there been any word from our friends in the Forest of Teteunxx?" asked Derrott.

Cantana shook his head.

"Very well," said Derrott, "Let's go. I want everyone ready for tomorrow." He started walking back to the house they had acquired on the outskirts of town. Without turning round he said, "You Ryszard, should be thinking about the four gold pieces you owe me. The interest is already accruing."

* * * *

It was not till they were clear of the town that Stilgoe breathed a heavy sigh of relief. Coulan marched on, his usual untroubled self, but it was Freyla who spoke first. "Is it safe to leave Kirin on his own?"

Stilgoe nodded but he wasn't smiling. "They will be watching him, but that will be all. If we're lucky they'll think he's just trying to raise money with his auditing." He laughed. "And if we're very lucky they may even try to recruit him."

"And if we're not lucky?" said Freyla, a hint of concern in her tone.

Stilgoe looked across at Freyla and the back over his shoulder towards the town, a small crease now marked the spot between his eyebrows.

"He can handle himself pretty well." Stilgoe nodded as if to convince himself as much as anyone. "At least they didn't question the venue."

"Yes but we were supposed to switch certificates at that meeting," said Freyla

"I know," said Stilgoe, "We'll just have to do it tomorrow during the commotion."

"As if tomorrow isn't going to be complicated enough." said Freyla to no-one in particular.

* * * *

Kirin felt bad about taking the woman's money. He would much rather have bartered his audit for goods or services. But he couldn't use any more stationary. Also he knew that he was being watched. It was important to keep up the pretence that he was trying to raise some money with his audits. If he was lucky, they might think that was exactly what he was up to. If he was very lucky they might be laughing to themselves at the impossibility of the task. The town was near bankrupt, which just made it worse taking this poor Mrs Magellan's money. In the end she still insisted on giving him three silver pieces which he suspected was more than she could afford.

The night sky was cloudy, he couldn't see the stars, but it felt like it was still before midnight as he made his way to his next audit. The hairs on the back of his neck felt the presence of unseen eyes upon him so it was a great relief as finally arrived at the ladies' dressmakers' store of Mrs Babington.

"Oh do come in master dwarf, I'm so glad you could come. Mr Shivers spoke very highly of you." Mrs Babington curtsied as she held the door open for him. That was not something Kirin thought he would ever get used to.

"Sorry about the lateness of the hour," he said giving a curt bow in return.

"Oh not at all master dwarf. It's not often an opportunity like this comes along," she said closing the door on the darkness. "I'm afraid I haven't too much to pay you with, I don't suppose you're interested in ladies apparel?" she asked hopefully.

It was then that he suddenly remembered.

"Well its funny you should say that," he smiled, unfolding a piece of paper from his pocket.

Mrs Babbington put on her glasses and began reading, she looked up curiously at Kirin.

"Eh, it's for a friend," said Kirin.

* * * *

The moonlight, finding a break in the clouds, picked out sharply the short white hair of a man riding a mule. He was trailing three additional, heavily laden mules along a dirt track by some woods. He was stopped by some shadowy figures and taken into the woods. After a brief discourse with the shadowy figures he returned to his animals tucking a letter into his jacket. He continued on his way with hardly a glance at the bulging saddle-bags on the mules behind him.

HIGH NOON

The sun was riding high in the sky as Stilgoe, Freyla and Coulan crossed the bridge into town. They were met by a bleary eyed Kirin, who had been watching for them while sitting outside the Green Man Tavern.

"You look terrible," said Freyla.

"Thanks," said Kirin with an attempted grin. "I guess I'm not really a morning person."

"You up for this?" asked Stilgoe.

"Sure," said Kirin squinting up at the noonday sun, "Besides I don't *really* have to do anything till the afternoon."

Stilgoe laughed and clapped his friend on the back and the four of them strolled casually towards the dock. When they were passed by a cart, heavily laden with a bulging tarpaulin heading out of town, Kirin took the opportunity to unobtrusively slip Freyla his pen set. At the entry to the dock were half a dozen Dividend-orcs. They stood blocking the way, more intent in hurling black looks at the dwarfs than in greeting potential business partners. Stilgoe's comment about Derrott not being happy about being kept waiting led to a reluctant parting of the way.

When they reached the Harbour Master's hut there

were another four Dividend-orcs outside it. Stilgoe smiled like he was greeting old friends and leant in the doorway letting his eyes adjust to the light inside. Derrott, Cantana, Ryszard and another four Dividend-orcs were inside, waiting.

"Gee," said Stilgoe, "I'm beginning to think I should have brought more dwarfs."

Sitting by the table Derrott spoke, with a calm assurance, "Speaking of such, where are your compatriots."

Stilgoe tilted his head to one side. "Well some weren't quite so happy about cutting a deal with orcs, so I'm afraid there's been a parting of the ways there." He entered and sat down facing Derrott across the table. "We're a party of four now. Five if you count him twice." Stilgoe jerked his thumb behind him at Coulan who had entered along with Freyla. Kirin had remained outside. "However the deal still remains the same."

"And as for the other dwarfs...?" said Derrott.

Stilgoe shrugged. "When the deal's done they'll come around."

Derrott nodded, "Very well let's get down to business then."

Stilgoe half turned holding his hand out for the package. As he did so he said to Coulan. "Why don't you keep an eye on things outside." Stilgoe gave a short laugh, "Eye on things, get it?" Derrott showed no sign of getting it. Coulan glowered round the room before trudging outside to join Kirin. Stilgoe placed the tracker firmly on the table and waited, with a detached curiosity, while Derrott eyed it hungrily. Derrott raised a finger and one of the Dividend-orcs behind him stepped forward and placed a white envelope in his hand, before melting back into the shadows. Derrott then placed the envelope on the table and pushed it forwards. Stilgoe picked it up and removed the Property Certificate from inside. He then nodded to Freyla who carefully untied the string and unwrapped the sealskin covering revealing the tracking device. There was a collective intake of breath by the orcs.

Stilgoe took the document in his right hand. He held it up to the light, looking through the paper, he rubbed it carefully between his thumb and forefinger. His left hand which held the envelope was not doing much of anything at all. Of course his left side was towards the door and partly obscured by Freyla. Not that it mattered much to Derrott who only had eyes for the device. He was practically drooling. He moved his hand to touch it.

"Uh. Uh." said Freyla, "Not till he's finished.

"Can I just push the button?" asked Derrott.

Freyla looked to Stilgoe who looked up from his reading for a moment and nodded.

If a hushed room can suddenly get even quieter, then it did. Derrott flipped the switch. Nothing. He flipped it again. Still nothing. He flipped it a third time.

"We told you it didn't work. This doesn't change anything," said Freyla.

Freyla grabbed the device back and carefully began wrapping it up tying the string tightly.

"What are you doing!" said Derrott. The other orcs took a half pace forward.

"Hey! You've verified the device, for all I know that document could be a fake. Till *he* verifies it, the device is still ours!"

Freyla glared at Derrott, who held her stare before leaning back in his seat, smiling. He raised a finger and the other Dividend-orcs immediately stepped back. All the while his eyes never left Freyla and the tracking device. Stilgoe coughed and looked angrily across at Freyla. Kirin who had been listening just outside the door then casually walked across the dock to where Coulan was standing, taking it in turns to out-stare each of the Dividend-orcs.

"From what I can tell this *appears* to be the genuine article." Stilgoe paused for a second. "Of course the paper doesn't seem to be quite as old as I would have thought for a document such as this, but then again paper does age differently depending upon how it's stored—"

"Are you satisfied or not!" said Cantana.

Stilgoe raised his eyebrows, then looked across at Derrott who said nothing, his attention now on Stilgoe. "As I was saying," Stilgoe eyed Cantana disapprovingly, "all things considered I am of the opinion that—"

There was the sound of distant shouts. Almost all eyes turned to the door. A Dividend-orc rushed in to the hut shouting that the dwarfs were attacking.

"What! Is this some kind of trick? You'll regret this," said Derrott.

"No trick," said Stilgoe, "In fact, truth be told, they're probably here for the package themselves." Stilgoe sighed and wafted the envelope in front of his face. "Is it just me or has it suddenly got a lot hotter in here." Outside the noise of conflict was getting louder. Derrott looked towards the door, Stilgoe could see small beads of sweat slowly make their way down the side of his face.

"I don't trust you," said Derrott.

Stilgoe shrugged, "I don't trust you either. But we came here to do a deal, now what's it to be, deal or no deal?" He waved the envelope in front of Derrott.

There was no mistaking the sound of fighting now.

"What's it going to be?" said Stilgoe

"OK, it's a deal!" said Derrott.

"Good we have a binding contract then?" He looked round he room. "You're all witnesses to it." A contract, even a verbal one was an ancient thing, sacrosanct even amongst Dividend-orcs. He tossed the envelope at Derrott and got up.

"Aren't you forgetting something?" That slimy voice was back.

Stilgoe nodded to Freyla who casually tossed the device on the table and followed Stilgoe outside on to the dock.

Stilgoe took in the situation at a glance. At the far end of the dock, the six Dividend-orcs had been scattered like broken pins. Two or three of them were already out of commission and the rest were in the water. The four Dividend-orcs who had been outside the office were now halfway down the dock battling Talia, Bashka and Dargo. Stilgoe shouted loudly that they'd done a deal, and were siding with orcs. With a loud battle cry Coulan, Freyla and Kirin rushed down to join the fray.

Stilgoe leaned on his staff as Derrott and the other Dividend-orcs surveyed the scene. Frankly it was not going well for them. Dividend-orcs were no taller than dwarfs and a little bit lanky. Their quarter staffs were more for show than actual fighting. Their problems were further compounded by all the action taking place on a ten foot wide dock; half the time they were getting in each other's way and ending up in the water. Talia, Bashka and Dargo were a skilled, fighting unit. They had quarter staffs and knew how to use them and on the dock the Dividend-orcs couldn't use their superior numbers. However with the arrival of Coulan, Freyla and Kirin as well as a couple of Dividend-orcs (who had been in the Harbour Master's hut) the tide looked like turning. But then a blow from Bashka's staff sent Kirin reeling towards the edge of the dock. For a moment it looked like he had regained his balance but then he toppled over. Sunk like a stone. Freyla ran over to see if she could help him. Coulan then went crazy, whirling his staff around his head like a lunatic. This was a very indiscriminate tactic. While he did hit Dargo knocking him over, he also clobbered another two Dividend-orcs.

Derrott seeing the danger, immediately sent a reluctant Ryszard and the two remaining Dividend-orcs to join the battle, only Cantana stayed with him. In Coulan's defence, he was not looking behind him when he accidentally hit Ryszard in the midriff with his staff, winding him. As for the other two orcs, somehow their forward momentum carried them past Coulan and indeed all the dwarfs. Talia, Bashka and a badly limping Dargo were now on the same side of the dock as Derrott, facing half a dozen confused

Dividend-orcs and a frankly completely out of control Coulan who was wailing like a mad thing. Freyla was still bent over the side of the dock calling for Kirin.

"You're idiot of a dwarf is hitting my orcs!" shouted Derrott at Stilgoe.

"Yes, but he's hitting the others as well," said Stilgoe. "Did you see what happened to the Chartered Accountant?"

"Oh him, he went over the side," said Cantana.

"What!" said Stilgoe.

"Yeah pity dwarfs can't swim." Cantana laughed.

"I don't care about your accounting *friend*," Derrott spat out the word. "Call off your idiot. He's hitting my orcs."

Stilgoe wasn't smiling now. "Without Coulan it's only five against three down there. You want that?" This was true Talia, Bashka and Dargo had dispatched another two Dividend-orcs into the water and Ryszard was cowering behind the others not really taking part.

"Well at least go and help then," shouted Derrott at Stilgoe. "Don't just stand there."

Stilgoe turned to him, "I'm not standing, I'm defending you. If I go and one of them gets past me who's going to save your ass then. Him!" Stilgoe indicated Cantana with his staff. Before Derrott could answer Talia broke away from the fight and came running up the dock towards them. Stilgoe approached her, hands outstretched. "Talia, look it's OK, we've made the deal, for the levy, the fine, everything."

She grabbed a handful of his jerkin, "And who made you the boss of this outfit?" She spat the words in his face before shoving him away and hitting him hard in the stomach with her quarter staff. Stilgoe doubled up his face a curious mixture of pain and disbelief. He hovered for a moment before crumpling to the dock like a rag doll, helped by Talia's clenched fist to his jaw. She turned to Derrott, "Give me my device." She didn't threaten, her voice was not raised, but Derrott could tell she was not going to take no for an answer.

"It's mine, we traded Stilgoe for it like he said." Derrott looked at the crumpled body of Stilgoe moaning on the ground. He gulped. "Look, possession is nine tenths of the law. This is a matter for—"

"Let's say you argue the law with the end of my quarter staff here," with that Talia poked him in the chest forcing him back to the edge of the dock. Derrott looked about him, he was teetering on the edge, literally he had nowhere else to go. Cantana was standing to one side doing nothing.

"Cantana! Do something," shouted Derrott.

Talia swung her quarter staff in his direction. Cantana swung his eyes down to his feet.

"You can't do this. I, I'll have a warrant issued for your arrest. You, you won't be able to show your face in any of the five kingdoms by the time I'm finished with you." Derrott's voice was slipping around, much like his feet, trying to gain purchase on anything.

Talia looked at him with contempt, she looked at the package he was gripping tightly in one hand. "You know what? You want it so much? Why don't you just keep it." With that she poked him hard in the chest with her staff. With a look of disbelief Derrott went over the edge. Talia turned to Stilgoe who was half sitting now. "As for you, You better keep out of my way cause if I ever set eyes on you again..." She didn't finish the sentence but strode off down the dock. From over the side they could hear Derrott thrashing about in the water crying for help. Stilgoe pulled himself over to the edge to see.

"Looks like your boss needs a hand," Stilgoe said to Cantana.

"I, I can't swim," said Cantana.

Stilgoe, shaking his head at Cantana, reluctantly grabbed his quarter staff and dangled it down towards the struggling Derrott. In his endeavours to rescue the orc it is not beyond the bounds of possibility that he may have poked Derrott in the chest once or twice. "Grab it you idiot!" A thrashing Derrott was trying to keep afloat and hold on to the package. "Use both hands," shouted Stilgoe. Eventually with a little help from Cantana they dragged a half drowned Derrott back up on to the dock. In the process the package had been cast aside and had drifted slowly down towards the sea bed.

Freyla and Coulan joined them shortly after. The fighting had stopped when Talia, Dargo and Bashka had left. None of the Dividend-orcs had the stomach for more and had not pursued them. Freyla was distraught, couldn't talk for crying. Eventually between sobs she managed to tell Stilgoe that Kirin was gone. "He just fell." She gulped "Into the water." She looked up at Stilgoe a bewildered expression on her face. "Disappeared."

Derrott had by now regained some of his composure. The Dividend-orc's were all standing about unsure of what to do next. "Arrest them. Arrest them all," he said. A couple of Dividend-orcs seized Stilgoe and Freyla by the arms, the rest looked at Coulan a little uncertainly. Derrott stepped forward grabbing Stilgoe's jerkin in both hands. "I don't know what part you had in this but I don't trust you. You're a player. Always looking for an angle." He shoved Stilgoe away.

"You don't trust me!" said Stilgoe "Well you seemed to trust me when I dragged your sorry ass out of the water a minute ago. Didn't see any of your trusted colleagues doing that for you. And as for my angle? We had a deal I gave you the package to offset the money owed you. And I told you the other dwarfs weren't happy about it. And as I recall it was *you* that suggested the deal in the first place." Stilgoe looked Derrott right in the eye. "Your problem is you think everyone's as twisted and devious as you are."

Derrott said nothing his face once again impassive.

Stilgoe snorted, "Fine, arrest us. Kirin's dead. Someone should pay for that. I'll welcome a trial. Get everything out in the open."

Freyla was now squirming against the orc holding her, trying to get free. An elbow to his stomach later she ran to Stilgoe, embracing him, sobbing on his shoulder.

"Don't worry Freyla we'll get justice for Kirin, if it's the last thing I do."

Derrott nodded to the orc still holding Stilgoe to release him. That calm assurance was once more in evidence as he spoke. "On second thoughts, you're more trouble than your worth. Just get out of my sight. I want you out of here by the end of the day."

"What!" Stilgoe turned on Derrott. "But we've paid for the boat to take us east, to the Land of the Caucasians!"

"Oh I don't think so," said Derrott. "That'll help cover my expenses for this... escapade."

"Listen you thief, we paid—"

"No, leave him. It's not worth it," said Freyla between her tears.

"Oh I see. We can't go south cause then we incur more levies. That only leaves us the option of going west along the coast. And that's the way Talia and the others went," said Stilgoe.

"Not my problem," said Derrott.

Stilgoe glared at Derrott who waved a hand dismissively at them. He turned and stared down into the black water. "Think yourselves fortunate to be walking away at all."

* * * *

Kirin swam on his side gently under the surface using the hollow reed stem, he had cut earlier, to breath. It was a long way to the woods but he didn't want to risk being seen, even though he suspected no-one would be looking in his direction with all the commotion back at the dock. Once past the river mouth the current pushed him further out to sea but also pushed him further westward. He allowed himself to drift floating in the water. Everything felt very serene compared to the adrenalin fuelled action that had played out on the dock. Now the water soothed aching muscles and a tired mind. His movements all felt sluggish, his water-logged clothes made him feel heavy and slow. He felt he could just sleep forever and a day.

He opened his eyes, rotating on to his front he lifted his head just enough above the water to get a good look. The good news was there was no-one in sight. The bad news was that he had already drifted past the little natural harbour in the woods where the others were. In addition he was dangerously far out to sea. He took the risk and began swimming on the surface, heading back to shore, ending up several miles away from the harbour. He rested up for half an hour, ringing as much water out his clothes and letting them dry as best he could.

When he entered the clearing at the little harbour he saw a fully built raft or boat before him. He was not quite sure what to call it. It was flat like a raft, lots of logs lashed together. But it had a pointed end like the bow of a boat. It had sides made up of two rows of logs (forming a wall) which interlocked at the corners like a log cabin. In the centre of the craft short cross logs formed a slot about a foot square and three foot deep. into this a tall mast had been slotted. However there was a problem.

It was only later after he was welcomed back with much back slapping and hugging, especially from Coulan that he got to ask Bashka about it, "It's good that you've got sides to stop you all getting washed overboard but I can see a design flaw," he said.

"Oh yeah? So what's that Charter-mouse," said Bashka laughing.

Pointing, Kirin said, "There's holes in the sides of the boat/raft thing where the water can get in."

Bashka shook her head, "Two things Charter-mouse: first, the boat/raft thing is called the Esmeralda; and second, stick to your numbers and leave boat-building to the experts, the holes are to let the water out."

AN EXIT STRATEGY

The swooshing sound of the Esmeralda cutting through the choppy waters and that tang of salt in the air reminded Kirin of those few occasions when he and his father had ventured out of the Tervent estuary, sailing their little boat just for the thrill of it. He leaned lazily on his elbows staring over the side, where the moonlight glinted carelessly on the wave-tops of the Big Water, but Kirin's gaze was further abroad, focused on the fast disappearing coastline.

Stilgoe approached and stood beside him.

Kirin winced, "How is that?" he pointed to the large red mark on Stilgoe's chin.

Stilgoe rubbed his chin. "Yeah, had a little talk with Talia about that. Clarifying her interpretation of a pulled punch."

Kirin smiled. "What did she say?"

"Apparently it's a fine line between fight choreography and spontaneous realism." He laughed, "Next time Talia gets to play the inside-man."

Kirin returned his gaze to the coast. "The people back there. You think they'll be OK?"

Stilgoe produced a deep puff of smoke from his pipe.

"Article seventeen, clause three. Levies are *not* applicable to permanent residents of the aforementioned area bounded by the Property Certificate," he said.

Kirin raised an eyebrow. "So, what, they shouldn't have been getting levied in the first place?"

"That's a standard clause in most property contracts. Makes sense really when you think about it. That fact that this Property Certificate," he tapped his jerkin pocket. "did not have the word *not*, along with a few other things makes me think that actually *it* was a forgery."

"Wait. So, let me get this straight. We stole a forgery, only to replace it with another forgery?" Kirin shook his head.

"Technically, but our forgery was probably closer in spirit to the original." Stilgoe slapped Kirin on the back. They both laughed.

A little later Freyla came and joined them as they stared out across the dark stillness of the Big Water. The three of them stood quietly, soaking in the calmness of the evening.

"So how did it feel taking part in your first scam?" said Freyla.

Kirin recalled how after he had been knocked into the water he had swum up to the Harbour Master's hut and waited. It was difficult as he could only see fragments between the wooden planks of the dock. When he finally heard Stilgoe's voice, he honed in on it, and beside him his target, that snake Derrott. Then there was the interminable wait for Derrott to get pushed in and for Kirin to retrieve the device, once Derrott had dropped it.

Kirin smiled. "Actually I have to confess, I rather enjoyed it."

He thoughts though turned once again to the people of Helsinagar. Stilgoe reassured him that when Bart returned from his fruitless delivery of the rocks in his saddlebags, Mr Shivers would get the letter Kirin had written. And when he and the other townsfolk demanded to see the Property Certificate (in particular article seventeen, clause three) then, well, Derrott and Co. would have no hold over them and the town any more. Even if Derrott suspected that they had switched certificates there was nothing he could do about it, not having presented it to the townspeople as the genuine article.

"I'd so like to see the look on his face though when he finds out," said Kirin

Freyla shook her head, "In the perfect scam, that's a pleasure you have to forgo."

Kirin sighed, "Numbers are my thing, you know that." Stilgoe nodded while puffing on his pipe. "But this? Oh, it's a close second. Very close."

"Kirin my boy." Stilgoe put his hand on Kirin's shoulder. "This could be the start of a beautiful apprenticeship."

* * * *

Waking late Kirin squinted his eyes in the bright morning sunshine, as he looked about the raft, everybody seemed busy with some small task or other. Bashka was at the tiller, Stilgoe was making some adjustment to the sail, Freyla was doing something with a rope. Talia was at the bow dropping a knotted rope into the water. Coulan was fashioning something out of a long piece of wood and Dargo seemed to be organising their supplies. Kirin realised he was seeing the dwarfs in their natural habitat, for they loved the sea in the same way as he loved the woods. He recalled his father's casual mastery of a boat. Attuned to its every movement like it was a living creature. He could sense a change in the wind before it occurred. Watching his father at such times reminded Kirin, as it did now, that he was not a dwarf.

"Hello sleepyhead," said Dargo.

Kirin waved.

"Some breakfast or should I say lunch," laughed Dargo looking up at the sun.

Kirin grinned and nodded. He was famished. Judging by the sun, they were still heading due north or there abouts. Bashka, at the tiller, had the compass around her neck.

He wandered across to Dargo who poured him a large drink of milk.

"Won't keep long so may as well enjoy it," he said

Kirin gulped it down in one go. When he had finished the others all laughed.

"What?" said Kirin

Freyla took pity on him "Nice moustache," she said.

Kirin grinned sheepishly wiping his mouth with the back of his hand.

After breakfast Kirin regarded their makeshift sail. Mrs Babington had really done an amazing job. In terms of the quality of her work, he had no criticism. Though to his way of thinking the black polka dots on a yellow background did clash somewhat with the red and green stripes next to it on the patchwork quilt of a sail.

He checked their progress with Talia and Bashka. According to their calculations they had travelled about twenty miles due north since they'd set sail last night. That was not the interesting bit though. It was the tracking device. It had read 026 degrees back in Helsinagar but now it read 045 degrees. Their target was moving or rather since they were moving their target was getting closer. When the tracker device was pointing 090 degrees then it would be due east of them. This confirmed it. Their target was Bank Island. For the rest of the day Kirin mooned about trying to help out the others but was of little use. Dargo already had their food and supplies stored away and lashed down and was busy helping. Coulan shaping another long piece of wood, both of them demonstrating a mastery Kirin had not seen before. Talia and Stilgoe were making adjustments to the rigging keeping the Esmeralda running fast and true. But it was Bashka who was master here, her hand that rested on the tiller, firm but gentle, ready to respond. A nod, a whistle, a clipped command from her, all carried out by the others without question, even Talia.

Eventually he sat with Freyla. She was untwisting one of the ropes the Mr Given had sent by cart along with Mrs Babington's patchwork sail. Once this was done she spent a lot of time pulling and stretching, getting the kinks out them. Then she began tying knots. Her expertise with these mystified Kirin. He knew a few tried and tested ones but she showed him a range for all occasions. She showed him one, a non-slip Mono Loop, which did just as its name suggested. He spent an hour practising to get it right. His success though felt like a child's. It hadn't occurred to Kirin to ask why she was untwisting the ropes.

Late in the afternoon Kirin's attention was drawn to Stilgoe and Dargo who were arguing about something. Whatever had started it, probably some light-hearted throwaway remark, was of no importance now for it had gone too far and the good natured banter had now descended into personal insults. The only way this was ending was badly.

"You don't fool me. Your problem's the size of your head," said Dargo.

"My head? What about your brother's head? Now that's a big head!" said Stilgoe.

"The both of you just cut it out." said Freyla putting down the rope she had been working on.

But the two duelling dwarfs were in no mood for listening to reason, they were now pushing each other and throwing mock punches. With a shake of her head Freyla moved aft and picked up a bucket with a short length of rope attached to the handle. Dargo and Stilgoe had now escalated to grabbing each other's jerkins as they continued to hurl insults at each other. Casually Freyla holding the rope, tossed the bucket over the side. Hauling the bucket back into the raft she laboured to carry it over to the two protagonists, whose faces were now inches apart. With a lazy swinging action she swung the bucket back and forth a couple of times before emptying the water over the pair of them. After an initial exclamation of surprise the bedraggled pair just stood, frozen to the spot staring at Freyla, while everyone else burst out laughing.

"Dargo don't let Stilgoe get under your skin like that. He's just trying to needle you." Freyla turned to Stilgoe. "And as for you. You think you're being clever but sometimes it comes across as just plain mean." Freyla walked away, throwing the bucket noisily into the corner and sat up by the bow attending to her ropes once more.

Stilgoe dripping wet himself, casually brushed a little of the water off Dargo's shoulder and soon the pair of them were laughing too. He then came and sat down beside Kirin, creating a small puddle in the process. Stilgoe pursed his lips together and winked at Kirin, nodding in the direction of Freyla, "I think she likes me."

"I heard that," said Freyla.

Stilgoe smiled at Kirin. "She didn't deny it though," he whispered.

"I'm denying it." said a far away voice.

Kirin slapped a somewhat stumped Stilgoe on the back. "You know what, I think you'd better quit while you're behind."

As he lay down that night Kirin felt himself being lulled to sleep by the gentle motion of the sea but something was troubling him and would not let him rest. Reluctantly he fished out the little black book and had another go at figuring out Sang-gast's code. The range of characters used was from 1-9, from a-y and from A-Y. That added up to 59 characters in total. This all suggested that it was written in sexagisimal, that is the base 60 (as opposed to decimal base 10). But even if that was true he was still no nearer a solution. Why would Sang-gast be using sexagisimal wondered Kirin? Was he doing some kind of arithmetic with it? Kirin shook his head. Too many questions. What he needed was some handle on what Sang-gast had been doing. He looked at the doodle page once more.

Freyla was wandering round everyone before she went

to sleep. Having used her own pack as a rope bag, she was now distributing what had been in her pack among the others.

"Would you take my sleeping mat," she asked. Kirin looked up, eyebrows raised. "Obviously not now," she added.

Kirin could think of nothing to say and so both nodded and shook his head. They both laughed followed by an awkward pause.

"Er, working on Sang-gast's code?" she said.

"Er, yes. In fact it's sexagisimal," he said.

There was another moment of silence.

"What is sexagisimal?" she said.

"Ah yes, it's the base 60. A very interesting base. Divisible by 2, 3, 4, 5 and 6," he said.

"Is that good?" she said.

"It's not bad," he said.

Freyla shook her head as if to clear it. Looking down at the notebook she said, "Sang-gast's doodles? You should really let Coulan have a look at them. He's good with pictures."

"Coulan really?" he said. "This the same Coulan who named the raft Esmeralda?"

Two red spot appeared on Freyla's cheeks. "Maybe you're so wrapped up in your numbers that you miss the big picture," she said.

"You mean like the one Coulan carries around with him," he said laughing.

"You think you have all the answers don't you?" she said. "Well maybe you should ask why he was given the honour of naming the raft!"

"What? No but—"

Freyla got up and left. Kirin looked after her and then across at Coulan who was lightly snoring till his brother gave him a slight kick with his foot. Coulan rolled on to his side.

* * * *

Bashka had been the first to spy it, just a haze on the horizon. Over the next hour the haze became a smudge and then the smudge became a line of rock, rising up out of the sea to greet them. Bank Island. Bashka gave the word to lower the sail. They even lowered the mast. Talia and Bashka wanted as low a profile as possible, in more ways than one.

It was at this point that the paddles Coulan had been working on got put to the test. Kirin was surprised at how efficient they were and was finding it hard going even with six of them paddling as Bashka barked out encouragement from her position aft by the tiller. As they got closer they could see the impregnability of sheer cliffs towering above them. Kirin had already rechecked the tracker device and it was pointing straight at the island. There was something else too. It was now bleeping louder and the blip that moved across the screen was moving faster. Everyone was focused now. No mistakes, not this time. Sneak in, get whatever was there, and sneak out. No-one the wiser.

Approaching from the west it was obvious that the island's sheer cliffs offered no easy landfall so they began paddling south. Eventually the western cliffs dwindled down to a low ridge of rock that extended southwards. At the southern end of the island the ground gently sloped down to a white strip of beech and the sea. The rocky peninsula in the west partially protected this, helping form a natural harbour. Bashka's binoculars were called upon once more and poking over the top of the western rocky peninsula they could just make out the mast of a tall ship. The Red Witch? As they paddled further south they could see that further up from the harbour and built into the hillside was what looked like a massive metal door set in concrete. They could also make out a hole next to it, very reminiscent of the vault they had discovered earlier only much, much bigger and annoyingly crawling with Dividend-orcs. What were Dividend-orcs doing there? Had the orcs already discovered the islands secrets? Did they suspect this was the destination they had been headed to all along? Bashka gave a quiet command to paddle and they steered back north, keeping their distance.

It took the rest of the day paddling to circumnavigate round to the southeast corner of the island. Having now examined almost the entire coastline of bank Island, clearly the south end was the easiest place to land and just as clearly out of the question. But there was another possibility. Freyla had spotted a possible route up the north-west cliff face. She had the ropes and reckoned she could climb it. There was a problem with it though, there was almost no shoreline to speak of and the heavy swell was crashing violently onto the base of the cliffs. There was no way they could get the Esmeralda in close enough. They would need to split into two teams. One to stay with Esmeralda, keeping it safe out at sea and out of sight. The other team to do the climb. Kirin knew which team he would prefer to be with. There was however one further problem.

"You don't have to do this you know," said Stilgoe. "No-one will think the worse of you if you say no."

"Oh well in that then case I say no," Kirin smiled.

"I'm serious," said Stilgoe. "None of us would do this. Could do this."

Kirin eyed the task in front of him. With the tide, currents and waves dashing against the rocks this was the closest Esmeralda could safely come. That still left over thirty feet of open sea to the foot of the cliffs. He was stripped down to his shorts. He had a loop of fishing line tied round one wrist. The other end was tied to a length of rope still on the Esmeralda.

Kirin turned to his friend and laughed, "Between you and me it's the climb afterwards that worries me."

Stilgoe clapped Kirin encouragingly on the back but neither of them were smiling.

Kirin dived in the water. The cold hit the back of his neck like a sledgehammer causing him to gasp and take in a mouthful of sea-water. He broke the surface gasping and spluttering but it didn't take long though for him to acclimatise. The effort of swimming in the large swells of six feet or so was all that consumed Kirin now. He stopped, treading water with about fifteen feet to go. Timing was everything. It would be the difference between being stood safely on the rocks at the foot of the cliffs or being smashed to pieces upon those self same rocks.

Kirin hesitated, and missed his chance, he needed to wait for the next big wave. His plan was to let it take him just to the edge of the rocks and then he could clamber up to safety before the next big wave hit. A simple enough plan. The next wave came and once again Kirin almost went. He stopped himself, he would only get one shot at this, he needed to be perfect. Third time he went. He timed it well and got to the edge of the rocks just as the swell died and secured a good hand hold he'd spotted earlier. But then as he tried to climb up he lost his footing on the slippery rocks. He hung for a moment by his arms, as legs scrambled for grip against the rocks. All the while the next wave was coming. For a moment his whole body went still. Looking down he calmly selected a foothold and lifted his left leg on to it, then feeling with his right foot he found another crevice. There was no time for anything else, Kirin hugged the rock for dear life. When the wave hit it felt as if some giant unseen hand was trying to prise him off the rock the way he used to prise off a mussels from his father's boat. He knew that to do that he would get his knife under the mussel, lever between it and boats hull, then exert all his force. He wasn't going to let that happen. He squeezed his body into the rock. If it was possible for human flesh and bone to meld into the very rock, then he willed it so. With his eyes shut tight, the crashing sound of tons of water all around him filled his ears for what seemed an eternity till he heard it, shouts and familiar voices. He dared to open his eyes and look round. He saw the others on the Esmeralda, jumping up and down, shouting. About what he had no idea, till he saw the next wave approaching. Quickly he scrambled up and across to the relative safety of the tiny strip of rock at the base of the cliff.

He'd been lucky. Apart from a few cuts and scratches there was only a shallow gash on his shin which was bleeding a bit. It took him a few minutes to get his breath back. He still had the fishing line round his wrist. For the first time since he's left Esmeralda he smiled. It didn't take long to pull the fishing line across and then the rope attached to it. Someone had thoughtfully attached his pack to the rope. A little way up to his right there was a suitable rock to tie the rope round securely. Stilgoe, Freyla and Talia, shimmied across, and joined Kirin at the base of the cliffs. The others remained on Esmeralda. While Freyla was bandaging Kirin's shin Bashka cut loose the rope attached to the raft and Stilgoe pulled it ashore. They were going to need all the rope for the ascent.

It was Freyla who led the way. She had little metal clips that she hammered into cracks in the rock with a tiny little hammer. The ropes were threaded through these clips and in addition all four of them were roped together. This secured them all in case of a fall. All of them that is, apart from Freyla. It was almost a sheer rock face, a much harder climb than that narrow ledge on the Crumbling Mountains of a few days ago. Kirin gripped the rope tightly, focused on the encouraging voice and firm pull the at the other end of it. Fortunately for Kirin it was a night-climb so that though he could hear the waves crashing into the cliffs below him, all he could actually see was the rock face a few feet in front of him. He focused on the next handhold or foothold, his world reduced to just the four feet of rock that surrounded him. The climb was made more difficult by the moon which from time to time disappeared in the half cloudy night sky leaving them in almost total darkness, then they had no option then but to stop and wait, till it lit the way once more. During the ascent there were a couple of large ledges where he and the others sat and rested and even had some water and something to eat. All of them that is but Freyla who was always up ahead out of sight when Kirin got there.

After forever and a day, or four and a half hours as time is sometimes measured, Kirin dragged himself over the top on to the blissfully flattish, grassy mound above the cliffs. Stilgoe and Talia, who were the freshest, had already taken the tracking device and headed into the night for a reconnaissance. Freyla and Kirin got some well needed sleep.

A hand on his shoulder woke Kirin. It felt like he had only just closed his eyes but the sky was noticeably lighter, dawn was nearly upon them. Stilgoe and Talia had managed under cover of darkness to get quite close to the orcs at the southern end of the island and had overheard some conversations. It seemed that the only luck they were having was of the bad variety. The landlord of The Green Man and a few other notable citizens of Helsinagar had demanded to see the Property Certificate when Bart had returned with the letter (explaining about article seventeen clause three). Apparently all hell had then erupted when they'd seen the phrase 'not applicable to permanent residents'. Derrott had tried to bluff it out but the townspeople were having none of it demanding their money back. A mob had formed in no time at all, and things had turned a little ugly. Derrott and the Dividend-orcs had decided to cut their losses, but their only escape had been to take the Red Witch and sail to the normally uninhabited Bank Island to consider their next move. And there was one other thing, they were apparently awaiting the arrival of 'the Dwarf'.

"Sang-gast?" said Kirin

Stilgoe shrugged, "Maybe. Don't like the idea of those two getting together."

"Anyway Derrott and most of the orcs seem to be berthed on the Red Witch, leaving just a few in the vault or whatever it is," said Talia

"Right," said Kirin even though it was very far from right.

"Oh, haven't got to the interesting bit yet," smiled Stilgoe. Kirin and Freyla looked at each other then at Stilgoe. "We used the tracker and it took us to a concealed door, not far from here on the west side of the island," added Stilgoe

"Great we can just—" began Kirin.

Stilgoe held up his hand and shook his head. "As our resident safe cracker you can have a look, but I don't think this door opens from the outside." said Stilgoe.

"Could still be a good exit strategy?" said Freyla.

No-one looked particularly hopeful.

Kirin briefly mooted a plan to capture the Red Witch and strand the Dividend-orcs on the island but no-one seemed very keen. Too many unknowns. A fight would be inevitable. And what if Sang-gast turned up with his dwarfs? No, the consensus was to wait till dark, then sneak in, get the Tral-fe-tigore (if it existed), then sneak out. Talia and Stilgoe had also come across some ruined buildings round the north side of the island where they could hide out for the rest of the day.

As they made their way to the ruins they passed the hidden doorway in the hillside, stubbornly shut its blank metal exterior forced Kirin to agree with Stilgoe about it. Any break-in would have to be via the front door. He did find it interesting though how far away this side-door was from the main entrance. It was possible inside the hill was completely hollow or possible a maze of tunnels. He cursed inwardly that they had left the compass with Bashka. The ruins on the north side of the island reminded Kirin of the building they had found by the Maze, they seemed to be of a similar construction, from that long lost era, before 'the Fall'. These buildings though were in a far worse state, most of the roof was gone and the whole front concrete wall had collapsed, leaving its steel skeleton exposed to all that the north wind and rain could throw at it.

Kirin took first watch, crouched below the brow of a low hillock where he could see anyone approaching them, while Stilgoe and Talia got some much needed sleep. Even from his concealed position he felt the chill of a gusty wind that was bringing in dark clouds from the west. 'There's a squall coming right enough' would have been what Bashka would have said. Kirin laughed to himself but it occurred to him that he wasn't just at the mercy of the weather, there was a far more dangerous storm that was in danger of carrying him away. The quest for the tral-fe-tigore itself. It had all been so simple and clear back in his parents' cottage where they'd gone over the plan time after time, till he was sick of it. He'd laughed at the suggestion by his mother that he could become ensnared by the excitement of it all. And despite finding the tracker, he still hadn't dared to really believe. But now with the importance Derrott had placed in it and the fact that it had brought them to this very island. An island that had an enormous vault built into it, to protect... something? Of course the smart move would be to avoid further encounters with Derrott and Sang-gast, to walk (or rather sail) away. The Tral-fe-tigore didn't exist. It was never his objective, but... A rumbling stomach reminded him how hungry he was, the next meal was all he wanted now. A light rain began to fall almost unnoticed in the buffeting wind.

It was around one pm and Talia had already left to give a prearranged signal to the Esmeralda, holding position five miles out, off the north coast. At this point Stilgoe relieved Kirin who then eagerly trotted back to the ruined buildings for something to eat only to find Freyla frantically looking round all the junk cluttering up one of the buildings.

"What ya doing?" he asked.

Without looking round, she held up a thin black rod.

"See if you can find more of these," she said.

Kirin felt intrigued but said nothing and began looking. Soon he returned, quite pleased with himself after finding eight of them, though one was slightly bent. He found a pile of fifty or so in the middle of the floor. Freyla had cleared a space and was opening a large black bag made of some material he had never seen before.

"Oh good. Help me unfold this. Here grab hold of the bag, while I pull it out," she said

"Eh, sure," said Kirin holding on to the bag's handles. What did you say it was again?"

"A Rogallo wing, I think. OK now grab that end and walk that way," she said.

They pulled out a carefully folded and tightly packed light blue material, which gradually revealed itself to be a large triangular shape, maybe twenty feet across. Kirin refused to ask what a Rogallo wing was, though he did try to get a look at a small white book that Freyla was reading. Pretending to shield it from the rain, she very politely ignored his attempts and with an enigmatic smile, read out instructions for Kirin to follow. Soon the two of them had slotted numerous of the black poles together and slipped them into sheaths at the edges of the triangle of fabric, which was now resembling an enormous sky-blue kite. There was now a complicated assembly of tubular metal pipes, for this Freyla did relent and they both studied the instructions.

"What are you doing?" hissed Talia standing in the ruined doorway of the building. "What part of sneak in, sneak out without a trace didn't you understand."

Before he could say anything Freyla jumped in "It's my fault I—"

"I don't care whose fault it is. This! This I want gone. If they send a patrol round this end of the island, how are we going to hide... What is it anyway?"

"Eh I think you'll find it's a Rogallo wing," said Kirin.

Talia turned on Kirin. "I'm very disappointed in you. I

put my trust in you."

"It's my fault," said Freyla. "I asked him to do it, he said it was a bad idea but I told him you'd approve when you found out what it was."

Kirin's mouth was open but he said nothing.

Before Talia could say anything else Freyla blurted out, "It's an exit strategy!"

THE TRAL-FE-TIGORE

The arrival of the summer thunderstorm in full force had made the argument for dismantling Freyla's wing pointless. Not due to the wind powerful enough to blow a person over, or even the thunder and lightning threatening instant destruction, but because of the torrent of rain now pummelling the hillside within an inch of its life. Anyone would have to be crazy to venture out in a storm like this, or at least certifiable. Talia, Freyla and Kirin took what shelter they could in one small corner of the building, their argument over semantics on hold, as the battle of the elements took precedence. So when Stilgoe arrived back, saw the wing, and let out a long low whistle, it was much to Talia's annoyance. Freyla was adamant that she still wanted to use it. Apparently her course in aeronautics had covered such a wing, in theory. For Kirin the very idea of taking to the air in that flimsy blue construction made him nauseous, it was going to be hard enough climbing down the cliff face. He just didn't get Freyla's enthusiasm for something clearly so dangerous. And something else troubled him, why had she lied for him earlier?

It was always hard to figure how old a dwarf was. Especially the men with their smooth faces and long hair, they hardly changed much in appearance from 14, when they were full grown, to 40. Some said that once, long, long ago, they had beards like regular folks, but that was from the time when everything was different and the word 'dwarf' itself meant small. Freyla seemed full grown, Kirin figured her for maybe a few years older than himself, certainly younger than the others. It wasn't that though, there was something different about her. The others had tackled the climb like a task that needed doing; for Freyla it was a joy, an expression of being alive. He had seen it in her limber body swinging precariously by her fingertips as she angled for her next handhold and it showed again in her face when she had found the flying wing. Maybe other dwarfs were like that too, or maybe it was because what she loved terrified him so much, or maybe it was... Kirin shook his head such things were forbidden in the Fourth Kingdom. Dwarfs kept to dwarfs and regular folks kept to regular folks. Besides it was said that the offspring of such prohibited unions were, if they survived at all, feeble minded and hideously deformed. So it was said.

The thunderstorm brought dusk early. Throughout the day they had seen most of the Dividend-orcs seek refuge from the storm in the comfort of the Red Witch, which was relatively sheltered in its natural harbour. It was now impossible to see much more than a dozen yards in front of them, much less where the orcs were now; so they decided to wait no longer. They carefully made their way round to the south side of the island and the main entrance to the vault, which was deserted. Quietly Kirin slipped through the large hole by the massive steel door. Inside was a large concrete room with, at the far end, a tunnel leading off downwards into darkness. The room was lit from a strange light emanating from round glass discs in the ceiling, giving a quite unnatural glow. The light did however reveal that the room was empty. Kirin signalled the others.

The tunnel was in darkness but upon entering it more

of the ceiling lights came on as if sensing their presence. As they moved tentatively forwards more of the ceiling lights came on, but at the same time the lights behind them switched off plunging the tunnel back into darkness. No-one said anything but from the looks on their faces Kirin was pretty sure they felt like he did, that they were being lured into a trap by this small bubble of light. At the bottom of the tunnel it opened up into a large cavern which now had two more concrete tunnels leading off it, down into the bowls of the island. Since no-one was about they decided to risk the tracker. Kirin had muffled it by wrapping a piece of old cloth round it. He switched it on and off quickly, allowing one beep only. The underground tunnels seemed to amplify and echo the noise, carrying it away into the darkness. For a moment they all looked around and listened, but nothing stirred. The tracker had indicated the tunnel on their left.

This tunnel was of the same design as the previous one, only smaller. They all entered it hesitantly, especially Freyla who hunched her shoulders and proceeded with a grim expression. Kirin wondered idly how many hundreds of feet of rock were above them now. He reached up to see if he could touch the ceiling and the strange lights, but they was still just tantalisingly beyond his grasp. As they went deeper and lower into the island, it occurred to Kirin that at some point they might pass below sea level. Eventually their bubble of light led them to yet another vault-like door. This one though had three lines of writing above the doorway, and though many of the letters had faded away completely, what they could make out had Kirin and the others transfixed to the spot.

TR AL   LF
E   TI G
OAR

They looked from one to another and even the

ubiquitous dwarf-shaped hole next to the door could not break the spell the letters held over them. Talia was the first to come to her senses and nudged the others forward and through the opening and after a wary glance behind her, she followed. The lights above them all blinked on all at once, and they found themselves in a large room, maybe 100 feet across, constructed from thick steel girders arching up from the floor, forming a low curved ceiling. In between the girders, metal panels lined the walls reflecting back the light from above, but all this extra brightness only revealed the stuff that broken dreams were made of. The room was full of metal shelving that had once been the orderly home of hundreds upon hundreds of cardboard boxes. Most of these boxes were now on the floor and had spilled their contents of small paper packets, many of which had been ripped open, perhaps in some act of fury, frustration, or futile hope, leaving the metal floor covered in a crunchy layer of tiny, worthless, seeds.

For a while they ran around looking in boxes, opening packets of seeds, trying to sniff out any traces of Ko-Ko beans, like so many others must have done before them. Worse still, a quick examination of the room confirmed what they had feared, that it was a dead end. If this room had been the resting place of the Tral-fe-tigore, then it was no more. Questions on Kirin's proficiency in reading the device were whispered harshly with adamant replies hissed angrily back. Freyla remained by the door her hands pressed against the walls, while Stilgoe and Talia debated going back to the other tunnel. Kirin wandered off towards the back of the room and decided to activate the tracker device again, this time though he allowed two beeps, just to be sure. The device indicated sharply to his left, there was no mistaking it. He turned to face the exact spot on the shiny surface, but all he could see was merely a dull reflection of himself. Then something clicked. As if by magic a heavy looking, metal door sprung open from the wall in front of him.

No-one spoke for a moment.

"Well that looks promising," said Stilgoe.

The others laughed, even Talia.

Stilgoe cautiously popped his head through the doorway for a moment before progressing. Each of them in turn tentatively followed Stilgoe into the tunnel beyond. Kirin lingered though, he ran his fingers over the door's edges that had been cunningly concealed between two girders and then tried to push it. It wouldn't budge, it was stuck fast in a half-open position. He wondered what force had been able to move it so easily? Who had built this ancient place and what knowledge did they possess? He looked up at the artificial light above him. How did that work and what controlled it still after all this time? There was so much about this place he didn't understand. He shook his head and followed after the others.

The tunnel had led them away at right angles to the room, by Kirin's calculations they were heading east. Then the tunnel took a left turn and headed north before finally entering another room. It was just like the previous room only much, much smaller and, to their disappointment, empty. It had shelves in it and unlike the other room they were all still upright but there were no boxes. It had not been ransacked because there was nothing to ransack. Whatever had once been here had been carefully removed long, long ago.

Kirin sat down. He had felt sure there would be something there. Especially when the tracker device opened the door. There should have been something there. It wasn't fair. The others checked the room thoroughly. Stilgoe found a door that led to a tunnel that seemed to lead upwards.

"Think I may have found our exit," said Stilgoe.

Kirin wasn't listening.

Talia and Freyla double checked the room. A quiet shake of their heads confirmed it. Nothing.

"Come on we'd better go. No sense pushing our luck,"

said Talia.

Kirin got to his feet. He still had the tracker device in his hand all wrapped up in the cloth to muffle its sounds. He looked down at it for a moment before suddenly flinging it across the room where it bounced off the wall and on to the floor. Somehow this must have switched the device on for it was now beeping like crazy, many times a second, its sound echoing noisily down the tunnel.

"Fool of a dwarf!" hissed Talia who took off after the device and eventually managed to switch it off. "Freyla, go, check if anyone heard." Freyla nodded, she stared for a moment into the darkness beyond the bubble of light, before jogging back down the tunnel. Talia was about to exercise her vocabulary more fully on Kirin when there was a hiss like escaping gas and a circle appeared in the metal floor. This circle then became a column of metal slowly rising upwards. A slight hum accompanied the metal column as it rose to a height of about five feet, then it stopped. Kirin felt a wave of cold air spill over his feet but his eyes were riveted on the metal column for just about a foot below the top was an alcove containing a small black casket.

For a moment Kirin, Stilgoe and Talia just stood there as if the ancient machinery had frozen them to the spot ensnaring them in its power, then slowly they looked at each other and after a brief nod from Talia, they approached it. There was just the faintest smell of Ko-Ko beans. A smile appeared on each of their faces as they looked at it and each other.

"You should open it." Stilgoe gestured towards Kirin. "You've earned the right."

"No." Kirin shook his head. "Talia leads the quest. The honour falls to her."

Stilgoe looked to Talia and nodded. Talia stepped forward and carefully took out the casket and opened the two catches, after a quick smile of anticipation to the others she then pulled back the lid. The others saw the puzzled look on her face as she stood motionless.

Stilgoe moved forwards. "It's a cardboard box!"

It was indeed a plain brown cardboard box measuring about six inches long by two wide and one deep. On the outside was some black writing, it was difficult to read as some of the letters were very faint or faded completely. The first word said 'TR' something 'AL'. The second word said something, something and what might have been an 'L' and then an 'F'. The third word was also faded. The first letter may have been a 'G'' but they couldn't be sure but it was followed by 'ERM' then it was something, something 'ATING'. The final word began something, something then 'OAR' something. There had possibly been other writing below this, but it was lost now. When Stilgoe picked it up there was a slight noise.

"There's something inside," he said.

"There at the bottom," said Kirin "I think you pull that little tab."

Stilgoe, who hadn't noticed this, looked down his nose at Kirin. "Yes, I knew there was a reason we brought you on this quest."

Kirin shrugged his shoulders. Stilgoe pulled the tab and a small cardboard drawer came out of the box, and in it a single bean. He tilted the cardboard box tipping the bean into the palm of his hand. Talia grabbed the box from Stilgoe and began shaking it but there was nothing more inside. They all examined the bean in Stilgoe's hand. As beans go it was a sorry looking, poor excuse for a bean. Only about half the size of a normal Ko-Ko bean and instead of having a healthy deep brown sheen, it was all shrivelled up and light purple in colour.

"It does smell of Ko-Ko, a little." said Talia sniffing the bean. "But whatever it may once have been, it is too old to be of any use now." She shook her head.

"All this way and not even a single Ko-Ko bean!" Stilgoe opened his hand letting the bean fall. Kirin quickly caught it. He gently rubbed it between his thumb and forefinger, it was wrinkled the way your fingers get when they've been in the bath too long.

"You don't think maybe?" The others just shook their heads.

Freyla appeared at the door.

"Orcs coming," she said.

Kirin slipped the bean into the little corner pocket of his trousers.

"What's that?" asked Freyla, her eyes fixed on the metal column.

"No time to explain, " said Talia. "How many?" she asked.

"Eh, at least two, but they came from the other tunnel, and they were calling for others. If we go now we might make it out before the rest arrive," said Freyla.

"No! Don't want to get into a fight unless we have to. We'll see if Stilgoe's exit strategy works first. Everyone through the door now," said Talia.

Stilgoe's door led to another tunnel which went encouragingly upwards. Kirin was so turned around now he was not sure which direction they were heading, but up was certainly good. They could hear a dull commotion behind them. It was still far away though. At some point, Kirin hadn't noticed where, the concrete walls had given way to living rock. There was still the same artificial light in the ceiling but the tunnel was now a natural one winding its way through the island. Eventually the tunnel stopped at a sheer rock face, clearly man-made, with a steel ladder attached leading up into the darkness.

They began to climb, Stilgoe leading the way, Kirin bringing up the rear. They stopped and for what seemed an eternity were left hanging. There were hissed whispers above him. Kirin looked down below, straining to hear their pursuers. Eventually Talia who was immediately above him whispered to him that the door was locked. Kirin thought for a moment, how could it be locked? It was supposed to open from the inside?

"Oh! Maybe the tracker device opens it, like the other door?" whispered Kirin.

"Try the tracker device," hissed Talia.

"Use the tracker," said Freyla.

"Great," said a muffled Stilgoe, "Pass it up."

"Hand it up to me," said Freyla.

"OK, give it to me," hissed Talia.

"Aw nuts!" whispered Kirin.

Kirin slid down the ladder and was running back down the tunnel before the others realised what he was up to. He slowed his pace treading quietly as he approached the door. Listening, he could hear the two orcs in the room talking. It didn't seem like the orcs had spotted the second door yet. He could see one orc at the main entrance to the room, the other, by the sound of him, was out of sight towards the back of the room. But where was the device? He racked his brain to remember where it was. He had thrown it against the back wall, then Talia had picked it up. Where did she put it. Stupid! He should have asked Talia before he ran off. No time now. More orcs could be here at any moment.

He was about to risk it when he heard a gentle pad of feet behind him. Talia. He had never been so glad to see her, he could have kissed her. Instead he indicated silently the position of the two orcs. He mouthed silently the question 'tracker device'. She mouthed back silently 'on shelf next to column'. Kirin indicated he'd take the orc by the door, and in they went.

Kirin was lucky, his orc was looking down the tunnel for reinforcements, twisting the orcs arm up behind his back he forced the orc across his own outstretched leg and onto the ground where Kirin quickly restrained him with bark-ties. He was crying out for help but that was drowned out by the considerably louder noise of crashing shelves as Talia dispatched her orc in a less precise but equally effective manner. After a scrambled look amongst the fallen shelves Kirin found the device. Quickly the pair of them were back inside the tunnel and sprinting for the ladder. There was no sign of pursuit, but it would just be a matter of time now. Kirin got to the ladder first and handed the device up to Stilgoe who tried it. There was no satisfying click. The door did not budge.

"So what now?" said Stilgoe.

"It's got to work! Let me try!" said Freyla.

She grabbed the device from Stilgoe and reached up past Stilgoe and tried the door again. And this time it sprung open a fraction and Stilgoe was then able to push it fully open. No-one, not even Kirin, stopped to ponder the intricacies of this door's mechanism and why it worked for Freyla but not Stilgoe. They all hurried up the ladder and out the door, which did indeed turn out to be the door in the hillside they had found earlier.

Stilgoe closed the door. Frustratingly though it wouldn't seem to lock, no matter how many times he beeped the device at it. There was not enough time. No time to figure out how to lock the door. No time to get to the cliffs, without being spotted. And no time to get down safely before being pummelled by rocks from above. One person though, could hold the orcs back at the door, long enough for the others to escape. Someone was going to have to stay behind.

"I'll do it," said Freyla. "I've got my escape route," she smiled. "It makes sense."

"No! No way," said Kirin. The others looked at him but he could not supply any logical reason.

"Stilgoe," said Talia. We're wasting time. Go signal Bashka that we need her now."

Stilgoe hesitated for a moment before nodding and running off to the north end of the island.

Talia gave Freyla a long hard look. "How confident are you about this wing thing?"

"Talia we can't leave Freyla. Not here. Not with them." Kirin pleaded.

"It'll work." Freyla placed her arm on Kirin's "It's Ok

I'll be fine. Now what I could use is something to discourage anyone coming up the ladder," she said.

There were few loose stones on the hillside, which they scurried about collecting till Stilgoe returned and asked what they were doing.

"Come on Kirin," said Stilgoe. "There's plenty of bricks in the old buildings." He pulled at Kirin who reluctantly went.

"We'll be right back," said Kirin.

The pair of them sprinted off, returning shortly carrying the black bag that had contained Freyla's exit strategy and which now contained her rear guard action. As they approached Kirin saw Talia and Freyla standing still, their heads inclined towards each other, touching. Talia then turned and told them to say their farewells and follow. She jogged off to check the ropes at the cliff edge. Kirin started arguing with Stilgoe about the impossibility of leaving Freyla behind when they were interrupted by noises from the shaft. Someone was climbing up. Stilgoe quickly grabbed a brick from the bag, opened the door and dropped it down. There was a cry of anguish followed by what might have been the sound of someone falling off a ladder.

"Well that appears to be discouraging them nicely." Stilgoe handed another brick to Freyla. "We'll need twenty minutes to abseil down then another ten to shimmy across the rope to the raft." He looked into the bag. "I reckon that's a brick every thirty seconds. You think?" He smiled.

Freyla nodded then tossed another brick down, which added to the commotion at the bottom of the ladder. "I think we may have a few spare."

Kirin had suddenly gone very cold. "Abseil? Twenty minutes?"

Stilgoe and Freyla looked at him. While Stilgoe and Freyla argued, Kirin diligently chucked a brick down every thirty seconds. They could see Talia who was waving from the cliff edge like a dwarf who wants to get down in a hurry.

"He can come with me," said Freyla.

"You're crazy, it's not even designed for two," said Stilgoe.

"We can fit, besides we're light and it's weight that counts," she said.

"No, he's safer trying to abseil. You can do it, can't you Kirin?" he said.

Stilgoe turned to Kirin who had been trying not to think of hurling down a sheer cliff in a matter of minutes. A cliff that it had taken him five hours to go up. And all in broad daylight! He chucked another brick down the shaft.

Kirin gulped. "Look it's simple I'll stay. Buy some time. You guys go abseiling. If you get the chance, come back and rescue me sometime. No pressure."

"He goes with me. That's final," said Freyla.

"I don't want to worry anyone, but we do have a limited brick supply," said Kirin.

Stilgoe clasped Freyla's arm and they bowed heads as Talia had done. Then he clasped Kirin's hand. "Don't forget to hang on tight." And with that he was gone running across the grassy hillside. Kirin thought he heard the wind scatter the words, 'some people get to have all the fun', but he couldn't be sure.

There was more activity below them. This time they were using some kind of shield and it took a concerted effort and a large portion of their bricks to dislodge the climbers. Now they no longer had enough bricks to buy the time for Talia and Stilgoe to get safely away.

"Of course we could make it forty five seconds between bricks," said Kirin.

"Why are you *so* obsessed with numbers," said Freyla, "I'm going to prep the wing. When you get tired of chucking bricks, head back. I'll be on the slope leading to the north cliff."

Kirin still had a few bricks left when he realised that he'd been out-flanked. Coming along the side of the hill were a dozen Dividend-orcs. On a positive note none of them were looking over the western cliff edge at the escaping Stilgoe and Talia, and, it had also stopped raining. Kirin popped his last few bricks down the shaft and with a cheerful wave at the approaching orcs, started running.

Coming round the hillside he saw Freyla and the wing some thirty yards from the cliff edge. She was like some giant butterfly, with the wing perched on top of her, she also seemed to be wrapped in some kind of cocoon. He headed straight for her. When he got there he saw she was wearing what looked like a large bag with her feet protruding out of the bottom. Round the middle of the bag a harness of sorts connected it to the wing.

"Quickly," she said, "Get behind me. Take this rope and tie it tight round both our waists." Freyla pushed the harness ropes out of his way as he hunched under the wing right up behind her and quickly looped the rope round them twice and knotted it. "OK, now hold on to the bar." Kirin gripped the bottom of the triangular frame outside of where Freyla was holding it. "Now walk with me left leg then right."

They started to walk, then to jog, and then to run. Kirin closed his eyes knowing the edge of the cliff was only yards away. At any moment he expected that sudden sinking feeling as he fell off the cliff. But then the exact opposite happened, he felt himself rise up into the air. His feet were off the ground and for a second he almost lost hold of the metal bar as their two bodies, now suspended from the wing by the harness, swung into a horizontal position. He tightened his grip and opened his eyes, then quickly closed them. He had been looking straight down thousands of feet onto the sea below, watching it crash on to the rocks. There was nothing between them and certain death. He felt the cold wind rushing past his body, he wasn't falling though, he was flying.

WIND AND WAVE

Kirin's eyes were shut tight, trying to imagine that he was just lying on a grassy hillside on a windy day, he could feel the air rushing past him but it was so cold, so very cold. All this air and he couldn't breathe. His heart was beating so hard he felt sure Freyla must feel it beneath him. He forced himself to recite his father's manta over and over. Stay calm, accept your fear.

He peeked open an eye for a moment, making sure his head was tilted upwards. Something caught his eye, there just above his head dangling from the apex of the tubular triangle. It was a tiny miniature of the Rogallo wing itself. Gazing at it Kirin, despite everything, managed a smile. In one way it made him feel like a giant looking down on this tiny contraption dangling in the air, but at the same time it made him appreciate his own smallness amidst the vastness of the world. His father had once told him, to know you place, however small, in the great scheme of things can be comforting. Gradually his breathing returned to something approaching normal, and his heartbeat slowed to that of merely a small demented woodpecker in his chest.

Dawn had broken and the aftermath of the

thunderstorm had left clear skies. But everything was wrong up here: the way the horizon kept shifting on its own, that he was supported by only the wind, and that his stomach kept lurching behind him. He steeled himself to look down once more, those figures on the cliff looking up at him, they were people! Was this how a bird felt? He laughed. He was pretty sure a bird didn't feel like throwing up. Someone was calling his name.

"Kirin! Kirin! Can you hear me?" shouted Freyla. "Are you all right?"

Kirin was suddenly conscious of Freyla below him. His body pressing on to her. He looked at his hands gripping the bar and there just inches away were hers.

"Kirin! Can you hear me? I need your help to steer," shouted Freyla.

"I'm OK," said Kirin.

The wind took his voice and threw it carelessly away behind him.

"What?" shouted Freyla.

"I'm OK," shouted Kirin this time directing his voice to Freyla's ear.

"Good. Listen we need to use our combined body weight to steer. When I shout left, lean left with me till I say stop. Understand?"

Kirin nodded, then shouted, "Yes."

"OK we need to go up. We can use the up-currents of air at the cliffs to climb." she shouted.

"Up! Up! You want to go higher?" he shouted.

"We need to gain height, trust me on this Kirin," she shouted.

Kirin gulped, this was going to get worse before it got better. "OK, tell me what to do." he shouted.

"OK first off, lean left now," she shouted.

Together they engaged in a series of manoeuvres going back and forward in a pointless waste of time it seemed to Kirin. He risked looking down once more and was shocked to see the whole island below him like he was looking down at it on a map. Freyla explained that climbing over the east of the island kept the eyes of Derrott and the Dividend-orcs on them, not looking for the others on the raft. If they were to head for the raft now and ditch in the sea, they would lead Derrott straight to the others and he still had at his disposal the Red Witch. The Esmeralda was no match for her.

They continued gaining height over the eastern side of the island. As they rose higher and higher, with every bank of the wing, it was like someone was twisting his insides. Each turn he tried to brace himself, to anticipated that horrible churning feeling in his stomach, but it was useless. Surely this was high enough? Certainly they were safe from Derrott, he couldn't touch them up here. Safe? He laughed. It seemed crazy to think that. Why go higher still? Part of him knew why, Freyla had explained the higher they were the better their chances were of making the mainland 30 miles away.

Even through the cold Kirin could feel the pain in his arms, he was gripping the bar too tightly. He looked at his hands, the skin was turning blue except where the white of his knuckles showed through, but the pain was coming from the tendons in his forearms which were beginning to spasm. He took a deep breath and relaxed his right hand. Immediately it felt better. He focused on this. He tightened the grip once more and this time relaxed the left hand. This was crazy, he needed to get a grip. He laughed despite himself. Freyla was securely strapped in and he was lying on top of her. Lashed to her. He could even let go with both hands and he would still be OK. The thought made him nauseous. He shut his eyes tight.

"Left," shouted Freyla.

He opened his eyes and leaned into the bank till she shouted to stop. Bad as these continual turns were, they were much worse with his eyes closed. He looked down once more.

"Where's the island?" he cried out.

"It's still there," shouted Freyla.

Kirin peered down, but it was difficult to see, there were wisps of cloud now between him and the ground. Clouds! He was above the clouds! He thought he could just about make out a green spot on the grey seascape below him. This was *so not*, the quiet walk in the woods he had signed up for.

"We need to try to get up to 13,000 feet, higher would be better but then we risk running out of air to breath," shouted Freyla.

How is it possible to run out of air screamed a voice inside Kirin's head.

"We'll need all the height we can get if we're to glide the thirty miles back to the mainland, even then we're gonna have to rely on some thermals from the sea later on," shouted Freyla.

The mention of thermals reminded Kirin how cold he was. It was then that he remembered about his fleece lined gloves. Silently he thanked his mother for making him pack them, even though it was summer. The only problem was, they were in his pack. This just gets better and better, thought Kirin. If he could only get his feet back on the ground once more he would never complain about climbing a mountain ever again.

"I think we're about as high as we're going to get," announced Freyla.

They were high but Kirin had no idea if they were high enough, clouds now obscured everything. They were gliding due south, as best as they could figure using the sun for a compass, which was the shortest route to the mainland. Freyla started prattling on about thermals and ridge lifts and how they would now be losing height, one foot for every ten feet travelled. Despite his normally inquisitive nature he'd rather she hadn't told him that. She had sounded anxious. Kirin suspected that was because he was here. If she was on her own, he didn't think she would be worrying about crashing into the middle of the sea. She would be feeling the exhilaration of being a bird in the sky and having the time of her life. There were so many unknowns, so many estimates. This flight was like an equation. All the variables plugged in to it: initial height; wind speed and direction; any possible thermals they might encounter; the weather conditions; the size and specification of the wing itself. He tried hard to remember the map. He had the notion that the coast extended due east of Helsinagar, but he could not be sure. If it fell away to the south, then that meant further for them to travel.

It all came down to faith. Faith in Freyla, her judgement, her skill. Kirin needed to take a leap of faith himself. Slowly he loosened the grip of his left hand and then released it, leaving it hovering inches from the bar, ready to grip in an instant. His right hand though seemed to have a will of its own and was now gripping the bar tighter than ever. He closed his eyes and recited his father's mantra till he felt some measure of control return. Then he let go. For a moment his heart was in his mouth as the wind whistled by his head, just as it had before, but his body still lay securely strapped to Freyla, just as it had before. He was still flying. He fastened his jerkin up tight and pulled his hood over his head against the cold before gripping the bar once more. He then tapped Freyla on the shoulder and as she turned her head slightly he extended his hand beside her and gave her the thumbs up.

* * * *

Speed was of the essence. Stilgoe followed Talia across the rope to the Esmeralda, hand over hand letting his feet dangle in the heavy swell, and scrambled over the side in an exhausted heap. Talia immediately cut the rope and Coulan and Dargo were already paddling as Talia grabbed Stilgoe and shoved a paddle into his tired hands. Soon Bashka had steered them safely away from the crashing breakers, but with dawn upon them they were still a sitting duck for anyone looking out west from the high cliffs of Bank island.

It was Bashka's keen eyes that spotted it first. A small triangle of paler blue, hard to see against the morning sky. For a moment they all stopped paddling, marvelling at the sight, till Talia barked the order to keep going. Freyla's wing was now above the far side of the island. They knew this was drawing eyes eastwards, buying time for them, time needed to put as much distance between them and the island as possible.

It was only after a couple of hours paddling due west, with the island now a faint blip on the horizon, that they felt they were safe enough from prying eyes to risk their multicoloured sail. They now steered southwest plotting a course back to Helsinagar, whence they had come, knowing that if Freyla and Kirin made it back to the mainland safely, they'd make a beeline for the town. There had been no vote, no discussion, but they were not leaving anyone behind. They were five now and if they had to battle Derrott and all his Dividend-orcs, then so be it. But it would be on dry land!

To maximise their speed they had continued to paddle all day. Stilgoe stood next to Bashka at the tiller, as the sun was setting. Bashka looked up and could just make out the appearance of the evening stars.

"Do you think they'll make it?" he asked in a hushed tone.

Bashka glanced towards the setting sun. "There's bad weather closing from the west."

"But will they make it?" he said.

Bashka focused straight ahead on her course. "Freyla has knowledge of such things. If anyone can make it, they can," she said.

"And if they can't? If they go down in the sea? What then?" he turned away biting down on his lip.

Bashka's immediate concern though was for their sail. It was perfectly fine for a gentle breeze, and even in a good wind it could hold its own, but for the storm that was coming it would be useless, ripped to shreds in minutes.

The Esmeralda may have been up the creek, proverbially speaking, but at least they did have paddles. They would need them. Indeed, a stern test awaited both design and construction of the good ship Esmeralda as well as the seamanship of her crew. The wind would be against them and also the tide. If they could just hold on till the tide turned, then they had a chance.

Talia, stood beside Bashka at the tiller. She had the binoculars trained on the waters behind them. "No sign of the Red Witch."

Bashka looked over her shoulder scanning the horizon. "She's out there, but pity them if they don't foreshorten sail and head for cover."

Talia nodded. There was no love lost between them and the Dividend-orcs but the sea was a common adversary. They respected it. None of them would wish ill of a fellow sea-farer. It was an unwritten code for all who risked life and limb across the Big Water. The sea was a cruel mistress and they all sailed at her mercy.

"What about the sail?" said Talia.

"We'll keep it up while we can," Bashka glanced at the sail straining hard as they tacked against the wind. Progress was slow but they were making headway, every hour brought them closer to the mainland. "Take the tiller for a while, I'll help paddle for a bit. When it comes time you'll need all your strength."

Talia nodded. As she steered Esmeralda, Talia had little need for commands. Coulan, Dargo, Stilgoe and of course Bashka were as fine a team as she could wish for. They worked the raft as one, each knowing their place and what was required. Small shouts and gestures, acknowledging cries and nods, problems spotted before they arose, an economy of effort and efficiency. Talia watched the black clouds beginning to darken the sky, the wind was picking up.

Within an hour of Bashka observing its first signs, the storm arrived. It was an epic one. The sort where if you had any hatches you would have battened them down. With the tide against them they were struggling to make headway, but make headway they must in order to steer, otherwise they were doomed. First came the wind, full of strength and fury whipping the sea into a frenzy, foaming water breaking over the bow of the Esmeralda drenching them. Everything inside the raft had to be lashed down, even the dwarfs themselves. The ropes that bound them to their craft would, if it came to it, also bind them to a watery grave. Then the rain, echoing the sea, it too came in waves that lashed their backs, and numbed their bodies with the cold. The swell of the Big Water deepened and widened, pitching and tossing their tiny craft like so much driftwood. Soon rolling troughs had opened up into which the Esmeralda fell helplessly, mountains of water rose impossibly high above her before crashing down upon wooden timbers and dwarfish backs alike. But each time she somehow managed to emerge, spilling water from her sides, poised for a moment atop the crest, before once more slipping downward in a stomach wrenching plunge.

A howling wall of wind and pulsating rain engulfed their senses in a primordial world of darkness, as if the sun had never been. Lightning flashes revealed only a seascape of greys and five wretched figures striving to survive the turmoil of a sky and sea battling for dominion over each other. All they existed for now, was to paddle. Though only a few yards separated them, each was alone in a world of their own pain as they pitted aching muscles and near exhausted bodies against wind and wave. Their collective will reduced to a single common imperative. To endure.

They lost all sense of time, even of each other, but their resolve never faltered. Each thing in the world has a time accorded to it. A time for even the mightiest of storms to vent its rage, and a time for it to wane. No more, no less. And so, almost imperceptibly at first, there was a lessoning. The waves still broke across their backs, the rain still whipped across their bodies, but the wind was dropping. Eventually the sea's ferocity relented, its stormy waters settled and even the rain ceased. The clouds then cleared away to reveal a newborn sky and an untroubled sun to set in it. The tide had turned in their favour. Nature having asserted her power was now in abeyance, leaving in her wake, a frail wooden craft and her pitiful dwarf crew.

Wearily they went about their business of getting the mast back up and hoisting the sail. They checked what damage had been done, and reviewed what stores and provisions they still had left. None spoke of it openly but each gave silent thanks to the sea for permitting their safe passage. Bashka alone stood watch as her exhausted comrades then gave themselves up to the gentle, soothing, respite of sleep.

FOOD FOR THOUGHT

"Kirin! Kirin! Wake up!" shouted Freyla.

"Wha?" Kirin blinked his eyes open and tried to focus on the long greenish line in front of him. Whatever it was they were heading straight for it. At first he felt euphoric, an end to the relentless grey sea below them, but there was something in Freyla's tone that alerted him to danger. The easy flying part was about to be over and the hard landing bit was about to begin.

"Just get ready to do what I say, when I say it," shouted Freyla.

Kirin gave her a thumbs up.

He was suddenly conscious of their speed. It seemed faster now, faster than ever. They were also dropping lower so that the cliffs appeared to be moving by themselves, physically rising up from the sea. At their base there was no soft sandy beach or even rocky shoreline to land on, other than ditching in the sea, their only option now was to make it over the cliffs. Looking down he estimated they were no more than 300 feet above the water. Making it over the cliffs no longer seemed the simple task it had appeared only a few minutes ago.

"We need to gain a little height. It'll kill our speed but I think we can make it over the cliff," shouted Freyla.

Kirin gave a thumbs up.

"OK get ready to lean back, on my command."

Kirin poised himself ready to react instantly. On Freyla's command he leant back hard, along with Freyla. The wing tilted upwards, a wall of cliff now filled his vision. They were moving slower and climbing now but still hurtling straight at the cliff. He could make out details in the rock; cracks and fissures; some tiny plants eking out a precarious existence; water dripping down into the sea below. The wind was gushing all around him now intent on dashing the two of them against the cliff like rag dolls in the hands of some petulant child. Freyla had now angled the wing upwards, aiming at the line of green just above them. Kirin could not take his eyes off the cliff, they were so close now, they must hit it. The line of green widened to a wedge. They were still gliding quickly, too quickly to survive a crash. Then with what seemed like seconds to spare they were over the top. Breathing air again. Air from the earth, from grass and trees. Air he was used to. Air that meant they were safe.

Too late they realised they were not. There was nothing Freyla could do and no time to do it. The trees were upon them like rampaging monsters of bark and wood. Their branches clawing and tearing, leaves lashing faces and arms. Kirin let go the bar and covered his face. His screams the only defence he had. A large thick bough came hurtling towards him and didn't stop.

* * * *

An eye opened, then promptly closed. It opened again briefly only to be confused by an upside down image of Freyla. She said something. It might have been his name. The eye closed again. Inside his head someone was playing the drums. He wanted them to stop. He shouted at them to stop but they took no notice. Kirin was in darkness, it was cold and still, almost like he was floating but he knew that was an illusion. He was falling and all he could do was brace himself for the inevitable impact. All the while the crazy drumming in his head was getting louder and louder. He squeezed his eyes shut tight, as if that might help. Finally he gave up and opened his eyes.

Freyla was over by a small fire warming her hands. He tried to ask her what was going on but all that came out was a groan.

"Kirin. How are you feeling? Are you OK?" she said.

Kirin tried to nod and immediately regretted it. He tentatively touched the top of his head where someone had placed what felt like a rather large hen's egg.

"Argh."

It was more out of anticipation than real pain. Something that big had no place being there.

"You took a bit of a bump to the head I'm afraid," said Freyla, touching his arm. "How do you feel apart from that?" she said, indicating his head. "Anything else hurt?"

Kirin gingerly moved his arms and legs, but was careful not to move his head.

"No, apart from a bump the size of Coulan's fist on my head, I think I'm OK," he mumbled.

"Here have some water." Freyla brought a cup up to his lips and Kirin sipped at it tentatively. Apparently this did not seem to provoke the crazy drummer so he had a little more. After a while Kirin felt emboldened enough to ease himself up into a sitting position leaning his back against a, now thankfully stationary, tree. His resident percussionist throbbed back into action once more, though perhaps not quite as bad as before. He took a few deep breaths.

"You OK?" he asked.

"Yeah, pretty much. It was quite a day all things considered," she smiled.

Freyla put some more wood on the fire. The wind was picking up now battling the fire. There was a deep rumble of thunder in the distance, and in the far west the sky was dark and ominous. For a moment Kirin felt relieved that they had not flown in to that, then he remembered that their friends were still out there.

"How long was I out?" he said.

"A little while. I was worried." Freyla turned away.

"I am so hungry right now," he said.

"Me too. Sorry. Fraid we've got nothing to eat and it's getting too dark now to go foraging." she said.

Kirin went into the pocket of his jerkin. His hand closed around the small package of elfin biscuits. There were two of them left. He looked at Freyla sitting slumped forward in front of the fire her arms hugging herself. He suspected she was in worse shape than she let on. He bit his lower lip.

"Um, eh, I know they taste terrible n'all but, I've got these." Kirin brought out his hand with the elfin biscuits still wrapped up.

Freyla looked from his hand to Kirin and back to the elfin biscuits. She nodded and slowly made her way across to Kirin. Opening the package he gave Freyla one. He took his and broke it into three pieces. He began eating one, putting the other pieces back in his pocket. He watched as Freyla did the same. Neither made any signs of displeasure and with hardly another word they both turned in for the night. Despite the storm raging in the west they fell asleep instantly and slept soundly through the night.

By the next morning the hen's egg had reduced in size that of a plover's and the throbbing had gone. Strangely for something that large it was not sore to the touch, though Kirin still explored it very gingerly. Even so he felt very out of sorts. Perhaps flying thirty miles through the air into a tree had something to do with it. Freyla went foraging for breakfast. Kirin had not felt up to it, but while waiting he spotted some Stevia leaves, and with a little extra effort soon found some wild strawberries. The fruit were past eating, but the leaves, together with the Stevia could still make a passable strawberry tea. Kirin busied himself and soon had a nice herbal brew going over the fire. Freyla had found plenty of wild raspberries and some blueberries which together with the tea took the edge of their hunger. Neither of them had much to say, as Freyla packed up their stuff there had only been a brief acknowledgement that they should start out for Helsinagar right away, to try and meet up with the others.

Before they left Kirin observed the remnants of the Rogallo wing. The whole structure was mangled and ripped apart like some giant's plaything that had fallen out of favour and taken the brunt of some momentary rage. And then as if some guilty conscious was at work the remains had been gently placed, cradled almost, in the branches of a handy oak. Freyla still thought it was salvageable, Kirin was not so sure. Anyway that would be for another day.

They set off in silence their long shadows pointing the way. Kirin still had his backpack which fortunately also had Freyla's sleeping mat. Freyla's pack which had been used as a rope bag was back on Bank Island. They kept close to the coast where the woods were not too thick. Pausing only to refill Kirin's canteen from a stream they continued on in near silence. Now that the mad drumming in Kirin's head had been reduced to a mild headache, waves of wildly conflicting thoughts and ideas began to batter his beleaguered brain. He was still processing the ten hour flight in the flying wing; it hadn't killed him, but whether it had made him stronger he had no idea. Could a fear of heights ever be cured? Then there was the concern for his friends, trying to weather that storm in a homemade raft. And as if that wasn't enough there was Derrott maybe chasing them down in the Red Witch. If he should catch them while they were still at sea! And then there was Freyla...

She had always seemed different, certainly harder to read than any of the others. Had he really known all along. He thought back to all those hours he had lain on top of her. His face blushed at the thought. He put a hand to his cheek feeling the warmth of the blood beneath the skin. He almost looked round at her but stopped himself in time. He shook his head. This was all speculation based on, what? That she had no reaction to elfin biscuits? She was starving, had hardly had anything to eat for an entire day. But then there were other little things, undwarf-like things: her knowledge of herbs and plants, the salve she'd given him; her love of climbing and flying; she'd been apprehensive being underground in the tunnels. On their own maybe nothing but— Wait a minute the salve? Had she known about *him* all this time? He could not resist a glance round at her.

The woods began to peter out and were soon replaced entirely by open grassland. The cliffs on their right had fallen away before eventually breaking into a jumble of large boulders tumbling down to a thin strip of beach. Further ahead they could see the beach widen giving way to grassy dunes. These curved away to a point some five miles or so distant. Kirin stopped to take in the scene, quietly rubbing the bump on his head. Freyla came up beside him.

"Sorry," she said.

"What for?" he said.

"Well if we'd come ashore here..." she said.

"You couldn't have known." Kirin shrugged. "Besides you got us both down alive didn't you."

"Yeah, I suppose," she said.

He turned away and didn't see that telltale little crease between her brows.

They continued on with no more than a curt word between them. Last night's storm had cleared the sky and by mid-morning it was already hot. They stopped only for a brief rest and finished the last of their berries. They were sitting opposite each other and Kirin watched as she took out another piece of elfin biscuit. Her eyes flashed at him as she bit into the biscuit. She munched it noisily before wolfing it down.

Once they got past the headland of the bay, the land sloped downwards and they could now see beyond. In the distance maybe seven or eight miles away, was Helsinagar. They should make it there in time for lunch. Whether it offered safe haven or harboured danger they could not say. However as they made their way towards it, yet another barrier became apparent.

Kirin stopped by the riverbank it was no more than ten yards across. It was slow and muddy, couldn't say how deep but there didn't seem to be much current to speak of. He looked across at Freyla.

"Don't worry about me," she said.

Kirin took off his jerkin, shirt and boots, but not his trousers and stuffed them in his pack. Freyla took off her jerkin and sat down to take of her boots. Silently he stuffed her jerkin in his pack as well. Her boots wouldn't fit so he hurled them across the river. Freyla looked at him as if he were chucking them off a cliff, but said nothing. He flung his pack across and then eased himself into the water. It came up to his chest, chances were it was deeper in the middle. He said as much to Freyla. Sure enough he soon had to start swimming. He swam side stroke all the while looking back. Freyla was still sitting by the river bank. He swam back to her side of the river but as he was finding his feet Freyla got up and eased herself tentatively into the water. That stubborn crease between her brows was back as she waded past him before promptly disappearing underwater. Quickly he swam to her side. She surfaced spluttering and doing some kind of doggy paddle.

"Kick your legs," he shouted. "That's it use your feet to push the water." Freyla was still spluttering straining to keep her head above water. "Listen to me I want you to take a few deep breaths then on the third deep breath hold it." he said. Freyla did as he suggested. "Now don't worry about letting your face go below the water. You've got breath enough for at least a minute. Concentrate on your arms now. Cup those hands Slow steady strokes." Freyla did as she was told and began to make forward progress in surges. "That's it you're doing fine. Now next time your face surges up above the water I want you to take a breath OK?'

Unfortunately by the time she'd breathed out she was back under water and breathed in a mouthful of it. She was struggling and panicking so Kirin, who was by her side throughout, grabbed hold of her by the waist supporting her. "Stand up. Put your feet down." She continued to panic, arms flailing and splashing at the water but as soon as her foot touched bottom she became calm. She stood now on the bottom with the water no higher than her chest. Kirin was stood slightly behind her to one side, his hands still round her waist.

"Thanks I'm fine now," she said.

She moved away from him wading the last few yards to the far bank. They rested on the grass letting the sun dry them off, feeling it's comforting warmth, but saying nothing. Kirin was first to stir collecting his pack and Freyla's boots. He dropped her boots beside her on the grass and began getting the rest of her gear from his pack.

"Look I'm a girl OK. If that's a problem for you then... Then tough! You're just going to have to deal with it!" she said.

"I, eh, um," he said.

Freyla stomped her feet into her boots and glared at him.

"Look I'm sorry," he said. "I have no idea what for, but I'm defiantly sorry OK?"

For a moment that swirl of emotions on her face remained, then collapsed into a smile. "I have no idea either, but for what it's worth I accept you apology," she said with a confident nod of her head.

"Well that's... good," he said. He paused. "Though since we're clearing the air... Perhaps there's something I should say..."

"What that you're not a dwarf either?" she said.

"Oh, right. Eh, so you figured that out?" he said.

Freyla looked at him and rolled her eyes. "You know for someone who's supposed to be *so* clever. At times you're really *not* so clever."

As they made their way to Helsinagar Freyla, began to tell her story, slowly and haltingly at first but as Kirin listened attentively it soon all spilled out. Her mother had been skilled in the way of forest plants, much like his own mother, Riverna. Their life together involved travelling from village to village in a large, colourful, wooden wagon, which was their home. It was from this same wagon that her father also sold her mother's herbal remedies. She told Kirin of how her mother had died when she was still young, six or seven. The wagon had thrown a wheel, pitching her mother to the ground where she hit her head, and that had been that. Afterwards it was a struggle. Her father was no herbologist, he was a salesman. They had worked as a team but without Freyla's mother now, he was lost. More and more he sought solace in local taverns. As she got older Freyla used her mother's books to learn about plants and help out more and more. By this time she was ten, she was practically running the operation, her father often too drunk to even sell the remedies.

One night he had just disappeared on his way back to the wagon after a hard night's drinking in a village tavern. His body was found later, drowned in a local river. A kind couple they knew slightly had offered to help, to take Freyla in and raise her as their own. But village life was not for her, she had gotten used to the open road. She had continued on her own, posing as a dwarf as it led to less awkward questions being asked. Not long after she had bumped into Talia and her band of accountants. They needed someone with her herbal knowledge and despite her not being a dwarf had offered her an apprenticeship in Certified Accountancy in exchange.

It turned out Freyla had sussed Kirin almost from the off. Takes one to know one she had said. Apparently she had been covering his ass from the beginning. As for the others Freyla thought they suspected, at least Talia and Bashka.

Kirin sighed, life would have been so much simpler if he had been born a dwarf. He thought back to his parents, Shalako and Riverna. But then if he had been a dwarf he might never have come on this quest in the first place. He would never have met Freyla, Stilgoe and the others. And what of his birth mother, who had died bringing him away from who knew what danger?

"Penny for them," she said.

"Oh you know just the usual, smart guy stuff," he said.

"Uh Huh? You just keep on thinking there Kirin," Freyla slapped him on the back, "that's what you're good at." They both laughed. In the distance down the slope, Helsinagar lay nestled by the shore waiting for them like an old friend.

* * * *

Far along the coast to the east, further east even than where Kirin and Freyla had come ashore, shallow blue waters lapped gently along a stretch of sun-kissed white sands. Half way along the beach, lying on her side, lay a boat like some stranded whale, out of her element. A sixty foot schooner. A once beautiful boat, lovely lines, sleek and fast, perhaps none faster. But now, of her three masts and sails, only ugly wooden stumps remained. Shattered timbers, broken apart like matchwood, marked where once her stern had been. Seagulls and crabs explored the detritus she had coughed up during her demise and the tide slopped against her exposed underside as if mocking her, reminding her that in the end there is only ever one winner.

There was a hollow victory of sorts for the now humbled boat. Its cargo had not been entirely lost. Leading away across the sand towards the woodland that bordered the beach was a trail of footprints.

* * * *

Kirin and Freyla entered the Green Man Tavern a little after midday. The landlord wasn't there but Bart was serving behind the bar. He was astounded to see Kirin of course, as was everyone, and there was a great deal questioning as well as celebrating of his return. By way of explanation Kirin told of how in the midst of the mayhem on the dock that day, he had quietly swam away to safety. This was of course entirely true, if not perhaps the whole truth. In any event everyone agreed it was a most sensible course of action. Bart did seem genuinely glad to see them again and offered them some very welcome milk on the house. He did rebuke the pair of them, in a good natured way, for his being sent on his way with a saddlebags full of rocks to non-existent dwarfs. But the letter, of course, had been most useful. As Bart filled their tankards he confessed that his main regret was missing all the excitement on the dock that day but Kirin and Freyla weren't really paying attention as they watched him pour the cold white milk. They paused for a moment watching the condensation form on the outside of the tankards, before gulping it down. Kirin had never tasted better. Soon Kirin and Freyla were laughing at each other's milk moustaches. Then there was a moment of silence between him and Freyla. She raised her tankard again.

"To absent friends," she said

Kirin raised his tankard. "Absent friends."

There was something, a little voice inside Kirin's head that was saying something wasn't quite right, something about the milk. What was it? Before entering town they'd checked that the Red Witch was not tied up at the dock. So wherever Derrott was, he wasn't here in Helsinagar. Bart was still prattling on about how the towns folk had banded together and driven the Dividend-orcs out. And all down to the letter *he* had carried.

Kirin smiled only half listening, he was missing something.

"What is it Kirin?" said Freyla

"I don't know? It's just... What did you say?" he said turning to Bart

"I just said a lot of folks were worried about the orcs returning but then when your friend turned up—"

"Our friend!" said Kirin and Freyla together.

"Yes, well, he said he was a friend of a friend of yours. Oh, here he is now," said Bart.

"Hello old friend."

Kirin and Freyla both turned round to find Sang-gast standing facing them. His face a picture of brotherly love and innocence. The rest began to emerge from the shadows like a bad smell. They had them outnumbered. There were three dwarfs by the main door but as Kirin checked out the exit behind the bar he saw one of dwarfs with a knife at Freyla's throat. Too late, that little voice was shouting at him now. Too late. He raised his hands in a gesture of surrender as Sang-gast's dwarfs closed in around him. Sang-gast's smile grew bigger and bigger, filling the room. There was a high pitched scream that wasn't his. The last thing he saw was the confused look on Bart's face before a large black puddle began to form in front of him. He didn't hesitate, not for a second. He dove straight in, swallowed up in the deep dark nothingness.

* * * *

This was a very strange bed, thought Kirin. It was hard in all the wrong places. At times it even seemed to be hitting him. Beds were not supposed to do this. They were soft, yielding places. They were comfortable and warm. The sorts of places you didn't want to leave. This bed was none of these. It felt like parts of it weren't even there at all. There was defiantly something wrong with this bed. This bed was most peculiar, unlike any other bed he had ever known. It moved!

He was dreaming! That was it. It explained everything. Even that crazy drummer that was back in his head again. Though why would he dream about that? And why did it feel so bad? It must just be a bad dream that was all. What should he do? Being aware in your dream was a rare thing. He could do anything he wanted, after all it was only a dream. He could go flying again. Hmmmm maybe not. Save that one for the nightmares. Still there should be nothing to fear. Not in a dream. Oh, but why did his head hurt so much? Maybe he could find the drummer. Stop him somehow. Smash the damn drum anyway. This was not fun. Dreams were supposed to be fun. Weird maybe, but still fun.

"Argh."

What was that? It felt like his bed flung him up in the air and then let him fall onto a hard stone floor. What kind of bed would do that? It was a bad bed. He'd had enough of this, he was going to get up. Hmmmm. How do you wake up from a dream? People do it every day but that's just because they've finished sleeping or maybe someone wakes them up. How do you consciously will yourself to wake up? This was a problem. Still he was good at problems. He could solve this. he just needed to concentrate. If only that crazy drummer would stop!

* * * *

Kirin half opened one eye. Then it just closed shut again. There was something there, he couldn't quite make it out. It looked like he was looking down at the ground. Was he flying again? His stomach churned at the thought. This was impossible. He willed both his eyes to open this time. There was something close to his face obscuring his view, but in front of him it was definitely the ground. A stony track only a few feet away. He couldn't be flying. Then he saw it. A strange brown hairy thing. It came towards him. He flinched but then it retreated. What the heck was that? He watched as it repeated the same attacking and retreating motion several times. He closed both eyes and fell back once more on to his strange bed.

* * * *

He woke with the pain throbbing in his head. For a moment he thought he was back at the coast with Freyla after the crash. He was lying flat on the ground, his head propped up on something. There was a chill in the darkening air. Ahead of him he could see an open plain, no trees. The Plain of Angaurd? Also he was not alone.

"Oh so you're awake at last." Sang-gast's face loomed over Kirin. "We were all very worried about you. Would you like a little water?" The smile of relief on Sang-gas's face, that tone of concern in his voice. Kirin knew he was in trouble, big trouble.

"Leave him alone you creep," said Freyla.

Kirin turned his head to see. The crazy drummer didn't like that.

"Freyla?" he croaked.

"Cut me loose. Let me take care of him. I don't want any of your brutes touching him."

"Will you give me your word as a Certified Accounting Dwarf not to try to escape?" said Sang-gast.

Her eyes flashed at Sang-gast but she nodded.

Sang-gast indicated to one of his dwarfs who cut the ropes binding her. She rushed to the mule where their stuff was and brought back a canteen, gently cradling Kirin's head, she held it up to his mouth allowing him just a few careful sips to begin with.

"Very touching," said Sang-gast.

Freyla talked quietly to Kirin as he drank, filling him in on what had happened after one of Sang-gast's dwarfs had hit him on the head from behind. They had had to beat a hasty retreat from Helsinagar as Sang-gast hadn't counted on the outrage of its good citizens. They were now halfway to Angaurd Castle. Freyla slipped her last fragment of elfin biscuit into his mouth. As Kirin chewed his eyes closed once more and he descended into a nightmarish world: one of impossibly high castles, of being bound and helpless, and of falling into a giant smiling face that slowly began to scream.

Kirin woke to find the camp preparing to move on. He squinted up at the morning sun, he felt much better, the crazy drumming now a mere dull throbbing. He gingerly touched the back of his head where another small bird had decided to lay its egg. He resolved to no longer make his head available for nesting purposes. He laughed to himself. If this did not cure him of having a big head then nothing would.

Today he got to sit astride the mule instead of being slung over it, though Sang-gast had made sure his hands were securely tied. In addition his mule, like Freyla's, was tied to the one in front. Angaurd Castle loomed large now and they should reach it by midday. He peered at the north side of the plateau trying to make out the torturous route up to the top. Another fun filled afternoon he thought. He looked ahead at Freyla, her shoulders were slumped, her head down, occasionally jolted as her mule lumbered forward with its uneven gait.

* * * *

"Are you comfortable?" asked Sang-gast.

Kirin looked round. The room had a high vaulted ceiling constructed from large stone blocks like the rest of the castle. This part though was underground, in places water oozed down the walls leaving a dull green slime in its wake. It was lit by a few torches his captors had placed in holders on the wall. Kirin shrugged, as much as a person can whose manacled arms are secured above his head.

"Where is the book you stole from me?" asked Sang-gast.

"Whoa there, stole? Did you say stole?" said Kirin shaking his head. "No, no, no, I think if you remember you *gave* me the book. There was no stealing. In fact as I recall you then proceeded to stamp on my foot and run away." Kirin nodded to himself. "Incidentally an apology for that would not go amiss." He needed to stall for time. But what he really needed, was to come up with a plan. Where was Freyla he wondered? In another dungeon? He couldn't ask. He mustn't show he cared for her. Sang-gast would use that against him.

There was a small guffaw of laughter from one of the two dwarf guards. Sang-gast fired a glance in his direction silencing him. "I'm not going to argue semantics with you. It's my book, you had it, now give it back to me."

"This book, it's important to you?" asked Kirin.

Sang-gast took a step towards him.

"OK. OK. Let me think."

Sang-gast nodded to one of the dwarf guards who punched Kirin hard in the stomach.

"Argh!"

"We've searched you and your friend, *Freyla*. We know you don't have it on you." Sang-gast stepped closer, his face inches from Kirin's. "Where is it?"

Kirin did not like the way Sang-gast said 'Freyla'.

"Look it got wet. I mean it was useless anyway. Why should I care?" said Kirin.

Sang-gast indicated that Kirin should be made to care.

"Argh! Hey I'm telling the truth here," lied Kirin. "I went in the water, the book was in my pocket and it got wet."

Before leaving the Esmeralda Kirin had taken Freyla's advice and left the book with Coulan. Whether that was for good or ill, he now had to switch Sang-gast's attention away from the book. The rudiments of a plan were beginning to form. For it to work he'd need Freyla to play along. But would she get it? This was crazy, thought Kirin. Stilgoe and the others carefully planned their scams. They were the experts. And here he was trying to run one off the cuff with Freyla, who didn't even know he was doing it.

"Now could you please tell this guy to stop hitting me," said Kirin.

Sang-gast indicated Kirin should be hit again.

"Argh!"

"It's a very simple question. Just tell me where the book is, and he'll stop."

"I'm trying to. As I said it got wet, the pages were all

stuck together, the ink was running, I mean it was useless to me anyway. You said so yourself—"

"Where is it!"

"Well when it dried out, it was still a useful source of paper, if you know what I mean." Kirin left the sentence hanging there, like it had run off a cliff with its legs still going, waiting for gravity to take effect. He tried to maintain an apologetic expression on his face as he watched the cogwheels whirr and click behind Sang-gast's eyes.

"You, you *used* the paper?"

Kirin attempted another shrug.

"You used the paper for *that*."

"Well you know, when nature calls. And compared to a bunch of leaves..."

"Hurt him!" Sang-gast started walking away.

"Wait. Where are you going? I told you the truth!" lied Kirin. "Argh!"

He needed to get the hook in and preferably before he got beaten up. "Come on now, we're both Chartered Accountants. We can do business here."

"Business?" Sang-gast looked down from the steps. "You have nothing I want."

"Really? Ask yourself why a Chartered Accountant would go on a fool of a quest for the Tral-fe-tigore," said Kirin. "You think I don't know it's just a PR exercise by Queen Zehalani to divert attention from the kingdoms economic woes? I'm a Chartered Accountant and a damn good one." Kirin was gambling here. He didn't know for sure if Sang-gast had heard from the townspeople of Helsinagar about his accounting abilities or not.

Sang-gast motioned the others away. The count of sullen dwarfs in the dungeon rose to at least two. He approached Kirin. "You could have made a very good living as a Chartered Accountant. What *are* you doing with a bunch of idiot Certified dwarfs?"

"I'm not with a bunch of idiot dwarfs. I'm just with

one."

"Who? The female?"

Kirin watched as Sang-gast tried to put the puzzle together. Stilgoe had told him it's always better for the mark to think he's smarter than everyone else.

"She seems to care for you but..."

"You're asking the wrong question," said Kirin.

"No, no more games. You destroyed my book *and* my smelting operation. Now you pay."

"Forget the book? It's history! If that's a problem for you then... Then tough! You're just going to have to deal with it!"

"What!" said Sang-gast. "How dare you—"

"You really don't know who she is, do you?" said Kirin.

"What, I eh..." Sang-gast turned, looking up the stairs, then back at Kirin.

"She's the reason I'm on this stupid quest for something that doesn't even exist," said Kirin.

"She, she's nothing just another certified idiot..." said Sang-gast.

"Not her exactly..." said Kirin. If Sang-gast didn't connect the dots now thought Kirin, he would seriously have to consider reporting him to the Institute of Chartered Accountants.

"Her family?" said Sang-gast. "Who's her father?"

Kirin smiled, "Now you're asking the right question."

JUST BUSINESS, NOTHING PERSONAL

The new day revealed to Talia and her exhausted crew a view of a white sandy bay. Cliffs in the east tumbled down to the beach that curved round to a headland in the west. Talia looked to Bashka who shook her head. They had attempted to steer southwest, but had no idea how far east the storm had blown them. There were many dissenting opinions but none voiced with any degree of certainty. Indeed there more suggested courses of action than dwarfs to utter them.

All agreed their priority was to find Freyla and Kirin. What was certain was that if the two of them had made it to shore they would head for Helsinagar. Assuming that is, the Red Witch had not made it there before them. But the question now was, where exactly were they? Were they west of Helsinagar or east of it? The arguments might have continued for sometime had Stilgoe not remembered that he still had the tracking device. When they had used the device in Helsinagar it had pointed 026 degrees (north by northwest) to Bank Island. This time from their present position it pointed 024 degrees to Bank Island. This was the start of more arguments as to exactly what the two degree difference signified. In the end a vote was taken and it was decided, they were east of Helsinagar. There were grumbling acknowledgements by some and jubilant cries by others when, after an hour's sailing they cleared the headland and saw Helsinagar in the distance.

The sail was lowered and they approached cautiously, Bashka's binoculars were employed by more than one but could detect no sign of the Red Witch. Of course this was not to say that she had not disembarked her cargo of orcs and then departed. They tied up at the dock, it was early still and not a soul stirred, the only sound a gentle breeze blowing in from the sea. They made their way cautiously through the deserted streets till suddenly Talia halted, frozen to the spot. The others all on tender hooks did likewise. Mr Dombie was opening up his bakers shop, wedging open the main doors. He arched his back and raised his hand up to shield his eyes for the sun. He turned to go back in the shop when he saw the dwarfs. He too froze for a moment before dashing back inside. Talia looked to Stilgoe who shrugged unhelpfully.

A moment later Mr Dombie's head appeared round the door, "Master Stilgoe? Is that you sir?"

The others looked to Stilgoe who shrugged again but he stepped forward, or more accurately was pushed. "Eh, good day to you sir. Yes I am Stilgoe and these are my companions," Stilgoe gestured rather theatrically. "Eh, we come in peace," he added thoughtfully.

Mr Dombie welcomed the dwarfs into his shop and offered them some freshly baked bread to which the dwarfs helped themselves rather more than polite hospitality dictated. As they did so Mr Dombie related the events that had occurred to Helsinagar since their absence. He confirmed what had happened to Derrott and the Dividend-orcs. Then he hesitated looking uncomfortable as he told of the arrival of Kirin and Freyla.

At the mention of their names there was general rejoicing, much back-slapping, cries of incredulity and not a few barely concealed tears. It was Talia who was the first to notice the wan smile on Mr Dombie's lips. One by one the others stopped and listened to Mr Dombie's tale.

Mr Dombie explained that when the other dwarfs arrived, they had appeared very friendly, especially their leader, a Mr Sands he called himself, the townsfolk had thought perhaps this was the other group of dwarfs that master Kirin had spoke of. Anyway they (the townsfolk) had no way of knowing... The poor man was nearly in tears as he recounted how Kirin and Freyla had been captured, with poor master Kirin taking such a blow to the head. Talia questioned the distraught baker extracting all the details she could. Sang-gast's group (Talia and the others felt sure, based on the description, that it was indeed he) consisted of more than a dozen dwarfs, armed with clubs and knifes, though they had concealed these at first. When the outraged citizens of Helsinagar had risen up against them the dwarfs had retreated south, taking Kirin and Freyla to Angaurd Castle.

The others were all for moving out immediately, after all Sang-gast had a twelve hour start on them already. It was Talia though who shook her head, as she looked at her companions. Since the storm they had sailed a day with little food or water. There was another days march ahead and perhaps a fight at the end of it. They needed rest, provisions and a plan. A plan that might involve storming Angaurd Castle.

* * * *

The hazy afternoon sun found them resting behind the low stone wall that marked the boundary of Helsinagar. Above and beyond the Plain of Angaurd stretched far away to the foot of the Crumbling Mountains. There was only one small blot on the landscape, sticking up like a sore thumb, Angaurd Castle. Even at this great distance they felt its eyes upon them, scouring the land for any movement, any sign of life.

Talia had insisted they wait there till dark. There had been a quite serious argument with Dargo and Coulan who said they should press on regardless. None were happy at the prospect of sitting doing nothing while Freyla and Kirin were in the hands of Sang-gast. The numbers though, were not in their favour, by all accounts they were outnumbered three to one by Sang-gast's dwarfs. In addition they did not know how many Dividend-orcs Derrott had left behind in Angaurd Castle.

Stilgoe had some business to attend to in town, which if nothing else kept him busy. While not strictly essential to his current undertaking he was enjoying a refreshing tankard of Mr Shivers' finest in the Green Man Tavern when Mr Shivers and Mrs Magellan approached him. Representing the good citizenry of Helsinagar, they felt bad that they had not done more to protect Kirin and Freyla, especially after all that they had done for the town. Despite having already furnished them with enough food for a week, they now additionally offered them the services of Mr Shivers' mules and a dozen of the townsfolk, who'd volunteered to take part in the rescue the dwarfs were planning. Stilgoe listened carefully to the offer from the good landlord but politely declined. He explained that they were not planning on a fight but to sneak in quietly, so the fewer the better. He thanked them again for their hospitality but insisted that what he and the others had done was no more than any honest dwarf would have done and to consider any debt more than repaid. What he did not say was that despite the best laid plans of mice and dwarfs things were almost certainly going to get messy, very messy and they would work better as a tight unit, without civilians.

Waiting is often the hardest part of any operation. They all recognised the logic and necessity of Talia's decision but that did not make it any easier to deal with it. As usual Dargo was the most on edge but even he had managed some fitful sleep, his body demanded that. Coulan too was not his usual placid self, his yo-yo nowhere to be seen. After taking considerably longer over his business than was strictly necessary, Stilgoe arrived at the wall but now he too was conscious of the delay and like each of them in turn was now willing the sun to drop below the horizon, to set their enterprise in motion.

"So we just sit here on our hands doing nothing," said Bashka. "Twiddling our thumbs!" she added. It was an indication of how solemn the mood was that Stilgoe did not make a joke at the impossibility of this.

Dargo then spoke. "So, for the record, we don't *actually* know that Freyla and Kirin are in Angaurd Castle. We don't know how many dwarfs and orcs we're up against. We don't know where or when Derrott may suddenly appear with more orcs. And even if we do somehow sneak into the castle, we don't know where they're being held. And our only exit strategy is to... run away. Is that right?"

"Yes," said Stilgoe glaring at Dargo.

"This is your plan?" Dargo addressed Stilgoe directly matching him stare for stare.

"Yes," said Stilgoe, his body was poised ready to pounce. Everyone else was silent waiting for the inevitable.

Dargo sighed, "And this is why we give you an equal share?"

"Yes," said Stilgoe his fists now clenched.

Dargo paused, looking down at his feet as if readying himself.

"Good! I like this plan." He burst out laughing. Soon everyone was laughing even Stilgoe.

Talia smiled as Dargo and the others poked fun at Stilgoe. She looked south towards the imposing Angaurd Castle, her smile gently fading to an expression of resolve.

＊ ＊ ＊ ＊

"Her father is one of the dwarf Guildlords you say? Hmmm. It's possible I may have misjudged you. That is not something that happens often."

"Oh, don't worry about that. Now if you could just see your way clear to..." Kirin looked up hopefully at his manacles. Sang-gast ignored him but Kirin could see that though he hadn't swallowed the hook yet, he was giving it a good chew.

"Of course what's to stop me just taking your place?" Snag-gast smiled amicably. I'm sure my associates here could eh, extract all the details if I ask them nicely. For instance, exactly which Guildlord?"

"Well apart from being very bad form, it's not a good percentage play. The odds are much better with my plan and me as your partner."

Sang-gast shot him a contemptuous look.

"Eh, your junior partner, that is," added Kirin.

"Now you're beginning to bore me. I don't need you or your plan."

"Course you could go straight to torturing the female," said Kirin.

Sang-gast raised his eyebrows at Kirin, who shook his head.

"You'll have to trust me on that one. Firstly she doesn't know my plan, obviously. But more importantly she is..." Kirin looked around the dungeon to check he wasn't being overheard. He motioned with his head for Sang-gast to approach closer. He then whispered "sweet on me. Or hadn't you noticed?"

Sang-gast stepped back from Kirin. "You think that'll save you? We don't really need her co-operation. Just so long as the goods are still alive, so to speak. I'm sure her father will cough up the cash." Sang-gast looked quite pleased with himself.

Kirin shrugged again. "You could play it that way but..."

"But what?" said Sang-gast.

"You're still not seeing the big picture. If we use my plan, with a cooperative Freyla, we don't just get a measly ransom with a high risk of getting caught. No! We get it all. And the beauty of it is that we..." Kirin nodded to Sang-gast, "are completely legit. If anyone takes the fall it's her." Kirin stretched both manacled arms up in the air and yawned.

"What is your plan, tell me," Sang-gast commanded.

Kirin smiled to see the little cogs whirring and clicking behind Sang-gast's eyes. Well, he's definitely beginning to swallow now. Just feed him titbits, gotta be careful not to choke him. Let's see. A trust fund. Uh huh, a very lucrative trust fund. An only daughter, yes that's good. A father on his last legs, that's better. Naturally no pre-nuptial. Let Sang-gast imagine the details, his greed will do the rest. Of course his next step will be to talk to Freyla. It will all depend on her.

As Sang-gast stood listening to Kirin his scowl changed to a smile once more. "You know you're an interesting fellow. You intrigue me. You really do. Now that's not something that happens a lot in the circles I move in." He looked pointedly at the two guards. "I could really use someone with your flair in my organisation. You've no idea what it's like being surrounded all the time by the... unimaginative."

The problem is..." Sang-gast nodded to one of the guards who then punched Kirin in the stomach.

"Argh."

"The problem is, I just can't quite get the idea out of my head that you're lying to me." Sang-gast nodded to himself as if confirming this regrettable fact. "As one accomplished at the art, you're good, I'll grant you that. Possibly there is even some truth in what you've told me. But...

"Ah. If only I could *believe* you really meant that," said Kirin.

Snag-gast smiled. "Yes indeed, all in all a most remarkable dwarf. Intelligent, perhaps even with a flair for business and able to handle yourself with that fighting technique of yours. Incidentally you must teach me that some day."

"I'm afraid my *self-defence* technique doesn't involve the use of teeth." Kirin did his best to shrug.

Sang-gast laughed and regarded his fingernails. "Yes, well, when push comes to shove it does rather bring out the primitive in me. A fact you will discover to your cost if your story doesn't check out." He signalled one of the dwarfs to give Kirin another punch.

"Argh."

Kirin rolled his eyes towards the ceiling. After a pause he said, "You know what dungeons make me?" As no-one else seemed interested Kirin answered his own question. "Very, very hungry."

* * * *

Sang-gast returned and gave the signal for Kirin to be unchained. Kirin rubbed his wrists where the manacles had left some ugly looking bruises, before following Sang-gast to the steps. Inside he had a hundred questions but on the outside he was nonchalance personified. "Told you she was crazy for me. Don't beat yourself up about it. You know if you want my advise the best—"

Sang-gast stopped in his tracks and turned round, grabbing Kirin's shirt. "Listen to me very carefully. I trust you about as far as I can throw you. One wrong move and you're back in the dungeon."

Sang-gast's face was so close, Kirin could tell what he'd had for lunch.

"Maybe there is some profit to be made out of you. Maybe! But don't think about crossing me or both of you will regret it."

"Sure, sure," said Kirin looking Sang-gast in the eye. "This is just business, nothing personal."

Outside the dungeon Kirin found himself in a long damp stone corridor, which had a few torches flickering at intervals along the walls. Kirin figured they were still underground. "Not to sound ungrateful, but this place is a little on the chilly side, so where's my stuff?"

Sang-gast turned on him again, poking Kirin in the chest. "Your stuff! You should feel lucky to have your life!"

Kirin kept his eyes fixed on Sang-gast. " Look if you don't believe me then take me back to the dungeon. Otherwise I want my stuff! I'm freezing here. I'm no use to anyone if I get pneumonia. I want my jerkin. And my pens. We're either doing business or we're not." He stood toe to toe with Sang-gast. A flash of something unpleasant swept across Sang-gast's face only to be just as quickly replaced by that fake friendly smile. On reflection Kirin preferred the former. At least it was honest.

"Of course," he said. "That doesn't appear... unreasonable."

Sang-gast indicated to one of the dwarfs who thrust Kirin's jerkin and pack into his midriff. "Consider it a gesture of good faith."

The lining of his jerkin had been ripped to shreds. The pack was a jumble of his clothes, the sleeping mats and a few personal items, among which he was relieved to see his pens. His bark-ties, fishing line and hooks were missing. They'd even taken his wire coat-hanger. Kirin put on his jerkin and slung the pack over his shoulder as he walked behind Sang-gast.

"Just so as you know, the cost for my missing stuff comes out of your end."

Sang-gast said nothing.

They went upstairs, through more corridors and anti-rooms before coming to a large hall where a long table was laid out with food. Kirin waited till Sang-gast had sat down and started eating, before he tore into the food. The one thing he hadn't been lying about was being very, very hungry. He was still stuffing himself when Freyla was brought in.

"Oh. Hi Freyla, how are—"

"You, you're eating with this, this creep!" she said.

Kirin gave Freyla a lingering, condescending look.

"That's a little harsh, don't you think?"

"Harsh! Harsh! I'll give him harsh." She grabbed a knife from the table and lunged towards Sang-gast, giving him quite a fright. The guards escorting her managed to catch her before she could get close enough to do any harm.

"How dare you attack me!" said Sang-gast.

"Why don't we all just calm down, and have something to eat, we'll all feel the better for it. I know I will," said Kirin

Freyla flashed her eyes at Kirin, but did as he suggested, all the time keeping Sang-gast pinned to his chair with her angry stare. After they had had a little to eat Kirin started the conversation once more, emphasising to Freyla Sang-gast's good qualities. How there had just been a series of unfortunate misunderstandings and of how after all he *was* a Chartered Accountant. Freyla looked at Kirin as if he was trying to convince her to sell her grandmother for a bag of worthless beans. All the while Sang-gast was eyeing them both carefully, very carefully indeed.

"I'm not saying he hasn't made bad decisions. Money Laundering is against the law." Kirin looked at Sang-gast as if he was disappointed in him. Sang-gast glared angrily at some of his guards who were now nodding at Kirin's mastery of the facts. "But he's never really hurt anyone," added Kirin with a knowing nod to Sang-gast.

"He hit you didn't he? And... And what about Talia," she said, "He bit her!" She glared angrily at Sang-gast once more.

Kirin had to hand it to her. She was really good at this stuff, especially considering she was improvising off the cuff, without even a clear idea of the plan. Kirin rubbed the back of his head. "That was more of a... miscommunication. The dwarf in question has been dealt with and Sang-gast himself has personally apologised to me. Haven't you?" Kirin looked over towards Sang-gast.

"Eh yes, yes indeed." Sang-gast nodded and continued to eat.

"And Talia?" said Freyla menacingly.

"Eh, Um..." Sang-gast looked to Kirin.

This was good Freyla was keeping him nicely off balance. There should be a name for this where one of them plays the bad guy and the other plays the good guy. Anyway it was his turn.

"Look there was a bit of a fracas and someone accidentally got bitten. I mean who would deliberately bite someone," Kirin gave his incredulous expression a try out. "Anyway it's all water under the bridge now." He looked towards Sang-gast who nodded. "The important thing is that we all try to behave like reasonable people. We don't all have to like each other." He now looked towards Freyla who shrugged non-committally. "But we can do business together, after all we all have a mutual goal."

* * * *

The guard stopped Kirin entering Freyla's room, pushing him away from her.

"Orders," he said, with a hesitant look across to Sang-gast, who had been trailing behind the two of them all the way, to their rooms.

"What!" said Kirin in his most flabbergasted voice. "How dare you treat the daughter of a Guildlord this way."

The faint trace of a smile playing across Freyla's lips vanished and that stubborn crease between her brows returned, but this time directed to the dwarf guard who was looking distinctly uncomfortable at the mention of Guildlord, "Eh, orders is orders," he said.

"Well good night my love," said Kirin in a voice he was quite unsure of. He also wafted his arm in what he hoped was a romantic flourish.

"Good night my darling. Sleep well," she said in a much more convincing voice.

With that she stepped forward past the guard, wrapped her arms around his neck and kissed Kirin on the lips. For a moment his eyes opened wide and it was fortunate for him that Sang-gast was behind him and could not see the expression on his face. At first her lips felt hard against his but then she pulled back slightly brushing her lips against his and he felt the tension in him ease. She pressed her lips firmly against his again but this time he softened his mouth slightly and they seemed to meld into each other and then his whole body began to relax into Freyla, his arms encircled her waist pulling her even tighter to him.

Sang-gast's face gave nothing away as he silently scrutinised them, the guard looked distinctly uncomfortable, as for Kirin he wasn't sure what was happening, who was fooling who or how this was all playing out with anyone.

ANGAURD CASTLE

Talia halted, at her signal so did the others and looked up at the black monolith towering over them. All remained still amid the gentle hush of the swirling cool wind that had followed them from the sea. There was no indication that they had been spotted. Of course if they were heading into a trap that was just the impression the castles occupants would want them to have. At the base of the plateau, where it sprang out of the plain, a path had been cut into the living rock. It switched back left and right continually, with sharp hairpin turns, but always going upwards disappearing into the darkness above. They would have to go unheard now as well as unseen, if they were to have any chance they would need the element of surprise. Talia turned to the others and gave the signal. They began to pad silently up the rock.

The builders had done their work well. It was a gentle climb. In easing the gradient the builders had sacrificed speed for endurance but this was easy fodder for the feet of Certified Accounting Dwarfs. Their pace hardly slowed from the one they had set across the plain below. Indeed it was not the terrain that necessitated their slight slowing, but vigilance and their desire for stealth, even Coulan was being careful to tread quietly on the hard rock surface. Shy of the top, the path disappeared into a large tunnel that delved into the heart of the mountain; five hot and sweaty dwarfs, ready for action, peered into the darkness. They sheltered here, out of sight at least, but the sound of their heavy breathing was caught by the wind and sounded unnaturally loud as it blew up through the tunnel. The night was still warm but now they felt cold as the wind chilled the wetness of their bodies. Their muscles yearned for release, straining against this enforced inaction. Once again Talia waited patiently, listening for the slightest sound.

It was Bashka who tapped her on the shoulder, pointing not towards the castle but down to the plain below. She passed Talia her binoculars. At first Talia could not locate them, but then they swept into view. Figures, carrying flaming torches, moving towards the castle. They came from the northeast. There was no mistaking their destination. It could only be Derrott. They counted eleven torches.

"How long?" said Talia handing Stilgoe the binoculars.

"Depends, how quickly they ascend," said Bashka "Two, maybe three hours?"

Talia nodded.

The continued on into the tunnel. It too was carved into the living rock of the plateau and sloped steeply upwards for about fifty yards to a small patch of night sky at the far end. As they walked they were soon immersed in almost total darkness. Every so often they felt a cold draught of air blow across them. There were recesses cut in to the rock and within these, small openings that led up, presumably to the surface. Perhaps in days long past, having fought their way up the tortuous path, assaulting solders may have charged through here in the darkness, only to be assailed by something very nasty indeed coming down these chutes.

The end of the tunnel opened into a large courtyard.

They were now not only on top of the plateau but they were inside the castle itself. Once again Talia had them huddle inside the tunnel patiently watching and listening for signs of the enemy and noting the layout of the castle. Above them a large portcullis had been conveniently raised. Surrounding the courtyard were the outer castle walls, built on top of the rock at the edge of the plateau itself. From below they looked in ruins, but up close they were still a formidable barrier. Directly across the cobbled courtyard was the castle keep, a large square building three stories high with a large tower at its centre. Unlike the outer walls it was mostly intact. It too had a large entrance with a portcullis also conveniently raised. There were no guards to be seen.

They knew from the townsfolk of Helsinagar that Sang-gast had more than a dozen dwarfs with him. How many more were in the castle or how many Dividend-orcs they did not know. It was not likely that there was an army to defend a ruined castle but it was a safe bet that they were seriously outnumbered. They reasoned that Sang-gast would not be expecting an attack and apart from a few look-outs what forces he had would be concentrated in the keep. Time though was not on their side. Derrott and more Dividend-orcs would soon be ascending the path to Angaurd Castle. Not only more potential foes to fight but cutting off their only escape route.

As the moon disappeared behind a cloud, Talia signalled Stilgoe and Dargo who slipped noiselessly across the courtyard. They entered the keep. Going through the entrance they found themselves in a passageway made from the same large stone blocks as the rest of the keep. It was shorter than previous tunnel, maybe only twenty yards. They padded silently on the cobbles to the far end, where they halted, melting into the walls, one on either side. There were voices. Two guards.

As they looked out they saw yet another courtyard and yet another (inner) keep, This was the tall round tower they had already seen. More importantly there were two guards patrolling this courtyard between the inner and outer keeps. Stilgoe and Dargo waited patiently till the guards crossed the courtyard once more, towards them. As they turned Stilgoe and Dargo pounced. There was little noise. Stilgoe used some of the bark-ties that Kirin had given him. They pulled the helpless, gagged dwarfs into the darkness of the passageway. Stilgoe waited patiently once more for a small cloud to drift across the moon before slipping across the courtyard to investigate the inner keep while Dargo went back and signalled Talia and the others to approach.

Huddled in the passageway under the outer keep, it was Talia who spotted it, high up on the tower of the inner keep. Something out of place amid the relentless dark, grey stone. It looked for all the world like a set of bed sheets knotted together. For the first time since entering the castle Talia smiled. Then all hell broke loose.

* * * *

Kirin woke from a fitful sleep, his head still filled with crazy swirling thoughts. Trapped in an ancient castle full of ghosts, a prisoner of a vicious dwarf, his friends maybe lost at sea and trying to run a scam with someone he couldn't even tell it to. And then there was that kiss. His mind normally so ordered, so logical couldn't think straight about anything. He was in over his head and couldn't afford to lose it. He needed to keep his wits about him, keep focused. Not just his life but Freyla's depended upon it. He shook his head as if that would clear his thoughts. It was then that he heard it.

He lay still, unsure if he'd imagined it. Then he heard it again, a scratching noise. He got out of bed and went to the window, a tall narrow slit in the thick stone walls of his room but still wide enough for him to fall out of. There it was again. It was coming from outside the window. Just as he was about to poke his head out, a hand appeared clutching at the window sill.

He jumped back from the window, his heart racing and held his breath. Then a head appeared. There was a grunting noise and a face looked up and grinned. The face belonged to Freyla.

"You wanna give a person a hand here?" she whispered.

Kirin sprung forward and helped pull her over the sill into his room. He hugged her close before standing back awkwardly. He looked out the window at the sheer drop below. "You're crazy. You know that right?"

"Me crazy?" she laughed quietly. "I'm not the one trying to convince Sang-gast that we're lovers." She paused looking at Kirin and tilted her head to one side. "That was what you were doing, wasn't it?"

Kirin suddenly realised that he was just wearing his shorts and quickly started dressing. "Eh, well, um, yeah I was trying to keep Sang-gast confused."

"Keeping Sang-gast confused?" said Freyla.

Kirin felt himself blushing.

"Eh. He's smart though. I don't think he's entirely buying into it."

"Oh I think between us we managed to sustain his interest in the affair."

"Oh, yeah, eh, sorry if that was awkward for you."

Kirin turned away and busied himself with getting his stuff together and didn't see the expression on Freyla's face. As he finished dressing Kirin explained to Freyla his plan about how the three of them would acquire the Guildlord's money.

"Really that was the best you could come up with?" she said.

"OK, OK, you're here now and at least it got me out the dungeon." Kirin peeked out the window again, this time looking along the wall to where Freyla had come from. He saw that between the massive blocks of stone there were gaps, they were only one or two inches at most, but still enough for determined fingers and toes. He surveyed the wall in all directions. "So do you think you could make it along to the next room along? I could call the guards inside—".

Freyla was shaking her head.

"Oh don't give me that, we never leave one of our own behind line," he said.

"If our positions were reversed, would you leave me?" she said.

"Sure." He shrugged his shoulders. "In a heart-beat."

"You are such a bad liar." She shook her head. "How you ever convinced Sang-gast of anything is beyond me."

"I'm not sure he is convinced. He is however very greedy."

But Freyla wasn't listening, she was looking out the window herself. "I've got an idea." From out of her sleeve a knife suddenly appeared.

"Where did that come from?"

She shrugged. "Oh, eh, I liberated it from the dinner table."

"You know that's stealing don't you.,"

"Shut up you idiot," she said smiling. " Look it's too risky to try and get past the guards at the door, one peep out of them and the alarm will be raised." He nodded. "So that just leaves the window."

"Look you might be able to—"

"You can climb a rope can't you?"

"What?"

"We don't go across. We go down."

Kirin went to the window again. He looked down and instantly felt nauseous. Just for once he wished Freyla would come up with an exit strategy that involved staying on the ground. Her plan, as she explained it to him, was relatively simple. Kirin began shredding the bed sheets and Freyla knotted them into a rope. The ceiling in this room was made from wood and there was an exposed beam not far from the window. This would do to anchor the bed sheet rope. Then they would make their way down to the room on the floor below, which hopefully was empty. In a castle this size it was a good bet. As Kirin quietly slit the bed sheets he wondered if he would ever have a restful night's sleep between sheets again. He steeled himself to look outside the window once more. They were on the northwestern side of the round inner keep. It looked as if they were on the third or fourth floor. It was still a sheer drop though on to the cobblestones below. If he fell, it would kill him just as surely as if he fell all the way down to the Plain of Angaurd itself.

"I'm telling you, next quest I'm going to insist on no mountains and no buildings over two stories. I'll have it written in the small print," mumbled Kirin.

"Oh quit whining and grab the other end of the bed sheet."

* * * *

Freyla hissed something about the bed sheet rope. Kirin could not make it out, there was just something about holding tight. That, had always been part of *his* strategy. The next thing he knew she was kicking off against the wall swinging the rope out. Kirin gripped the rope very tightly indeed with hands and legs. The next thing the rope went sickeningly slack and he was banging against the castle wall. He ventured a look down. Bad idea. She must have made it in the window below he told himself. He shuffled down the rope. Disconcertingly his legs ran out of rope to grip.

"It's a little short," hissed Freyla her head popping out from the window. He was now gripping the last two feet of a knotted bed sheet with nothing between him and the ground below. His legs were dangling in front of the window, his upper torso still above it!

"Em, can you push off the wall? Then as you swing back let go and you should drop right in," whispered Freyla, not entirely helpfully.

"What? How can I push off? My legs have nothing to push off against," hissed Kirin. As if to demonstrate this

Kirin kicked his legs in the empty space of the window.

"Er, yeah you should have done it a little higher up and slid down at the same time," whispered Freyla, again not very helpfully. Kirin felt a pair of arms grab his legs. "OK, I'm going to push you out from the wall. When you come back in just let go," said Freyla.

Kirin, his face pressed against the wall above the window tried to protest but then he felt himself being pushed away from the wall. As he swung back he gritted his teeth and let go the bed sheet. He felt arms grab him, pulling him through the window. He collapsed in a heap onto the hard stone floor.

"What did I tell you, never even touched the sides," said Freyla.

Kirin picked himself up off the floor nursing a buzzing elbow. He gave the back of Freyla's head a very unsympathetic look as she padded to the door. The room they were in was smaller than the one they had just escaped from and completely empty. However it did have one redeeming feature that the other one did not; it didn't have a locked door with dwarf guards outside it. Quietly he slipped outside, following Freyla into a dark stone corridor. Coming from their right they thought they could hear the sound of voices. Kirin wanted to go in the opposite direction but Freyla insisted they should keep going that way. Treading cautiously, they continued one behind the other, snaking their way along the wall, as the voices got louder the cold damp air that seemed to emanate from the very stones of the castle also began to change. Kirin exchanged a look with Freyla, she had noticed it too. It was getting warmer. They came to a corner, they sneaked a peek round it, and saw a flickering light coming from an opening at the far end. This proved to be a large room with a very distinctive feature. It had a functioning chimney. A huge roaring fire occupied the large open fireplace that was just inside the opening. For the first time since he had arrived at the castle Kirin actually felt warm. There was a problem though, the room was full of around twenty Dividend-orcs.

They slunk back into the corridor again.

"You have no idea where you're going do you?" hissed Kirin.

Freyla turned on him, "Oh and do you think you could do any better?" she hissed back.

"Hey I'm still a little groggy from being knocked out," lied Kirin. "I could show you the way to the dungeons if that would help?" he added truthfully.

"Idiot," she smiled. "I'm sure that's the way out. Beyond that hall is a corridor that leads to the courtyard between the two keeps. I'm sure of it," she whispered.

"Yes, but it's full of Dividend-orcs," he hissed

"So, they're mostly asleep," she whispered.

"Mostly asleep is not all asleep," he hissed.

Yes but they've stopped talking. Looks like the last of them are bedding down," she whispered.

"We should go back, find another way," he hissed.

"I'm not going back," she hissed back at him.

"Hey what are you Money Laundering dwarfs doing here?"

Kirin and Freyla both turned to confront a Dividend-Orc eyeing them suspiciously.

"Who are you calling Launderers," said Freyla standing up straight. Kirin began sidling away. Freyla poked the Dividend-orc in the chest. "You guys think you own this place but we've got every right to be here just as much as you," she said moving round slightly, in the opposite direction to Kirin. "Listen buster—"

Kirin grabbed an arm of the hapless orc while kicking her in the back of her knee. As she went down Freyla clapped her hands over the orc's mouth. Soon the orc was prostrate on the floor, tied and gagged with strips of her own shirt. They stood wondering what to do with her for a moment before remembering the empty room they'd just come from. They struggled back along the corridor, Kirin grabbing the mumbling orc under her armpits while Freyla had her feet.

"I told you we should have gone back," he whispered.

"And I told you, that's going in the wrong direction," she hissed.

"Oh, OK, so you want to put this one in with all the sleeping ones?" he whispered.

"Very fun... Oh hello there," she said.

"What?" said Kirin, he followed Freyla's gaze round to see the Dividend Orc behind him.

"Eh. Well don't just stand there gawping. Give us a hand with your drunk friend here," said Kirin. "Here grab her, watch out she's heavy." In the darkness of the corridor Kirin handed over the immobilised Dividend-orc to the gullible Dividend-orc and then casually stepped behind him. The inevitable followed. Kirin almost felt sorry for him.

"So is this your brilliant plan, then. We just gradually fill up an empty room with Dividend-orcs," hissed Freyla as they made their way back to get the second orc.

"Well, leaving them in the corridor is just a trip hazard. Anyway have you got a better plan?" he whispered.

"I believe it was my brilliant plan that got us out of the room," hissed Freyla.

"Oh, so it's my turn is it," whispered Kirin.

"Share and share alike, turn and turn about," hissed Freyla.

"Yeah? So why is it I always seem to end up with the heavy end then?" whispered Kirin.

Freyla dropped the second orc's feet, "Fine," she hissed and moved round to the other end.

"Fine," hissed Kirin dropping his end and going round to pick up the feet.

They continued carrying the orc in silence. As they got to the room, Kirin spoke. "You know, they've got this reputation for being financial wizards but the ones we've encountered so far don't seem any brighter than your average dwarf."

Freyla who had been struggling with the heavy end dropped it "Who are you calling average." She grinned.

"Wait," he said

"I said who are you calling—" Freyla stopped as she looked at Kirin. "Oh. You've got an idea, haven't you." Kirin looked up at her. He was the one grinning this time.

Beside the fireplace where the Dividend-orcs were sleeping was a large stack of logs, it stretched nearly to the ceiling, which like the ceilings elsewhere in the castle, was made of wood. Kirin and Freyla crept into the room, in which now all the orcs were asleep, they were tempted just to sneak across but it was too good an opportunity to pass up. They had bound their hands with strips of cloth and as quietly as they could they began moving burning logs from the fire to the wood stack. It was a slow business as they could only take logs that were burning at one end only. It was going to take forever and the orcs might wake up at any moment. After the longest five minutes of his life, Kirin was beginning to think that perhaps this was not such a good idea when he noticed a tankard of something on the table. It was still half full. He brought his nose to it, recoiling in disgust, alcohol. He took it and flung the contents on the wood stack. Instantly the small flames at the base shot up. Quickly he searched for more of this magic fuel. Soon the wood stack was burning fiercely. So much so that Kirin and Freyla could no longer bear to get close to it.

Freyla nudged Kirin and pointed to something in the far corner that had been lurking in the shadows. It was a large tarpaulin covering something substantial. Freyla was pointing at a small corner of it that was uncovered, a small corner that now glinting gold in the light of the blazing fire. A cry of alarm behind them brought them back to the real world. The Dividend-Orcs were waking up.

"Fire! Fire!" yelled Kirin, helping a startled orc to his feet.

"You," Kirin pointed at Freyla, "Get water! Now!" Freyla nodded , running off to the doorway at the far end of the room. "Are you OK?" Kirin asked the confused orc. "Quick go, get help now!" He escorted the stumbling orc to the corridor and propelled him back the way he and Freyla had just come. "I'll wake the others. Go!" As the orc stumbled down the corridor shouting fire, Kirin turned around and fought his way back through half-asleep panicking orcs rushing past him. The room was now beginning to fill with smoke. Half the orcs had already fled and Freyla was at the far exit directing any that came her way back, telling them it was not safe and to use the other exit. Kirin helped the last of the orcs up and propelled them in the right direction and as he joined Freyla he noted that the ceiling had well and truly caught fire now.

"Aw nuts!" said Kirin.

He slipped off his pack and thrust it at puzzled Freyla before sprinting back through the smoke filled room. Once in the corridor, he quickly located the room where they had stashed the two orcs. He cut their bound feet and got them up and out into the smoke filled corridor before shoving them off in the direction of their fellow orcs with cries of 'fire' ringing in their ears. The air was so full of smoke he was now having to breathe through a strip of cloth held over his nose When he got back to the room a large beam on fire came crashing down and the rest of the ceiling did not look like it would hold much longer. To his left the woodpile was a roaring inferno and from it long fingers of yellow and red flame licked across the remaining part of the ceiling. He could feel the heat even from the doorway. Through the smoke, across the room, he could make out Freyla waving franticly. Without thinking twice, he took a deep breath, pulled his jerkin over his head and made a dash for it.

At first he thought Freyla was hugging him till he realised she was patting him down. His jerkin was on fire. Coughing and spluttering Freyla helped him rip it off, leaving a charred, smoking mess on the floor. He looked back at the now impassable room of fire and then to Freyla.

"C'mon," she said and grabbed his arm.

They ran along the corridor away from the fire, strangely though, the noise of commotion seemed to be getting louder the further they got from the fire. Freyla had been right about the corridor leading to the courtyard between the keeps but there was something happening there, something very loud indeed. They slowed as they approached the end of the corridor which turned sharply right before opening on to the courtyard. The peeked round the corner. Not ten feet in front of them was a quite animated Sang-gast shouting instructions to his dwarfs, intent on directing their efforts, as they battled the Company of the Quest in the open courtyard.

After a silent mime to Freyla, the two of them crept up on the unsuspecting Sang-gast. Each of them grabbed him under the armpit lifting him up slightly before dumping him flat on his back. Sang-gast looked on open-mouthed as the two then ran past him to join their friends.

Things had not been going well for the Company of the Quest. Caught in the open space of the inner courtyard they were scattered, waging individual battles with Sang-gast's forces, who must have spotted them and had been lying in wait. Many of Sang-gast's dwarfs had quarterstaffs and knew how to use them and on top of that they had numerical superiority by almost three to one. Freyla immediately sped off to help Talia. In front of Kirin, Bashka was surrounded by three dwarfs. Kirin took out one, from behind, pulling him down heavily on to the cobbles, the dwarf fell awkwardly with his wrist making a horrible crunching sound. The second dwarf swung a club at Kirin who ducked beneath it. Quickly he was up grabbing the swinging arm by the elbow and wrist, twisting it round behind his back. Then he propelled the off balance dwarf, crashing him into the remaining dwarf attacking Bashka. This gave Bashka the opportunity to give her attacker a hefty swipe with her staff, knocking him flying. Kirin forced his dwarf down on to the cobbles, knocking the wind out of him as he landed on top of him. With a brief nod to him, Bashka raced off to the aid of a beleaguered Stilgoe.

As Kirin got up he was now faced with a dwarf with a viscous looking scar that started above his eyebrow and continued on to his cheek. He felt the sharp streak of pain along his forearm before he even saw the knife. A warm trickle of blood ran down on to his hand. The scar-faced dwarf looked at the bloody knife in his hands and then up at Kirin and smiled. Scarface swung the knife wildly at Kirin who jumped back out of the way but then immediately moved forwards grabbing the wrist of an off-balance Scarface and twisting it and the knife downwards. He was now face to face with Scarface, and could feel his stinking breath on his face as they struggled for control of the knife. With his other hand he pushed Scarface's elbow up, turning and forcing him forwards. Kirin used his leg to trip Scarface and soon had him pinned down on the cobbles with his arm twisted up round his back. Kirin then did something he had been taught never to do. Something he had promised his father never to do. Instead securing the prone dwarf with bark-ties, he leant all his own weight on the struggling dwarf's arm till something snapped. With an anguished cry the dwarf went unforgivably limp.

Gradually the tide was turning, with the seven dwarfs of the quest reunited back into a fighting unit, their opponents were scattered and in disarray. Talia shouted that they should fall back to the passageway beneath the outer keep. Once there, Coulan, Dargo and Stilgoe defended the entrance while the others made their way through to the far end. There were a few hugs and back-slaps for Kirin and Freyla but they were not out of the woods yet, or rather the castle. At the far end of the passageway, the outer courtyard seemed deserted. Kirin was about to rush across when Bashka placed her arm across his chest. Kirin followed her gaze to see a couple of Dividend-orcs dash across the outer courtyard to the exit tunnel. Seconds later there was a great clanging noise as the portcullis over the tunnel crashed into the cobble stones below causing the whole ground to shake. The two Dividend-orcs were now running away, keeping to the far wall. They watched as the two of them crossed back over the outer courtyard a hundred yards away and disappeared into a doorway. Why? Wondered Kirin. It didn't make sense not to guard the portcullis. Bashka and Kirin at a signal from Talia ran across the outer courtyard. The exit was deserted. There was no-one else there. As soon as they got there they realised why. They hadn't lowered the portcullis. They'd cut the ropes. They were trapped.

They tried for a while to hold the passageway between the keeps, but it was futile. Sang-gast's dwarfs found other ways through the outer keep and soon they risked being outflanked and trapped in the passageway. Talia gave the order to abandon it, then they all made their way across to join Bashka and Kirin by the portcullis. Sang-gast and the other dwarfs spilled out on to the outer courtyard. Many were limping and looked the worse for wear. They knew they had been in a battle right enough and there was fear to be seen in the defensive stance of their bodies, none dared to cross the courtyard. Sang-gast's forces still had numerical superiority, but only by three or four and now they faced all seven members of the Company of the Quest. Sang-gast started to rail at them but to no effect. Of course Kirin and the rest had nowhere to go, trapped as they were by the portcullis. Sang-gast's dwarfs still did not attack even when their numbers were swelled by the arrival of a dozen or so Dividend-orcs which seemed to cause even more disruption as they then started arguing amongst themselves. In the air there was now a strong smell of burning, smoke was drifting through the air. The wind was carrying burning embers on to the roof of the outer keep where now the first few flames were taking hold.

* * * *

Sang-gast's forces fell back for the third time. Some of the Dividend-orcs must have been tackling the fire and others, thankfully, seemed to feel that fighting dwarfs was dwarfish business. Their opponents may have been suffering more casualties, but then they could afford to. Unfortunately another attack was inevitable, the fire, which was now out of control would see to that. While dealing with the fire was occupying most of the orcs for the time being, ultimately it would focus all of their attention on the portcullis; the only exit from a fiery death. Kirin could have kicked himself. And on top of all of that Derrott would be here soon. Freyla, slim enough to slip through the portcullis, had been keeping tabs on his approach. Kirin surveyed the damage. It was not good. Most of them were battered and bruised, even Freyla had a nasty looking bump above her eye. Kirin's head had not added to its collection of bumps but his forearm ached from the viscous gash inflicted by the dwarf with the scar across his face.

It was not Kirin's arm that worried the company though, it was Dargo's leg. He was supporting himself on Coulan's shoulder while Freyla and Bashka had a look at it. A shake of Freyla's head to Talia confirmed it was broken. He was going nowhere fast. In truth none of them were. Their backs, whilst not against the wall, were against the next worst thing. A dropped portcullis. They could feel the draft of cold air coming up from the tunnel, escape tantalisingly only inches away. And now the news about Dargo. Between them they could lift the portcullis but Sang-gast's dwarfs attacked the minute they tried that. Some of them might get away while others engaged Sang-gast's forces but there was nothing that could be done for Dargo.

"I'm the one who has to stay. Can't run and you can't afford to nursemaid me." He gave a hollow kind of a laugh. "I'll buy some time for you at least," he said.

Coulan was looking around at everyone's faces.

Dargo put his arm round his brother. "You've got to go with the others now, they'll take care of you."

Leaving Dargo behind was not an option! Kirin looked about wildly at the others. Bashka was looking hopefully at Talia who just shook her head, her mouth a grim, thin line. Freyla was trying to explain to a bewildered Coulan while Stilgoe just stood looking out across the courtyard chewing nervously on his lip. There had to be another way. Kirin tried to think, he closed his eyes to concentrate, but unbidden, an image of Scarface appeared before him.

Stilgoe suddenly turned round, a faint smile now on his lips.

"What?" said Talia

"It's a long shot and we'll need to time it just right but... it might just be possible." Stilgoe quickly explained his plan to the others.

* * * *

Freyla appeared back at the portcullis out of breath, she nodded to Talia before squeezing back through, concealed by the others. Talia then gave the signal to attack. Along with Stilgoe and Kirin, she launched a frontal assault on Sang-gast and his dwarfs, who were caught unawares by this unexpected development. At the same time Bashka and Freyla ran towards an old cart lying unnoticed by the side of the keep wall. It was small enough to be pushed by a couple of determined dwarfs but still large enough for their purposes. With only the injured Dargo to encourage him, Coulan put all those workouts and strength building exercises to the test. He got down on his haunches, bracing his back against the portcullis, getting a good grip he tensed his muscles then heaved. The portcullis lifted but only a foot or so before falling back.

Sang-gast must have figured out what Bashka and Freyla were up to with the cart for he sent three dwarfs to stop them. Kirin seeing this, immediately split away from

Talia and Stilgoe, chasing after them. He clipped the heels of one with Dargo's quarterstaff causing him to fall heavily on the hard cobbles in a crumpled heap, from which he did not get up. The other two stopped running and turned to engage with him, they were competent enough but predictable with their moves. Even with only Stilgoe's basic training, his superior speed allowed him to more than hold his own and crucially it left Bashka and Freyla free to begin pushing the cart towards the portcullis. Meanwhile Sang-gast was now shouting and screaming at the remaining dwarfs fighting Stilgoe and Talia, pointing at the portcullis and Coulan, telling them to attack it.

Coulan tried again. This time it rose a little more before falling back. Bashka and Freyla were now only twenty yards away, with the cart. A third time Coulan raised it, this time by two feet but it needed to be higher still. The cart was now only ten yards away, with its momentum Bashka and Freyla could not stop it now even if they wanted to. Finally with one last effort Coulan straightened his legs and his straining arms held the portcullis three feet above the cobbles just as the cart came crashing in at an angle. There was a ear-shattering sound of hammering iron and splintering wood as Coulan let go and the portcullis tried to crush the cart into nothingness. The laws of physics however prevailed and the solid object of the cart was not compressed, certainly not to nothingness. The cart was smashed and splintered, its functional days over, but it now provided a two foot gap between the bottom of the portcullis and the ground. When this happened, those of Sang-gast's dwarfs that had heeded his command to attack were caught halfway across the courtyard, they stopped unsure of what to do. Sang-gast was still screaming at them to attack but they had lost their impetus now and their hesitation proved pivotal.

Bashka and Freyla helped Dargo get under the portcullis and into the tunnel before following, and shouting to Talia and Stilgoe. Coulan was next to get under, he however proved a very tight fit and got jammed, only with Kirin's arrival to help push did he manage through. Kirin quickly followed. and finally Stilgoe and Talia squeezed under with only seconds to spare as Sang-gast himself and the rest finally arrived.

Kirin and Freyla helped Dargo on to Coulan's back then Talia led Coulan and Freyla silently in single file down the left side of the tunnel. Stilgoe, Bashka and Kirin stayed at the portcullis discouraging any other dwarfs and orcs from squeezing under. At a signal from Talia they too slipped silently into the darkness down the right side of the tunnel. Halfway down the tunnel, from the far end, they heard voices approaching. Talia and the others stopped, flattening themselves into the recesses in the walls and waited. The advancing Dividend-orcs had just passed them in the darkness when they stopped, alarmed by the commotion coming from the castle end of the tunnel where Sang-gast and his dwarfs had now gotten past the portcullis. The Dividend-orcs were close enough to the outside for their silhouettes to be highlighted to Sang-gast and his dwarfs, who then fell upon the orcs attacking them. Confused and unable to see, the Dividend-orcs fought back defending themselves against Sang-gast's dwarfs, perhaps taking them for Talia and the Company of the Quest.

Quietly, one by one, Talia, Coulan and Dargo, Bashka, Stilgoe, Freyla and Kirin slipped by in the dark and confusion. When they got outside they increased their speed, jogging back and forth down the switchback road. Going downhill their pace was good, it would be a different matter on the plain, but they were out of the castle, all seven of them. A hour ago that did not look a likely prospect. Not very likely at all.

At the bottom while the others retrieved their packs from where they'd been hidden, Kirin held Dargo's leg straight while Freyla make a splint for it. She thought it a simple fracture below the knee. And had brought a couple of splintered planks from the ruined cart that suited her purpose. Kirin looked up at the rock and castle towering over them. Could they really have been so lucky? He looked down at Dargo grimacing in pain but he was pretty sure, before the assault on the castle, even Dargo would have traded his broken leg to be where they were now. The others made a stretcher from a couple of staffs and Coulan's jerkin. They were heading south now, the direction of home. It is too dark for him to see anything especially so close to the base of the rock but a little while later there was a call from Bashka. No emotion, just the reporting of a fact. Movement from the top of the path.

BROKEN THINGS

They made good time, even through jogging was not an option because of Dargo's injury. This caused a big argument with Dargo and it was indeed fortunate that silence was no longer a necessity. But Freyla had insisted, and there was to be no dissuading Coulan, who would also not let anyone help with his end of the stretcher. The rest of them organised themselves into shifts helping carry Dargo, they all took a half-hour rest break every four hours. But there would be no real rest until they had put some water between them and the pursuing dwarfs. At walking pace it would take them two days to get to the junction of the rivers and all that way Sang-gast and his dwarfs would be just a few hours behind them, probably Derrott as well.

As they journeyed due south, Freyla filled in the others on what had happened since they had left Bank Island. The others tried to joke with Kirin about how funny it was that he of all people had ended up flying. Kirin rebuffed these entreaties with gruff monosyllabic replies. The others soon reserved their enquires for Freyla. When they found out that it was they who had started the fire Stilgoe let out one of his long low whistles.

Kirin turned on him. "It was a bad idea. OK I get it! Now they won't stop now till they catch us."

Stilgoe tried to tell Kirin that he had not meant it as a criticism. On the contrary he tried to explain how impressed he was till Talia laid a hand upon his arm and shook her head. Kirin spent the rest of that shift immersed in his own thoughts. All he could think of was that dwarf, the one with the scar across his eye, the one who had cut him. He tried closing his eyes but that vicious Scarface would appear before him, snarling and cursing and then he heard it. That gut wrenching noise, the sickening crunch of broken bone.

It was not long after dawn when they had their first rest break. There was no wind, and the pale blue sky held the promise of a warm summers day. A day like any other, except for the black smudge of smoke, smearing the skyscape behind them. At the base of the smoke were small, unreal-like, flashes of orange and yellow.

"Looks like Derrott is gonna have to find himself another castle," said Dargo twisting round. He laughed then immediately winced and clutched at his leg.

"Stop moving you idiot," said Freyla,

She was doing the rounds of the wounded, checking out each of them in turn.

"Let's have a look at that arm," said Freyla looking at the makeshift, bloodstained bandage wrapped round Kirin's left arm. He shook his head.

"Here let me see," she said gently taking his arm.

"I'm fine!" He jerked his arm away. "Leave me. I just need some rest." With that he turned away lying down onto his side, his back to Freyla.

When they started up again Talia insisted Coulan share stretcher duty. She argued that they might need his strength before long and they could not afford to spend it needlessly. Dargo did his bit by telling his brother not to be an idiot. Even so it was not till Freyla laid her hand gently on Coulan's fist, gripping the stretcher, that he relented.

It was mid-morning when they stopped again. Kirin was sitting with his back to the others as Stilgoe was doling out food and water to everyone. As he handed Kirin some bread he laid a hand on his shoulder, "Back there was... It was tough, but you did fine. You did what you had to do."

Kirin could not look him in the eye. He just nodded and took the bread ripping a chunk off with his teeth. He chewed and swallowed. His body needed nourishment, that was the only reason he ate.

Freyla looked across at Kirin's hunched back and then to Stilgoe who shrugged. A stubborn crease formed between her brows. She got up and went over to Kirin. "Arm!" she said.

"I'm fine," he said.

"That's for me to decide," she said. "Now let me have a look at that arm."

"Just leave it," he said. "Check on the others."

"I've checked the others, now show me that arm. We can't afford to have you slowing us up."

Kirin flashed his eyes angrily at her but Freyla remained perfectly determined. She took his arm and began unwrapping the shirt bandage. He did not resist but turned his head to look at the tiny orange and yellow glow below the pall of smoke.

"Can you make a fist?"

Kirin clenched his fingers tightly, the dull throb of pain in his arm became a searing agony. Kirin jerked round expecting to see Scarface again. There was only Freyla with a concern etched in her forehead. He watched disinterestedly as the blood oozed out the gash in his forearm.

"You were lucky, a little deeper and it would have been much worse. You'll still need stitches though. It will hurt." Her voice calm and steady.

"Fine," he said.

The wound was about four inches long running from

just above his wrist diagonally up his forearm. As she cleaned the wound Kirin did not say a word, he just stared off into the distance. Even when she began stitching up the wound, not a sound escaped his lips. She tore a strip of her own shirt to make a clean bandage before gently placing his arm back.

"I'll check it again when we reach the river" She brushed back the hair from his eyes. "Any other lumps or bumps?" she asked.

Kirin shook his head. He turned back to stare at the burning castle. Everything that could burn there was now aflame. His arm too felt on fire.

* * * *

Dusk was fast approaching when they halted for their next rest break. Most of the company had not had a proper rest since the previous day when they'd lain below the wall complaining about inaction. Since then they'd had a forced jog to a castle, stormed it, battled dwarfs and orcs and walked for almost a day carrying a stretcher with only four half-hour rest breaks.

Stilgoe joined Talia and Bashka.

"What do you think?" asked Talia passing Stilgoe the binoculars.

"Three, maybe four hours behind us?" said Stilgoe lowering the binoculars.

"Three at most, never four" said Bashka, putting out her hand for the binoculars.

"You think they're getting closer?" asked Talia.

"Hard to say, maybe" said Stilgoe passing the binoculars to Talia.

"They're not making jogging pace. That's for sure," said Bashka putting out her hand once more.

"Hmmm. We don't know if they'll keep going through the night or not." Talia put down the binoculars. "We can't risk stopping, even for a few hours. We'll keep to the four hours on, half-hour break, through the night. Dargo can keep watch. At dawn we'll see where they are." She handed the binoculars back to Stilgoe and went to get some food. Stilgoe smiled innocently at Bashka as she snatched the binoculars from his hand and followed Talia.

Kirin practically collapsed in a heap. In the gloom he was only dimly aware of the others doing likewise. He managed to drag himself a few feet away and rolled out his sleeping mat and had just laid his head on his pack as a pillow when the hairs on the back of his neck suddenly stood upright. Suddenly he felt the weight of a body, heavy on top of him. He opened his eyes to find Scarface, only inches away. But it was the flicker of the blade tapping his forehead that had his full attention. Scarface smiled and brought a finger up to his mouth indicating Kirin should remain quiet. A hush fell upon the camp. Kirin's eyes darted around the huddled backs of his slumbering companions. He could see no-one else. Then the knife flashed. Aimed at his face, all he could do was raise his arms in token defence. The knife slashed first one way then the other. His mouth widened in an anguished cry that never came. For though he could see the blood streaming down his forearms, he felt no pain only a strange numbness that was spreading, with every heartbeat, like a poison throughout his body. He tried to shout on the others but it was too late, no words would come. Scarface was laughing silently at him. Kirin tried to make a grab for the knife but his movements were sluggish now and with hands so slippery that he couldn't hold on. His mind too was clouding over with a fogginess that was strangely soothing as it crept softly over him, enshrouding him. Scarface was hacking at him again and again with his knife. Dimly he was aware, as if watching from afar, that his arms were being ripped to shreds...

"Argh."

Kirin was suddenly awake. He looked about wildly but there was only the sight and sound of weary dwarfs getting their stuff together.

"You OK?" asked Stilgoe. "C'mon breaks over."

Kirin nodded. The night air felt cold against his skin. He realised that his shirt was drenched with sweat. He shivered like someone had just walked over his grave.

* * * *

The next time they stopped, Kirin dared not sleep, even though his body craved it. He lay on his side with his back to the others in a pretence of sleep. Back in Angaurd castle, even when Sang-gast had held him prisoner, it had been a game of sorts, a battle of wits with his jailor. He'd busied himself solving the problem of getting out of his manacles and out of the dungeon. Trying to prove he was the smarter of the two. And with only a bump on the head for his troubles he'd succeeded. But in that courtyard he'd come face to face with reality. It all happened so quickly, no time to think, to apply reason and logic, he'd reacted instinctively; his actions, the most honest reflection of who he truly was. His father had said that a man is defined by what he does, Stilgoe had said he'd done what he needed to do and the logical part of Kirin understood that breaking Scarface's arm had stopped him knifing, maybe even killing someone. But there was something else. Throughout the battle he hadn't been scared, not really, not even of Scarface. His father's training had helped of course, but even so he'd handled himself with a calm, almost detached, ruthless efficiency There had been hints of this before but the battle in the courtyard had confirmed it. There was no getting away from the fact. He had a natural ability for violence.

Most everyone, after a few bites to eat, fell asleep where they lay except for Dargo who was keeping watch. Suddenly there was a tap on Kirin's shoulder. It was Coulan. He had in his hand a small black notebook. Kirin looked down at it not recognising it at first. Then he remembered he had given it to Coulan to look at the doodles. That seemed so long ago now. So much trouble caused by so small a thing. Why was it so important to Sang-gast? What secrets did it hold that caused so much pain and misery? He had half a mind to throw the thing away. Cast it into the darkness.

"Pretty triangles," said Coulan as he handed the book back to Kirin. Coulan returned back to his sleeping mat and was soon fast asleep, snoring loudly. His brother beside him gave a grunting laugh but did nothing to stifle his brothers snores. Dargo looked across at Kirin and nodded. Kirin nodded back then rolled on to his front. Perhaps it was the problem solver in him, perhaps it was a stubborn streak determined not to let Sang-gast win, or perhaps it was just distracting his mind from other things but Kirin took up the book and the enigma of Sang-gast's code once more.

He looked at the doodles, he didn't remember any triangles. He looked carefully. There he spotted one. Well not a triangle exactly but... It was where three circles intersected, Sang-gast had filled in the intersection. Strictly speaking a non-Euclidean triangle, the kind you get if you draw a triangle on the surface of a sphere. Interesting. Kirin checked carefully, there were many intersecting circles but it was only where three of them intersected that he'd filled in the intersection. Triangles? Everywhere he looked now, the number three jumped out at him. There were squares within squares within squares, the intersecting circles and underlining things with three sets of parallel lines. How could he not have seen it?

He went back to the coded part of the notebook and redrew a page of the book this time grouping the characters into sets of three, He took a mental step back and looked at it. He focused hard, there had to be a pattern here. Something was telling him it was there but he just couldn't see it. The numbers and letters began to swirl about on the page. He blinked his eyes and tried to concentrate but now he was getting a headache. He closed his eyes just for a moment, just to collect his thoughts.

"What!"

Stilgoe was shaking Kirin gently on the shoulder.

Kirin sat up, his head buzzing with scarred faces and doodles, knives and numbers, and a million whirling little black books.

"Time to go," said Stilgoe. He patted him on the back.

Kirin nodded. As he was getting up. He saw it. The book. There it was lying right beside him. He opened it up and went to the back where he thought he had redrawn the code. It was there all right, taunting him.

All that Kirin could think of over the next four hours was the code. What was he missing? What was the significance of the number three? His mind was running through different possible solutions, but without the data in the book, it was impossible. He tried holding the book in one hand while carrying the stretcher but the constant movement and poor light made it impossible. It was so frustrating. The others tried to talk to him but all he could think of, wanted to think of now, was the book.

At the next break he looked up at the sky, he saw a few familiar constellations and figured it was about four in the morning. Close up there was just enough light to work. He sat down with the book once more. Clearing his mind he opened it at the page where he'd written out the code in sets of three characters. For a moment he didn't believe his eyes. There it was right in front of him. He blinked and looked again. The hairs on the back of his neck stood up and a nervous tingling sensation coursed through his body. If the characters represented sexigisimal numbers (which he was sure they did) then...

In each group of three numbers the first two were small but the third one almost invariably bigger, much bigger than the previous two. This wasn't random. This was a pattern. Sang-gast was doing arithmetic within the code. That was why he translated everything into sexigisimal. And that was why he hadn't hidden the structure of the original text with its columns of amounts and dates. That was a trap for any potential code breaker to fall into.

The groups of three sexigisimal characters could be a Fibonacci sequence of sorts. When he subtracting the first two numbers from the third he got the true value of the third number. Occasionally this resulted in a negative number but this could be where the original sum was greater than 60. Sang-gast wouldn't want to betray his arithmetic by having a two digit number, he would just omit the leading 1. Yet another level of disguise. Quite brilliant really. All he had to do in these instances was add the leading 1 (or 60) back in.

Doing the subtraction in his head, he rewrote one line of code to show the true value of the third number. In every instance this formula consistently worked. The dates and amounts now had ten or less characters meaning they were numbers He'd done it! Of course he would still have to work out the simple substitution code to get to the original text, but with the original structure of the code indicating words and dates, that wouldn't be too difficult. The code was broken. He smiled to himself feeling good about something for the first time since they had left Angaurd Castle.

Back on stretcher duty it didn't take long before the elation wore off, a puzzle solved was no longer of interest, like yesterday's news. His body too was feeling the strain. It had become leaner and stronger but it still needed food and above all, sleep. The others had taken advantage of the last two rest stops to catnap, something he craved now above all else, despite whatever else sleep might bring.

Freyla was beside him on stretcher duty. She tried to talk to him but he could not talk to anyone, least of all her. Inside everything was mixed up: fear and anger, the pain in his arm, that sickening crunch of broken bone. He was not sure who he was any more. Perhaps Freyla was right about him. She had said Sang-gast and he thought alike, maybe it went much deeper than that. All he knew was that he could not talk about it. She said 'she understood'. How could she when even he didn't? He just shook his head and said he was tired, which was true enough. He focused on the task of carrying the stretcher. For the final hours of this stint he was free from stretcher duty, immersed in his thoughts. Stilgoe joined him, walking in silence by his side.

* * * *

During the night Talia had changed direction, heading southwest towards the river junction where they had crossed before. With the light of a new day their pursuers had discovered their mistake and were now following them once more, but a small number of them had remained headed due south. None of the dwarfs could agree as to the reason for this but one thing they were sure of, it did not bode well.

"Sorry if I've been a bit of a..." Kirin looked across at Stilgoe.

"I think idiot's the word you're looking for," said Stilgoe.

"It's..." Kirin sighed, "complicated."

"Sorry my mistake. Complicated idiot," said Stilgoe. "But don't worry we're getting used to it."

Kirin gave a half smile despite himself. They continued on in silence for a while.

"Back there," Kirin gave a slight indication of his head towards the plume of smoke behind them. "I.. I hurt one of them." He made a slight gesture with his hand as if that explained it all.

"They broke Dargo's leg. And the guy who sliced your arm wasn't playing around either. Everyone of us has got an injury of some kind," said Stilgoe. "And don't forget they were lying in wait, they attacked us."

Kirin looked across at his friend. "I didn't realise—" He shook his head. "It doesn't matter who attacked who. I hurt him... deliberately."

Stilgoe looked across, a puzzled look on his face. He said nothing. They continued walking.

"Look all I know is that they were trying to hurt us, and succeeding. If you and Freyla hadn't turned up when you did..."

"You don't understand," said Kirin.

"Apparently not," said Stilgoe.

They continued walking in silence.

"Look I don't know what's going on in that overly smart head of yours. But perhaps you should try talking to Freyla," said Stilgoe.

Kirin looked across at Stilgoe. "What! No. No, I can't talk to her about it."

Stilgoe sighed. "You know you're not the only one who's had a hard time of it." He paced a hand gently on Kirin's shoulder before moving away back to the others.

Kirin watched him go. What was he talking about? He and Freyla had been together throughout it all. Though he'd lost track of her during the fighting in Angaurd Castle. She'd got that nasty bump on her head. He looked across at Freyla. He saw that small crease just between the eyebrows. As if there was something not quite right with the world and she was determined to fix it. What had it been like for her? All this time making her way in the world with a bunch of tough no-nonsense dwarfs. He'd been doing it for just a few weeks. She'd been doing it for years.

He remembered the joy on her face when they'd found the wing. How she'd loved flying that thing. She was born for it. She had such courage, more than him. She'd even learned to swim. They had just been getting to know each other when Sang-gast had arrived. Then. Then what? He'd been unconscious for hours. What had happened then. Sang-gast had been looking for the book. He'd searched Kirin. He remembered the lining in her jerkin, it too was ripped. Even worse, when he'd been in the dungeon, he'd actually sent Sang-gast to her. To question her, confirm the story he'd made up. He pictured Sang-gast leering over her, his face close to hers.

He looked over again. She saw him looking and waved.

At the next rest break he laid his sleeping mat beside

Freyla's and forced himself to smile. "How are you feeling?"he said.

"Fine." Freyla too forced a smile.

"I just wanted to say I'm sorry," he said looking down at his feet.

"Eh, OK. Not sure what for, but apology accepted," she said.

Kirin glanced up to see the puzzled look on her face.

"I mean for Sang-gast and everything that happened back there I was just... stupid."

"Stupid? You're one of the smartest people I know and I keep pretty good company." Freyla gestured with her arm towards the others.

"Yeah smart like Sang-gast."

She gently touched his arm. "Yeah you are as smart as him but with you it's a good kind of smart."

Kirin looked back down at his feet shaking his head. "It wasn't a good kind of smart that sent *him* to you to question you about a plan you knew nothing about."

"No it wasn't a good kind of smart. It was brilliant kind of smart, you idiot!"

"What?" Now it was Kirin who looked up with a confused expression.

"Things were not looking good back there. Sang-gast had made it clear that if I should prove no further use to him in getting his precious book back he was going to let the guards have me."

"What?' Kirin suddenly felt his face flushing red.

"So you're plan of setting me up as your love interest, kept me out of their clutches."

"Really? But it was just a spur of the moment thing"

"Well then you've got good instincts. We may make a scam artist of you yet." Freyla clapped Kirin on the back. This though only made Kirin frown.

* * * *

They had been making good time and expected to reach the river junction where they had crossed before by midday. Angaurd Castle was behind them but the river lay ahead and though no-one said anything Kirin could feel the weight of expectation on him to get them across but they didn't even have a rope, till Freyla came up with an idea. She figured having made one out of bed sheets, she could make one out of shirts and clothing. As they marched along she used Dargo's stretcher as a work table as she shredded and plaited and knotted, every shirt the company possessed, spare or otherwise.

Kirin's plan was simply the reverse of how they had gotten across before, but with a few variations. He would swim across both rivers as before. Then the others would tie the rope to the tree on the east side of the tributary as before and fling it across to Kirin (on the west side). Then the dwarfs would use the rope to shimmy themselves across the torrent of water.

"But there's no tree on that side to anchor the rope too. You're not Coulan, you won't be able to hold the weight of a dwarf," said Talia.

"No, but two of us can." Kirin looked at Freyla.

"No way. You've got to be kidding." She shook her head. Everyone now looked at her.

"You managed the other river and with hardly any help from me, and this time you'll have the empty canteens to help you float. You can do this," said Kirin.

"No, no I don't think—"

"Hey if you can fly across thirty miles of water, you can swim across thirty feet." He held out his hand to her. "It'll be OK."

While the others used their remaining staffs and the few remaining bark-ties to make the stretcher into a raft, Kirin and Freyla set out, first crossing the River Kirin, which was fairly straightforward as it was only 30 feet wide and did not have much of a current. Freyla managed a passable doggy paddle and only required a little help from Kirin towards the end. The second river that flowed west in to Teteunxx Forest was a bigger kettle of fish. Kirin had

Freyla lie on her back in the water and tied, with a shirt-rope round her chest, the two bunches of canteens which then floated at her armpits. Kirin did a side stroke across the river with one arm, while with his other he pulled Freyla by the shirt-rope. As they crossed he talked to her encouraging her to kick her kegs. When he told her to stand up she didn't believe him. But they were across, about 500 yards downstream, but they were across.

As they walked back to the junction of the rivers, Kirin spoke.

"I don't think my instincts are good."

"What. Why would you say that? What's wrong? Is it to do with your nightmares?

"How do you know about them?"

"We're all sleeping a few feet apart. It's not easy to keep secrets."

"It was my instinct to break that dwarf's arm."

"What dwarf? The one that cut you?"

Kirin nodded.

"Well maybe your instinct was good there too."

"How can you say that. I deliberately broke his arm!"

"What I mean is that at some level you understood how dangerous he was to you. To all of us."

"But that makes me just as bad as them."

"Look I'm not going to sugar-coat this for you. In this job there are hard choices. Choices where no matter what, someone gets hurt. But we're not like Sang-gast and his crew. They don't have hard choices because they don't see the difference any more. We still do. You still do."

They walked on to the sound of the tributary getting louder and louder.

"Does it get any easier?"

"No."

* * * *

With the shirt-rope tied to the tree on the far side of the tributary, and Kirin and Freyla anchoring the rope on their side, Stilgoe was first to try. The rope did sag as Kirin and

Freyla strained every muscle, and Stilgoe did get soaking wet, but he made it. Once he was across it was easier to get Bashka over and Talia followed soon after. Despite the combined strength of five dwarfs to support him, Coulan showed a distinct lack of confidence in the enterprise and needed a great deal of encouragement and the use of the (unbeknown to him) now empty aqua-stick, before he finally crossed. Kirin once more swam across the two rivers to get back to Dargo on his stretcher/raft at the mouth of the tributary. He tied the rope to the stretcher/raft and gently pushed it into the water. Dargo was decidedly not happy when it was swept out into the river by the current but the others had a firm grasp of the rope. Kirin, in the water helped steady the stretcher/raft as the others hauled it back to the safety of the bank.

Everyone felt better now that water separated them from Sang-gast. They decided to have an hour's break for some food and sleep. Kirin asked Coulan for his yo-yo. In response to the suspicious look, he explained that if he could borrow the string he could use it to fish. As usual it took Freyla to convince him. Of course she took a little convincing herself when he said he needed to borrow one of her needles. Technically she would get it back albeit a bit bent out of shape.

They continued on for the rest of the day heading toward the Forest of Teteunxx. By dusk they had put a great deal of distance between themselves and their pursuers. From what they could see they were still at the river junction. There did seem to be some figures on their side of the river but most were not. This meant they had at least a good six hours advantage over them. A few days ago they had been only too eager to escape the forest's eerie silence as they carried a stricken Talia away from it. Now they were rushing towards it, carrying the injured Dargo, seeking the safety its unnatural canopy provided from the vengeful eyes behind them.

They continued their strength sapping pace of half an

hours sleep for every four hours travelled. Kirin tried to fish during these breaks but was too tired to catch anything. Indeed it was a struggle to force himself even to eat. He was catnapping now like the others but only Dargo was managing to get enough sleep, the instant he laid his head down one of the others was shaking him awake, no time for dreams or nightmares. Everyone was feeling the pace and after Dargo had been dropped for the third time Talia gave the order to stop. It was still over four hours till dawn but they had to risk it.

Four hours sleep was like gold dust. But like gold, a little is never enough. For Kirin though it was a double edged sword bringing a renewed attack by Scarface, once more catching him incapacitated and unable to defend himself. Helpless he watched Scarface's leering face get bigger and bigger as he leaned in for the kill. Then with a jerk he was awake, breathing heavily. He looked round warily, no-one seemed to have noticed anything. He roused himself to his feet feeling just as exhausted as he had been four hours ago. The others were grunting and groaning throwing around a few half-hearted jibes but getting on with the business of breaking camp. Each of them part of the team, willing to do what was necessary, sacrifice themselves, even Dargo. What was it his father had said noble is as noble does.

By mid morning they entered the forest, its eerie presence engulfing them once more. They found the fortifications they had built just as they had left them. Once there the plan was to get a good night's sleep, secure in a place they could defend. There were however two problems with that plan. Firstly, though they reset the traps, they were designed for an attack coming from the forest not from the plain behind them. And secondly they were gambling that Sang-gast had taken most of his dwarfs with him. They had counted fourteen plus Sang-gast himself but how many more might he have left behind?

A RIDE HOME

One pair of black eyes, bright and alert, scanned the darkness, ever vigilant. Watchful for danger from the plain but also from the forest itself lest its unnatural malevolence should roll over the recumbent, helpless Company of the Quest, and bind them to it, trapping them forever. Suddenly a noise startled the bright eyes. Quickly they darted locating it's source. Then they relaxed in much the same way as the dwarf who had just snored.

No attack had come. and it was dusk when Dargo woke them. If Kirin had dreamt of Scarface he did not remember it. He had the uneasy feeling that this was not a good thing. He stretched his body which felt better than it had for days, but even this felt like a betrayal. The business of the day took over with more immediate concerns to worry over. Talia sent Kirin and Stilgoe out to scout ahead and behind them respectively while the rest set about preparing some food.

An hour later they were on the move once more. Stilgoe had counted over twenty pursuers, they had crossed the rivers and were now only a couple of hours behind them. Kirin had better news, reporting that the way ahead lay clear. Aware that they could be heading into more of Sang-gast's dwarfs, Talia gave the order to proceed. They had no choice but to head west into the forest. Eastwards was barred to them by their pursuers, and southwards by the Crumbling Mountains (the only pass they could get Dargo across was at the far end of the forest). Since Kirin best knew the way to Sang-gast's camp, he was on point about five minutes ahead of the others. Their plan was to skirt round the edge of the camp, without being seen, and head west towards the edge of the forest then make a dash for the mountains.

A few hours in they came across where they had stashed Dargo and Talia's packs. And Dargo's stash of gold. Talia was glad to get her pack and her old quarter staff which was far superior to the one she had cut to replace it. She was even OK with getting Dargo's gear back as well, even if it meant carrying the extra weight. What she was not OK with was carrying the two gold ingots. A hushed argument ensued beneath the forest canopy. In the dark, the heavy boughs of trees seemed to bear down upon them unnoticed, listening as they squabbled amongst themselves. There was a stalemate with Talia, Freyla and Stilgoe arguing against and Dargo, Bashka and Coulan arguing for. Kirin arrived back from scouting the trail ahead to find himself in the middle of it. His would be the deciding vote. Kirin didn't hesitate. He was not a dwarf, but he had come to know them and understand them a little. He didn't always agree with their ways but he respected them.

"We'll take one gold ingot. It can be carried on the stretcher. It shouldn't be too much more weight to carry. The other we stash again," he paused, looking at Dargo. "For a rainy day."

Everyone looked at each other considering the compromise. There was general nodding and agreement. No-one had won at the expense of another, but no-one had lost either.

"OK now let's get moving, we've wasted enough time.

We want to reach the smelters camp just after dark, said Kirin. He started forward on the trail again.

Talia and Stilgoe looked at each other. Stilgoe smiled and began whistling.

"And keep quiet back there," hissed a voice from up the trail.

* * * *

Kirin appeared gesturing to the others with his finger to his mouth. They put down Dargo's stretcher and hunkered round. "Sang-gast's camp is just a couple of hundred yards up ahead," whispered Kirin. "If we go left here we should be able to keep a hundred yards of forest between it and us till we're clear."

"Good," whispered Talia getting to her feet.

Kirin remained hunkered down.

"Is there something else?" she asked hunkering down again

"Well, you're not going to like this but there is an alternative..." whispered Kirin.

"We don't have time for this Sang-gast is snapping at our heels as it is," whispered Bashka.

"Exactly," said Kirin.

The alternative or cunning plan B as Kirin labelled it was fairly simple. Tied up at the jetty was a raft. It was just sitting there all ready to float effortlessly all the way to the western end of the Forest of Teteunxx. Kirin had seen three dwarfs sleeping by the jetty, snoring the night away, he had not seen any others. In the cave all was quiet, no-one was working, though there was a light on in the shack. He had not risked going near the shack only observing from the bridge. They would not even be stealing the raft, merely borrowing it leaving it at the far end of the river. The river had hardly any current, though what it did was flowing westwards. The raft was propelled by large poles that were pushed against the river bed. There were still several days of travelling through the forest to contend with. With a raft they could travel continually, sleeping in shifts, and they would be much safer on the move all the time. It's hard to sneak up on someone in the middle of a river. Everyone liked this plan.

Talia, Bashka, Stilgoe and Kirin, armed with his last two remaining bark-ties, slipped across the bridge. Coulan, Freyla and Dargo waited, watching, concealed in the trees close to the bridge where they could see both the cave and the three dwarfs by the jetty without being seen themselves. This was the most dangerous part of the plan as the others crept along the river bank towards the sleeping dwarfs.

It was not an even contest. The end result was never in doubt. But could it be done in silence? Talia, Stilgoe and Bashka positioned themselves at each of the three dwarfs. They pounced, pinning them to the ground with their bodies while clapping hands over their mouth. This was where Kirin came in. His job was simple, quickly restraining their hands with bark-ties, but this would be the first action he was involved in since Angaurd Castle and he couldn't stop thinking about what might happen if something went wrong. He secured first one, then a second. The third was more awkward as he'd had to tie his hands with some strips of willow, he'd cut and corded earlier. But all went smoothly enough and importantly with only a few muffled grunts for their troubles. He finished by binding their feet and cut strips of their shirts to gag them. Despite the cool night air he felt his back wet with sweat.

Kirin crept back to give Freyla and Coulan a hand with the stretcher. The others began untying the raft from the jetty. In the middle of the raft there was something under a tarpaulin. Bashka lifted it up. Her eyes opened wide like saucers. She motioned to Stilgoe who started to let out a long low whistle till Bashka clamped her hand over his mouth.

"Fool of a dwarf," hissed Talia. "What are you two..."

Pulling aside the corner of the tarpaulin Bashka showed

Talia.

"What should we do?" whispered Bashka.

"It's a conundrum right enough," whispered Stilgoe stroking his chin.

"She'll weigh us down we could throw it overboard?" whispered Talia.

"No!" hissed Bashka and Stilgoe together.

"The raft's obviously built to carry her," whispered Stilgoe.

"Right enough," whispered Bashka. "She's a sound enough craft."

'Well if she's sound enough..." whispered Talia stroking her chin thoughtfully.

Kirin and the others arrived at this point. The tarpaulin was carefully replaced and the stretcher and their gear was carefully stowed on the raft. Bashka took the tiller and the others all grabbed a pole and Talia cut the last remaining rope and they poled the raft out into midstream where the current took her.

Within a minute they were round the bend in the river and heading westwards. They quickly got the hang of using the poles apart from Coulan who was too enthusiastic and got his pole stuck in the mud of the river bed. They had to abandon it in the end. As they drifted away it stood up in the middle of the river, a rebuke to their enforced piracy. Everyone breathed a sigh of relief, all that is but one. They felt more at home on the raft, safe within the river's flow, and slept soundly through the night. In the morning the forest still encroached on either side but up above there was the clear blue sky of a new day.

"We could have taken the other. With the raft we could have taken it." Dargo spoke to no-one in particular. He sat upright gazing back whence they had come as he clutched the gold ingot to his chest.

Stilgoe gave a sly wink to Bashka then looked long and hard at Dargo. "What shall we do with it?"

"The weight will slow us down right enough," nodded

Bashka. "We should stash it on the bank some place."

"What?" said Dargo tightening his grip on the gold ingot. "What are you talking about?"

"No," said Talia shaking her head. "We don't have the time not with Sang-gast on our tail."

"Too right we don't," said Dargo glaring at Bashka.

"You're right," said Stilgoe. "Over the side with her then." He moved towards Dargo.

"You're crazy," said Dargo looking at the three of them. "You're not getting it."

"Wait!" said Talia. "We should pick a good spot first."

"Aye, so we can come back and reclaim it," Bashka winked at Kirin. "On a rainy day."

Stilgoe nodded sagely, stroking his chin as he contemplated Dargo. Turning to the others he said, "I think we should tell him."

"Tell me what?" said Dargo.

Talia nodded and looked at Bashka who spoke. "Dargo you see that tarpaulin beside you?"

Dargo glanced at it, "So?"

"Have a look underneath," said Bashka.

Dargo, suspiciously tucking the gold ingot by his side, pulled aside the tarpaulin revealing the large, very large, neatly piled stack of solid gold ingots.

* * * *

For the rest of that day they travelled swiftly and without incident. The river, now officially named the Golden River, had many twists and turns but its general direction was ever westward. Even taking into account its meandering they were making good progress, much faster than if they were travelling on foot. More importantly they were getting two days rest and recovery. They split themselves into shifts with at least two of them punting the raft along at any one time. Even Dargo proved useful taking his turn at the tiller whenever he could.

As for the gold, in the end they did throw it overboard, but in a good way. They spotted a giant dead oak tree by a bend in the river. They waited till they got to the next bend then found a deep spot not too far from the bank. The tarpaulin had a rope threaded through its edges, used to lash it to the raft. They turned it around using it as a giant bag for the gold. They sunk it down to the riverbed. Kirin managed to swim down and tie the bag shut, knotting it carefully. From the surface nothing could be seen. Dargo however refused to part with his single ingot. Everyone was feeling good swapping stories about what had happened to them but it was Talia, as ever, who pointed out to them that they were not out of the woods yet.

Freyla was resting, sitting on the edge of the raft. She had her boots off and was dangling her feet in the cool water. She sat propped up by her arms facing the sun now low in the sky, her eyes were closed. It was Kirin's time too for a rest period.

"Mind if I join you for a bit," said Kirin.

She put her hand up to shade her eyes from the sun. "Sure," she said.

"The water looks cool," he said.

She nodded.

He took of his boots, rolled up his trouser legs and sat beside her both of them dangling their feet in the cool waters of the Golden River.

* * * *

Bashka and Talia estimated they would get to the western edge of the forest of Teteunxx by the end of the day. In his spare time Kirin decided to finish the job of breaking the code. He wrote out a whole page of Sang-gast's book. Applying the Fibonacci arithmetic to it. With that much data, and the original structure of words, dates and amounts he soon cracked the simple substitution code. He began the tedious process of transcribing the whole book. Still wary of sleep, the nightmares had not gone away, Kirin worked in to the night, finishing the first page which was a list of names and businesses and amounts paid for them and the dates of these transactions. Presumably the rest of the book was the same. The book was a coded record of the end use of all Sang-gast's Money Laundering activities. This explained Sang-gast's eagerness to get it back. The authorities back in the Fourth kingdom would be only too keen to get a hold of this. Chances were all these names were the Shysters, the ones who had swindled the money in the first place.

The next day Kirin called Stilgoe across and filled him in on what he had discovered. Stilgoe listened intently his eyes gradually becoming as wide as saucers. A long low whistle ensued.

"You realise what this means," said Stilgoe.

"Yeah, it's a record of criminal activity," said Kirin.

"Oh it's much more than that, potentially," said Stilgoe stroking his chin.

"How so?" said Kirin.

"Well of course it depends on the rest of the book panning out," Stilgoe was not listening.

"I understand that these people can be prosecuted but..." Kirin shook his head.

"It's almost worth hanging around to see the look on his face. Losing his smelting operation, the gold and now this book." Stilgoe had a wistful look about him.

"I thought the mark wasn't supposed to realise what had actually happened," said Kirin.

"Well that's more a guideline than a rule," Stilgoe got out his pipe.

"Of course technically he believes the book to be... eh, lost," said Kirin.

"What? Even better," Stilgoe nodded to himself.

Kirin sighed. "You know my original plan was just to wander round the woods for a couple of weeks, put in an effort of course but ultimately come back empty handed. A gallant but fruitless quester."

"And how's that working out for you?" Stilgoe puffed at his pipe.

"It's been... educational," said Kirin.

Stilgoe clapped Kirin heartily on the back and Kirin could not help but smile back.

A HERO'S WELCOME

It was Bashka who caught sight of it first. The Tower, poking above the trees in the distance, the sun glinting off its metal structure. Kirin stared at it. There it was, the goal they had first sought only a few weeks ago, but so much had happened since. And here they were approaching it, floating gently on the waters of the Golden River. Perhaps it still held secrets. Perhaps Sang-gast had lied about it. Perhaps...

When the Tower was due south of them they beached the raft on the river bank, lashing it to a tree, Stilgoe and Kirin went to scout ahead while there was still daylight. They knew they were close to the edge of the forest but this was also the place where people were *made to disappear*.

The Tower was made entirely from metal and stood in the centre of a square clearing of sorts. Four legs tapered up into the air joined by metal struts criss-crossing with one another. At the top, perhaps 150 feet up, was a metal cabin. It appeared deserted. Marking the boundary of the clearing there was still the remains of what had once been a metal fence. It had long since collapsed to the ravages of time. Strangely though the forest had not encroached over this boundary. The clearing was not devoid of trees but the ones that grew there were sparse, stunted and deformed, like malnourished and diseased cousins of their neighbours.

Kirin and Stilgoe observed the Tower from the clearings edge. Kirin was curious as to what was in the cabin, but not curious enough to want to climb up the metal ladder that led all the way to the top. Besides now was not the time, he told himself. They circled round the eastern edge of it, taking care to keep hidden in the trees. As they crept forwards it wasn't long before their noses detected woodsmoke ahead. Approaching stealthily they found the dwarfs camp. There were four of them, judging from the rough wooden shelter and sleeping mats inside. Only two of them were in plain sight, making Kirin and Stilgoe nervous. Nothing much was happening so Stilgoe kept watch while Kirin reported back.

There was a brief discussion as to the relative merits of tackling the dwarfs versus sneaking by unnoticed. There was an even briefer vote and with just an hour's daylight left, they prepared for some sneaking. As darkness fell they ate a cold meal, not risking a fire, and waited. Stilgoe joined them with the good news that the other two dwarfs had turned up and all four were now fast asleep.

Sneaking involved sacrificing their speed for stealth. They gave both the Tower and the dwarfs' camp a wide berth passing a hundred yards to the east of it. The forest was, as ever, eerily quiet. Stilgoe had point while Kirin padded along their right flank. In the moonless dark he was forced to rely on his other senses, he focused with his ears. Despite their care, his companions footsteps seemed loud and careless but from the dwarf camp all was quiet.

After an half an hour Kirin reckoned they were well past the dwarfs encampment and he rejoined the others. It was then that they came upon it. A path. A well trodden path. It must have been the same path that led all the way back to Sang-gast's camp and his smelting operation. If he were chasing them, this is the path he would be using.

They all stopped, peering uselessly into the darkness. All was still. With the path only a few yards behind them, it felt to Kirin like they had breached some unseen barrier. Their enemies were all behind them now. With every step they took, it was a step further away from danger and up ahead, the way home now lay clear. Clear that is if you didn't consider the Crumbling Mountains much of an obstacle.

Within an hour they were in grassy scrub land. It was cloudy overhead but occasionally the moon shone through and they could see a path leading to the mountains. Once more dwarf etiquette dictated a short discussion over whether to risk taking the road, or stumble slowly across the rough terrain. It was dark, no-one was about and they were still carrying a stretcher, decidedly it was worth the risk. The Crumbling Mountains were their last big hurdle. If they could get across them under cover of the night then so much the better. Kirin too was glad, climbing at night meant he couldn't see how far below him the ground was.

They travelled all through the night with the same half an hour's rest in every four. The mountain path this time though, was wider, lower and not so perilous as their previous crossing. Despite his recent couple of days rest on the raft Kirin was tired. Trudging up the mountain he felt the weight of the stretcher in his legs, so much so, that the enormity of the mountain itself was almost forgotten, his only focus the unending patch of ground just a few feet in front of him. He hadn't even noticed the slope of the path levelling off till one of the others commented on it. They were nearing the top. The pass they had chosen was just below the snowline; he could feel the freshness and chill in the air now. Two white topped peaks now loomed on either side of him, like sentinels, but in between the top of the path was only a couple of hundred yards away. When they did crest the summit, Talia had them continue straight on to the descent, not wishing to expose them to any eyes that might be scanning the skyline. At their rest break a little way down the other side, Kirin slumped to the stony ground lying flat on his back, gulping in deep breaths of the thin mountain air. Most of the others were doing the same. They had a five minute break, time for some food, water and a little rest, then they were on the move again. All were conscious that Sang-gast was still on their trail and that at some point a reckoning was coming.

"Well that's that then," said Stilgoe.

Kirin gave him a wan smile.

"Come on cheer up, we're on the descent," said Stilgoe.

To Kirin's way of thinking it wasn't over till the ground was flat.

"Oh leave him be," said Freyla. "You've done really well." She patted Kirin gently on the shoulder. "We should be down in a few hours."

Kirin looked up. The sky was beginning to lighten. Going up he had been staring at the stretcher or the mountain just a few feet in front of him and all in darkness. Going down his gaze extended out over the vast panorama of the Fourth kingdom laid out before him and dawn was breaking.

"I'll be fine." He smiled at her.

Daylight soon illuminated their descent. Actually it was not as bad as Kirin had imagined. He could see the tree line now, not too far away. After all, he told himself, he had flown at over 10,000 feet, what was this mere mountain to him. He snuck a glance at the mountain behind him while he carried the stretcher. He stumbled a little. Quickly he focused on the ground in front of him.

"You OK?" said Freyla.

"Oh fine, fine," he said in his best nonchalant voice.

From far away mountains seemed such inconsequential things; a hazy blue outline on the horizon edged in white. But close to and looking straight up their enormity was beyond his comprehension. He couldn't believe he had just come down that. And carrying a stretcher! It had been steep but not that steep. It must be his eyes. Somehow they told his brain things were much more scarily high than they actually were. He'd climbed mountains, scaled sea-cliffs and scrambled down castle walls. He'd even flown thousands of feet up in the sky on a wing and a prayer and after all that he was still afraid of heights. Probably always would be. He gave a metal shrug and half-smiled to himself. But maybe, when absolutely indispensable that he do so, he could, if not master his fear then at least not let it master him.

By ten o'clock they were safely under cover of the trees and it felt safe to stop for a rest. They had a quick meal, the last of their provisions from the good landlord of the Green Man Tavern, and then slept for two hours. Dargo who had been the only one to get any decent sleep kept watch. Their luck was holding: first the raft with the gold, second sneaking by the dwarfs' camp undetected, now no pursuit over the mountain. In any event they seemed in the clear. Though as Talia was fond of saying they weren't out of the woods yet.

By midday they were once again on the flat and even Kirin was beginning to believe that the worst was over. At this point there was a parting of the ways. Stilgoe insisted he had some important business to attend to in the south. He said he would meet up with the others in Agra-nore in two days time. He asked Kirin for his notebook before he left said it might prove of interest to someone he knew. Kirin gave it to him gladly, he had finished transcribing it and if truth be told was glad to be rid of it. The remaining Company of the Quest headed west towards Agra-nore and a hero's welcome. The sun was shining out of a clear blue sky and though it felt a little sad that Stilgoe would not be with them for their return, the atmosphere among the rest was good natured and light hearted. Even Dargo was making jokes claiming his broken leg would get him all the sympathy and attention especially the female kind.

They had crossed the Crumbling Mountains much

further to the west and consequently were much closer to Agra-nore. Even allowing for their reduced pace carrying the stretcher they should reach it tomorrow by midday at the latest. Sang-gast was not forgotten but they were in familiar country now. Should he come upon them, now they would have home advantage. That night as they bedded down Kirin realised, tomorrow it would be all over. The quest for the Tral-fe-tigore would be no more. He wondered for the first time what would become of the friendships he'd made, what different paths their lives would take after tomorrow.

They were just breaking camp the next day when Bashka, who had been scouting ahead, burst in to the camp. "Solders coming from the west," she said. "Palace Guard."

"How many?" said Talia.

"Looks like a full company, forty plus officers," said Bashka.

Talia nodded, once again she had her customary serious demeanour.

"OK everyone get your stuff together. Now!"

She looked at Bashka. "How long?"

"Fifteen maybe twenty minutes," said Bashka.

They started out along the road towards the approaching troops. Kirin felt an elation inside. Here they were about to be escorted back to Agra-nore in triumph. His head was buzzing, wondering what everyone there would make of their exploits. At the beginning his objective had been to just get his education paid for, but so much had happened since then. He looked at Talia acting like it was just another ordinary day. He should follow Talia's lead, not let himself get carried away. After all he still had secrets to keep. She'd have them march in on their own two feet. A band of Certified Accounting Dwarfs. The Company of the Quest would end, just as it had begun.

The Palace Guard were in sight now, marching towards

them all shiny and bright in their bright red uniforms with two sets of brass buttons stretching up from the waist to the shoulders, one half of which weren't even real, just for show. They halted ten yards in front of them on the road. Talia gave the signal to stop and Kirin and the others put down Dargo's stretcher. The captain of the guard advanced, his uniform like the rest but adorned by gold braid stitched across his shoulders, and took from his tunic a document which he unfolded and glanced at. He seemed uncomfortable as if unsure how to proceed. He saluted Talia who nodded in return.

"Am I addressing Talia Grimthold, leader of the Company of the Quest for the Tral-fe-tigore?" he said.

There was a little suppressed laughter, some of which came from Kirin.

Talia ignoring the sound behind her nodded and gave a slight bow.

The captain stood to attention and continued. "By the authority of Queen Zehalani I am placing you and the members of the Company of the Quest under arrest for crimes against the Fourth Kingdom."

* * * *

All in all as dungeons go this one had a great deal going for it. For one thing Kirin wasn't chained to the wall, indeed he wasn't even wearing manacles. Compared to Sang-gast's dark, dank, health hazard of a dungeon with its serious condensation problem, this was positively luxurious. It had beds, was relatively clean, even had fresh air, indeed if anything it was perhaps a trifle draughty. But that was only because it had a window. Of course you had to grip the bars and haul yourself off the floor to see out of it, and even then all you could see were the feet of Palace Guards in a courtyard, but a view is a view. Best of all though (apart from not being tortured) Kirin was not alone. He shared the prison cell with Dargo and Coulan. Next door to them were Talia, Bashka and Freyla. All in all apart from being detained against their will and facing some quite serious criminal charges, it wasn't that bad.

Talia had said, just to confirm your name and that you're a member of the Company of the Quest for the Tral-fe-tigore. Apart from that all she would say was, wait for the legaliser. She'd sent word for someone she knew, a dwarf who specialised in such matters. Kirin had his doubts that anyone had ever come across such a matter before, much less specialised in it. It was a very serious situation. He had been in shock thinking there must have been some mix-up, some misunderstanding all the way back to Agra-nore. He figured it would all get cleared up once they got there. Stilgoe would arrive, if he was not there already, and explain everything. Of course when they had arrived it was not Stilgoe who was there to greet them, but Derrott.

He had that same non-smile on his face that Kirin had remembered from Helsinagar. His voice that same oily quality that made you trust him about as far as you could throw him. The only consolation for Kirin was seeing that look of disappointment on his face when he counted only six and not seven of them.

But how had he got there ahead of them? What power did he have over the court of Queen Zehalani that allowed him to stand there ordering about the captain of the Palace Guard? And then there were the charges. They still did not know what they were but Kirin could imagine. Though he could hardly charge them with stealing an already forged Property Certificate. Of course they had burned down his castle...

The days passed slowly. It was a trial in itself to fill the hours. Kirin paced the jail cell till it drove the others mad and he was forced to stop. He then practised the techniques his father had taught him. This proved less annoying for Coulan and Dargo, who were eager to learn. Dargo of course was unable to practice them but Coulan proved a willing pupil. What he lacked in dexterity he made up for in determination. Despite his repeated failures and Dargo's verbal battering, slowly but surely, Coulan began to learn. In a way it was harder for him not to use his strength, which must have been so tempting. It was only a few basic techniques that Kirin taught and Coulan had by no means mastered them, but one thing Coulan was very good at, was practising.

That may have been the tedium of his days but his nights were still dominated by his nightmares or at least the fear of having them. Some nights the nightmares were just as fresh and vivid as that first time, others less so and sometimes he awoke unaware of having dreamed at all. Maybe in time they would fade but they felt a part of him now, like his fear of heights, just something else he would have to deal with. His father had always taught him to master his fear not let it give way to anger, not to make it personal. But one thing his father hadn't been able to teach him was what it was like to be fighting for your life, for your friends lives.

They had one hours communal exercise each day at midday. They all looked forward to this, even Dargo who had been given crutches and hobbled out to the heavily guarded courtyard. The very first time Kirin had sidled up to Talia and asked about escape.

"Escape?" said Talia, "Escape to where? The Fourth Kingdom is our home. Would you have us become outlaws?"

"No! Of course not, but..." said Kirin.

"But what? Run off back to the Plain of Angaurd? Let Derrott win?" said Talia.

Kirin said nothing his mouth set firm.

"Listen, just bide your time. Remember we still have an ace up our sleeves." Talia tapped the side of her nose.

Kirin nodded. She meant Stilgoe of course. As long as he was still free he would work tirelessly to help them. But what could he do? One dwarf against, well, everyone. Leaving their defence to wiser more experienced heads was difficult, but these midday meetings helped. The long hours of tedium in his cell made bearable by that single hour each day even though it sped past so fast. They fell into a pattern. Kirin, Freyla and Coulan would walk together pacing round the courtyard. Freyla in the middle linking arms with the other two. Dargo hobbled round on his crutches at his own pace for a bit, but mostly just sat enjoying the warm sun on his face. This left Talia and Bashka strolling arm in arm some way ahead of them. Once Kirin suggested they all walk together but Freyla shook her head and said this way was better.

For the most part Coulan seemed content just to listen as Kirin and Freyla talked. They told each other more about their past and, assuming they ever got out of this mess, their plans for the future. Freyla joked that she would one day even build her own Rogallo wing, she had that far-away look in her eyes as she spoke and despite her laughter Kirin suspected she might actually be serious about it. Later she told him that she too wished to go to university, her dream to study engineering. Kirin wondered if this might mean something more and sneaked a glance across but as ever Freyla had that same enigmatic smile which he just couldn't read at all. He wanted to speak to her about other things, more personal things, but it felt awkward within the confines of their present situation or so he told himself.

It was four days before Tartattle arrived. She was Talia's legaliser friend. A small dwarf with spectacles and halo of fluffy black hair. Till then there was nothing to do except speculate. The others had pumped the guards for all the information they could get, which was precious little. The one piece of information they had found out was that Derrott was the duly designated magistrate of all the land north of the Crumbling Mountains to the Big Water. A fact that was greeted by the dwarfs with despair. Kirin insisted that it shouldn't make any difference. Dargo called him a naïve fool and even Coulan looked at Kirin and shook his head.

Within an hour of Tartattle arriving they were on the move. A preliminary hearing, according to her, to see if there was a case to answer. They were all brought out and handcuffed and proceeded single file to the court (apart from Dargo who was carried on a stretcher by two Place Guards). The high court in Agra-nore was a separate, square box of a building next to the palace itself, its plain brick walls contrasted sharply with the ornate stonework of the palace. It was presided over by the chief magistrate of the Fourth Kingdom herself, the right honourable Judge J. K. Crabtree. As they exited the palace the noise hit them like an ocean wave, only drier. Two lines of guards lined the way to the courthouse. Either side crowds of people thronged trying to get a glimpse of them. Kirin was unsure if they were cheering or jeering. He was tempted to wave, but it felt wrong somehow in handcuffs.

Inside the main part of the courthouse was a single large room. The walls were covered in dark wooden panelling, light streamed in from windows, too high to see out of, and a series of murky skylights in the roof above them. They were shuffled down an aisle, past a series of long pews on either side of them for the public, till they got to a wooden balustrade. This separated the public gallery from the official part of the court, they trooped through a swing gate in it and sat along another pew. At the far wall, facing them and dominating the room was a kind of a pulpit, for the judge. Beneath that was a small desk where the clerk of the court sat and next to him the court stenographer, who basically wrote down everything that was said and done in the court. To their left was the witness box, basically a chair walled in on three sides by wooden panels that came up to waist height. To the right of the pulpit stood a very fierce looking man with his arms folded. This was the court bailiff. The courtroom was completed by two sets desks and chairs for the prosecution and defence which were directly in front of where Kirin and the others sat.

They had no sooner sat down when the judge arrived and they had to stand up till she sat down, apart from Dargo (on account of his leg), who seemed to find this all very amusing. The judge was wearing dark red robes and seemed to conduct the whole affair by a series of nods to the concerned parties accompanied by banging a small wooden hammer. There were a lot of preliminaries and protocols between the judge, their defence attorney Tartattle Thicket, and the prosecuting attorney, a man called Mr Walker. He was a tall thin man with a bald head and sunken in cheeks. Both attorneys and indeed all the court officials were wearing black robes. Over the course of proceedings Kirin learned that the judge was called m'lord (even though she was a lady) and that the pulpit, where she sat, was called the bench, whereas the attorneys were referred to as m'learned council, or by their surnames. At one point they, the accused or the defendants (depending on who was talking about them) were each asked to stand, confirm their name and sit down again. Then there was the interesting bit. A small, flustered looking man wearing spectacles, who was the clerk of the court, at a nod from the judge stood up and spoke.

"The aforementioned accused also known as the Company of the Quest for the Tral-fe-tigore are hereby charged with the following:

1. Breaking into a safe belonging to a one Derrott Lankane;

2. Non payment of property land levies due for the property known as the Plain of Angaurd;

3. Non payment of fine, for the non payment of property land levies for the property known as the Plain of Angaurd;

4. Non payment of interest on aforementioned levies and fines;

5. Assault and battery of duly appointed officers of the court in the performance of their duties on the docks of Helsinagar;

281

6. Breaking and entering into the vault on Bank Island belonging to one Derrott Lankane;

7. A second count of assault and battery of duly appointed officers of the court in the performance of their duties on Bank island;

8. A third count of assault and battery of duly appointed officers of the court in the performance of their duties at Angaurd Castle;

9. Arson at the aforementioned Angaurd Castle."

Kirin bristled as the charges were read out. What annoyed him most was that they had traded the payment of levies, fines and interest in exchange for the tracker device. They had shaken on it before witnesses. What was the world coming to if people just reneged on deals? That they had *reacquired* the tracker device, unknown to Derrott, was neither here nor there. Besides a deal was a deal. But then it struck him, there was no mention of Sang-gast. No mention of his smelting operation. No mention of the gold. While Kirin was pondering all this Tartattle was having a whispered consult with Talia.

"How do you plead," said the judge.

Tartattle looked up at the judge, "My clients do not wish to enter a plea at this time," she said.

Kirin looked a across at Talia mouthing the words, 'we don't?'

"Clerk of the court, record that the accused made no plea at this time." The judge eyed them all rather suspiciously. "Mr Tartattle, do you have anything to say concerning the charges laid against your clients?"

Tartattle shook her head. "Not at this time m'lord."

The judge then nodded to Mr Walker, who stood up, gave a little bow of his head towards the judge, then slowly shook his head and sat down again. The judge banged the small wooden hammer she had on the bench. "I find there is a case to answer in the matter of the Company of the Quest versus the state. Trial to start one week from today." With that she banged her little hammer again and with barely a nod they were all ushered out of their pew, and back to their jail cells. As they trooped out of the courthouse Kirin was looking over his shoulder trying to catch Talia's attention, who was whispering something to Tartattle. Turning round he suddenly, for a moment, found himself inches away from the sympathetic smiling face of Sang-gast.

TRIAL AND RETRIBUTION

Kirin was just getting used to the casual routine of life in his jail cell when the day of the trial arrived, and it all became real again. They all trooped into the courthouse once more but this time there were many more formalities and procedures to be gone through, the reason for which was beyond Kirin's understanding, and which lasted the entire day. He sat between Freyla and Talia to whom he occasionally whispered some query but they were as much in the dark about it all as he was. One thing he did learn to his cost was that the judge was very keen of hearing and had, on more than one occasion, shouted at him to be quiet.

On the second day of the trial the case for the prosecution began. Kirin found himself clenching his fists as Derrott and the others took to the stand to give evidence. What was so frustrating was that Derrott would take some small thing that was true, twist it together with lies and half truths and then wrap it all up in web of plausibility. This he would then present to the court, emphasising that tiny kernel of truth, as if somehow by association it made all the rest of it true. And to make matters worse their legaliser Tartattle said practically nothing. All she would say was, no questions at this time m'lord. With every witness it was the same thing. No questions at this time m'lord. And then she just sat down. She didn't even make any notes, so far as Kirin could see, on the pad of paper in front of her. This continued day after day till Kirin became resigned to it.

His previous trip to Agra-nore had been a such a whirlwind of confusion and choices that there had been no time to appreciate the splendour of Queen Zehalani's court. But now he found his attention drawn towards the public galleries and the good citizenry of the Fourth Kingdom. The otherwise drab courtroom was awash with colour, with flashy golden embroidery sitting alongside simple brown homespun, as crowds of people jammed into it every day, keen to get a good seat. Regardless of rank everyone seemed to regard the trial as a great spectacle, but not for the reasons Kirin at first supposed. Overheard mumbles of conversation about which of the witnesses were the better dressed or whether the judge was in a good or bad mood came in equal measure from both lords and ladies and the common folk (to guess from their simple attire). People were arguing as to which of the defendants were their favourites, Dargo (who was playing up to the galleries) was getting the sympathy vote and there were even wagers being made as to the outcome of the trial.

After four days of falsehoods, forgeries and fabrications the prosecution rested. Finally it was the turn of the defence. That day began just like all the proceeding days. They trooped into the courthouse. They took their seats. They stood up. The judge came in. The judge sat down. They sat down. The judge banged her little hammer. Silence ensued and, with a nod from the judge to Tartattle, the proceedings got under way. Then everything changed.

At the back of the court there were murmurs and people began to talk openly, careless of the judge's wrath. She brought her hammer to bear and shouted for silence.

Her attention now focused on a man in a blue uniform and a peaked hat walking down the aisle escorting a handcuffed dwarf wearing a dishevelled, green hooded jerkin. They halted by the little gate in the wooden balustrade. The clerk of the court fluttered across, from his desk beneath the bench, and engaged the man in whispered conversation. With an alarmed look upon his face and his robes flapping around him, the clerk of the court scurried back to the judge and whispered in her ear.

"What!" said the judge venting her full wrath on the hapless clerk.

"Technically he is within his rights," said the clerk.

The judge now glared at the dwarf who had entered her courtroom, much to the clerks relief.

The courtroom was alive with murmuring.

She banged her hammer. "Silence in court!"

For what seemed an eternity but could only have been seconds, she glared at the hooded dwarf.

"It is a fool of a legaliser that has himself for a client," she said.

"You are most probably correct m'lord," said the dwarf bowing slightly.

The judge nodded and the man in the blue uniform unlocked the dwarf's handcuffs. As he sat down beside Tartattle, the dwarf lowered his hood, twisted round and gave the defendants a huge wink. It was Stilgoe.

"Let the record read that Stilgoe Lee, member of the Company of the Quest and one of the accused is duly appointed co-counsel for the defence," said the judge and banged her hammer down hard.

* * * *

...

"I make reference to the, so called, arrest warrant presented by the prosecution," said Stilgoe

"Objection m'lord. Council for the defence is questioning the integrity of this court," said Mr Walker.

"Sustained. Do not make a mockery of this institution

sir." The judge addressed Stilgoe.

"With respect m'lord. This arrest warrant only makes mention of nine charges against the defendants—"

"Well I'm sure I could have come up with more if I had put my mind to it," said Derrott. He was sitting in the witness box, leaning back on the chair, he opened his hands in a futile gesture, looking up towards the judge. The public gallery responded to Derrott's comments with a wave of laughter.

The judge banged her hammer. "Silence in court."

"Mr Lankane!" The judge addressed Derrott by his surname. "This is no laughing matter. Please restrict yourself to answering questions asked." Derrott nodded deferentially to the judge.

Stilgoe then started going into detail about how the arrest warrant contained no mention of destroyed smelting equipment, assault on dwarfs or stolen gold. The counsel for the prosecution, Mr Walker, objected and Kirin could not help but agree with him. Even the judge warned Stilgoe to stick to the charges detailed on the arrest warrant.

"Indeed m'lord," said Stilgoe. "Mr Lankane can you confirm that there are nine charges on the arrest warrant. Nine charges only?"

Derrott gave his most condescending smile. "Yes I'm sure. There is no mistake"

"What's he doing?" whispered Kirin. "Isn't he supposed to be on our side?"

Freyla shrugged, "He knows his stuff, just wait."

Kirin was not so confident. Surely it would be best to concentrate on getting the existing charges dismissed. Why even mention new ones? Kirin had the horrible feeling that someone would stand up and agree with Stilgoe that there should be twelve charges against them instead of nine. If that happened they may as well throw away the key.

Stilgoe then took a different line of questioning, accusing Derrott of doing a deal with the defendants, trading a tracking device against any outstanding property levies, fines and interest owed by the defendants. Stilgoe then produced the tracking device and entered it into evidence as exhibit A. He even switched it on briefly, allowing a few beeps, which was greeted by a gasp of awe from the public gallery and then by a round of applause. The judge too appeared impressed momentarily before she banged her hammer for silence once more. During this Kirin had kept his eyes in Derrott, observing his reaction. Derrott denied that there had been any deal, denied that he knew what the device was, denied that he had wanted it, but the condescending smile was now gone.

This is more like it thought Kirin, Derrott hadn't expected that. He looked at Freyla whose eyes were glued to Derrott. Yes, he thought, this was definitely better. Why Stilgoe had bothered talking about those extra three charges, Kirin had no idea, but now he was on the right track. Derrott had done a deal with them. He should admit it and that would be at least three of the charges gone, dismissed or whatever they called it.

Stilgoe grabbed the tracking device and strode across the courtroom to the witness box. He slammed one hand down hard on the banister and brandished the device only inches away from Derrott. "I put it to you that a deal *was* done between yourself and the defendants! You wanted this device! Didn't you!"

"Objection m'lord. Council is badgering the witness. The witness has already answered the question," said Mr Walker.

"There was no such deal," said Derrott looking straight at Stilgoe.

Stilgoe seemed to falter, like the wind was taken out of his sails. He turned to the judge. "I must remind the witness that he is under oath." Stilgoe's words felt more like a plea for help.

"Council for the defence," said the judge. "the witness has answered your question. Please move on."

Stilgoe returned to his seat and began a mumbled discussion with Tartattle which involved a degree of searching through the various papers on their desk. There seemed to be a muted disagreement between the two after which Stilgoe angrily strode back to the witness box, clutching the charge sheet, with a stern look upon his face.

"If as you say there was no deal between you and the defendants then pray tell the court what caused the assault on the officers of the court on Helsinagar docks, eh..." Stilgoe looked down at the piece of paper in his hand. "Charge five on the arrest warrant. I put it to you that it was as a result of a broken deal that the subsequent fight on the dock—"

"Quite correct," said Derrott.

There was another outburst of noise from the public galleries. After it subsided Judge Crabtree addressed Derrott directly. "Let me remind you Mr Lankane that I will not stand for contempt of this court by anyone. Now in your previous testimony you said there was no deal."

"M'lord if I may elucidate? I'm sure it will satisfy the court."

Derrott gave a slight deferential bow of his head to the judge, who after a narrow-eyed stare, nodded.

"If it please the court there was a deal." Derrott paused making sure he had everyone's attention. "And that deal was between the accused and parties representing myself. But that deal was for a simple boat hire for an agreed sum of eight gold pieces. The accused only paid four, the source of the dispute which given their violent natures escalated into the assault as stipulated in charge five."

Kirin sat there fuming. He felt like standing up and shouting liar. How could this be allowed. He looked around the courtroom. Could no-one see that Derrott was lying through that fake smile of his? Freyla placed a hand on Kirin's arm. Her eyes seemed to say be patient. He took a deep breath, closed his eyes and recited his father's mantra in his head.

Stilgoe seemed lost for words. Since to some extent what Derrott had said was true. He returned to consult with Tartattle, still clutching the charge sheet in his hand. Stilgoe leaned on the banister of the public gallery as he addressed his question to Derrott. "Eh. You say there was no mistake on the arrest warrant," Stilgoe paused. "Tell me Mr Lankane I imagine in your role as magistrate you deal with a great many arrest warrants. How can you be *so sure* that there was no mistake with this one?" Stilgoe turned to face the public gallery, with his back to Derrott, as he waited for an answer.

"Objection the witness doesn't have to answer that question," said Mr Walker getting out of his seat.

"Oh that's all right," said Derrott looking directly at Stilgoe's slumped shoulders. "I think you'll find the paperwork is perfectly in order. I should know, I wrote out the charges myself." He looked round the courtroom milking the ripple of laughter that followed.

Stilgoe returned to his seat without looking at Derrott. He sat down and directed his attention to the judge. "No more questions for this witness at this time m'lord, but defence requests the right to recall the witness at a later date."

The judge instructed Derrott to step down from the witness box but reminded him that he was not yet excused from the court. There then followed a very dull and boring part of the case where Stilgoe called first Cantana and then Ryszard to the stand. They were asked the same questions about the same deal and the tracker device. Just like Derrott they denied everything. They had been very well schooled, even using the exact same language to describe the events, 'I have no recollection of the aforementioned deal', which raised some laughter in the court, when Stilgoe pointed it out.

"I'd like to call my next witness Mr Sporakas, m'lord. Also at this time I wish to introduce exhibit B, the original pink form of the Property Certificate for the Plain of

290

Angaurd for which the levies in the second charge relate to," said Stilgoe.

There was a great deal of murmuring in the court at this announcement, as no-one had any idea of who this Mr Sporakas was. It took a deal of banging from the judges hammer to restore order once more. Mr Sporakas, who it turned out was senior clerk at the land registry office, testified to the veracity of the pink document (meaning that it was the original and not a forgery). This document (the pink form) was always retained by the state he informed the court, the owner being issued with a copy of it, the white form. He then read into the court record article seventeen, clause three which made mention of the levies *not* applying to permanent residents.

Stilgoe then called the Chancellor of the University of Shang-nam as a witness. There was a gasp of awe from the packed courtroom as his imposing figure strode down the aisle. Kirin watched as the Chancellor's black gown billowed out behind him like a sail and those darting blue eyes took in all the chief players in the court, as he approached the witness stand. He and the judge exchanged a barely perceptible nod. Perhaps the prosecutor felt intimidated or perhaps he was just stunned like everyone else in court. In any event he neglected to object.

Stilgoe also introduced exhibit C, the forged white copy of the Property Certificate that he had *acquired* from Derrott. The prosecuting council had recovered sufficiently to object to this. The judge allowed it on the grounds that it be entered as a forged document with no proven provenance i.e. it was not the proven private property of Derrott. Though, at this point, the judge warned Stilgoe of the dangers of making a mockery of her courtroom. Stilgoe got the Chancellor to read out article seventeen, clause three of the forged document which said that levies *did* apply to permanent residents, into the court record. Another gasp of awe from the courtroom. A now nervous Derrott watched proceedings from his seat. Kirin wasn't sure if Stilgoe knew his stuff or not, but he was up to something.

"Objection m'lord. Relevance of this document?" said Mr Walker.

"Sustained. Council for the defence will come to the point here. I will not have you waste both the courts and the Chancellors valuable time on a document whose provenance is unknown," said the judge.

"Yes m'lord. A couple more questions and I believe it shall become clear to the court," said Stilgoe. The judge nodded and Stilgoe continued. "Chancellor, you are, among other things, the foremost authority on handwriting in the Fourth Kingdom?"

"Yes," said the Chancellor.

"You have had a chance to compare exhibit C, the forged copy of the Property Certificate and the arrest warrant, with the nine charges on it. Were they written by the same hand?"

The courtroom filled with noise as everyone seemed to talk at once. It took repeated hammering by the judge to restore order once more. "I will have quiet in this courtroom or I will have it cleared. The judge glared at the public galleries which had a more sustained effect than her hammer.

"Objection m'lord," said Mr Walker.

"Mr Walker are you objecting to my having silence in my own courtroom?"

"Eh. No, m'lord. To the last question m'lord."

"On what grounds?" said the judge.

"Eh..." Mr Walker looked angrily at Derrott who was looking straight ahead at the Chancellor.

"Overruled!" The judge looked down at the Chancellor. "You may answer the question Chancellor."

"Yes. There is no doubt. Both documents were written by the same person," said the Chancellor.

The court room erupted into another racket of chatter once more.

"No more questions for this witness," Stilgoe tried to say over the din in the courtroom.

In the ensuing uproar Derrott tried to sneak out the courtroom but the judge in the midst of her hammering spotted this and gave a nod to the two officers of the court by the door who escorted Derrott back to his seat.

When things calmed down Stilgoe repeated his question for the record

"So just to be clear the person who wrote the arrest warrant against the defendants, also forged this Property Certificate for Plain of Angaurd," said Stilgoe.

"Yes," said the Chancellor.

"Your witness," Mr Walker.

Mr Walker had no further questions for the Chancellor who was excused and took up a seat in the public gallery. During this pause in proceedings Mr Walker franticly leafed through the pages of a large book till he found what he was looking for. He got to his feet still holding open the book. He then proceeded to argue what he called a 'point of law' stating that this forged documents existence was not necessarily proof of any wrongdoing on Derrott's part. Since there was no proof that it had actually been used. He also added the inescapable fact that Derrott was not on trial, the accused were. When the judge then agreed with Mr Walker, the courtroom let out a collective audible gasp. Kirin stared hard at the judge who in turn was staring hard at Derrott. She did not appear very happy with Derrott, not happy at all, but as she herself said, the law is the law.

Stilgoe slowly got to his feet once more and addressed the judge. "M'lord, m'learned council for the prosecution makes a good point, according to the letter of the law. But there is also the spirit of the law, which, as m'lord is well aware of," Stilgoe gave a slight bow towards the judge. "holds equal sway over the deliberations of this court. Our courts are here to dispense justice. But on rare occasions our courts are also called upon to see to it, that right is done. This I believe, is such an occasion. Now since m'learned council has already brought up the matter of wrongdoing. Asserting there is no proof. I would like to present evidence to the contrary. Proof that Mr Lankane did not only forge this document, but used it fraudulently and therefore charges against the defendants relating to this fraudulently used forged document are non-founded," said Stilgoe.

The courtroom erupted once more. This time the judge did not use her hammer to quieten the court. Though her stillness, as she stared at Stilgoe, had the same effect, and once again the court fell silent, all eyes now on the judge.

"Objection m'lord. Whatever the conduct of Mr Lankane. It is not he who is on trial here, it is the accused," said Mr Walker.

"On the contrary m'lord it is the wrongdoing of Mr Lankane and the subsequent chain of events that followed from it that have led to the defendants being in this courtroom today," said Stilgoe.

The judge sat still, deep in thought. The courtroom too held its collective breath, waiting. "Mr Walker you did bring up the matter of proof of Mr Lankane's wrongdoing. In the interests of justice and of right being done, I will allow the defence some latitude in this matter. Objection overruled." Cheers rang out throughout the courtroom. It took a great deal of hammering and threatened ejections from court before order was restored.

Kirin thought he could detect the tension ease from Stilgoe's shoulders as he casually introduced exhibit D. A sworn affidavit by a Mr Albert Shivers of the Green Man Tavern in Helsinagar. It testified that Derrott has been levying the residents of Helsinagar for some years now. Mr Walker objected, claiming a single affidavit was hardly proof, his objection was quickly followed by Stilgoe introducing exhibits E, F, G and H, more affidavits from the good townspeople of Helsinagar. This in turn was then followed by much laughter from the public gallery, till the judge silenced it. Once again Mr Walker objected, claiming that these documents too could be forgeries, though Kirin felt his heart was no longer in it.

Stilgoe got to his feet. "If the court pleases," Stilgoe turned to the prosecutor and bowed, "And at m'learned council's insistence. Mr Shivers is in court today and is prepared to testify if required." A stunned Kirin, along with the rest of the court turned to see a slightly embarrassed looking Mr Albert Shivers stand up at the back of the courtroom.

"Objection!" said Mr Walker, getting up on to his feet.

"Mr. Walker are you objecting to your own objection?" said the judge.

At this point The prosecuting council sat down and put his head in his hands. When his objection was overruled he looked across angrily at Derrott. There then followed a slight delay while the prosecutor and the judge examined the affidavits. During this Derrott got up and tried to excuse himself to go to the bathroom. The judge was not inclined to acquiesce to this exit strategy.

"Mr Walker. Have you anything to say regarding these affidavits?" said the judge.

"No, m'lord," said Mr Walker shaking his head. "I have nothing further to add at this time."

"Very well there will be a short recess while I consult with counsel. Bailiff! No-one is to leave the court without my permission." The judge nodded to Stilgoe, Tartattle and Mr Walker, who followed her through the door beside the bench to her chambers. After they left the clerk of the court sat down, for a moment a little uncertainly, before jumping up and rushing after the others.

In the absence of the judge and her hammer the courtroom buzzed with the general hum of murmuring. No-one quite dared to raise their voice and risk the wrath of the absent judge, even Kirin and the others found themselves talking in whispers. None of them were sure exactly what was happening but the look on Derrott's face told them he was not pleased with proceedings.

Suddenly there was a commotion when the clerk of the court came hurrying out of the judge's chambers. He approached the man in the dark blue uniform with the peaked cap (who had delivered Stilgoe to the court) and who had been sitting at the back of the court all this time. The crowd were quiet for a moment watching, listening to their hushed conversation. Then the two of them made their way to the judge's chambers, the clerk's birdlike gait struggling to keep pace with the tall man's long stride. Once they had left the courtroom the murmuring began once more.

This unexpected pause in proceedings left Kirin's head buzzing with questions. Did this mean Derrott was guilty of lying or did it depend on some 'point of law'? What could the Judge and Stilgoe possibly be talking about that would take so long? And who was that man in the blue uniform? He looked at the others. Talia as ever seemed detached and thoughtful with Bashka by her side. Dargo from his position slightly away from the rest of them was chatting with a female dwarf in the public gallery behind him, like he was just in some tavern or other and as for Coulan he was playing with his yo-yo! Freyla had a cool look of curiosity about her as if she found the whole proceedings intriguing.

She laid her hand on his shoulder. "It'll be all right," she said "You do have to admit Stilgoe knows his stuff." She smiled.

Kirin smiled back but inside his stomach was churning. He was about to say something when the door opened and the tall man in blue came out. There was a collective deflation in the court as he walked straight through the court and out the door. The waiting continued.

"Who is that guy?" whispered Kirin.

Freyla shrugged.

"He's the constable," hissed Talia.

"Oh," said Kirin none the wiser. He was going to ask what a constable was but Talia was already engaged in a whispered conversation with Bashka.

"What is taking so long?" whispered Kirin.

"Oh legal stuff," sighed Freyla. "They have their way of doing things. Their protocol. Everything by the numbers, as you would say."

This was nothing like *anything* in his world. It reminded him of that day at the palace of Queen Zehalani. This was a world beyond his ken. A small crease formed between his brows. How come Freyla seemed so at ease. Had she had dealings with the law before? He recalled what she had told him of her early life travelling from village to village. It must have been a tough life. Her face was calm and sanguine with just the faint trace of a smile. He smiled back at her.

Eventually the judge and the others returned. Everyone stood up, the judge sat down, everyone else sat down, the judge banged her hammer for silence, but in between Stilgoe had given them all a wink. Though the murmuring had stopped the judge banged her hammer twice more for good measure. The court fell deathly silent.

"In the case of the state versus the Company of the Quest I find the integrity of the state's case sufficiently compromised to warrant dismissal of all charges," she said. "The defendants are free to leave."

The courtroom erupted with cheering. People were even throwing hats into the air. Kirin sat open mouthed staring at the judge, even when Freyla hugged him. He thought he detected a faint smile on the judge's lips as she seemed to look right back at him. In any event it seemed to Kirin that she allowed the court its moment of noisy celebration before she brought the court to order with a great deal of judicious hammering. She then continued.

"However this case has brought to light certain other matters and pertaining to these I am convinced that there is sufficient evidence to warrant the arrest of Derrott Lankane and other associated individuals." With that she nodded the man in blue at the back of the court. "Court dismissed," she said and with that she banged her hammer one more time and got up and left.

Pandemonium broke out as more blue suited constables flooded into the court and arrested Derrott and all his so called officers of the court. Kirin watched in dismay at one point as Sang-gast took advantage of all the mayhem to make his way through the crowd to the door. But just as he was about to sneak out a long blue arm clapped a handcuff round his wrist, Kirin saw his snarling face as he twisted around then the constable bundled him away.

ALWAYS READ THE SMALL PRINT

The next few days were a bit of a blur for Kirin. Things were moving at a fast pace and Kirin always seemed to be the last to learn what was happening. Even after they had been released from their handcuffs Kirin suspected that they were still not yet out of the woods. There had been so many charges against them and he was pretty sure they had done some of them, so when they were marched back to their jail cells this did little to dissuade him of his suspicions. However this was only to collect their stuff, after which they were escorted to more luxurious palace accommodations and from there to a celebratory buffet in the very same banqueting hall where it had all began, a few weeks and a lifetime ago. All of them that is except Stilgoe. Talia explained that he was helping the constables with their enquiries. Kirin didn't like the sound of that but Talia assured him it was a good thing.

For two days they stayed in the palace, honoured guests, the Palace Guard assured him. But still, to Kirin's way of thinking, prisoners in a gilded cage. There was lots of coming and going by Palace officials but Kirin and the rest spent most of their time in the Banqueting hall. The others did not seem to mind, especially Dargo and Coulan, who were making full use of the free buffet. Dribs and drabs of information however did trickle through to them but Kirin was more preoccupied with another matter and had been trying to contrive a chance meeting between him and Freyla. Eventually he did catch up with her alone in the corridor, where she stopped, leaning back against the wall. He stood directly in front of her.

"Eh, there's something I wanted to talk to you about."

Freyla waited.

"Eh, it was just that, eh I mean, we're friends right?"

Freyla tilted her head in consideration before replying. "Yes. We're friends. We've been through a lot together," she acknowledged with a serious look.

Kirin frowned.

"Eh you know I'm fifteen in a couple of weeks?"

"Uh huh." Freyla smiled and brushed the hair from his forehead. The touch of her hand dissolved all the carefully worked out and rehearsed words in his head.

"Eh... Back in Angaurd Castle. I know we were fooling Sang-gast n'all but..."

Freyla placed her finger against his lips and whispered for him to shush. Then she leant in closer placing her hands on his shoulders, bringing her mouth slowly up to his. He did the same till their lips gently brushed then his body took over, remembering that first time, and he fell into her feeling that surge of excitement spread throughout his body, but this time there was just the two of them.

As he drew back he looked into that perfectly calm face with its enigmatic smile. "Does this mean..."

Freyla laughed. "How old do you think I am anyway?" With that she grabbed his hand and ran back along the corridor with him.

Back in the banqueting call there was at last official news of what was happening. Firstly there was confirmation that both Sang-gast and Derrott had been arrested. It seemed that Cantana and Ryszard, his lieutenants, had turned state's evidence and were testifying against Derrott in return for a reduced sentence. In addition Derrott's assets had been seized by the state including the Plain of Angaurd and Angaurd castle itself. There was even talk of the townspeople of Helsinagar being reimbursed from their illegal taxation from the sale of these assets. Kirin wondered idly if the authorities knew about that large pile of gold that had been in the castle. Secondly and more importantly they, the Company of the Quest, had definitely been cleared of all charges. Cantana, and Ryszard had confirmed the deal they had made (trading the tracker device for the levies) and the lack of evidence put paid to any of the other charges being brought. This was welcomed in particular by Kirin who did feel responsible for burning down the castle. The reason for their being kept in the palace was that a grand reception that was being planned in their honour. Kirin was still a little dubious since the quest for the Tral-fe-tigore hadn't really ended the Kingdom's economic woes and he was not at all comfortable with all the interest their dramatic return had generated. A simple thank you and by the way, consider your fees paid to Shang-nam University, would have done for Kirin. The others though, even Freyla, seemed to revel in all the attention.

It was still a mystery to Kirin and the others what Sang-gast had been arrested for. The others thought it must be to do with his Money Laundering activities. Kirin thought it might have to do with the little black book but then again Sang-gast's name was not mentioned in the book. There was nothing to tie him to the businesses it mentioned. Kirin had the uneasy feeling that this particular dodgy dwarf would weasel his way out of it all somehow.

The evening of the grand reception was upon them and still there was no Stilgoe. No-one seemed to know where he was. All their enquiries were met with shrugs, shakes of heads and blank stares. They were having a quick bite to eat, taking the edge of their hunger, before going to the grand reception in the throne room when the door opened, and in walked a very tired looking Stilgoe.

"How about a tankard of milk for a thirsty dwarf!" said Stilgoe.

The large banqueting hall had only seven small figures in it but it can rarely have seen such an eruption of rejoicing as Stilgoe received a hero's welcome. Even Dargo was hopping around on one crutch attempting some sort of jig with Stilgoe as he tried to make his way to his requested refreshment. Everyone was asking questions at the same time. Poor Stilgoe, clearly exhausted, was being clapped on the back and hugged so much it took him five minutes to get to the table. Bashka poured him a tankard and for a several long seconds there was just the sound of Stilgoe gulping down his milk. Stilgoe slammed the empty tankard down and brushed aside his milk moustache. "So, questions anyone?"

The place erupted once more. Eventually Talia restored some order by suggesting Stilgoe tell his tale which would probably answer most of the questions in the telling of it. Everyone settled themselves round the table and listened to Stilgoe's story.

"Well, after I left you on the road to Agra-nore, my business in the south was with my old friend Constable McClintock. I had a few matters that I thought might be of interest to him. As it turned out he was looking for me, he already had the arrest warrant from Derrott."

There were gasps from the others. Shouts of how did he get back before them? What happened next? Talia once again called for silence.

"Constable McClintock's a good man. I showed him the forged Property Certificate and it didn't take a handwriting expert to see that it and the arrest warrant were written by the same hand. That and the affidavits I'd collected in Helsinagar was enough to convince him of the merits of our case. Officially I was under arrest but I gave him my parole and he allowed me my freedom to do a little investigating. Especially once I showed him what

Kirin had done."

"Kirin?" said a multitude of voices. Suddenly everyone was looking at Kirin.

Stilgoe smiled at the look on Kirin's face. "Yes indeed, we may not have found the Tral-fe-tigore as such, but thanks to Kirin we may have just solved the Kingdom's economic woes."

Kirin tried to speak but only a spluttering noise came out, helped by Stilgoe's repeated clapping him on the back. It took a long time to tell the story and parts came out in all the wrong order, as some wanted him to start in the middle, rather than at the beginning, which is generally the best place to begin. But eventually they discovered just what had happened. The key to it all was Sang-gast's book. The forty or so names in it were all owners of businesses throughout the kingdom that had been procured from the proceeds of illegal Money Laundering. While Sang-gast's name was not mentioned in the book, closer examination of the businesses themselves proved that either he or Derrott were silent partners in all of them.

These businesses had all been bought with gold ingots. Perhaps they had just been extra greedy or perhaps merely careless or maybe both but when they had recorded the transactions, no purchase tax had been paid. Thanks to Mr McClintock's constables, mass arrests were made the morning of the final day of the trial. Caught bang to rights, and with the demise of Derrott for other crimes, many of the Shysters who had bought the businesses had plea bargained for a lighter jail sentence. They confessed not just to the felonies of money laundering and tax evasion but gave details of hundreds of cases of fraud against the individuals who had been swindled out of the money in the first place. So with all these charges piling up against him Sang-gast was going away for a very long time. Bizarrely he was also charged with the somewhat obscure crime of 'defacing the Queen's face', as the coins he'd melted down had, rather appropriately, a quite cross looking Queen Zehalani on them.

There was a note of discord raised when Stilgoe revealed that he had given up their stash of gold. However there was some consolation in that he had negotiated a ten percent finder's fee for it. Dargo was not well pleased till it was pointed out that his personal stash had not been mentioned to the authorities. Also as Stilgoe made clear, Constable McClintock after consulting with judge Crabtree, had agreed that this gold would be ring-fenced as compensation for the victims of the fraud swindle. At Stilgoe's suggestion a contingent of constables had been dispatched to the Forest of Teteunxx where they'd arrested the Money Laundering dwarfs and also seized Sang-gast's smelting equipment. Meanwhile Stilgoe and Constable McClintock, had skirted the still smouldering Angaurd Castle on their way to Helsinagar. There Mr Shivers confirmed Stilgoe's version of events and was only too happy to agree to do his bit and testify in the trial in Agranore. Stilgoe concluded by bringing them all up-to-date with the latest happenings. The state had appropriated the gold ingots paid to the original owners of the forty businesses. In lieu of compensation (to the original owners) the businesses then reverted back to them. So all in all Queen Zehalani was quite pleased with the whole situation. There was still one thing though that played much on Kirin's mind.

* * * *

Once again Kirin stood in the throne room of the Queen Zehalani. This time though he was not alone. He stood shoulder to shoulder with the other members of the Company of the Quest for the Tral-fe-tigore. He stood with his friends. Queen Zehalani raised her arms to bring silence to the assembled beings of the Fourth Kingdom. As the crowd began to hush, Kirin looked around. He made out some familiar figures and faces. The tall unmistakable figure of the Chancellor, next to him judge Crabtree. Round to his left near the front he saw

Constable McClintock and standing beside him, slightly overawed, was Mr Albert Shivers proprietor of the Green Man Tavern. And there to his right and a little behind him, were his parents Shalako and Riverna looking over at him. Kirin smiled.

"The Fourth Kingdom is grateful to have such heroes as the Company of the Quest. It is in no small measure due to them," The Queen gave a careless gesture with her arm towards the dwarfs. "for the uprooting of that insidious growth of corruption and illicit behaviour that extended even to one of our own magistrates!" The Queen paused at this point apparently overcome with emotion. The crowd responded.

"Who does she think she's kidding?" whispered Bashka.

"Most of them apparently," whispered Stilgoe.

"Now as to the matter of the Tral-fe-tigore." The Queen seemed to have recovered herself. "A gallant though alas unsuccessful effort." There was loud applause.

Dargo snorted. "How long is this going to last?"

"Shhhh," hissed Talia.

"Of course we understood the enormity of the challenge they faced," said the Queen.

Dargo accidentally dropped one of his crutches with a loud clatter. The Queen gave him her stern eye. Dargo grinned back at her while Kirin and Freyla helped to pick up his crutch.

"And we pay tribute to their courage, resourcefulness and determination," said the Queen through gritted teeth. More applause followed during which the Queen and Dargo had a staring match.

"Nevertheless." The Queen addressed the crowd once more. "The terms of the contract are quite clear." The crowd begins to murmur. The dwarfs begin to nudge one another.

"I'm afraid the contract clearly states that upon failure to—"

A ripple of nudges, bumps and elbows concluded with Coulan bumping Talia out from the line.

"Yes?" said the Queen.

"Eh. Ahem." Talia coughed and gave Coulan an angry look before facing the Queen. "Eh, um Your Majesty," said Talia. Kirin and the others tried to not to snigger.

"Yes? What is it?" said the Queen.

"Eh, it's just that, eh, well that is to say, we did find it." Talia quickly stepped back in line. She popped her head back out of line adding "Eh, that is if it pleases your Majesty."

"What!" The Queen did not look at all pleased. She glanced at her Chamberlain who took a step back shaking his head.

"Eh, the Tral-fe-tigore that is, your Majesty," said Talia.

"You *found* it. You *found* the Tral-fe-tigore," repeated the Queen.

The crowd began to cheer. The Queen kept her gaze fixed firmly on Talia and raised her arm for silence.

Talia shifted uncomfortably from one foot to another, Dargo was balancing on one crutch as he had one hand clapped over his mouth to stop from laughing and the others were not much better. Kirin felt it wrong to find Talia's discomfort so funny, but to see the serious, unflappable Talia so unsure...

"Well it was Kirin who found the tracker device, and ultimately discovered it. Ahem, so credit where credit's due. " Talia looked across at Kirin and so did everyone else in the room.

Kirin gulped. "Eh. What!" He gave Talia an angry look. "Eh, it was a group effort, your Majesty .It required *every single member* of the Company of the Quest, if it pleases your Majesty," said Kirin bowing his head and hoping everyone would stop looking at him.

The Queen looked up and down the line of dwarfs. "Well?" she said.

The dwarfs looked at each other and then at the

Queen. There was an uncomfortable silence.

"Well what your Majesty?" said Stilgoe who thought someone needed to say something.

"Where is it?" said the Queen.

The dwarfs all looked down the line to Talia. The Queen then looked at Talia. All the assembled beings of the Fourth kingdom, now looked at Talia. Slowly she reached into her jerkin and withdrew a small, battered cardboard box. The Queen nudged her Chamberlain who scurried forward. Hesitantly he took the box from Talia and examined it closely. The sound of the Queen's tapping foot sent him scurrying back to her. Gingerly she took it from the him, carefully turning it over. After peering at the writing on it she then lifted it up to her ear and gave it a shake.

"It's empty," said the Queen looking at Talia.

"Eh, um. Yes, your Majesty," said Talia.

"No Ko-Ko beans?" said the Queen.

"No Ko-Ko beans, your Majesty," said Talia.

Kirin did not regard himself as a great student of human nature and human emotions. Indeed the past few weeks had taught him just how inexpert he was in such matters, but even he could tell the Queen was not happy.

"She's not going to be able to pull the old 'hunt for the Tral-fe-tigore' next time the Kingdom needs distracted from its economic woes," whispered Stilgoe to Kirin.

"I see," said the Queen not really seeing at all. She handed the box back to the Chamberlain glaring at him. "Where was I?"

"Eh a gallant but ultimately *fruitless* attempt, you Majesty," whispered the Chamberlain winking at the Queen.

She narrowed her eyes at him but stuck out her hand for the box once more. "Yes a gallant but," She shook the box at her ear in a rather theatrical fashion. "alas fruitless attempt." She discarded the box which was caught, after a little juggling, by the Chamberlain. The crowd sighed in unison. The dwarfs begin to murmur amongst themselves.

"However," The Queen raised her arm. "Endeavour must always be rewarded." The crowd cheered once more. The dwarfs began a series of back-slaps and 'I told you so's'. "As your contract dictates even in the event of *no Ko-Ko beans*," She looks pointedly at Talia. "The Company of the Quest still receive minimum rewards and benefits etcetera, etcetera—"

Kirin decided he needed to strike while the iron was hot, so to speak.

"Excuse me your majesty!" said Kirin.

"Yes?" said the Queen.

"I just wanted to confirm that as an alternative I could claim educational expenses?" said Kirin.

The Queen gave him her stern eye. During this the Chamberlain suddenly produced a document from inside his robes . He whispered something in the Queen's ear and pointed to the document. The Queen peered at it uncomprehendingly, till the Chamberlain produced a magnifying glass he also had secreted about his person. She took the glass and read where the he was pointing. After consulting in hushed whispers for a moment, she looked up and regarded Kirin, her expression all condescending sympathy.

"Ah yes. I'm afraid young Kirin, that as an associate member of the Company of the Quest you are not entitled to full member benefits," said the Queen.

The crowd began to get restless.

"It's all there in black and white in the small print. And that is you signature is it not?" The Queen held out the contract.

Kirin stepped forward and peered at the grey smudge above his signature. The Chamberlain helpfully handed Kirin the magnifying glass. He realised that the smudge was actually writing. Very, very, very, small writing. He took his time to read it all. Even the Queen's tapping foot did not distract him. Shoulders slumped he stepped back into line. Stilgoe took the contract and magnifying glass from his unresisting hands as Freyla put her arm round him

"Look, I'll give you my benefits. You can still go to the University." said Freyla.

"I couldn't take your chance away from you," Kirin smiled wanly. "Besides benefits are non-transferable. It says so."

"You guys are forgetting, we've still got the ten percent finder's fee for the gold," said Dargo.

Kirin shook his head. "Not according to the small print."

"What! What do you mean?" said Dargo.

"He's right," said Stilgoe, who had been reading the small print.

"I don't understand, what's the gold got to do with the contract. It's ours! We found it!" said Dargo.

"When we signed the contract, we became employees of the state for the duration of the quest. Anything we acquired during that time belongs to our employer," said Stilgoe shaking his head.

The crowds restlessness was now generating a few boos and jeers. The Queen looked around the room with a distinctly cross expression. This was not going according to plan. The Chamberlain stepped forward and whispered in her ear. Immediately she brightened up. She raised her arm for silence once more.

"Regardless of the stipulations of the contract," This was greeted by more boos and jeers, despite the Palace Guard's attempts to stifle it. "Signed by all parties in good faith." The crowds derision was now out of control and the Queen was having to shout. "The state has decided to grant a boon to the Company of the Quest! Anything they wish!" The crowd went wild, there was so much noise hardly anyone heard her add the phrase, 'within reason'.

The dwarfs went into a huddle. There was only one shot at this they had to choose wisely. Everyone was talking at once. Dargo just kept repeating the gold, the gold. Stilgoe said it was a once in a lifetime opportunity, but couldn't think what to ask for. Freyla said they should ask for Kirin's university fees. Bashka said they should let one person choose for them. Kirin said as their leader it should be Talia's decision. Coulan said nothing at all. Talia thought for a moment then said, no, Kirin should be the one to choose. Each in turn looked from Talia to Kirin and then back to Talia and nodded. It was decided.

"Well Company of the Quest, what will you choose," said the Queen.

Kirin was pushed forward. A hush fell softly upon the room like a blanket of snow. All eyes were on Kirin, but he was oblivious. He knew what it was he would ask for.

"The ownership of the Plain of Angaurd now belongs to the state," said Kirin. He looked the Queen in the eye. She nodded. "I ask that it be declared conmen land, free for everyone to use without let or hindrance," said Kirin.

The Queen narrowed her eyes and looked at Kirin. After a quick look at her Chamberlain, who merely shrugged, she said, "So it shall be." and bowed her head towards Kirin.

* * * *

The cheering of the crowds still echoed down the palace hallways as they made their way back to the banqueting hall, where a celebratory buffet had been prepared for them. They walked in silence except for the clicking noise of Dargo's crutches on the marble floor. A solitary Palace Guard greeted them with a curt bow of his head and opened the door for them and stood aside. The Company of the Quest entered. It was a time for farewells.

It was not long after their arrival that Kirin's parents also turned up and were admitted. There was a subdued silence in the room while a distinctly overlong hug took place between Kirin and his mother Riverna. During this Stilgoe took the opportunity to present himself to Kirin's father, Shalako, who had many questions, as only a very sketchy account of events concerning the Company of the Quest was generally known (and most of that related to the criminal charges laid against them). In response Stilgoe attempted to fill him in on some, but by no means all, of the details of what they had done. Riverna too was full of questions though mainly concerning Kirin's health and whether he had been injured at all and if he had been eating properly. Kirin assured her he was fine an all accounts but he could feel her eyes appraising him sensing he was not the same boy she had bade farewell to only a month ago. Riverna also had news of her own to impart. The Chancellor had told her at the reception that the Professor of Mathematics at Shang-nam University, having seen Sang-gast's notebook, was sufficiently impressed with Kirin's work on code-breaking that he was prepared to offer, on behalf of the university, a partial scholarship for Kirin. In response to the blank faces round the room as to what a scholarship was, Riverna explained that it meant Kirin would get part of his fees paid for him, assuming of course he worked hard and passed all his exams and visited his parents regularly. Kirin suspected his mother may have made that last part up, but gave her a long hug anyway. As he did so Kirin raised an eyebrow in Stilgoe's direction regarding how the Professor of Mathematics had gotten hold of a book that was still such a vital part of a police investigation. Stilgoe however just smiled and began whistling out of tune, much to everyone's good natured annoyance.

While there was general rejoicing at this news, there were some within the company who were also saddened as they hoped Kirin might remain within their band of accountants. But even these sad thoughts were soon banished when Kirin pointed out that his course did incorporate rather extensive summer vacations which could be devoted to accounting activities, should they choose to consider him an associate member. This was indeed agreed by all without even a discussion much less a vote leading to smiles and cheers all round, though Kirin's mother did look a little apprehensive.

There was also other news that was not so good. They learned that Sang-gast had escaped police custody. There was much confusion concerning the details of this; stories of bribed guards and secret passageways conflicted with others of viscous attacks, bitten fingers and hasty getaways. Kirin was not at all surprised at the news and suspected that their paths would cross again one day.

As everyone mingled round the table eating one last meal together Freyla came over and introduced herself to Kirin's parents and during the ensuing conversation just happened to drop in the fact that she too had decided to go to university in the fall, studying engineering. There then followed an awkward silence during which his mother looked at Kirin very inquisitively before peppering the pair of them with questions, lots and lots of questions. Freyla bore them with her usual good nature and quiet smile but after a while Kirin conveniently remembered something very important he needed to ask Stilgoe about. Excusing himself in a hurry he left Freyla behind with his mother, the dwarf code in this instance downgraded to optional guidelines. The 'something' was not quite so important as his hasty departure implied, but it was still something that had been bothering him. In all the confusion and commotion since the trial he had almost forgotten about it. How had Derrott and Sang-gast gotten back to Agranore before them? Stilgoe did happily know the answer to this puzzle. It turned out that there was an ancient passageway beneath the Crumbling Mountains. A secret way that linked the main part of the Fourth Kingdom to the Plain of Angaurd. It was too small for gold laden mules but big enough for a dwarf, though quite a tight fit according to Stilgoe. He had used the shortcut himself to lead the constables to Helsinagar while Kirin and the others had been languishing in jail. Indeed as part of their punishment, it was expected that Sang-gast's dwarfs would be set to work widening the passageway under the mountain. Making it a regular throughway so that all might pass easily to and from to the Plain of Angaurd. If it meant avoiding the mountain-top crossing Kirin was all in favour of it.

Finally before Kirin parted from them, there was the traditional dwarf exchange of gifts. Bashka went first. Standing before Kirin she presented him with his white gold Chartered Accounting ring. She said Kirin had repaid it's two gold pieces in full many times over, she glanced across at Talia who nodded. In answer to his mother's speechless question that he had pawned her ring for two gold pieces, Kirin merely shrugged, thinking it best not to mention that he'd needed the seed money for a scam.

Next was Coulan who after a shove from Dargo stepped forward. He delved into his pocket and slowly began to draw something out. Everyone was jostling, trying to see what it was that would emerge. In the end it was the wonky compass. Everyone laughed so much, even Coulan, that in the end he did not mind parting with it so much, though it was one of his treasured possessions. Someone cried out, whatever you do, don't give him the magnet as well, causing a look of alarm to pass over Coulan's face, but Kirin shook his head to indicate that the compass was more than enough and a relieved looking Coulan gave Kirin another of his bone crunching hugs.

Freyla was next up and presented Kirin with literally a small memento of their flight from Bank Island. It was the tiny replica of the Rogallo wing that had dangled from the apex of the tubular triangle. Kirin laughed to see it again for it reminded him of his place in the world, which was not a very big one and he was content with that.

Stilgoe gave Kirin the strangest of gifts. It was his favourite pipe. Indeed it was his only pipe. Kirin at first refused but seeing the hurt look on Stilgoe's face accepted it graciously. Stilgoe assured him that he would not find a better pipe anywhere in the entire Fourth Kingdom, Kirin was a little confused as he did not smoke and Stilgoe knew this. It was only when Shalako, Kirin's father came and put his arm round Kirin and examined the pipe carefully and declared it a most excellent pipe that Kirin fully appreciated his friends gift.

Talia was next, and she presented Kirin with a silver Certified Accountant ring. She had even had his initials engraved upon it, as was the custom. Kirin was speechless. He tried to say that he was not worthy of such an honour, that he had not done anything to deserve it. He tried to say that and more but failed as a mass hug ensued, leaving poor Kirin able only to honour his friends by simply accepting it with a silent nod and a wipe of his eye with the back of his hand.

Finally It came to Dargo's turn. He passed his crutches to Coulan and with Freyla and Coulan's help balanced on his one good leg. He then took off his grey accounting hooded jerkin and handed it to Kirin, who had lost his own during the fire in Angaurd Castle. Dargo stated that he was not afraid to admit that Kirin had proved him wrong and turned out to be a pretty competent Accounting Dwarf after all. There was general nodding and agreement to this and indeed not a few dwarfs who suddenly found something in their eye that required their immediate attention.

In the face of his friends generosity Kirin was initially at a loss as to how to reciprocate. But then he remembered Dargo's two gold ingots, that had been stashed away for a rainy day. Kirin offered up his seventh share of this gold to the others as his parting gift. There were general nods and agreements regarding this and Kirin was assured that his gift was indeed most generous.

It was late, and night was already upon them when all was said and done. Too late to start out on a journey when warm, soft, comfortable beds awaited them nearby. It was agreed, without even a vote, to spend one more night in the palace. Whether this was also agreeable to Queen

Zehalani and the other palace officials was unclear. In any event no-one was there to say positively that they could not. There was a spare room next to Kirin's where he escorted his parents who settled down for the night, albeit a little uncomfortably as they were not used to such lavish surroundings. Soon everyone was asleep, and this small corner of the palace echoed to the sound of snoring dwarfs.

It was early, before the good citizens of Agra-nore were awake, and a small troop of dwarfs could be seen moving through the town, their grey jerkins merging in with grey light of dawn. All that is but one, who also limped a little.

EPILOGUE

Kirin stood at one corner of the newly ploughed land breathing in its earthy smell, a strong wind fluttering at his back. Kneeling down in front of him Stilgoe was getting a fire started, beside him Freyla opened her pack and drew out a small ceramic bowl, she handed it to Kirin.

"Are you sure about this?" she asked.

Kirin took the bowl, his fingers rubbing its smooth surface absent-mindedly. He looked into her eyes and nodded. Stilgoe placed a small tripod over the burgeoning fire, taking care to shield it with his body from the wind. Kirin took out what looked like a small wizened bean from the corner of his trouser pocket, he rolled it between his thumb and forefinger, feeling the burr from its wrinkled surface before placing it in the bowl. Then he bent down on one knee and handed the bowl to Stilgoe.

"You know once we do this it can't be undone." It wasn't a question from Stilgoe. The three of them watched as the bowl containing the wizened bean heated up. Every so often Stilgoe nudged the bean with his knife making sure the heat was being applied evenly. Then it happened. There was a sudden crack, the wizened bean burst open and what looked like a puff of smoke popped out. It wasn't smoke though that the wind caught and lifted up in the air. The little cloud of particles hung there for a moment, like a sharp intake of breath, then a stiff breeze swept them away, dispersing them high and wide, carrying them to the awaiting earth.

Stilgoe and Kirin stood up. They took a step back to stand either side of Freyla.

"All those Ko-Ko beans. It'll cause the economy to boom," said Stilgoe.

"Perhaps, but in time, they'll be valued less and we'll be right back where we started," said Kirin

"Oh I don't think that's where we'll be," said Freyla. "Not even close."

Freyla linked arms with Kirin and Stilgoe as they looked out over the plain. The wind flapping round them quickly blew out the fire.

The End

31154651R00188

Printed in Poland
by Amazon Fulfillment
Poland Sp. z o.o., Wrocław